, Kathlee

CROW
MARY

ALSO BY KATHLEEN GRISSOM

The Kitchen House

Glory Over Everything

CROW
MARY

❧ A Novel ❧

KATHLEEN GRISSOM

ATRIA BOOKS

New York • London • Toronto • Sydney • New Delhi

ATRIA
BOOKS

An Imprint of Simon & Schuster, Inc.
1230 Avenue of the Americas
New York, NY 10020

First Atria Books hardcover edition June 2023

ATRIA BOOKS and colophon are trademarks of
Simon & Schuster, Inc.

For information about special discounts for bulk purchases,
please contact Simon & Schuster Special Sales at 1-866-506-1949 or
business@simonandschuster.com.

The Simon & Schuster Speakers Bureau can bring authors to your
live event. For more information, or to book an event, contact the
Simon & Schuster Speakers Bureau at 1-866-248-3049 or
visit our website at www.simonspeakers.com.

Interior design by Yvonne Taylor

Manufactured in the United States of America

1 3 5 7 9 10 8 6 4 2

Library of Congress Cataloging-in-Publication Data has been applied for.

ISBN 978-1-4767-4847-4
ISBN 978-1-4767-4849-8 (ebook)

To my beloved daughter, Erin Plewes.

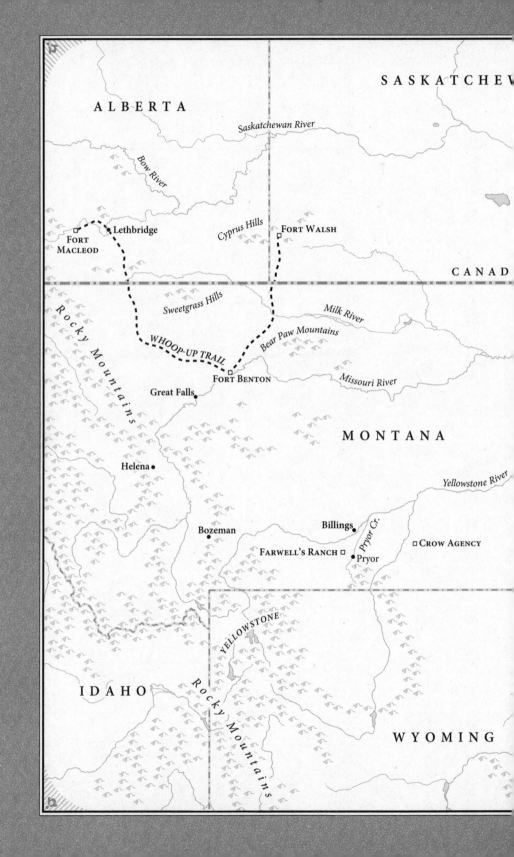

MONTANA AND
THE NORTHERN PLAINS
late 1800s

Qu'Appelle River

MANITOBA

• Winnipeg

UNITED STATES

MINNESOTA

Red River

NORTH DAKOTA

Missouri River

0 Miles		50		100		150
0 Kilometers			150			

Black Hills

SOUTH DAKOTA

Missouri River

NEBRASKA

© 2022 Jeffrey L. Ward

NEDRA'S FOREWORD

I HOPE THAT AS you read the amazing story of Crow Mary you felt her spirit and her courage and strength as she fought to do what she knew to survive in the 1800s. Both the author, Kathleen Grissom, and I, Crow Mary's great-granddaughter, felt her overwhelming spirit for the first time when we visited Fort Walsh, aka Fort Farwell, a historical site in Saskatchewan, Canada. There I learned about the Cypress Hills Massacre and my great-grandmother's part in it.

It was exciting for me to learn more about my Crow great-grandmother, as my father, Bud's son—named Abe Farwell after his grandfather—died at the age of forty-four when I was only twelve years old, and with him went much of my family's history. I am thrilled that my children and their families will have this book to refer to so Crow Mary's story might live on.

I was contacted by Kathleen when she was doing research for this book, and after reading her other two novels, I felt in my heart that she was the person to tell my great-grandmother's story. I knew that she would do justice to her spirit, and also give tribute to the courage of the Crow tribe. Kathleen is gifted in her ability to make you feel what is happening at that time in history that she is writing about. My great-grandmother, Goes First, who became known as Crow Mary, was a beautiful, strong young woman who married a white man she did not know. That she faced this world with such bravery makes me proud to think I carry her blood.

It is my hope that now that you read this story, you will look at our world and the people who live in it with more insight and compassion.

Nedra Farwell Brown

PROLOGUE

1891

I T WAS DARK and hot at the back of the big barn as I rolled aside a heavy wagon wheel that leaned against the entry to the storage room. A slam behind me made me jump, heart hammering even more, but it was only a stall door caught by the wind.

Careful of the bottle of whiskey that sat at my feet, I worked a key in the rusty lock. Finally, it clicked and the log door moaned open. This room had been built with one high, small window so none of the ranch hands, drunk or daring, would be tempted to break in, and I squinted into the dim light.

A fine dust covered everything, though the air smelled clean enough. A wood floor had been put in to keep the pelts dry, and the chinking along the logs had kept out the wet ice of our brutal Montana winters and the worst of our hot sun. Leftover goods from our fur-trading post were scattered on the pine shelves. A comb, a few bars of soap, and even an old can of sardines lay next to a mouse-nibbled red blanket and the remainder of one last buffalo hide. But there—there in the corner on the second-highest shelf, two tiny blue bottles shone in the pale yellow light.

Mice scurried when I pushed aside empty liquor barrels to get to the shelf, and as I reached up, my hand trembled. The tiny bottle was no heavier than a pinecone, but the enormity of what it held almost put me on the floor. With great care, I set it next to the liquor, unplugging first the whiskey bottle; then, before I could hesitate, I picked up the strychnine and held it to the light. How much did I need to kill a man? Just a small amount of this would take down any number of animals.

I shrugged and tipped the entire contents of the blue bottle into the whiskey. "Dead is dead," I told myself. "You can't overkill him."

As I was locking up again, I heard the horses circling the corral, answering a whinny that had come up from the direction of my tipi. Was he early? Was he already waiting? My legs went weak, and I leaned against the wall. I was no match for him. I was as good as dead. But then I remembered what he had done to Song Woman, and what would happen to Ella, and rage straightened me.

I gave the whiskey bottle a last shake. "*Awe alaxáashih*! Hold firm," I said to myself, and then I went out to greet him.

CROW
MARY

PART ONE

CHAPTER ONE

1863

I T WAS THE beginning of April, the moon of the first thunder, when the man rode up. The air was crisp outside our tipi, but Mother had seated us in the warm afternoon sun.

"Now watch, Goes First," she instructed, threading three tiny blue beads. "I was about seven snows, just like you, when I first learned to bead moccasins for my doll. . . ." We both glanced up at the approach of a horse, and as Mother took in the state of the rider, she handed me the pan of beads and got to her feet.

"Red Fox?" Mother asked, unsure if she recognized the visitor.

Father stepped from our lodge, carrying the musket he had been cleaning.

"Horse Guard," the man greeted my father.

"Red Fox! Where did you come from? How did you find us?" Father looked pleased to see our visitor until the gaunt man suddenly tried to catch the gray blanket that fell from his shoulders. He moaned when it slipped to the ground, and his hand went to the deep gash across his chest.

Father grabbed hold of the reins. "You're wounded! What happened?"

"A raid," the man said. "Sioux—our old enemy. There were only four of them, but we were just three lodges and they caught us unprepared. We were heading down here, camped just below the Elk River where we were waiting out the snow. I was coming. . . . I wanted my sister to meet my new daughter. But they wiped us out. Killed . . ." He leaned forward in an effort to breathe, and I was afraid he was going to tumble off his horse. "My sister, your mother," the man murmured. "Where is she? Is she well?"

Father's face went tight as he glanced back at me. "Red Fox," he said, "there was a battle not far from here, a year ago. Mother was . . . it was a bullet. She went to the Other Side Camp."

On hearing the news, the man slumped forward. Father caught him and tossed the reins to one of the young boys who had come to investigate our visitor. "Take the horse to the water and then pasture it with mine," he instructed. "Lean on me, Red Fox," Father said, and half carried the injured man into our lodge, where he set him close to the fire.

"When did the Sioux attack?" he asked.

"Two days ago, if I'm remembering right," Red Fox said.

"Where were you?"

"In that ravine where your father used to trap."

Father nodded.

"They got our horses. Lucky for me, mine circled back."

Exhausted from talk, the man listed to the side, and Father helped him lie back. "We'll set up a lodge for you next to ours. You'll stay here with us." He glanced up at Mother, who nodded back.

"Go ahead. I'll take care of him," she said.

When Father leapt away, I had no doubt of his purpose. If he, chief of our fifty lodges, led a war party, I knew that the Sioux men did not have long to live.

Mother hurried to the back wall of our lodge, where a tripod held her medicine bag.

"Here, hold this," she said, handing me a wooden bowl of water. Red Fox grimaced as Mother cleansed the deep knife wound, but when she dusted black root powder over the reddening gash, the old man sighed in relief.

"Rest now," Mother said, and then nodded for me to follow. Outside, Mother stamped off a circle, and then I tramped down the dried grass while she uncovered and brushed the snow off Grandmother's dismantled tipi. News of Red Fox's arrival had quickly moved through the village, and before the two of us had all the lodgepoles in place we were joined by two of Mother's friends. Together the women lifted the tipi covering. Fifteen buffalo hides stitched together were heavy, but this was familiar work for women who could put up or dismantle a lodge at a moment's notice.

I helped by bringing in kindling and getting a fire started, and soon Mother and I had Red Fox settled in his tipi.

"He needs a good marrow broth," Mother said, and with that the two of us went out to split some buffalo bones. These we covered in water, and as they simmered over our campfire, we began to hear our braves gathering. The men set up a sweat lodge close to the river, and as they prepared for war, they smoked and prayed and painted themselves while sending up animal calls as they sought help from their animal spirits. Their cries reminded me of the battle fought the day Grandmother went to the Other Side Camp, and as my fear increased, I stayed close to Mother.

When the marrow broth was ready, we filled a horn cup with it and brought it to Red Fox. Twice he refused to take it from Mother, and frustrated, she handed me the cup while she tended the fire. When the old man glanced at me, I didn't ask, but pushed the drink toward him. Surprisingly, he took the cup and drained it, then handed it back before he lay down and fell into a deep sleep.

Mother and I returned to our own lodge just as Father appeared, painted in dazzling yellow zigzag stripes and as charged up as a war horse.

"What do you think? How bad is his wound?" Father asked.

"It's bad, but I think it will heal. He doesn't speak, though."

Father shook his head. "He was always shy with women, just like me."

Mother thumped his shoulder with her hand, and he laughed as he caught her arm and pulled her into a tight embrace. There was one steady argument between the two of them, and that was Father's flirtation with other women. Dalliance among the Crow men was not uncommon, and at forty snows, not only was Father chief of our village, he was also taller than most, and handsome. Mother was a good wife and took great pride in caring for his clothing. His deerskin shirts and breech cloths were always clean, and she made sure there were no beads missing from his leggings and moccasins. I liked to watch the two of them in the early mornings as Mother used her porcupine brush to care for his long black hair, braiding it, still damp from his early morning swim in the cold waters of the creek.

Now Father kissed her, his hands on her cheeks.

"How long will you be gone?" Mother asked.

He shrugged. "Depends on the amount of snow and the weather. They'll have a few days on us, but I'm only taking six of our best men so we can move fast."

"Come back to me," Mother said, and they kissed again. As he turned to leave, he nodded toward me. "Don't baby her," he said, and I was hurt once more when I was reminded that he had wanted me to be a son.

With a great war whoop, Horse Guard leapt onto his gray horse. He called out again, waving his rifle with four eagle feathers attached, a reminder to everyone of the coups he had won in past battles. His shrill warrior's cry sent shivers down my back, but to the other warriors it was like a hot flame set to dry tinder. Their answering cries reminded me again of the battle I tried so hard to forget, and when Mother left me to go and see to Red Fox, I climbed under my buffalo robe. There, trembling, I squeezed my head tight, trying to keep the memories away.

ONE YEAR BEFORE, I had gone with Grandmother to spend the winter at the camp of her younger son, Bears Head. I happily waved goodbye to my parents, reassured that I would see them again when the snow melted.

We Crow were one large tribe, made up of many villages that came together in the summer months, not just to visit and have fun, but because there was safety in numbers from our enemies. In winter we dispersed again into small villages to ensure that everyone could find good shelter, a sufficient wood supply, and plenty of elk and buffalo for food.

Over those cold months I enjoyed meeting Grandmother's old friend, Sees Much, and her grandson, Big Cloud, but our good time was brought to an abrupt end in early spring when our scouts brought word that the Sioux, the Cheyenne, and the Arapaho had joined forces and were amassing with the intention of wiping out the Crow people. Being forced from their own land by the Yellow Eyes, they now wanted to claim ours. Our caravan traveled north as quickly as possible, picking up other Crow villages along the way until we were almost four hundred lodges strong. Days later, though exhausted from travel, we hurriedly set up camp alongside our familiar Arrow Creek. There we were offered a natural barrier of steep banks to give us an advantage.

As the braves set up their defensive positions along the creek bank and in the surrounding ravines and bluffs overlooking the creek, the women quickly erected their lodges in tight circles and then skirted the creek with lodgepoles. These they covered with buffalo hides to create further fortification.

A huge cloud of dust rose from the corral that had been built to hold the horses not used for battle. There, hobbled and pushed onto their side so they wouldn't be hit by bullets or arrows, they struggled and screamed.

Along one side of the creek, braves prepared for battle, purifying themselves in sweat lodges before they opened their medicine bundles. From these, some took preserved pieces of their spirit animal and tied them to their hair, then painted their faces in vivid colors and called on their animal helpers to share their strength and courage. As the warriors took on the characteristics of their animal helpers, the air, already thick with the smell of sacred sweet grass and cedar smoke, now filled with the howling of wolves, the grunting and growling of bears, and the screeching of birds.

I lay between Grandmother and Sees Much as we peeked out from a trench alongside the fortified lodgepole barrier to see the enemy atop the hills. It was strangely thrilling to see the feathered war bonnets of hundreds and hundreds of our enemy as they rode back and forth along the bluffs. With frenzied war cries, they waved their weapons, taunting our warriors who waited below. Even I could see that we were desperately outnumbered. Some of our braves were mounted, but many were on foot, concealed in the trees and the tall grasses. Others, positioned in the hills, waited there for the attack.

"They say we're outnumbered twenty-five to one," Grandmother whispered.

"Is your knife sharp?" her old friend Sees Much asked, glancing at me. "You know what you might have to do."

I could smell Grandmother's fear when she stroked my head. "They won't take us."

AND THEN THEY came! The ground shook from the pounding of the horses' hooves, and I felt Grandmother's heart thump against her chest as she held me tight, trying to shield me from the war cries and the screams of pain. Too frightened to cry, I held to her, my teeth chattering uncontrollably.

"*Awe alaxáashih*! *Awe alaxáashih*! Hold firm! Hold firm!" came the Crow command as guns blasted amid the cries of hand-to-hand combat. The enemy charged again and again, and when we heard the men call for the women to bring ammunition, Sees Much and Grandmother both pushed to their feet. I clung to Grandmother, but she pried me loose and pushed me back into the trench. "Stay down! Stay here and wait for me!" she shouted.

I tried to call her back, choking on dust, but when she disappeared, I crawled out of the trench to follow.

I was frantic, calling out her name as I made my way past young boys who fought to hold terrified horses. Women raced to treat wounded braves—and I stopped to watch in disbelief as one of them, his shoulder shattered by a bullet, was bandaged and then tied back onto his horse. With a warrior's howl he reentered the battle, waving a hatchet that was tied to his one good arm.

"*Káale*!" I screamed when I finally saw Grandmother in the distance and I ran through the blue smoke of muskets and whistling arrows when she gave an answering cry.

"Get down, get *down*!" she called, waving her arms as though to push me to the ground. She was coming for me when a gun blasted, shattering her chest and turning it red. She crumbled, and I stopped running. I wanted to go to her, but my legs wouldn't move. An arrow whizzed by, and in front of me a rider fell from his horse. The panicked animal reared over me, and I stared up at the threatening hooves until an unknown hand pulled me back. I sat there, too stunned to move.

"Look! Look!" Thick smoke suddenly rose from the northern hills, where a Crow scout had set a fire. Our people's cry went up, leading the enemy to believe this was a smoke signal from approaching Crow reinforcements.

When a massive cloud of dust rose opposite the billowing smoke, our old men and women saw another opportunity to bluff.

Drumming began, and cries went out to the enemy that a second large war party of Crow was on the way. Incredibly then, another huge cloud of dust formed over the far hills and began moving in the direction of the battle.

Fear of what appeared to be approaching reinforcements rippled through the enemy, and when they turned back, our braves gave chase while our women shouted cries of victory. I was alone when Bears Head came with Grandmother's body.

WHEN MOTHER RETURNED from treating Red Fox, she found me damp and trembling, and took me with her to her pallet. There we lay as she soothed me with the lullaby Grandmother had given me, and slowly I came back to the present. As she grew tired, Mother's voice dropped off, but I wanted her to stay awake.

"Who is Red Fox?" I asked. "If he is Grandmother's brother, why don't I know him?"

"You met him when you were just a baby," she said, rousing herself. "He is a lot younger than your grandmother—only a few years older than your father. He lived on the other side of the Elk River and traveled around up there with our relatives, the River Crow."

"What should I call him?"

"You call him Grandfather," she instructed.

In the morning Mother insisted I come with her to dress Red Fox's wound and then to offer him more of the healing broth. He didn't speak but again, he would accept the broth only from me. We left soon after when we understood that he wanted to be alone.

The following day Mother sent me with some hot fry bread along with the broth. I stood close to the door while he drank the liquid, but he didn't touch the bread. His body was so thin that I could see all his ribs, and I wanted to tell him to eat the bread but the way he stared off in the distance frightened me.

Finally, on the third evening after his arrival, when again he did not eat the bread, I approached him. By now I recognized his grief for his wife and daughter, and I remembered how after Grandmother's death, I, too, had to be encouraged to eat.

"Here," I said, dipping a piece of bread into the marrow soup, kneeling in front of him, and feeding him as Mother had fed me. After I pushed the soaked bread into his mouth, he swallowed, and after finishing the bread he took the bowl and drank the contents before angrily shoving it back into my hands. But I was not frightened, because I understood that he didn't want to live.

The following day, when he turned away from a steaming bowl of elk stew, I pushed it toward him. "Grandfather, eat this," I said. "It is good for you."

He considered my words before he took up the food, and then nodded for me to sit. Before I took my woman's place alongside the lodge door, I threw more wood onto his fire. Then I sat as Grandmother had taught, with my legs and feet under me, carefully covered by my deerskin dress. He gave me a fleeting look when he handed back the empty bowl. "You have the same face as my sister," he said. My eyes filled, and afraid of my tears, I ran.

Mother insisted that I return the following day. "He doesn't take the food from me," she said, "but he'll eat for you."

"I suppose you will tell me to eat all of this?" he asked, receiving the bowl of plum pudding.

I nodded, though I kept my eyes down. It made me smile to think that I, a child of seven snows, was giving a grandfather orders.

※　　※　　※

AFTER FIVE MORE days, Father and the braves returned with four Sioux scalps. Red Fox attended the celebration that night, and the next day after finishing the meal I gave him, he stared into the fire. "I had a daughter," he said.

I was seated, but I was prepared to run, scooting closer to the lodge door. I couldn't bear to hear him speak of any violence.

"My wife and I were old when our daughter came. She was no bigger than a chickadee when she went to the Other Side Camp. She was only two snows."

I held my breath. I didn't want him to tell me more.

He cupped his head in his hands and rubbed his face. Then he sighed, and there was a long silence before he looked up at me. "You remind me of my sister," he said, his voice soft.

"How am I like her? How am I like *Káale*?" I asked, hoping to turn his attention away from his daughter.

His mouth curved up in a half smile. "She was bossy."

In spite of myself I smiled.

"She was more like a mother to me because she was so much older," he said. "She had her two boys, but she always wanted a daughter. You must have been very special to her."

I nodded but looked down, trying not to cry. I wanted to tell him about her and how I had caused her death, but instead I choked back the words and left at a run.

ONE OF MY last memories of Grandmother alive was when we arrived at the winter camp and she was reunited with her childhood friend Sees Much, who came to help us put up our lodge.

"Where is your husband, Goes First?" Sees Much asked me as she patted my head. "Is he out hunting?"

"I don't have a husband yet," I said, astounded that she should think I did.

"And why not?" she asked.

"Because I don't like boys," I said.

"And why don't you like boys?"

"Because they think they can ride horses better than me. But they can't. Right, *Káale?*"

I looked at Grandmother to see the two friends exchanging a smile. Then they got to work, and though they both carried weight they moved with the agility of younger women. I moved between them to do what I could, and soon the three of us had the lodgepoles in place. I groaned as I helped them lift the heavy cover, and again I saw them exchange a smile.

"So, do you have any news for me?" Sees Much asked Grandmother. "Have you found a new man yet?"

I gave a swift glance to Grandmother, who was pounding in stakes to hold the cover in place. After Grandfather died two snows ago, she had moved next to my parents' lodge and helped Mother care for Father and me.

"I told you that I was finished with that business. I don't want an old one, and the young ones don't want me." The two laughed.

"Well, you had a good one," Sees Much said.

Grandmother agreed. "Fine looking, too."

"And you are still beautiful! Between the two of you, you had some nice-looking babies. Horse Guard and Bears Head are handsome men." She puckered her lips and pointed them toward me. "Looks like she has some of that Métis blood, too."

"Métis blood?" I asked. "I don't want it. What is that?"

"Too late," Sees Much teased.

"*Káale,*" I complained.

"Ach, Goes First. Métis are just people who are part Indian with some French or English mixed in," Grandmother said. "Like your father."

"Are you Métis, too?" I asked her.

"No. I am Crow. Your grandfather was a Yellow Eyes. Don't you remember how he spoke to you in English?"

I nodded. "He always made me talk like him." But I had never thought of my grandfather as anything other than Crow. He smoked with the men, and he loved to talk about the raids that he had been a part of.

He was a tall, gruff old man, but he always had a smile for me, and whenever I was unhappy, he was the one I ran to.

"Ah, my little one. Tell your grandpop what's troubling you."

No matter what my complaint, his answer was always the same. "Now isn't that just the worst?"

"Dance with me," I'd plead, and I'd pull him to his feet while he moaned about his aching joints. Once standing, he'd reach for my hands. "Come on then, lassie. Let's dance your troubles away."

I loved to hop about with Grandpop, and soon I'd join him in song. "Ohhh, a-hunting we will go, a-hunting we will go. We'll catch a little fox and put him in a box and never let him go. Oh, a-hunting . . ." By the time we worked our way through the song, my unhappiness was always forgotten.

As the two old women bantered, I remembered how soft Grandpop's white beard had been and how Grandmother was always trying to get him to cut it off.

"He was a trapper who got trapped," Sees Much joked.

Grandmother poked at Sees Much. "He was happy enough," she said.

"And why not? You gave him two strong boys and a good life here with the Crow."

I DIDN'T WANT to be reminded of Grandmother again so I refused to take Red Fox his meal the following day, but when Mother returned from his lodge, she had a message. "He would like to take a walk, but he is not strong, and he asked if you would come with him."

I shook my head.

Mother sighed. "Goes First. He said he will walk only with you. He said you are bossy and you will know when it is time to return home."

Reluctantly I slipped on my fur-lined moccasins and mittens while Mother fixed my warm red blanket around my head and shoulders. It was a gray day with a chilly wind.

He was standing outside his lodge, dressed in Father's clothing. The leggings were too long for him and bunched around his moccasins, and the buffalo robe looked too big, but he was ready for the cold. He didn't smile when he saw me, but his look was kind and his hand shook when it reached for mine.

There was still snow on the ground when we began those walks. At first neither of us had a lot to say, but in the coming months we both began to take notice of Mother Earth's changing face. When summer came, I pointed to a cluster of tall purple flowers growing along the rocky slopes of a hillside. "If I had my digging stick, I'd dig up that root," I boasted. "*Kaale* always kept some of that, and she'd make me chew a sliver of it when I had a cough." I shivered. "It tasted bad, but it helped."

Red Fox nodded. "Black root is good for many things. When I was a young man, I was a good runner—"

"*You* were a good runner?" I asked.

He looked down at me with a slight smile. "Yes, I was a good runner, and when enemies were spotted, I was often sent to alert other Crow villages. I had to run fast, sometimes for days, so I carried nothing, but if I needed water and there was no stream to be found, all I had to do was to chew one petal of this flower and my thirst was satisfied."

"Only one petal?" I asked.

"Yes, one petal, and then I could run like a deer."

I didn't voice further doubt about his fleet-footedness, but said instead, "I wish I was a boy."

"A boy?" he asked. "Why is that?"

"Because I want to be brave, like a warrior."

He stopped and looked me. "You don't have to be a warrior to be brave. Women are as brave as any warriors."

"How can you say that?"

"Why do you think the men stay away from the birthing lodge? They can't bear the idea of a woman giving birth, never mind give birth themselves. If they had to do it, they would be crying like a bunch of Little Toes."

"Little Toes are just babies," I said, and he returned my wide smile.

I took his hand again, and we continued on our walk through the sunshine and the open meadow.

"Tell me, Goes First, what makes you think that you aren't brave?"

I shrugged, but remembered Grandmother's death. Suddenly I was choking back tears.

"Are you crying?"

"No," I said, turning away from him.

"Then what is that water running down your face?"

I shook my head.

"Let's rest," he said, and sat me down opposite him in the sun-warmed grass. With his thumb he reached over and dried each side of my face. "Now tell me, why you are crying?"

"Be . . . because I . . . made *Káale* . . . die." I sobbed out the terrible words. "She told me to stay in the trench, but I didn't. I followed her, and when she saw me, she came running and . . ."

"And she was shot by our enemy," he said.

"Yes." I leaned over in anguish, and the tears I had been storing poured out.

He waited until my sobs died down. "And then what? What happened then?"

"I didn't go to help her," I whispered. "I ran away."

"You couldn't have helped her. She had already gone to the Other Side Camp."

"But I didn't go to see. I *ran away*."

"We do things like that when we are young and afraid," he said.

"But I want to be brave," I said. "I want to learn to ride and shoot a gun like the boys do. Then if the enemy comes, I wouldn't be afraid and I could help to fight."

He thought awhile. "*Éeh itchik*. Good. I can teach you about horses and guns, and after I finish with you, you'll be able to outride and out-shoot any of the boys. But there is something just as important that I want you to know."

"What?" I asked.

"No one is without fear. There will be times in your life when you will be very afraid, maybe as afraid as you were with your grandmother. But the brave take action in spite of that fear."

"Will I ever be that brave?"

"You already are," he said. "It is the brave who tell the truth."

CHAPTER TWO

1865

I WAS NINE SNOWS when Mother finally delivered another child, but before I could resent the tiny boy for giving my parents such joy, I, too, fell in love with him. On the fourth day after his birth, a revered member of the tribe came to give him his name. He raised our baby in the air four times in a cloud of cedar incense and said his name for the first time: Strong Bull. It was a good name, and unless he became sickly, he would remain Strong Bull.

We all doted on my brother and would have created an unruly child if Mother hadn't insisted on teaching him when necessary. I remember well the day Mother and I were cutting up fresh deer meat and Strong Bull was squawking to get out of his cradleboard. He was around eight months by then, and his dark eyes and thick black hair made him the most beautiful baby I had ever seen.

"No, son." Mother always spoke in a quiet voice. "You must stay there. We need to keep you away from our sharp knives." She held up a bloodied knife to show him.

"I could take him out and play with him," I offered.

"No," she said, "he's been fed and he is comfortable. We need to get this meat cut and hung to dry." But my brother was used to having his way, and he began to cry. Again Mother explained to him that he must be quiet, but when his cries grew louder, she got to her feet. "Where is the water?" she asked, making a great show of filling a small cup with water. As his cries continued, Mother held up the cup and again repeated, "Where is the water?"

Strong Bull wailed louder.

"Do you have to, Mother?" I asked, hating to watch for I knew what to expect, as did all Crow children.

"You know I do," she answered. "It's for the safety of everyone." As my brother continued to cry, she took the cradleboard and tipped it back to pour water up Strong Bull's nose. He sputtered in surprise and then began to scream in fury as I fought to keep from rushing to console him.

"Where is the water?" Mother asked again, and when she repeated the action he stopped crying as he sputtered for air.

Twice more in the following days Mother had to use the water, but following that, if tears threatened, all Mother had to say to Strong Bull was "Where is the water?" and his tiny chin would wobble as his small round face scrunched up to hold back his tears.

RED FOX WAS true to his word, and in time I could ride as well as any boy my age. He often took me down to walk among the herd of horses where they were tended by Magpies, young boys my age who were in training to be warriors. They listened, too, as Red Fox pointed out the subtleties of a horse's communication. "See the way that one holds his ears? He's curious when he has them forward like that. But be careful when they go back flat. He'll come for you then."

The young boys watched with envy as I rode out on my pony accompanied by Red Fox. I didn't use a saddle because I wanted to ride like a boy, so the only riding gear we used was a war bridle—reins made of braided hide that were looped under the horse's jaw for control. Grandfather knew where our scouts were hidden in the high wooded bluffs, watching out for our village, and we might have gone out farther, but on Mother's request we stayed on the flat land of the valley and within easy riding distance of our village.

"Use your legs to feel her body. If she stiffens, pay attention. She'll smell a bear or hear the snake's rattle before you will," he warned.

I had never been so afraid, nor had I ever felt so strong as during those lessons.

"Stay low," he'd shout as we'd race each other across the flat land. "Use your legs. Pump them to get her to go."

Red Fox was like Grandmother in that he did not offer praise, but his approval came in subtle ways. One day he gave me a knife that he had made for me. "Look, Goes First," he said as he unsheathed it. "I made this for you so you will always have a weapon." He molded my hand tight over the handle of polished white bone. "Hold it firm and feel the spirit and strength of the deer. The deer is quick and fast. Can you feel it?"

I nodded. I could. I could feel the deer's strength through the bone handle.

"I will teach you how to use this, and whenever you do, you'll ask the deer for her help—for her strength and agility."

Later, Mother helped me suspend the sheathed knife safely from my child's belt. I was seldom without it.

STRONG BULL LOVED Red Fox as much as I did. Already at three snows, my little brother went everywhere with the small quiver filled with arrows and a right-sized bow that Red Fox had made for him.

Mother had me sorting berries the day Strong Bull came running. "Goes First," he called, and when he reached me, he leaned down close to my face. "Do you want to see how fast I can run?"

"Show me," I said, pushing his shiny black hair away from his eyes.

He shot away to run around and around our lodge until he finally dropped down beside me. His small chest and round belly heaved. "Did you see me?"

I widened my eyes in amazement. "I did. How did you learn to run so fast?"

"Red Fox had me chase butterflies, and when I caught one, I rubbed it here." He pointed to his young chest. "And then I asked the butterfly for its speed. I want to be able to run for two days without stopping and not get tired, just like Red Fox did when he was a scout."

"What a wonderful warrior you will be," I said, hugging my brother to me. I wanted to hold on to him forever, though I knew that once we were grown, as brother and sister we would not be allowed to see each other alone, nor would we speak directly to each other. But for now he was still mine.

CHAPTER THREE

1870

EVERY YEAR, AS summer approached, many of our bands gathered again. Some of the villages had wintered far away, and they came great distances, traveling across our vast Crow territory to the destination that our chiefs, the year before, had decided upon. Often it was in the foothills of the Shot in the Arrow Mountains, where the hot sun that scorched the grassy flatlands was cooled by the mountain air. Now in this awakened season, when hundreds of lodges came together, the men hunted the plentiful elk, deer, and mountain sheep, and the women gathered fresh berries and turnips and their all-important medicine plants.

I was always impatient for the arrival of my grandmother's best friend, Sees Much, and her grandson Big Cloud. The boy was four years older than me, and the first time I met him when I was six snows, I didn't like him. I was sitting in the shade of our lodge playing with my doll, Little Tree, while Grandmother and Sees Much were having a dull conversation inside.

"You sit here," I told my prized doll, propping her up amidst the fallen leaves, "while I set up your tipi." I was carefully wrapping a rabbit skin around the twigs that served as lodgepoles, when my play was suddenly interrupted by the nearing clomp of hooves and the barking of dogs. The rider, painted in gray mud, pulled up abruptly and slid from his horse. "Grandmother," he called to Sees Much as he ran by me, "Grandmother! I am fighting the enemy today, and I will need a feast this evening."

One of the dogs that had come with the boy jumped on me and, in his frenzy, knocked over my doll's tipi. "Get away," I scolded, but when I waved my doll's lodge cover at him, he grabbed hold of the rabbit skin and tugged at it like this was some sort of game. I held tight to the cover until the dog nipped at my wrist and then took off with my prize. My sobs brought everyone running, including the rider.

"Your dog bit me and he took my tipi cover!" I cried. The boy looked around helplessly. "Go get it," I said, pointing toward the pines where the dog had gone.

"But I am fighting the enemy," the boy objected.

"Go, Big Cloud," Sees Much said, pushing his shoulder, "or you will be fighting with me." At that, the boy sprinted toward the woods.

NOW, OLDER, MY opinion of him had softened, and my reunion each summer with Big Cloud and his grandmother was always the same. Sees Much would send her grandson to come looking for me, and when he found me, he would tease. "I'm looking for a little girl called Goes First? Have you seen her? She is so high—" And here his hand would go to his knees.

Then I would smile shyly. "Stop that, Big Cloud. You know who I am."

"Come then," he'd signal. "Grandmother is waiting for you."

But the year of my fourteenth snow, I didn't wait for Big Cloud to find me, and instead surprised the two of them in their lodge. I had grown tall, and my body had matured since the past summer.

"Can this be our little Goes First?" Sees Much stared in astonishment before she opened her arms. I ran to her and held her tight, holding back my tears and breathing in her scent of woodfire and tanned hide. It felt almost like holding Grandmother again.

After releasing me, Sees Much fingered my two shining braids. "Goes First, your *Káale* was always a beauty, but if it is possible, you are even more beautiful."

I felt Big Cloud studying me, and though I inwardly smiled, I scarcely glanced his way. He was already eighteen snows and had grown quite handsome, but he had always treated me like a little sister. Now, seeing his astonished gaze, I sensed a new power.

SUMMER WAS A time for the young braves to challenge one another. Their rivalry was fierce as they knew they were being carefully watched by the older Crow warriors, who were always on the lookout for the most promising young men to join their societies. They competed in footraces, contests with weapons, and other games, but it was the thrilling relay horse race that got everyone most excited. It was a fast and dangerous ride, and only the finest and most daring riders took part.

That summer, while getting ready for his first race, Big Cloud saw me and waved me over to where he and his relatives were preparing their three racehorses. His uncle was having a problem with the second horse, and Big Cloud handed me the reins of his lead horse. "See if you can get him to calm down," he said, leaning over me. He glanced toward the excited onlookers. "He isn't used to a crowd of this size."

"What is his name?" I asked.

"Tip Ears," he said, referring to the horse's black-tipped ears.

The big bay gelding nervously stamped and pawed, anxious to race, so I spoke to him quietly. "Tip Ears? I could have given you a better name," I said. "Look at those beautiful long legs you have, and just look at your shining coat. And who painted those pretty red and white handprints on your haunches? Was it Big Cloud? I'll bet he wanted you to have the same color that he has on his breechcloth and moccasins." After I had the horse's attention, I walked with him and sang to slow his dance, and by the time Big Cloud tugged one of my braids and took back the reins, the bay had settled.

"I heard how good you are with horses, and now I see for myself." He smiled. "You'll make a good wife," he said, teasing, and those few words snared my young heart.

The drumming, singing, and shouts from the crowd all receded as the riders took off, and I watched Big Cloud fold down onto his speeding horse. Without a saddle and with only reins for control, he leaned close to her neck, and as she pounded around the track, they took the lead.

At the end of the first lap, though he slowed her, she was still galloping when he hopped off and flew toward his uncle, who held the reins of a second horse. This required skill, for as his uncle tried to control the prancing, charged-up horse, had he touched Big Cloud in any way, they would have been disqualified. After Big Cloud leapt onto her back, the mount took the next lap at a dangerous speed. They circled the track, and again as Big Cloud came in at a gallop, he successfully leapt off and onto the third and last horse for the final lap. They raced onto the track and past a loose horse that had thrown off one of the other riders, while the other two competitors were still trying to mount their third horses. My heart was pounding and the crowd was shouting, and when Big Cloud won, I was cheering as loud as anyone.

THAT SUMMER, BIG Cloud went on to win many of the competitions, but I wasn't the only one who admired his strong muscled body, his flashing smile, and his growing confidence. As his popularity grew, I jealously watched other girls vying for his notice and I gradually felt his attention slipping away.

It was overcast and gray the afternoon Big Cloud won yet another horse race. I told my friends that I wanted to leave before the rain came, but truthfully, I didn't want to see Big Cloud once again basking in the attention of all those foolish girls. I walked alone, back to my lodge, muttering to myself and kicking at the dirt at the unfairness of it all.

"Granddaughter."

I turned back when I heard Red Fox's call. He'd been watching the race, too, and now caught up to me. "What troubles you?" he asked.

When I didn't answer, he glanced at me. "Big Cloud won that race again," he noted.

"That Big Cloud is such a fool. He thinks that all the girls like him."

"Then he isn't far from wrong," Grandfather said.

I shot him a look. "Well, I don't!"

He looked straight ahead. "Is that true?"

"Ohhhh," I moaned. "Grandfather, is it that obvious? What can I do?"

Red Fox chuckled. "Why don't you do as my wife did," he said. "When I was young— about Big Cloud's age—not only did I win every footrace, but I was very good with the bow and arrow." He looked over at me. "The mothers saw that I would be a good provider, and I became full of myself when young women gave me their attention. But there was one pretty girl who didn't seem to care about me at all. In fact, whenever I looked at her, she would be smiling at other young braves—usually competitors of mine. The more she ignored me, the more determined I became to have her notice me. In time, she was all I could think about, and by the time I won her, I had forgotten all about wanting attention from the easier women."

"So I should pretend not to care about him? Won't he know? Are men really that ignorant?"

"Yes," he said. "I'm afraid we are."

We caught each other's eye, and then we laughed.

THE FIRST TIME I gave a shy glance and a smile to Three Hawk, Big Cloud's main rival, the surprised young brave not only gave me a huge smile in return, he went on to win the challenge of the footrace. By summer's end, Big Cloud was competing for me. But I wasn't won easily, and I suspect many summer storms were ignited from the sparks that came from Big Cloud's dark looks as I allowed other braves to believe that I was interested.

CHAPTER FOUR

1871

THE SPRING OF my fifteenth year, Big Cloud and his father came to our lodge with ten horses for Father and a request of marriage for me. With my approval, Father agreed to the union, but he said that we must wait another year until I would be sixteen snows. But Big Cloud's age was an obstacle, too. In my sixteenth year he would be only twenty snows, and the Crow men did not marry before twenty-five, unless they had proven themselves by earning a coup against the enemy. At nineteen snows, Big Cloud was as tall as my father, and with his shining black hair, my sweetheart was in every way a handsome brave.

His nose might have been too prominent for some, and he carried the swagger of the overconfident, but to me, both only made him more appealing. Mother and Sees Much often mentioned what a striking couple we made, for I, too, had grown tall, and I was almost Big Cloud's height.

In that summer of my fifteenth snow, Big Cloud and I often went out berry picking or rhubarb gathering, as young lovers did, using it as an excuse to be together. Sees Much often came as a chaperone, but she usually found her own berry patch a distance away.

One warm July day, in the moon when the cherries are ripe, I sat with Big Cloud on a ledge that overlooked the valley. Yellow, white, and blue summer flowers gave color to the green grass in the sun-washed view below. We had just finished sharing a plum pudding with

Sees Much, and now our beloved chaperone napped in the shade of a nearby fir tree. As I looked out, I gave a deep sigh, still troubled by the argument I had had with my father earlier that day. We had disagreed about the value of a horse that he wanted to trade, and when I would not see his side, he accused me of being too outspoken and stubborn. I shared this now with Big Cloud, and he laughed. "Good. I want a wife who speaks her mind. When I'm chief, I'll need a strong woman beside me."

He turned to me then, and his kiss tasted of the plum pudding. When he ran his fingers down my back, my body tingled and I wanted more. But I remembered my mother's cautions and I pulled away. At first his kisses had been so light that I wondered if I had imagined them. Then, as time went on, he grew more ardent, but I always held back. Yet concerned when I began to hear rumors that he was being intimate with other girls, I went to my mother.

"Oh, Goes First," she said. "That is only natural for him to seek out other women. Men are expected to have sweethearts, sometimes even after marriage."

"Did Father have a lot of women?" I asked.

"He was a handsome man," she said, grinding the juneberries harder than I thought necessary. "He still is."

"What about you? Did you ever go with . . . ?" I didn't finish before she shook her head.

"No," she said, "and neither must you, especially before you marry."

"I know. I know. But some of my friends aren't waiting, and they're *happy*," I objected.

"Well, they might be happy for now, but think of what can happen to them later on," she said. "They're opening themselves up to being stolen."

Mother's reminder was always sobering. I knew the practice that we Crow lived by.

The Crow warriors had two special clubs—the Foxes and the Lumpwoods. All the young boys dreamt of being recruited into these societies, and already Big Cloud was a member of the Foxes. These two societies competed with each other in everything from horse raids to feats of bravery in battle. But in early spring the Lumpwoods and the Foxes competed against each another with the practice of stealing wives.

If a warrior was married to a woman who had had sexual relations with a member from the opposite society, the man who had been intimate with her during her youth had the right to steal her away from her husband and claim her for himself. Neither the wife nor the husband could object, and in fact, if the husband should object, he was ridiculed.

Increasingly, I heard talk of White Wood, a very beautiful girl from one of the villages who didn't often join our summer gatherings.

But this season her arrival was noted, for not only was she of marriageable age, she also claimed to have the power to entice any young man she chose. And she didn't care about her reputation.

High Rock, one of my closest friends, mentioned her one day when we were out gathering firewood. "Did you hear that girl White Wood has her eyes on Big Cloud?" High Rock asked. "She's saying that she might want him as a husband."

My face grew hot, and I used my knee to snap a fallen branch in two. This would not do. I knew that Big Cloud had been with other women, but rumor had it that White Wood was turning men from their sweethearts by using her advanced sexual experience. How could I compete with that? Until this point, I had been confident and comfortable with my strong body, but there was something about this girl's delicate features and perfectly proportioned smaller frame that made me question my own appeal.

The following day, White Wood happened to pass by where High Rock and I sat, each beading a pair of leggings. My friend poked me. "That's her," she whispered. "The one that claims she's going to take Big Cloud from you."

The girl, with hair shining like sun on river rocks, walked by while giving me sidelong glances. She raised her eyebrows in surprise when I waved her over.

"A group of us are going out tomorrow morning to collect wood.

We know of a good spot," I said. "It would be fun to have some new company. Do you want to join us?"

Again she looked surprised, but she agreed to come.

After White Wood left, High Rock turned to me. "Who's going with you tomorrow morning?" she said. "I can't come. Mother said . . ."

"No one else is coming," I said. "I'm going out alone with that girl." My friend looked me over before she gave me an uneasy smile.

"What will you do?" she asked.

I shrugged. "Gather wood, I guess."

White Wood met me the next morning at my tipi, and with hatchets in hand I led us toward a familiar mountain slope with a dense forest. It was a good distance away, but I knew there were scouts in that area, always on the lookout for our enemies and dangerous bears or angry buffalo bulls.

I said little as I led the way at a brisk walk, and we had almost reached the edge of the forest before she stopped to look around. "Where are your friends? I thought they might be meeting us here?"

"Oh, they couldn't come," I said. "But this will be good. We'll have a chance to get to know each other."

She hesitated as she looked around.

"Come," I encouraged her, but already she was claiming to feel tired. Before she could object further, I moved quickly into the woods and began to gather fallen branches and good-sized twigs. She did the same, but after gathering a small bundle she sat and watched me as I broke or hacked the large branches into a manageable size.

I looked over at her. "Are you tired?" I asked.

"Yes," she sighed. "I really don't like to gather wood. But you are so big and strong. I could never work as hard as you." Her voice came in whispery sighs, and her flushed face only emphasized her high cheekbones and large brown eyes.

"Well, why don't you stay here and wait for me? I want to go to a better spot up ahead."

"Oh, I don't want to stay here by myself. What if a bear came?"

I looked around. "Just climb this tree if you see one. Then wait for me and I'll come back and chase him away."

I turned to leave, when suddenly a startled deer with two babies crashed through the underbrush and ran by. White Wood squealed in alarm. "Oh, Goes First. Let's go home."

She was on her feet, but I sat down on the forest floor. "We can go back if you like, but I'll need to rest first. We have a lot of wood to carry."

She sat down again with an uneasy glance at the pile of wood I had gathered.

"Did you see those babies?" I asked.

She shook her head. "No. I was too scared to look."

"Next year they'll have babies of their own. By then I'll be married."

"To . . . is it . . . oh, yes, Big Cloud," she said, and I could have swatted her for her feigned ignorance. "Do you expect he will be a good husband?" she asked.

"Yes, I do. But especially so when he brings me help."

I knew for certain that one of her lovers was a man from the Lump-wood society, so I relished my next words. "Big Cloud is with the Foxes, and he has already told me that he has had plenty of lovers he could steal from the Lumpwoods. He said he would bring home any woman that I ask for so she could work for me."

"But if he took her to his home, she would also be his wife."

"Oh, yes, that is what she would be *called*," I said, getting to my feet.

"What do you mean?" she asked.

"Well, as his first wife I would expect her to do most of the hard work. I'd send her out for the firewood every day, maybe even twice a day—especially in winter—you know how we always need wood. And she would keep my mother and mother-in-law supplied as well."

"You'd send her out alone into the woods?" she asked.

"Why not?" I asked as I separated our gathered wood into two piles. "Look," I said, pointing. "You didn't collect very much, so I've given you some of mine. I don't want this to be a wasted day for you." As I considered the two stacks of wood, I began to wonder if they were going to be too heavy even for me to carry. But I was determined.

"Oh, I don't think I can lift . . . ," she began, but I didn't let her finish.

"Do you like to scrape and tan hides?" I asked as I tied the two bundles with strips of hide and secured them to our carrying packs, made of the same.

She sighed a beautiful sigh as she watched me work. "No. I don't like to get the smell on my hands."

"Oh, we are so much alike! I don't, either. Now you know why I'll need Big Cloud to steal one of those women he's slept with."

I straightened then, aware of her silence. "Are you ready to go?" I asked.

"Oh, Goes First, my bundle is too big," she complained in her wispy voice, so I pulled two small branches from her pack. Then, to further make my point, I tucked both of them into my bundle before I hoisted it onto my back. The weight of it might have done me in had my pride not lightened the load as the two of us shuffled back to camp.

CHAPTER FIVE

1871

IN SUMMER OUR warriors went out on horse-stealing raids. It was already toward the end of the season when Big Cloud was again invited to go out on a raid, and this time he was determined to win a coup so we might marry the following year. The evening before he was to leave, Mother was visiting a sick friend, and I was alone when Big Cloud arrived at our lodge. "Come," he teased, holding out his hand. "Quick, before anyone sees us."

I knew it was wrong, but I set down the grinding stone and dropped a cover over the chokecherries. Mother would be upset that I left without a chaperone, but I was in love, so I took up his challenge.

A half-moon lit our way as we raced hand in hand up the path that led to our favorite spot on the wooded bluff that overlooked our villages. Once there, panting from the run, we sat, surrounded by our sacred mountains. Below us our village campfires flickered against the white tipis that circled alongside the winding Arrow Creek. Meals were being prepared amidst the laughter and cries of children, where young boys played at pretend raids and girls sang war songs to encourage them on. I thought of how the night held everything I loved.

Big Cloud slid off the rock we were sitting on and pulled me down to lie on the grass beside him.

"We must marry soon," he said into my ear. "I've been with others, but I want you."

"I've heard stories," I said, my face turning warm. This was not a topic we talked about, and I would never have raised the subject.

His voice was low and deep when he reached for me. "I only want you." He kissed me hard, then teasingly, he bit softly at my lips.

My breathing quickened. "I'm so tired of waiting until we marry," I said, sighing.

He spoke into my neck. "I always think of how it will be with you as my wife—coming back from raids and finding you in my lodge."

"Big Cloud?"

"Yes?" he murmured.

"Why do you want me for a wife?"

He chuckled. "The first time I saw you . . . remember how you scolded me and then sent me out for a rabbit skin? You were so little, but you looked so fierce."

"I remember my *Káale* had to put a poultice on the place where your dog bit me."

"You are like your grandmother in every way. Sees Much tells me how she was so beautiful that a Yellow Eyes came with twenty horses and then won her heart. Did you know him—your grandfather?"

"Yes, he was Father's father. I was about five snows when he left for the Other Side Camp. He always made me speak to him in English. He had funny names for things—he called these mountains the *Pryor Mountains* and said that the Yellow Eyes called the Elk River the *Yellowstone River*."

"Maybe one day you can teach more of those words to me? It's good to know what those Yellow Eyes are saying."

Wolves howled higher up the mountain, and I had a sudden fear in the pit of my stomach when I thought of what could happen to him on this raid.

"Listen to the wolf." Big Cloud held me tight under his arm. "My spirit animal calls. He assures me that he will be with me tomorrow."

I was afraid for my lover, but I stayed silent for I knew what our future held. Big Cloud was a warrior and there would be many times he would leave and I would need to stay strong.

"Our scouts have seen the Sioux, and we are planning to surprise them. We're hoping to get at least twenty of their best horses. I have gone on other raids, but this time I will count coup."

I sat up and looked down on his face. "Surely the enemy will be watching for you," I said.

"I'll have my medicine to protect me." He sat up beside me.

I didn't ask about his sacred medicine, but instead stroked the long scar on his arm where he'd cut a strip of his flesh as a gift to the First Maker while on his spiritual quest for a vision.

When he looked away, I gazed at the beautiful profile of his angular face against the dark mountain behind him.

"You already know that the white wolf is my medicine—my protector and spirit animal. With his fur as part of my medicine bundle, I will never hunt him again. When you become my wife, I will ask the same of you."

I nodded my understanding. He leaned over to cup my face and kiss me tenderly. "You taste so sweet, but I have to go. Sweat lodges have already been set up."

"Wait," I said. "Before we go, I have this for you." I handed over a deerskin packet.

He unfolded the soft bundle and held up the small vial that I had fashioned from a deer joint.

"Mother helped me make this. Father has one just like it," I said. "He ties it around his horse's neck when he goes into battle. It is filled with black root that will stop any bleeding."

"This is beautiful," he said, carefully unplugging the chokecherry stopper and gently sniffing the herb. "I'll tie it around my horse's neck, just as Horse Guard does." He leaned over and kissed me. "You are right to make me wait for you, even though it seems like forever."

WE WAITED SIX days for the warriors to return. "Come, at least take some bread," Mother said, but each day that Big Cloud was gone, I found it increasingly difficult to eat. Though I knew these raids could take many days, as time went on, my fear for the safe return of Big Cloud grew.

The raiding party had gone to steal horses. Horses were our wealth.

We rode horses during our seasonal travel, and we used them to carry our sick, our children, our elderly, our lodges, and all our possessions. They were essential for raids and war.

Little was more precious to a brave than his horse, and with horse raids at night always a high risk, warriors of every tribe kept their favorite horses tethered safely next to their lodges. In fact, some slept with the reins snaked under the tipi and tied to their legs or their arms.

Big Cloud and the others had to wait until the village slept, then creep in without alerting enemy scouts, resting dogs, or nervous horses. Once there, Big Cloud's mission was to find a warrior's lodge and then cut loose and steal a tethered horse. Escaping with that horse would earn him a coup. But it was a very dangerous plan. If a Sioux warrior caught Big Cloud leading his horse away, it would mean death.

ON THE SIXTH morning I awoke to the sound of guns and shrill cries. Our scouts were alerting us to our warriors' return. I tried to see through the dust of the raiding party as they pushed forward a herd of new horses. When our men went to help corral them, I ran, too, but when I saw Big Cloud's spotted war horse among the herd, my legs grew weak. That could only mean one thing. Suddenly, though, through the din of hammering hooves and whinnying horses, I heard Big Cloud's call.

I didn't recognize the large buckskin that reared under him, but the spirited, tawny horse with its black legs looked an equal match for my handsome lover. Able to breathe again, I waited until Big Cloud pounded toward me and pulled me up onto his horse's back where I sat in front of him and took the reins. Then, amidst the cheering of our relatives and friends, we rode through the camp. Even Father looked pleased. I didn't need Big Cloud to tell me that he had earned a coup and now we could marry!

THE FOLLOWING MORNING, we learned that Sees Much was ill. She had pain in her chest and felt too weak to stand. Big Cloud was as close to his grandmother as I had been to mine, so I understood as he paced outside her tipi. Later that afternoon, she was feeling a little better and asked for some fresh buffalo liver. She felt it might give her strength, and Big Cloud was determined to supply it. He asked his friends Nest and Black Lake to join him in a hunt, and I rode out with the three of them to the meadow where their buffalo horses were pastured.

Big Cloud was on his fiery new buckskin, and I rode my older bay mare that Red Fox had given me. With Sees Much recovering and our wedding ensured, we were both in high spirits as we raced down to where Big Cloud's buffalo horse was enjoying the summer grass. She was not a pretty animal, but Big Cloud claimed there was none faster or more reliable when it came to chasing down a buffalo.

He was teasing me when he went for her, and she took advantage of his inattention and bolted. When she left at a gallop, he returned to his nervous buckskin. Frustrated, Big Cloud leapt onto his back and looked out at the dust trail of his disappearing buffalo horse. "I don't want to take the time to go after her. Would you bring her in for me?" he asked. "I know that you can handle her, but be careful. She has fire."

"But you'll need a buffalo horse," I said.

"I have this prize." He pulled back on the reins as the buckskin impatiently sidestepped. "He's fast and this will be a chance for me to see what he can do." His excited friends called out for him to leave, but before he did, Big Cloud reached for my horse's reins. He pulled me alongside him, then leaned over to kiss me with a passion that took my breath away.

I returned his kiss, and it would have gone on longer, but I finally pulled back. "I think you forget—I am a good girl."

He laughed aloud. "But I am a bad boy," he said, and with a whoop he swung his horse away. Armed with a rifle, he also had his beautiful buffalo horn bow and a quiver full of well-shaped arrows, and I didn't doubt his success.

Red Fox and I went out together to retrieve the buffalo horse. She was run out when we finally found her far down the river. Grandfather shrugged when I told him I would ride her back, though others might have discouraged me. Even tired out, if a buffalo horse decided to run, there was no holding her back. As it was, it took all my skill to keep her in check, but she was a good distraction from missing Big Cloud.

As expected, they were back within a few days, but the buckskin was missing and a packhorse carried Big Cloud's body. A crowd gathered round where I stood alongside Mother, trying to take in what Black Lake was saying.

"It was a . . ." He choked on his words, then looked back at his friend's draped body. He shook his head as though in disbelief and then he began again. "We found a large herd that was coming down from the Elk River. It's rutting season and the bulls were treacherous. But we had a plan and were heading in together aiming for a young cow when . . . when that buckskin of his went crazy. He started rearing up . . . there might have been a rattler, I don't know, but . . . the herd stampeded and two of the bulls charged. In the dust we lost sight of each other. When the herd thinned out . . . we found him. His horse was down and he had been thrown. A bull had gotten hold of both of them and . . . we had to finish off the buckskin."

"No one could have stayed on that crazy horse," Nest said, his eyes red and swollen.

"You're saying his horse threw him?" I shouted. "He would never have fallen off a horse!" Thinking it was a mistake, I ran toward Big Cloud, but close up I stared in horror at his torn body. Mother led me away.

Dazed by grief, I refused to believe he had joined his grandmother, who had also left for the Other Side Camp. I don't remember taking part in their death ceremonies, but once they were completed, I was free to leave. As I stumbled away from our camp, Mother followed and pressed a small parfleche of pemmican into my hands. "Take this," she begged. "You need to eat."

I shook her off as I tossed the bag of food aside and then left, heading to our special place on the bluff that overlooked our village. There, I told myself, Big Cloud would be waiting. But I was wrong. Unwilling to let go of my hope, I went in search of him, calling out his name as I fled farther up the mountain. Unmindful of jagged rocks tearing at my legs or the stones I sent tumbling down, I scrambled up higher and higher until, exhausted, I climbed out onto another ledge. The height was dizzying, but as I looked out into the vast emptiness, I realized the truth. Big Cloud was gone. Slowly I backed away from the steep drop and into the womb of a shallow cave. There, as nervous swallows swooped and dipped around me, I sat and screamed until my voice was gone. Then, unable to bear my thoughts, I reached for the deer knife Red Fox had given me, and I used it to slash at my arm. "Ahhh!" The pain of torn flesh gave me some distraction from my grief. The next day, the agony of losing him had only increased and, needing relief again, I slashed at my other arm. I watched the blood stream and wondered why it didn't hurt, until it did.

For two days I cried out for the Great Spirit to take me. During the day I suffered from the searing pain of my wounds, and at night I shivered uncontrollably from the cold mountain air. But then, during the second night, Big Cloud appeared.

"Don't leave me," I begged my lover as I reached for him. His face, painted in red and white, wore a sad smile, but I could see no wounds.

"Take me with you," I pleaded.

He didn't answer but instead lifted a small white wolf that he carried in his arms. The animal whimpered when he was handed over to me.

"What is this? Why do you give me a wolf?" I asked.

"It is not a wolf. It is a dog. He will bring you a new life."

"No, I want *you*. I want *you*," I cried. When he disappeared, the dog and I howled until we were both spent. Finally, I huddled close to the animal for warmth and slept, but when I woke the white dog was gone, too.

When Red Fox found me, I allowed him to take me home.

MOTHER CAME RUNNING when I returned to camp and reached for me in relief. I clung to her, my cut arms burning. "Come." Mother led me into our tipi.

She sat me down onto the folded buffalo robe. "You have spent enough time alone. You will come back to life when you are ready," she soothed. She sang Grandmother's lullaby as she heated water and then gently washed away the days of blood and dirt that were ground into my oozing wounds.

I had seen other women go off to grieve and always hated to see them on their return—their eyes dulled by pain, their hair chopped and matted, and their arms and legs bloodied. I hadn't understood, but I did now. What I didn't know, though, was how to go on.

PART TWO

CHAPTER SIX

1872

IN MY SIXTEENTH summer, two moons after I was to have married Big Cloud, a Yellow Eyes set up camp outside our village. Abe Farwell was a white fur trader who some of our people had met in the past when he had a trading post, up on the other side of the Elk River. He was known as an honest man. This July—in the moon when the berries begin to turn red—it was rumored that he had come looking for a wife.

As he smoked the pipe and exchanged words with my father and other esteemed men of our tribe, the women scurried to gather whatever they might have to trade, though everyone knew that they were using this as a means to parade their daughters.

The Crow had always been friendly to the white men because chiefs, like my father, saw the power in their weapons. A few years before I was born, many of our tribe died of smallpox, and because of our diminished numbers, we now needed allies to fight our many enemies.

The Sioux, the Cheyenne, and the Arapaho had always wanted to claim this Crow land that the Great Spirit had blessed us with. Here, we had high snowy mountains with goats and their tender meat and white hides. Below, across vast stretches of plains, rich grass not only fed our horses, but also supplied food for herds of buffalo, deer, and elk. Here, too, in our forests and along the banks of our clear rivers and streams, our medicines and food grew, and with each new season we traveled to gather from that abundance.

"Why does this Farwell want one of our women?" Mother asked Father that evening when we sat together on his return.

"He wants an Indian wife who can talk to other Indians when they come to his post to trade. And he says that the Crow women are much stronger than the white women. My Yellow Eyes father used to say the same thing. He was always surprised to see how quickly my mother could move a lodge and butcher a buffalo."

"Your parents lived with our people, though."

"In their first years Mother traveled with Father, but after my brother and I were born she wanted to raise us with her people. So, Father kept on trapping while she stayed back with her village."

"Did you miss your father?"

"Sometimes, but we had our grandfathers and our father was happy that his boys were being raised as Crow—he said there were no better people."

"So what are white women like? Are they sickly?" Mother said. "Have you seen many?"

"I've seen a few at forts, but they always stay back. I once came close when I found three of them picking berries outside a trading post, but when they saw me, they ran." He thought for a while. "They were underfed, but they were good runners," he added.

OVER THE NEXT days, many of the girls my age accompanied their mothers to Abe Farwell's lodge. The woman who married this wealthy fur trader would be held in high regard, for she could help the whole tribe. Everywhere Mother and I went, we heard nothing but whispers and giggles and gossip about this man. I wondered if I'd ever been that foolish about Big Cloud. Probably. But he was worth ten of this man, and I still ached with his absence.

One late afternoon, Strong Bull, now seven snows, convinced me to walk out with him to check on his pony, Smokey, pastured with Father's other horses. His pony happened to be grazing alongside Big Cloud's buffalo horse, and I was surprised at how round the buffalo horse had grown. "Is she with foal?" I asked.

"No, she's just fat," Strong Bull said. "No one rides her. They say the only one who could handle her was . . ." He looked away from me.

"That's foolish," I said. "I rode her. Let's go have a closer look," I said.

My little brother swung toward me in excitement. "Will you ride her?"

I thought of how patient my little brother had been with me throughout the long winter of my mourning, and I couldn't resist this boy who was as dear to me as my own child. "Maybe. Do you want to race?" I asked, knowing the mount would be slow because of her weight.

Strong Bull didn't bother to answer and instead ran for the halters.

Big Cloud's horse snorted on my approach, but she allowed me to stroke her spotted face and then slip the bridle in place. Strong Bull was right. She had gained far too much weight.

"She'll be hard to handle," my little brother warned, and I felt the stirrings of excitement at the challenge of riding her.

We used a nearby log to mount as the pony and horse eyed each other, both sensing the upcoming competition.

"Race you down to that cottonwood by the creek and back!" The words were no sooner out of Strong Bull's mouth than we were off, each of us leaning low as we gave our mounts their heads. I glanced over and saw how naturally my brother sat his pony. It had been only a few years since I had carried Strong Bull on my back and we pretended that I was his horse. Now my young brother rode fast and I gave him no advantage. Our horses pounded forward, side by side, and as the wind lifted my hair, for the first time since Big Cloud's death I had a moment of feeling alive. Suddenly my mount tripped in a prairie dog hole, and I was jolted forward onto her neck. I hung on, my heart in my mouth, but she recovered and we caught up to my brother as he raced around the faraway tree.

I suspected my brother had slowed, concerned for my safety, so I tossed Strong Bull an insult to spur him on. "You ride like my little sister," I called out.

"You ride like a grandmother," he shot back. I knew I needed only to tighten my legs around my horse's fat belly to move her forward, but I did not. Instead, I allowed my little brother the lead. He waited for me, panting at the finish line.

"You might have won if she hadn't stumbled," he said generously.

"Next time!" I promised, giving him a smile.

As we walked our damp mounts to cool them down, I caught sight of the fur trader standing back in the woods by the creek, near where he'd put his lodge. Angry to think that he had been watching us, I had us turn back toward our home. There, Mother looked up from her cooking fire and smiled to see us.

"My brother is fearless and one day will be a great chief, just like Father," I said, slipping from the horse's back. I handed my reins to Strong Bull, who grinned at the compliment.

"My sister rides like a warrior," he said, offering the highest praise possible, and I laughed aloud, maybe for the first time since Big Cloud's death.

Just then Father came around the corner of our tipi.

"Go, Strong Bull. Take the horses back to the pasture and then come join me. That trader, Abe Farwell, has shown me a new rifle. Let's see how well it works." My brother whirled away with the ponies, eager as ever to please Father.

I helped Mother clean and cut up the wild carrots and onions we had dug that morning. But the ride had given me a new energy, and as soon as I could I slipped away, curious to see what Father had called a Henry repeating rifle.

My father was thirty-three snows the year I was born, and he was already then a chief. Now at forty-nine snows, he was still a respected chief. Known for his fairness, I watched how he made certain that each man had a chance to try out this new rifle before they departed for their evening meal. Finally, the only men left were Red Fox, Father, Strong Bull, and Abe Farwell. I wanted a chance with the gun, and I signaled to Red Fox.

"Give Goes First a chance with this rifle," Red Fox said to my father. "I'd like to see how well she does with it. I'll bet she will handle it as well as any of the men."

Over the years, Red Fox had taught me to use a rifle, and he was proud of my skill. However, I had watched the men shooting with this new rifle and saw it was completely different from Red Fox's muzzle loader. That was a one-shot rifle, which took a long time to load with gunpowder, tuck the ball into wadding, and then pack it down with a ramrod. And after all that, you had only one shot before you had to reload all over again.

But with this new rifle, all you had to do was load bullets into a chamber and you could fire fifteen shots without having to reload. No wonder Father was so taken with it.

"It will throw you back, so be careful," Father warned.

"*Ahoo*," I said, thanking him. I carefully looked over the gun before I shouldered it, then aimed, fired, and splintered the first of two small logs set up as targets. I felt the force of its kick in the front of my shoulder, but after glancing at Father, I pulled the lever and shot again, splintering the second log. Red Fox nodded his approval.

Abe Farwell rubbed his hands together. "I'll be darned. That girl can shoot," he muttered.

Because of his Yellow Eyes father, Father spoke English better than most, and though he did not acknowledge Farwell's words, I knew he was pleased. My ability reflected on him and on our people.

As I handed the rifle back to Father, Farwell made an attempt to speak to me in Crow. "I saw you ride today. You ride like a horse."

My brother dropped his head to hide his smile, while Father replied in English, "Yes, my daughter is good with horses."

As I left, I felt the white man's blue eyes follow me.

I COULDN'T SLEEP that night, thinking about the day's events. As I lay on my pallet, snuggled deep into my buffalo robe, I overheard my parents talking quietly. "Wouldn't you know it would take a horse to bring her back to life?" Mother said.

"She got that love of horses from my mother," Father said. "No one could handle a horse like her."

"Well, she is also your daughter," Mother said. "And you are known for the same."

"And you are known as my wife," he said, and she giggled.

I pulled the robe over my ears when they began to make love.

OVER THE NEXT few days, Abe Farwell stayed at our village and traded with our people. Men offered pelts in exchange for knives and ammunition for their muzzle loaders, while the women traded their beaded work and tanned hides for blankets and more beads. Soon the whole camp was abuzz with rumors of who had traded what, and which daughter was certain to marry this Yellow Eyes. Even Mother got caught up in the excitement. She came to me one morning and held out the two pairs of beautifully beaded moccasins that we had just finished crafting. "Come with me. I want to see what the Yellow Eyes will give for these."

"But we made those for Father," I said. "And we used the last of the old tipi. That hide is hard to come by." And it was, for we had cut the moccasins from the upper part of our old tipi, where the escaping smoke made the buffalo hide more resilient and waterproof.

She waved my concerns away with her hand. "Horse Guard has plenty," she said, "and since he doesn't need them, he would only give them away."

"But it took us so long to do the beading," I argued, as I fingered the green and red floral designs. I sighed as I thought of the work. I wasn't that fond of beading. I preferred to dig for roots or pick the fruit that was in season. Better yet, I liked to work at tanning hides as Grandmother had taught me, leaning my whole body into it and rubbing the brain of the animal into the skin to soften it. "Rub it in good. Make it as soft as a baby's bum." Her words still made me smile.

"Yes. These moccasins are good quality," Mother said. "We won't trade unless he is fair, but I heard he has good blankets, and I guess you didn't notice that Red Fox needs another one."

Mother knew I would never deny Grandfather anything.

ABE FARWELL'S CANVAS lodge, just outside our village, was smaller than a Crow lodge, but it was set up so well that I wondered if he already had a woman with him. He looked surprised, but pleased, when we appeared through the trees.

Mother poked me. "Goes First, you go talk to him," she said. "Speak to him in his language. Maybe then he'll give us more for these moccasins."

"I don't want to," I said.

"Go on," she said, and poked me again. "If he was a horse, you'd be over there running your hands up and down his legs."

"Well, you can see he isn't a horse," I said. "And I don't want to talk to him."

"*Éekaawa*! This is too much! You are as stubborn as your father," she said, stepping forward.

The man greeted us with a smile, but I stood back and watched as the two of them began to trade. I was impressed with how well he knew how to hand-talk, but I wondered what he would think if he had known that I understood English well enough to have helped with the negotiations.

As Mother raised the stakes, he removed his worn leather hat and ran his fingers through his thick, close-cropped brown hair. Abe Farwell was approximately my height, with a solid build and a six-shooter wrapped low around a slim waist. He wore the dark pants of a Yellow Eyes, and although his shirt was buckskin, it could not have been from the Crow, because it was so poorly cut. Where had he come from? I wondered. Why had he abandoned his white man's home?

He had told Father that he was thirty-four snows, and though he was a Yellow Eyes, his square-cut face was almost as brown as my own. His heavy eyebrows were shaped in a way that gave him the appearance of frowning, yet when he smiled his eyes wrinkled nicely, and I saw that he had good teeth like the Crow.

"Goes First?" he said.

I nodded, surprised he knew my name.

"Come here." He waved me over with his hat.

It appeared he had something to show me inside his tipi, and I was reluctant, but with Mother there, I moved closer.

"I, Farwell," he said, pointing to his chest.

I nodded.

"And you, Goes First," he announced proudly, pointing at me.

Yes, I nodded again. I knew my name.

His hands nervously circled his hat until he seemed to suddenly recall why he had called me over. "Look," he said, and pulled back the door cover of his lodge to point inside, where a small animal slept. He gave a short whistle and the puppy yawned and wobbled to his feet. Then it yawned again and did a long, slow stretch before it came waddling out. My mouth opened in happy surprise at his all-white coat.

"Pick him up," Farwell said, and because he wasn't sure I understood him, he lifted the puppy into my arms. The small dog snuggled into my neck, and his rough tongue licked at me. At first I was shocked, but then I held the squirming creature tighter and stroked his head. There could be no other explanation. Surely this was the white dog promised me by Big Cloud. I felt the tears gathering behind my eyes.

"Come," Mother said in Crow, as she hoisted all she had gained from her trading. "Hurry," she said, handing over two prized trading blankets for me to carry. "Let's take all of this before he changes his mind."

Reluctantly, I set the dog down to do as Mother asked, but as we left, I looked back. The man had not offered the puppy to me, though I had hoped he would. Instead, Farwell had picked him up and was gently stroking him. I stopped for a minute to watch, disappointed, and yet surprised to see him express such tenderness.

That night there was a scratch on our tipi door, and when I lifted a corner, the small white puppy came tumbling in. I gave a joyful yelp as I scooped him up and laughed when he licked my cheeks and nose. Surely this dog had been sent to me by Big Cloud.

CHAPTER SEVEN

1872

I AWOKE TO MOTHER poking at me with my prized Shinny stick. Red Fox had spent days carving out the rounded pocket from the root end of the long willow branch, and now Mother was using it to wake me.

"Goes First. Come. Wake up."

I grabbed hold of the stick. "Don't, Mother," I said, but she had already awakened my puppy hidden under the covers, and now he was wiggling to get out.

"What . . . ?" Mother stared down. "Do you have that dog hidden in there? Goes First!"

I had smuggled him in every night since his arrival, cuddling him and trying to think of a name for him, but so far none suited. I had always taken him out before anyone woke, and now I had to get him out before he wet my pallet. Mother shook her head in disbelief when I threw back the covers and ran by her. I got him outside just in time, and after I quickly fed him some scraps from last night's meal, I went in to face Mother.

"I'm sorry," I said. I knew how hard she worked to keep our lodge clean, and dogs were never allowed in our tipis. "I know I shouldn't have brought him in, but he's so small to be outside alone."

Her face softened. "Well, from now on he stays outside where he belongs. But forget about that dog for now. I need you to come with me today. We need your help to beat those men."

"Is Father playing?" I asked, though I knew the answer.

"Yes, all the braggarts will be there," Mother said firmly, "and we will make those men eat their words."

Earlier this summer, after the men had finished a game of Shinny, they watched the women playing one of their own and began to poke fun at how slowly the women ran. "Even those white women at the forts can run faster than the Crow women," Father had called out, getting a huge laugh from the men, but upsetting the women, especially my mother.

This would be a serious game.

Reluctantly I left the puppy and went with Mother. "I haven't played yet this year. How will I know what your strategies are?" I asked as we walked toward the field.

"Our strategy is simple," she said, leaning into me. "The men will play by the rules, but we women won't. By the time they catch on, we'll have won the game," she said.

"But the men have already been out on raids, and they'll have more strength and stamina than us."

"That's why we got them to agree to play a shorter game—whoever gets the first twenty points wins. We women will start off slow to save our strength. The slower we move, the more the men will let us score, just so they can feel good about themselves. Once we have enough points, we'll put our strategy into play. The fastest runners will get the ball—you'll be one of them—while the heaviest women will block the men and then tackle them. And for those last points, if we have to, we'll use our sticks to trip the runners."

I looked at my normally compliant mother with surprise. "But tackling and tripping is against the rules."

"Yes, it is," she agreed, and I realized the depth of Father's mistakes. Mother was a dutiful wife, but he had pushed her too far. The last few weeks in our lodge had been tense, fueled by the rumors that he was seeing another woman.

The field had been sectioned off over a vast expanse of flat land with goals of buffalo robes set up on either end. Beaded belts, blankets, and pelts piled up as crowds of relatives and friends arrived to watch and bet on the game.

As the two teams lined up to face each other, I noticed the two young braves on either side of Father. Both had tried to court me, but neither interested me. The one who kept smiling at me now had teeth too big for his face, and the other was so full of himself there would have been no room in a lodge for anyone but him. My stomach did a funny flip when I saw Farwell come onto the field, but before I had time to wonder who had invited him to play, the sand-filled buckskin ball was pitched out. Forty players scrambled with their sticks to claim it. When the ball was sent to me, I scooped it up but was blocked by two of the men, so I whacked it across the field to another woman. She got hold of it, but she ran slowly and it wasn't long before the men had the ball and made their first score.

Just as Mother had predicted, after that first quick goal, the men gave the women an easy time and let them keep the score even. But at seventeen points apiece, the men arrogantly announced to the audience that they were ready to take the game. And that is when everything changed.

The women had been playing a casual game. Twice I had seen Father look confused when Mother and her friend jostled each other and laughed when the men scored. But now, as one, the women turned serious and surprised their opponents when they gained the next two points. After the men caught up again, they weren't quite as smug, and though they were still teasing, the women were now teasing back. The score was nineteen to nineteen, and the enthusiastic crowd was on its feet.

We were faced off again in the middle of the field when I looked up and saw Farwell position himself across from me. After he caught my eye, he winked, and then put his thumb up as though he meant to score. *We'll see*, I thought. The ball dropped, and after a wild scramble he actually won it. He was faster than I expected as he ran toward our goal, knocking the ball forward, but I caught up to him when he had to dodge women who were tackling the surprised men.

"Get the ball!" Mother shouted as she ran toward us. "Send it to me."

I whacked hard at Farwell's Shinny stick, and when the ball bounced free, I scooped it off the ground and whipped it toward Mother just as another player flew into my back. To stop myself from falling, I grabbed hold of another woman, and a pile of us went down. We were all laughing as we disentangled ourselves, and I was still sitting on the ground when I heard the roar of the crowd. I looked over to see my mother racing toward the goal with Father at her heels.

Mother was not tall, but she was quick and strong, and today her feet ran on air. All the players, men and women, now stopped to watch, with the women wildly cheering her on. Just steps in front of Father, Mother stopped suddenly and with full force swung her Shinny stick and sent the ball flying. The crowd watched in stunned silence as the ball flew and then thunked into the men's buffalo robe. She had made an impossible score, and as the crowd whooped and hollered, Mother, usually a humble woman, threw up her arms in victory. Then she proudly strutted by Father. I don't know what she said, but he suddenly caught her by the waist, picked her up, and lifted her into the air as everyone cheered.

"Put my hand up. Put my hand up." Farwell stood over me and was again attempting to speak Crow. I was reluctant to touch him, but I saw he wasn't going to move away. When I gave him my hand, he pulled me to my feet and smiled. My face went hot, and I didn't stop to brush myself off before I hurried away. There was something in his touch that disturbed me.

That night I agreed to come with Mother to celebrate the women's success as we feasted in the village circle on roasted buffalo ribs. Over the past year I had been too sad to attend events like this, and later, just as I had feared, when I heard the drumming and saw all the young couples dancing together, I missed Big Cloud more than ever. I was about to leave when the fur trader appeared, and I decided to stay and join Mother and the other women in their victory dance. In celebration we were all dressed in our finest clothes, and as the men drummed and sang of our good fortune, I danced with the women, aware that Farwell was watching me.

CHAPTER EIGHT

1872

THE FOLLOWING MORNING I was alone at the creek and on my knees, scrubbing at the grass stains on my young brother's leggings.

"Goes First?" A deep voice startled me. I dropped the pants and swung around with my knife in my hand.

Farwell's shoulders blocked the sun. *What does he want?*

"Whoa! I come in peace," Farwell said, his gaze on my knife. Then he pointed to my puppy, who slept nearby on a warm rock. "You like?"

"*Ahoo*," I said, thanking him as I sheathed my knife. He stood with the assurance of a successful brave, while I, unsure of what to do, turned back to the creek to continue my chore.

I sprinkled more sand on the leggings and scrubbed hard. Father was so impressed with this man that I didn't want to insult him. Over these past days he had learned that five snows ago, this Farwell had built Fort Peck, a trading post along what the Yellow Eyes called the Missouri River. Father knew of the place, and now, seeing Farwell as a man of wealth and power in the white man's world, he hoped to obtain some guns from him—with his eye on that Henry repeating rifle.

Farwell moved closer, then squatted near me. He was wearing that same buckskin jacket with fringes cut so poorly that they would not shed water as they were meant to do. He must have made a bad trade. I was tempted to explain this to him, when he suddenly smiled at me, causing his deep blue eyes to wrinkle. He was handsome for a Yellow Eyes, and my neck grew warm as I waited for him to speak.

He removed his hat and used it to flick away a bothersome fly, then nervously spun the hat on his index finger while he looked around. I gave him a glance, wondering if he would speak, but that only seemed to confuse him further, and he twirled the hat faster and faster until, of course, it flew into the water. When he went to fish it out, I scrubbed fiercely to hold back my smile.

"This is not going well," he muttered to himself as he set the dripping hat on the rock beside my puppy. He watched me scrub for a while before he began again. "Goes First. Do you understand English?" he asked.

I held my thumb and index finger up together, then opened them slightly. "A little," I said, but did not explain that I understood a good deal more, for my grandfather had taught me well.

Farwell nodded and again appeared to be struggling for words. He changed his position from squatting to kneeling, but grimaced when he found the pebbles uncomfortable. Finally, he sat back on the damp sand. Surely the wet sand was soaking through his pants. Behind him, the puppy had found his hat and was swinging it back and forth. When the pup started to run away with it, I motioned to Farwell, but he seemed not to notice.

"I don't know how much of this you will understand, but I've come with a proposal. I'm thirty-four years old and I'm looking . . ." He stopped himself and began again. He spoke quickly, as though afraid he would forget what he was trying to say. "I'll be going up north in a few months, into the Canadian wilderness. It's beautiful up there; much of it looks like this Montana territory, but without the mountains. Actually, it's flat like the plains down here—that is, most of it is flat land, but where I'll build my trading post is not flat—it's a bunch of hills—a place called the Cypress Hills, but that area's not flat. It is full of grizzlies—more than down here—but I don't suppose you need to hear that."

I listened to him talk about flat land and grizzlies, but my attention was increasingly drawn to the puppy, who, along with the man's hat, was getting closer to the water.

"I can give you a good life," he continued. "I'd need you to help me talk to the Indians who come to trade. And you could help me pick out the best pelts. I can do hand talk but I don't speak any of the Indian languages and I was hoping that you'd consider . . . well . . . would you consider marrying me," he blurted out, just as I jumped to my feet. The puppy had dragged the hat into the creek, and I ran with a cry of alarm when the current began to pull both the puppy and the hat away. As I stepped into the water, Farwell splashed past me. The current was swift, and the pup, though desperately paddling, was quickly moving downstream. Farwell was in almost up to his waist before he caught hold of the terrified puppy, but his hat escaped him. He sloshed out of the water, and I gratefully received the dog. Farwell looked back to where his hat had floated away, then shook his head before turning back to me. "My offer still stands," he said, and then, dripping wet, he left.

I sat on the rock to gather my thoughts. *Did he just say he wants to marry me?* Could I have misunderstood him? I rolled my puppy in the grass to dry him, and as he tried to wriggle away I lifted him up to kiss his round belly. Then, in spite of everything, I smiled as I thought of that Farwell walking away. "I knew his jacket wouldn't drain water properly," I told the puppy as I tucked him safely under my arm and hurried off to find Father and Mother.

OUTSIDE OUR TIPI sat a pile of blankets and two new Henry rifles. "It's a good chance for her," I heard Father's raised voice from inside our tipi. "He'll be a good provider."

"But will he take off and leave her alone with children?" my mother answered. "Like so many of those Yellow Eyes do?"

"No, he said he wants to marry her the white man's way. There will be a paper that she will carry. It will give her rights, same as a white woman."

"It will be a strange world for her," Mother's voice caught. "And she'll be so far away. . . ."

"It is what *my* mother chose, and she lived a good life with my father."

"But you said your father was never here."

"No, he was often out trapping. But he always provided for us, and then he lived here when he was old."

They came out of the lodge just as I was about to enter, and when they saw me they shared an uneasy glance. "Are those from Farwell?" I asked, pointing to the blankets and rifles.

"Yes," Father said. "And there is more to come. Farwell wants to marry you."

So it was true. He was serious.

"Why does he want me?" I asked.

"He thinks that you will be a good partner for him. He admires the way you shoot a gun and ride a horse, and he liked that you were strong when you played Shinny. He saw that you were respectful with me and your mother, and he knows you understand English."

Mother came and put her arm around my shoulders. "He also said you were beautiful," she murmured.

"Does he have other wives?" I asked.

"No," said Father. "He wants to live the white man's way and will take only one wife."

The puppy squirmed, and when I set him on the ground, still damp from the water, he shook himself dry. Had Big Cloud sent this puppy? Was it a sign that he was telling me to marry Farwell? A chill went through me as I considered the possibility.

I turned to Mother. "What should I do?" I asked.

"It's a Crow woman's right to choose her husband, so—" she began, but Father interrupted.

"You have already turned down two other braves, and you say you want nothing to do with my friend Runs Him Down."

"He already has two other wives," I said, but didn't add that he was also much older than my father.

"But he would provide well for you."

"No, Father, I will not marry Runs Him Down," I said, again trying to end an argument that had been going on since the beginning of spring.

Father looked toward the gifts that Farwell had already given. "This man is well thought of by the Crow," Father said. "And look at the guns he will give us."

How many guns am I worth? I thought. I looked over at my mother, but she wouldn't meet my eyes.

This was happening so fast. I had sensed that the trader was attracted to me, and maybe I was a little attracted to him, too, but that was a long way from considering marriage. "I need some time to think about this," I said.

"He wants an answer within two days," Father said. "He needs to get back to Fort Benton, needs to get ready for the winter trading post he's going to build up north."

"Give me until tomorrow," I said, scooping up the puppy. I needed to talk to Red Fox.

As I approached his tipi—what was once Grandmother's lodge—I was reminded of her. Why hadn't I questioned her more about her marriage to my Yellow Eyes grandfather? She must have been brave to take a husband from outside our tribe. "Life is an adventure," she often said, and I always wanted to be like her. But was I being foolish? I knew nothing about this man. How I could have used her counsel now, but I consoled myself that I had Red Fox, who, I had come to learn, shared her wisdom.

I found Red Fox near the woods, a short distance from his tipi where he was attaching some shafts to his hand-worked stone arrowheads. In fact, his arrows were so prized that he had once traded ten of them for a horse. On my approach, he smiled his welcome and set his tools aside.

"Grandfather, the fur trader wants to marry me."

"I know," he said. "I was there when he brought the blankets and guns."

"What should I do?"

"Come, sit," he said, stepping into the shade, where I sat alongside him.

"I don't know what to do," I said.

"What do you want to do?" he asked.

His look was so caring that I suddenly fought tears. "I don't know," I said.

We sat in silence until I spoke again, but this time my voice came out in a whisper. "Grandfather, I think that I am meant to marry this man."

"Why do you say that?" he asked.

"Because he brought me the puppy," I said. Red Fox was the only one who knew about my encounter with Big Cloud that night when I was grieving his death.

"And is this white dog the only reason you would go with this man?"

"No. Father said that he's a good man, and that our marriage could benefit our people."

"And there is no other brave you want to marry?"

"Grandfather, you know I'm not interested in another Crow man. None will ever measure up. If I go, I can leave all those memories behind. Everything here is painful to me. Every time our braves return from a raid and we dance and drum to celebrate their coups—over and over I'm reminded of what I'll never have. I'm thinking that if I go with this Farwell, I can move on to another life."

"I don't want to see you leave," he said, "but I have watched you suffer. Maybe a new start is what you need. A Yellow Eyes provided well for my sister, and it looks like this Farwell can do the same for you."

"But I would miss you," I said.

"I will always be your grandfather," he said. "That will never change."

I COULDN'T SLEEP that night. Father was snoring and my brother was kicking restlessly, as he did in his sleep. I wondered what my duties would be as Farwell's wife. How far away would we travel? When would I see my family again? At the creek, he'd said that we would go up north, where he was building a new trading post. What did that mean? And he said he wanted my help. Would I have to help him do business with the Sioux or the Arapaho, our old enemies? But if that were true, surely Father would not have encouraged this marriage.

Farwell was older, but at thirty-four snows at least he was younger than Father. He did not appear to be fierce or passionate like Big Cloud;

in fact, nothing about Farwell reminded me of Big Cloud, and in the end, it is what helped me make my decision.

Early that evening, after Farwell smoked and then ate with Father, I agreed to walk out with him. It was not yet dark, and I held my hands together so he would not see that they trembled.

We went down to the water and followed a deer path along the river. As we left the village behind, he spoke first, in English. "Your father said you agreed to marry me?"

I nodded.

"He also said that you speak and understand English."

"*Éeh*," I said. "Yes."

"I am happy that you will be my wife," he said, "but I'd like to know why you agreed to this marriage."

I glanced at him, surprised by the doubt behind this question. I had once asked Grandmother how her Yellow Eyes husband was different from a Crow man. "Oh, Goes First," she said, "men are all the same. Tell them every day that they are the biggest and strongest and the best provider, and they will seldom come home with a second wife."

I decided to give Grandmother's words a try. "You are big and strong."

If he was surprised by my English, he didn't show it. Instead, he straightened his shoulders and gave a smile. "I suppose I am," he said, and once again I found Grandmother's wisdom reliable.

"I hope you don't scare easy," he said. "We'll be going into some pretty rough territory, but I saw that you sure can ride and that you can handle a rifle. Do you have any questions for me?"

I shook my head.

"You don't talk very much, do you?"

"No," I said. I didn't say that words were sacred to the Crow, nor did I say that my agreement to marry him was still so new that I didn't know which questions to ask. He reached for my hand, but startled, I pulled it away. He looked at me with surprise and then spoke tenderly. "I won't hurt you," he said.

I fought back tears. What was I thinking, agreeing to go away with him? I knew nothing about him. Yet there was something familiar about him, and I couldn't deny that I was attracted to him. I suppose he reminded me of my English grandfather—a man I had trusted and loved.

"You are Métis?" I asked.

"No. All white." He pushed the sleeve of his shirt up past his tanned forearm to show me the startling absence of color to his skin. Is that what the rest of him looked like? I was glad his face was brown. Even with the darkening sky, that white looked sickly. "I was born here in the East, but my parents came from England. I don't have any Indian blood in me."

That's too bad, I thought. *Especially with that skin color.*

"Oh, I almost forgot," he said, and reached into a pocket. "Here," he said, handing over a small box covered in a soft, dark blue fabric.

It was as soft as finely tanned elk skin. I stroked it, turning it around and around. "*Ahoo*," I said. "Thank you."

"Open it," he said. "The box is not the gift." He reached over and lifted the top. Inside, on a shining bed of white, lay a beautiful piece of silver. "It's a bracelet," he said. "Do you like it?"

"*Éeh*," I said. Silver was highly prized by our people, and only a few men and women I knew had a piece. No one had anything like this.

"Should I put it on you?"

I closed the box before he could reach for it. Mother had no silver and I knew she would treasure this.

Farwell gave me a questioning glance. "I suppose it will take some time to get to know each other," he said as I stroked the blue fabric. "At least you seem to like that box?"

I tried to think of what to say, but it was complicated. The box made me think of my grandfather, and I didn't trust my English to explain, so I said quietly instead, "We'll catch a little fox and put him in a box and never let him go."

He looked at me in surprise when he recognized the ditty. "How do you . . . ah, yes, your grandfather," he remembered, and broke out in song. "Oh, a-hunting we will go, a-hunting we will go . . ."

He had a full, deep voice. It was comforting to hear the familiar melody, and this time when he reached for my hand, I let him take it. "Sing with me," he said, swinging our hands back and forth. Made brave by his lack of inhibition, I joined in, though I sang more quietly. He smiled at me then, and I liked the way his eyes wrinkled and warmed. We were both happy to have found this connection, and though eventually our singing stopped he held on to my hand.

Tall cranes picked their way on spindly legs through the grass on the riverbank, squawking to each other, the mothers staying close to their new chicks. The frogs had begun their evening song, and we turned back as the sun went down. As we approached our village, nestled in our summer valley, I looked up at the nearby mountain ledge that had been mine to share with Big Cloud, and again I felt the familiar pain in my chest.

BEFORE HE LEFT the next day, Farwell came to our lodge. He frowned and then looked at me in puzzlement when he saw the bracelet on Mother's arm, but he said nothing.

Farwell and Father decided that in another month's time, in August—the moon of wild plums—Father would bring me to Fort Benton, where Farwell would meet us and we would marry. Father had been to Fort Benton a number of times, but it was a long distance away—at least six or seven days of travel—and Mother and I had always stayed back with our village.

"I hate to leave, but I've got to get back up to Fort Benton. Supplies will be coming in," Farwell explained when Mother and I joined him. He spoke of the beauty of the Cypress Hills, an area that lay up north in the vast Canadian wilderness, and of the business we would run there. His enthusiasm ran high, and in spite of my concerns I began to feel some of his excitement. As he prepared to leave, he handed over a rifle. "I'll give you this now and I'll leave plenty of ammunition so you can keep practicing. When you leave, give it to Horse Guard and I'll get another one for you after we get married." Farwell saw Mother's look of alarm. "It's grizzly bear country up there, and we always have to be prepared," he explained.

Farwell awkwardly patted my shoulder on his departure. "Don't bother to bring much of anything. We'll get you outfitted up in Fort Benton."

What a strange thing to say, I thought. I had relatives who knew I was getting married.

OVER THE NEXT weeks, gifts kept arriving, as I knew they would. Women from the village presented me with a beautiful new lodge, while kettles and everything I needed for cooking were given by friends and relatives. Mother presented me with a white elk-skin dress, heavily decorated with prized elk's teeth, that fit me perfectly and was as soft as the blue cover on Farwell's box. My little brother shyly handed over a quirt. "Red Fox helped me make it, and it's as good as any that he makes for our warriors," he explained. Strong Bull fingered the long rawhide tails and then swung the carved wooden handle in the air. "We made it light enough for you to get your horse moving, but it has enough weight to smack an enemy over the head if you need to do that."

Red Fox gifted me two sturdy packhorses, one that he had recently won in a game of dice, and the other one of his favorites. Father presented me with my own horse.

She was a young filly—white, with a touch of black around her eyes and a black ridge running down the length of her snow-white mane. Her black hooves pranced as Father led her over to me, and when he handed me the reins, her ears perked forward and her intelligent eyes took me in. I stroked her muzzle. "Oh Father, she's a beauty," I said. "*Ahoo.*"

"He traded three good horses for her," Mother said, but in my estimation, this horse was worth ten more, for she was chosen for me by my father.

"I will call her Snow," I said, and Father nodded his approval.

But Mother found new things to worry about each day. "Farwell talked of all the grizzly bears, but what if any of our enemies come to trade? Could they steal her?" Father assured her that Farwell was well known among many tribes and that those who came to trade would not want to jeopardize their relationship with him.

I, too, came up with new doubts every sleepless night. But in the end, wanting to please Father was what convinced me to stay with the plan. For the first time I felt that he was proud to have me as a daughter, and that alone seemed worth the marriage.

CHAPTER NINE

1872

TEN LODGES FROM our village, each one sheltering between four and eight people, traveled north with my family to Fort Benton. We arrived after seven days and made our camp alongside a swift-running stream outside town. The next morning I rode Snow toward town with Father and Red Fox to find Farwell.

We avoided the deep ruts of the road, but before I had time to wonder what had cut so deeply into Mother Earth's face, we were met by the culprit. First there was a cloud of dust, then the shouting of men and the creak of wheels.

"They call that a bull train," Father said as a slow-moving parade made its way past us. I stared at the size of it all while I counted four eight-yoke teams of huge oxen pulling twelve massive wagons. The wheels of the enormous wagons—the back ones were taller than Father—made the cuts in the road, and each wagon was piled high with boxes and barrels.

Four men, two on either side of the laboring animals, shouted and urged the oxen forward with the crack of whips.

"They're bringing supplies to the white men in towns and outposts all across this land," Father said, answering the question I was about to ask. Another bull train followed the first, while smaller carts and wagons traveled more quickly past us. Finally, we arrived at the outskirts of town. Wooden structures lined both sides of the road. One, a large long building, had a painted sign. "Can you read that?" I asked Father.

I recognized English letters from Grandfather's teaching, but Father could read better than I.

"It says Overland Hotel," he said. "I think Farwell stays there."

Was I going to stay with him in that building? I couldn't imagine being so closed in, with no opening in the roof. Maybe I could convince him to camp outside the town?

We quickly came upon other huge structures with signs, but I was too busy trying to make sense of what lay in front of me to attempt to read them. Endless wooden buildings lined the busy road, with barely any space between them, while in front of them ran a narrow stretch of boards that connected them all. A number of men walking on those boards were watching those of us who rode by, and I felt uneasy when some trailed their eyes over the length of me. A rank smell permeated the air. It seemed to be a mixture of cooked meat and human waste, and I tried not to breathe in too deeply.

Father pointed out some buildings called saloons, where harsh music spilled through the open doors. I saw my first white woman in front of one of them. She was leaning up against a man who grinned down at her, and I didn't like the lazy look of him, with his one foot braced up against the building. The woman fascinated me, though, with her pale skin, red hair, and billowing blue skirts.

As we approached the river, we caught sight of a huge steamboat that was docked along the levee. Across from the levee was a massive structure of logs surrounding what looked to be a small village. "That's the fort," Father said. "If we had pelts, that's where we'd go in to do the trading."

But it was the river I had wanted to see. My English grandfather had always talked about traveling on the great Missouri River, but now there were so many people crowded around, and the din was so loud that any opportunity to see the beauty and hear the comforting song of the water was drowned out. The noise was shattering—squealing carts and wagons, horses, mules, and oxen were urged to move by men all yelling at the same time. I recognized English, but there were other languages, too. Men swarmed about the levee and called out to one another as they sorted through boxes and barrels before piling them high onto waiting wagons.

While searching for Farwell, my eyes were drawn to a small group of women who stood back, seeming to enjoy watching the unloading of the boat. All the women were clothed in full-skirted calico dresses with vivid-colored shawls around their shoulders. Some wore silver or gold earrings and bracelets and most had children in hand, but what really caught my attention was that all these women looked Indian. One held a small child, who, with extended arms, was calling out for his father. A white man, dressed like Farwell, came to take his crying son from the woman's arms.

Was that to be my fate? Did Farwell expect me to dress as a white woman? The thought worried me. Just then, I spotted Farwell. He was talking with two other men, both dressed in dark long-tailed jackets and dark pants, but as soon as he saw us, he came bounding over.

"It's good to see you, Horse Guard. Red Fox," he said, nodding at each. He reached up to touch my hand, but thought better of it and pulled his hand back again. "I'm glad you came, Goes First," he said, with a warmth that left no doubt he meant his words. He waved toward the levee. "This boat that just came in was late by three weeks because of weather. Two more were supposed to be here by now, but they're going to be late, too, so a lot of our supplies are held up. Now we're trying to get what we can from this shipment."

"Abe, I've found the blankets," a voice called over the din from the direction of the levee.

"Set them aside," Farwell called back, then came again to stand beside my horse. "That's Hammond," he said, pointing to a tall thin man who was stacking boxes. "You'll get to know him. He's agreed to work with me up at the post." The man had straightened and was staring at us.

Farwell looked around and shook his head. "What a hell-fired mess this is. I was hoping to introduce you to some of these folks, but they're as worried about their supplies coming in as I am. Horse Guard, how about I come out to your camp this evening, after I get some of this sorted out?"

Father agreed, and I could not leave soon enough.

❁   ❁   ❁

THE SUN WAS not yet on the ground when Farwell rode up later in the day. He joined the men for a smoke and then a meal, but after, when Father came to speak to Mother and me, Farwell remained seated with the other men.

"You will be married tomorrow. He wants you to go back into town with him this evening. He has friends there, and one of their wives has invited you to her home so she might help you take a bath and wash your hair and then dress in some English clothes. He says that this is customary."

I thought of the Indian women I had seen in town, and I pointed to the nearby stream. "Tell him that I have fresh water here and that it is customary for me to bathe myself. I'll wash my own hair, and Mother will gloss it with cactus pith and then will braid it in the way of Crow women. And tomorrow I will wear my white elk dress that Mother has taken so much time to prepare for me."

Father heard my tone and didn't argue the point. "Then I'll tell him that we'll meet him tomorrow in town? There's a man there who will marry you in the white man's way."

"I don't want to go into that town to get married. The odor sickens me and the noise hurts my ears. I want to get married out here where I can hear the birds sing."

Father eyed me. Then he took Mother aside, and soon after she came back to sit with me away from the others.

"Goes First, why are you unwilling to do anything Farwell asks of you? Have you changed your mind? Do you not want to marry him?"

"I don't like what I saw in Fort Benton," I told her.

"You won't live in town. You'll live out in the country, just as he said."

"But what if I don't like that life? And what if he isn't good to me?"

"Then you will come back to your father's camp. You know we Crow women are always free to leave a marriage if we're mistreated. There is no shame in it," she said. "You will have your tipi and your horses and always keep a parfleche of pemmican so you have food to travel."

At these words, I took a deep breath and felt my body relax. It was reassuring to be reminded that I could always return home.

Mother leaned over to my puppy, who rested on my lap. He had grown since Farwell had given him to me, and I was as attached to him as I had ever been to an animal. He had only one bad habit, and that was to eat anything he could find. I cuddled him now, remembering again that Big Cloud had promised that this dog would look out for me. I thought, too, of my past year of desolation, and I knew the emptiness that awaited me again if I returned now with my family.

"Will you still marry him?"

I nodded, and Mother went out to speak with Father.

I FELT REFRESHED the following day. It was late in August, in the moon of the wild plums—my favorite time of year. When the sun was high and hot, Mother and I found a secluded spot down by the water where we bathed together. But this day her mood was solemn. To tease her, I splashed water at her face, and when she scolded me I did it again. This time her fighting spirit responded, and after she splashed back, the battle was on. Mother laughed then, that girlish sound that always made others around her smile. Later, we sat on the riverbank where she dressed my hair into my usual two braids, and later still she helped clothe me in my white elk-skin dress. As I cinched my waist with my wide leather belt and hung my sheathed skinning knife from it, she stood back to look at me. "You look so much like your grandmother," she said, and wiped her eyes. "She would be as proud of you as I am."

I choked back tears as we embraced.

There was already a golden glow to the afternoon when Farwell arrived. This time he came leading five horses, each burdened with more blankets for Father and our relatives. Following him was a white-haired man on a skinny mare. After presenting the horses to Father, Farwell came over to me.

"Goes First," he spoke in Crow. "You look beautiful." He had clearly practiced this, and his pronunciation was improving.

My face turned warm, but I was pleased. Each time I saw him he seemed to grow more handsome, and though he had an odd woody scent, today he wore a different buckskin jacket, this one clean and the fringes better cut. He removed his leather hat and smoothed his hair back. I was glad that he had no bushy facial hair like so many of the Yellow Eyes.

"Are you ready?" he asked, and when I agreed, he waved over the white-haired man who stood awkwardly to the side of Mother's tipi, no doubt sweltering in his thick black shirt.

"This is a minister," Farwell said as the man approached us. "He'll marry us."

"Howdy," the man said after he cleared his throat. "You have a name?"

"Her name is Goes First, and her father's name is Horse Guard," said Farwell.

The minister unfolded a sheet of paper from inside a book he carried and shook it open to show to Farwell. "For the marriage certificate she'll need a white name," he said. "I already wrote down Mary. It's the name we give all Indian women. Easier that way. Who can remember names like Hits Him Over the Head or Runs the Land with the Buffalo?" He chuckled, but sobered when Farwell frowned.

"Let's get on with it," Farwell said.

The man cleared his throat again, then spit off to his side, before he began to read from a small black book. Though the ceremony was short, I noticed my little brother shifting from foot to foot in impatience. Later, when the minister addressed me as Mary Horse Guard, I turned around and glanced at Father to see what he thought of his name being used in this way. Father caught my eye and nodded his approval, but I was distracted when Farwell unexpectedly reached for my hand. I pulled it back, embarrassed that he should touch me with everyone watching. To my relief, he didn't try it again.

The words said by the minister meant little to me, but Farwell seemed oddly moved. In fact, at one point he wiped his eye, and I wondered at that. Surely it wasn't a tear? And if so, what did that mean? Was it possible that I was marrying a weak man? This time Father ignored my worried glance.

When the minister finished, Farwell took the wedding paper from the white-haired man and proudly showed it to me and then to my father.

"See there? Now we're legally married," he said. Father took a serious look at the paper. "It is good," he announced, and Farwell seemed pleased.

As the sun dropped, we feasted on fresh buffalo tongue and buffalo ribs, and though everyone else enjoyed the delicious food, my concerns about this marriage stole my appetite. Later, just as the drumming and dancing began, unsettling noise cut through the celebration. I knew little of the effects of alcohol, as Father and most of the elders of our village disapproved of it. But some of our men had a taste for the stuff, and earlier that day two had gone into town to find some. It was against the white man's law to sell or trade alcohol to Indians, but that law was largely ignored, and our men quickly found a saloon that traded to them through the back door. Now they returned, both wildly shooting their rifles into the air and disturbing our celebration.

One, a normally peaceful man, staggered into the camp and shouted at his sister and brother-in-law when they tried to wrestle his rifle from him. The other, shouting war cries, kept shooting his gun into the bushes by the stream. Our peacekeepers, chosen that spring from the leading society of the Lumpwoods, attempted to settle the drunken men, but in the end they had to be tied down in their tipis. As their inebriated shouts rang out across our camp, and gunfire from the town of Fort Benton blasted into the night, a low feeling descended on me.

Wanting to put an end to the day, I got up and went to my tipi to await my new husband. I sat awkwardly on my pallet, dreading what was to come. Was sex with a white man the same as it was with an Indian? Would he hurt me? There were rumors that some had hair all over their bodies like bears. I pictured a glowing white body covered with hair like a bear and shuddered to think of it. And how would he smell? Would this Yellow Eyes be dirty under his clothes? The Crow men bathed every morning and took great pride in their appearance, but did white men do the same?

"Goes First." Farwell startled me when he stood at the door. "Can I come in?" he asked.

I nodded.

He dropped down next to me on the buffalo robe. "I won't stay here with you tonight. I know it will be hard for you to leave your family, and I'm guessing you want this last evening with them. I'll come back for you tomorrow, when I've finished my business in town. Can you be ready to leave then?" He lightly cupped my chin with his hand and turned me to face him. "Don't be afraid," he said. "I'll be a good husband to you."

I understood all he said and I was grateful for his kindness. "*Ahoo*," I said, fighting back tears of relief. After he left, Mother came and together we moved my bedding back into her tipi.

There I lay awake, long after my parents stopped their nighttime murmuring, and realized that this was probably the last time I would hear my brother's soft whiffling snores and my father's louder ones.

THE NEXT MORNING, I woke early to rub Snow's white coat with a soft piece of deer hide until it shone. Later, Mother and I dressed her together. I put a buffalo-hide blanket across my horse's back, then Mother placed my new saddle over it. It had been made by a woman in our village whose saddles were highly prized, and it was a thing of beauty. She began with just the right box elder tree and covered the wood frame with stitched white buckskin, then finished it with colorful beaded pendants that hung from both the front and back horns. Mother ran her hand across the curve of the saddle and up the high back horn. "This should keep you secure," she said, trying to keep the worry from her voice. I ran my own hand up the high front horn and around the prong that would have held Big Cloud's war shield, had I married him.

Mother saw my stricken look and understood. She hugged me, but when Father waved at us she stepped back. "Come, Goes First. Our scouts signal that your husband is on his way. Father wants you to be ready. Let's finish up," she said, and together we fastened the red, green, and white beaded crupper that secured the saddle from the back end of my horse.

When we finished, my mother hung from my shoulder the small turtle-shaped bag that held my umbilicus. "Remember why you wear this, Goes First," Mother said. "It is to remind you that you are never alone. You have three mothers. You have me, you have your tipi, and you have Mother Earth."

I grasped hold of Mother's hand. How could I leave her? She had stood up to Father for me so many times and had so patiently helped me through my mourning Big Cloud. My throat felt tight from holding back tears.

Father came over and took the reins. "He's coming. It's time to go," he said, giving Mother a look that told her to back away. I raised myself into the saddle, and as I settled my feet into the wide stirrups, I looked around to see where Mother had gone.

As Farwell approached, Mother ran from her tipi and quickly hooked a small parfleche of pemmican to my pommel. "Keep this for yourself," she whispered. "It's good for over a year, and if you need to leave, you'll have it."

Father took Mother's arm and pulled her to his side as Farwell swung off his horse to meet them. Strong Bull handed up my yipping puppy, and Farwell turned to me. "Goes First, you and horse stand beautiful," he said, and his attempt at Crow words gave me a small lift.

Red Fox led over my two fully loaded packhorses, and Farwell's eyebrows rose when he saw they carried my tightly folded lodge and all the necessary cooking equipment. "You won't need most of that," he said. "I have more than enough pots and pans. And you sure won't need your tipi. I have a canvas one."

"I take my lodge," I said.

He looked surprised at my firm tone, but he mounted his horse and came up next to mine. "Well," he said, reaching for the reins of my packhorses, "let me at least lead these two then." He looked offended when I pulled them back, but Crow women took care of their possessions, and our men did not try to take them away.

He turned his horse to ride out then, and as I followed, my eyes blurred. What had I done? I dreaded facing Fort Benton. How long would we be staying there, I wondered?

"*Kalachíi diiawákaawik,*" Mother called. *I will see you again,* she had called, for we Crow did not like to say goodbye.

I looked back and gave a quick wave. Red Fox stood with his arm around my little brother's shoulders, his other hand raised in farewell. Together they called out, "*Kalachíi diiawákaawik.*"

I squeezed my eyes tight to keep tears from falling. I felt for Red Fox's knife that hung from my belt and checked again for my brother's quirt suspended from the horn of my saddle. I clutched hold of the puppy in my lap, and as we drew farther and farther away, it took everything in me not to turn back. I wanted to call out for Mother and tell her I had made a mistake. How could I live without her? What would I do when I had babies and she was not there to help me? And Strong Bull—I wouldn't be there to see him grow into a brave. Who would I turn to for advice? Red Fox had always been there to guide me. And though Father was often away fighting off our enemies, it was he we all relied on to feed and protect us.

What had I done?

CHAPTER TEN

1872

IT TOOK A while before I realized we were not heading in the direction of Fort Benton. Farwell saw my questioning look. "I guess you noticed that we're not going into town? Your father told me how you didn't like the place, so I made other arrangements."

I was so happy to hear his news that I smiled and began to relax as I took in the open countryside. We rode up and over some low hills and startled a herd of deer. Though they bounded away, they soon stopped to graze once more. A hawk swooped down into the tall grass and rose swiftly with a rabbit clenched in his talons, but as the rabbit's death-cry faded, the air soon sweetened again with the fluty song of the yellow meadowlark. In time, Farwell led us to the top of a small hill, where he pointed to the valley below.

There, in a grove of tall cottonwoods, some tipis set scattered among a settlement of about five small log cabins.

The deep lowing of oxen came from a nearby corral, and tethered horses fed on the surrounding green grass.

"These are some Métis who live out here. I've hired some of these men—they'll be bringing my supplies up north and helping build the fort. Since Horse Guard is Métis, I thought you might be more comfortable staying with them while I do my business in town." Farwell looked at me to gauge my response.

I understood why Farwell called Father a Métis, though I knew he didn't consider himself as such. Yes, his father had been a Yellow Eyes, but he had been raised as Crow and he considered himself Crow, as had I. I knew little about the Métis people but, relieved at not having to go into Fort Benton, I nodded my approval. "*Éeh itchik*," I said, and then remembered to speak so he could understand. "Yes, good," I said.

SHOUTS WENT UP as soon as Farwell and I were sighted. A river ran close to this small village that was laid out in a random way, though the cabins and tipis more or less circled the main yard. A few men came forward to greet us and take the reins of our horses, while the women stayed in the yard alongside open cooking fires.

"M'sieu Abe, we been waiting for you," one of the men said, patting the neck of Farwell's horse. "We been wanting to see the wife you got."

As they gathered around, I felt their eyes on me as we dismounted. When I faced them, they all grinned approvingly while looking me up and down. I didn't like their open looks. Did they think of me as a horse?

"She look strong, work hard, and give you plenty of *des enfants*," said a woman who stood with a baby of her own on her hip.

What unusual-looking people, I thought. I might have considered them Indian, but the women wore cloth dresses, and many of the men had bushy hair on their faces like my English grandfather.

"Her name is Mary," Farwell said, nodding toward me.

Mary? Was that what he planned on calling me? It was a solemn event when our Crow names were given to us after our birth, though those names might be changed if a child was sickly or later if an adult performed a brave deed. I hadn't minded *Mary Horse Guard*, given me at the wedding, especially after I saw Father's approval. Now, though, the single *Mary* felt foreign and lonely.

"We got you set up down there." The man pointed toward a dense thicket of chokecherry shrubs that bordered a stand of pines. The spot set close to the water and a distance from the village. "Nobody come to bother you and your new wife." He winked, and my face flushed. I understood only too well what he meant.

A young girl who looked to be about ten snows rushed over to me. "Hello, Mary. *Je m'appelle Lucille.* Jeannie and me, we come help you."

The girl pointed back toward a young woman, one closer to my age, but I was too tired and overwhelmed to pay much attention.

"Thank you, Lucille, for your kind offer," Farwell said, "but it's been a long day. I think Mary and I will go on our own to get our camp set up."

Lucille looked disappointed, but she said nothing more. Farwell grinned at an older woman who was stirring a big kettle over a fire in a corner of the yard. "If I'm not mistaken, that's elk you got in that stew, Lisette? We sure wouldn't mind some of that later on."

"M'sieu Farwell, you and your missus come get some anytime you ready," the woman replied.

A man slapped Farwell on the shoulder. "Go on now. Tomorrow, maybe, we roast some buffalo ribs and we celebrate the boss's new wife."

I was as tired as I had ever been, and I wished Farwell hadn't turned down Lucille's offer to help me get my tipi set up. After we watered the horses we rode to the campsite, but along the way I felt a pull on the reins when one of my packhorses tripped on a rock. She stumbled but regained her footing, and because she was only slightly limping, I continued on around the high bushes. There I was surprised to find a canvas tipi already set up next to a small covered wagon.

"I asked them to put it up for us," Farwell said. "I figured we'd be tired when we got here."

He was right. I was exhausted, but as soon as I dismounted, I went back to check my horse's leg. Relieved that I couldn't feel an injury, I straightened and patted her neck.

"Is she all right?" Farwell asked.

I nodded and then saw that Farwell was untying the load from my packhorse's back. "No," I said, touching his hand. This was my work. These were my belongings. A Crow man would never touch a woman's things like this.

"What do you mean, *no*," he said teasingly, even as he continued to untie and pull down the carefully bundled contents of my home.

"No," I said more firmly, as I pulled a backrest from his arms.

Still playful, he tried to take it back. "Come on," he teased, "I'm just trying to help."

I yanked it away. "No," I said again, and moved to stand as a barrier in front of my horses. I wanted to take my time, removing everything Mother had helped me pack. Every piece had been carefully made, and I wanted time to appreciate each one.

"Mary," he said. "What's wrong?"

How could this ever work? He didn't understand me, and I sure didn't understand him. I was too tired to leave, too tired even to put up my own tipi, but if my horse was all right in the morning, I would leave then. If I hurried, maybe I could still catch my parents before they got too far from Fort Benton.

Farwell threw his hands up in the air as I began to unburden my horses. He watched me for a while, and then after tending to his horse he announced that he would make some coffee.

"I know I could use some," he said. He lit the pile of wood that the Métis had collected for us, then got the supplies from the wagon. Out of the corner of my eye I could see that he knew what he was doing, and that made me angrier still. A Crow woman makes the food and here was this Yellow Eyes, cooking like a woman. Worse yet, while I didn't like the taste of coffee, it did smell good.

After I had everything unpacked and safely tucked under a cover, I straightened to rub my back. Farwell sat on a log by the fire, quiet, watching me.

"Why don't you come and have some of this?" He poured two cups of the hot black liquid and offered one to me. Why had I never noticed the hair on the knuckles of his hand? And what had ever made me think that he was handsome?

"Come, sit," he said, and patted a seat beside him on the log.

Exhausted, I sat.

"Looks to me like you got yourself tied into some knots?" he said. "You have anything you want to say to me?"

I couldn't answer. The English words I knew were all muddled. My stomach felt sick. I couldn't find the words to tell him that I had made a mistake and that I planned to leave. I got up and went over to check my horse's leg again. To my dismay, the bay pulled back when I touched her fetlock.

Farwell came over and squatted down beside me. "Can I have a look?" he asked. I nodded, and twice he ran his hand down her leg as I had. "It's a little swollen, but I think she'll be okay as long as she has a chance to rest it. I'll go over and get some ointment from the Métis." He lifted his hands into the air. "I'm sure you have some of your own, but this way you won't have to dig through all your things. Besides, you can always count on the Métis to know what to do for a horse."

I said nothing as I fought tears.

"Go on," he said, encouraging me to go back and sit by the fire. "Why don't you sit there and drink your coffee, and I'll go find some grub and get that ointment. I've got some business to talk over with the men, and that'll give you a little time to yourself."

I nodded, grateful for time alone.

He waved toward his lodge. "We'll get a good sleep tonight and start all over in the morning," he said. "I think maybe you're just tired."

He left then before I could tell him that come morning, I would be going home.

AFTER HE LEFT, I slowly sipped the bitter drink that matched my dark mood. My exhausted puppy slept at my feet while I watched the sun set. Though a brilliant orange colored the sky, I scarcely saw it. All I could think of was how I could catch up to my parents before they got too far away. If I left with only one packhorse, I would have to leave half of my belongings behind. Neither Father nor my relatives who had gifted me with so much would be happy about that.

Also, Father had made his support of this marriage abundantly clear. If I didn't at least give it a try, I doubted he would ever forgive me. But wasn't this my life? Shouldn't I be able to choose my own path?

As I debated with myself, I heard rustling in the shrubs. It was dark enough that I couldn't see far, and I unsheathed my knife as I got to my feet. There was a rifle leaning against my tipi, but I didn't know if it was loaded and I thought of it too late. My heart pounded in my chest.

"Hello, Mary," Lucille called as she and another girl, hand in hand, came through the bushes. Angry at being so scared, I swung my arms in the air. "Go away!" I called out. At the sight of my knife, their eyes grew large, and they ran.

It was dark when Farwell returned. I was still sitting at the fire, which had burned down to embers, and I was more unhappy than ever.

"You must be hungry?" he said, setting a small pot of elk stew next to me. Then he went to my horse and, without asking, applied some ointment to her leg. "It's a little more swollen than before, but this, and a few days' rest, should take care of it." He came back over to where I sat and filled two wooden bowls with the fragrant stew. It smelled of home, and my throat felt tight from holding back tears. He set a spoon in each one, along with a chunk of fry bread. I shook my head at his offer. "Come on," he said. "You need to eat something, and that Lisette's one of the best cooks I know." I shook my head again, and he set the bowl down beside me.

He lifted his own and began to eat. "It's good," he said, but I wouldn't look at him. After he finished, he put his bowl down, picked mine up, and came to kneel in front of me. He dipped the bread in the stew and offered me a bite. I remembered how I had done the same with Red Fox, and my eyes stung at the memory. Whatever would I do without Grandfather?

"Come," Farwell said, offering me the bread again, and because he looked so hopeful, I took a bite.

"Good," he said, but when he held up a spoonful of the stew, I couldn't hold back the tears. He set the bowl down and pulled me into his arms. "It'll be all right," he soothed, patting my back. "It'll be all right."

I couldn't seem to stop crying. Though I had been the one to leave my family, I felt abandoned. When my wave of tears finally eased, Farwell led me into the canvas lodge. There he settled me on a thick buffalo robe and handed over my tired dog. "I'll sleep here tonight," he said, laying out another buffalo robe an arm's length away.

Exhausted from the day, I soon fell asleep, but I awoke during the night, startled by a loud snore from Farwell. After that I stayed awake a long while, working out how and when to make my escape.

CHAPTER ELEVEN

1872

I AWOKE THE NEXT morning to hear Farwell whistling outside the lodge. My eyes still felt raw from crying, and then I remembered my dilemma. I was going to leave. I couldn't go without my pack-horse, so I would have to wait until she was fit for travel, but for the trip back to my parents, I had the stars to guide me.

I was afraid of Farwell's reaction to my leaving, so I didn't plan on telling him. But if he should catch up to me, what did Yellow Eyes do to their wives when they were angry? I had heard they could be cruel. But more than fearing Farwell, and even more than the fear of traveling on my own, I dreaded facing Father. What would he say if Farwell demanded the return of his horses and rifles? I would have to deal with that when the time came. Until my horse was ready for travel, I would try to get along with this man. He seemed willing enough.

I came out into the sunshine to find him with his face covered in a white froth. He was looking into a small mirror that hung from a tree, and with an odd-looking knife he was scraping the mess off his face. He didn't have a shirt on, and I tried to avoid gaping at his white skin and at how surprisingly broad and strong his shoulders looked.

"Ah, Mary," he said, noticing me. "I hope you had a good sleep?"

"Yes," I said, "I sleep good."

"Listen, Mary," he said. "René, one of the men I count on from here, came to tell me that a boat is supposed to come in today or tomorrow.

I'm pretty sure that you don't want to come into Fort Benton with me, so I'll have to leave you here alone for a day or so. Are you all right with that?"

"Yes," I said, and went over to check my horse's leg.

"I've already treated it," he said. "It's still a little swollen, and she'll need a few more days of rest." He winked when he saw me watching him dry his face, and I flushed.

"René will travel with me, but his wife, Jeannie, will come by later with some food." He went into the lodge and called out from there. "If you need anything else while I'm gone, look in the wagon. Take anything you need."

When he came out, he wore a blue cloth shirt that made his eyes look even bluer than before.

"I'll leave this one with you," he said handing over a rifle. "The Métis will be around if you need them, but just keep your eyes open. You've got the horses here, and there's always the danger of bears and cats—same as down where you come from."

Farwell surprised me when he suddenly leaned over and kissed my cheek, his lips soft and gentle.

He smelled of the woods—a clean pine scent, and in spite of my plans on leaving, I didn't find his intimate gesture unpleasant. I watched as he rode away and I was more confused than ever. I hadn't imagined he would be this thoughtful and kind.

I HEARD THEIR voices long before the two girls reached me.

"Hello," the older one called as she came forward with a smile. "I'm Jeannie, René's wife," she said as she set a blue-and-white tin plate of food down on a flat rock beside the ashes of last night's fire. "You must be hungry." She uncovered some fried pemmican and two pieces of fluffy white bread. "That's Bannock," she said. "I think you'll like it."

"*Ahoo*," I said, gratefully taking the plate. I had hardly eaten since the day before with my family. We Crow didn't fry our pemmican, but the familiar food made my mouth water when I sat to eat. When I finished, I set the plate down and sighed. "*Ahoo*," I repeated.

"Does that mean thank you?" Jeannie asked.

"*Éeh*," I said.

"Do you speak English?"

"My English not good," I said.

"Then we will speak slowly," Jeannie said. "Farwell said your father is Métis?"

"*Éeh*," I said.

"I'm Métis, too—but most everybody calls us half-breeds," Lucille offered. "My daddy, he's French, but he's dead, and my mama, she's Cree."

Jeannie cut in. "I am Métis, too, but my father was a fur trader from Scotland, and they said that my mother was Blackfoot. Last year I came down from Canada after I married René, Lucille's brother." The two girls exchanged a smile. "I was with the Grey Nuns in their orphanage until my René rescued me."

"*Oui*, our René, he fall in love," Lucille said, and the two girls laughed. Jeannie was older, though not much taller than Lucille, and both had dark eyes and a long braid of shining black hair that was interwoven with the prettiest red and yellow ribbons. Their dresses of deep blue cotton were of a length that showed off their brightly beaded moccasins and leggings.

Jeannie looked at my clean plate. "Lucille, would you please take this plate and bring back more for Mary to eat."

Before I could find the words to say I was full, Lucille was off and running.

Jeannie turned back to me. "I'm guessing you didn't want more, but Lucille tags after me all the time and I wanted to talk to you alone." She looked at me with such sincerity that I was taken aback. "Farwell told my René that you aren't happy? That maybe you think you made a mistake by marrying him?"

How did he know? When my eyes filled with tears, she put her hand over mine. "I know how you feel. Just one year ago, I felt the same way. I met René and I was so in love, but when he brought me here, to live with his mama who is not kind—God be praised—all I wanted to do was to run away." Her eyes moistened with the memory. "I cried at night for weeks, but René was good to me, and now I've even found a way to get along with his mother—that old crab." When she smiled at me it was as though the sun had come out.

"I cry, too," I said.

"Of course you will. You've had to leave your family, your people. But Farwell is a good man. You got lucky with him like I did with my René."

I glanced back at the lodge, then away again. I dreaded spending another night in that canvas lodge. It had a terrible smell.

"You don't like that tipi?" Jeannie asked, and I pinched my nose as I searched for the words.

"Sometimes those canvas tipis can smell musty," she said. "Especially once they get wet and aren't dried out the right way." She looked at my pile of belongings. "Mary, do you have your own tipi here?"

"*Éeh*," I said.

"So why don't we put it up? If the men are going to be waiting on those boats with their supplies to come in, the two of you could be here for at least a few weeks. Why not make yourself at home?"

Even if I planned to leave in a few days, the idea of having my own lodge with the fresh scent of clean hide gave me a lift. I could burn some of my cedar and . . .

Lucille burst through the trees. "Mama asking if we was feeding horses over here," she said, handing over more food on the blue and white plate.

"What a crab," Jeannie muttered under her breath. "Thank you, Lucy," she said aloud. "Just put it over here for now. First we're going to help Mary set up her lodge."

After we had my tipi standing, Jeannie, who was only as tall as my shoulder, stood next to me and put her arm around my waist. "There. You have your home now," she said. The gesture warmed me when I remembered how Sees Much had often done the same with Grandmother.

Relief had me again close to tears, so to distract myself I began to unroll the two willow backrests that Mother and I had made.

As soon as I suspended them from their tripods, Lucille plunked herself down in one, while Jeannie, with a happy sigh, sank onto a folded buffalo robe. She patted the space next to her, but when I sat, I was unsure of what to say.

Suddenly Lucille gasped. "Oh, I forgot! Mama said we have a bunch of berries that we got to sort through. She wants us back there to work."

Jeannie got to her feet. "Do you want to come with us?"

I shook my head. I had no desire to meet her mother-in-law.

"Then we'll bring you a meal again tonight." She reached for the young girl's hand. "Come on, Lucy, we'd better run," she said, and the two left, their skirts flying.

I HAD JUST finished tethering my horses after watering them at the nearby stream when my puppy came running. He had rolled in some animal dung and smelled so high that I had to take him down to the water to clean him. I had admired the rifle a few times already that day, but now I took it along and set it within easy reach.

It was secluded along that curve of the river, and after I washed him, I decided to bathe myself. There was good healing mud along the riverbank, and I used it now to scrub away the past few days. I sat on a flat rock on the bank and let the sun dry my hair before I returned to my lodge to put on clean clothes. Refreshed, I unpacked the rest of my belongings. Finally, with everything in place, I said the prayers that Grandmother had taught me as I cleansed my lodge with the smoke from burning cedar and sweetgrass. The familiar scents and Grandmother's prayers soothed me, and I felt more settled as I waited for Lucille and Jeannie to return.

The sun was already starting to go down when I heard the sound of hoofbeats and a whinny. When my horses answered, I stood, ready to go for the gun. But it was Farwell who rode up.

"Hey, Mary," he greeted me. "The damn boat won't be in for a couple more days, so I thought I might as well come home and see how my wife is doing." He nodded when he saw my lodge. "Good to see you settling in."

I had expected him to be angry when he saw my tipi and I was prepared to stand my ground, but with his approval, my fight left me and I felt oddly deflated. I wanted to be angry with him, but I could find no reason.

"I usually go down and join the others for something to eat," he said. "You want to come with me?"

"No," I said, expecting Jeannie and Lucille's return.

"Okay," he said, "I know it'll take a while for you to get used to all this. How about I just bring something back for you?"

I WAITED FOR Jeannie, but she didn't come. Instead, Farwell returned with a heaping plate of food. I had a fire going and I was hungry, but I waited until he took a seat across from me. "You want?" I asked, offering him the food.

He shook his head. "No, Jeannie fixed that for you. I've already eaten. I'll just sit here and keep you company."

It felt awkward to eat with him watching me, but I was hungry and I enjoyed the food.

"They're going to roast some buffalo ribs tomorrow evening to celebrate our wedding. Will you come along with me for that?"

"Jeannie come?" I asked.

"Yes," he said. "She'll be there."

I finished and set the plate to the side. "I come."

He yawned and stretched. "I'm ready to pack it in. Are you tired?"

My heart thudded and I shrugged. *Here it comes*, I thought. If I was going to stay, I might as well get it over with. Since talking with Jeannie, I had decided to at least give this marriage a few more days. If Jeannie had felt the same way when she first came, and it worked out for her, maybe it could work out for me, too.

Farwell searched my face for a long while but said nothing before he stood. He yawned again and then went into his canvas lodge. I heard him rummaging around and waited for him to call for me. My heart was pounding. Then I had another thought. Maybe he was going to come to my lodge. Of course. That was what he would probably do.

I swiftly doused the fire and went into my tipi. There, trying to stay calm, I stripped off my clothes and slipped into my bed. I had a fair idea of what to expect, but were white men like Indians? Did they have sex the same way, or did they do something that I didn't know about? I wished now that I had been intimate with Big Cloud so at least I would have something to compare it to. I lay there waiting, imagining every possible scenario. I kept trying to relax and reminded myself to listen to the night sounds. I could hear the frogs croaking out their mating calls, and if I listened carefully, I could hear the peaceful bubbling water from the river. Time passed, and I began to wonder where he was. Then I heard a sound coming from Farwell's lodge that had me lean up on my elbow to better listen. Sure enough, the man was snoring. I lay back down, first to smother my giggles of relief, and later to wonder if maybe there was something wrong? Was he too old to want sex?

But I doubted that was the reason. He was less than twenty snows older than me, and plenty of our much older warriors still had sweethearts. Was it possible that he had an injury? Maybe we would never have sex. But I wanted children, and I also wanted to enjoy sex with my husband as I knew my parents did with each other. Then I had another thought, one that troubled me the most. Maybe he didn't find me attractive enough to want me? Was that possible?

I LOOKED OUT in the early morning and saw Farwell heading down to the water with a change of clothes. *Good*, I thought. *Here is my chance.* Before I was completely sure about this marriage, I needed to know if all his parts were working. I quickly slipped on my dress and arrived just as Farwell was picking his way along the rocky river bottom toward the deeper water, his naked body tensed with the cold.

"Mary," he greeted me in surprise. I gave a wave to indicate I wanted him to turn away, and he dove into the water. As he swam, I undressed slowly, and after taking enough time for him to get curious, I stepped into the river. It was cool, and as I splashed myself, I gave little gasps when the water hit my hips and then my breasts. I didn't look directly at him, but I sensed him standing in water up to his waist staring at me. The water was so clear that I could see the mossy rocks and pebbles underfoot, and after wading closer, I dove in. There, seeing him underwater, in spite of the cold, any doubts I had about his virility were put to rest.

When I surfaced, he busied himself by rubbing a yellow piece of what looked like solid fat all over his body. After it frothed, he dove in and rinsed it away. He held it up to me. "Want to use this soap?" he asked. I shook my head. I would cleanse myself with the river mud, as I had always done.

I swam then, and he joined me, but whenever he came close, I swam away. Finally, he left the water, and after drying himself he again stood in front of a small mirror that he hung from a tree.

It was my turn to look then, and though he was pale as winter snow, he was unashamed of his body. He was more muscled than I had expected, and better formed, with a tight stomach and strong arms and legs. I watched curiously as he again rubbed his face with white foam and then scraped it off with the small sharp knife. As he did so, he glanced back at me, and again I saw that he was aroused.

I waited for him to dress, and though he might have stayed, I waved him away. After he left, I dove back into the water and welcomed the cold. I certainly had satisfied myself that Farwell's man parts were working, but what surprised me was the tingling in my own body.

WE COULD SMELL the buffalo ribs roasting, and by late afternoon I was more than ready to eat. When Lucille saw us walking toward their small settlement she came running. "*Bonjour*, Mary," she called, and I was happy to also see Jeannie's welcoming wave.

Jeannie led me toward the women tending large pots and pans over cooking fires while Farwell joined the men lounging over at the other side of the yard. Jeannie leaned toward my ear. "The one that looks like she was sucking gooseberries is Lucille and René's mother." Her voice took on a lighter tone when she brought me to stand in front of her mother-in-law. "Mama Rosa, this is Mary, Farwell's new wife."

A small woman, no taller than Jeannie, looked me up and down. "I know," was all she said.

When I saw her scarred face, I believed I understood her misery. I had seen other Indians who had survived smallpox, and I wouldn't have been surprised to learn that she had lost her family and most of her village to the disease.

The other women were quick to step forward and welcome me. I did my best to respond to their greetings, but because they spoke faster and with a French accent like Lucille, I found Jeannie and Farwell's English easier to understand.

"Here, have something to drink before we eat," Jeannie said, handing me a tin cup filled with something she called rum punch. I was thirsty and eagerly drank the sweet-tasting liquid without stopping to wonder what was in it. The women began to heap food onto platters and carry them to the long tables. I felt my cheeks warming and my joints loosening, though I didn't know why. I looked about for Farwell, and when he caught my eye, I returned his smile.

These men and women were certainly a colorful group—the men clothed in buckskin pants and brightly colored shirts while the women were dressed much the same as Jeannie and Lucille. Some wore full cotton dresses while others wore shirts that were tucked into long full skirts with petticoats that peeked out. Each had a vivid shawl around her shoulders, and I remembered those Indian women at Fort Benton who had worn the same. Both the Métis women and men wore beautifully beaded moccasins, and each man wore a wide colorful sash wound around his waist.

There were ten women, many children, and about fifteen men. The children were shy and stood back to observe both Farwell and me. Some of the families lived here in log cabins permanently, but the men who camped in the tipis were usually on the move, employed by fur-trading companies or independent traders like Farwell, to carry supplies from Fort Benton to fur-trading posts up north and into Canada.

There was much good-willed laughter and banter as we sat to eat. The buffalo ribs were flavored with salt and pepper, a new sharp taste for me, and there was fish served as well—a food that the Crow did not eat. But they also served something they called a meat pie, and that I liked very much. Then, after I thought I could eat nothing more, Jeannie brought me another dish—a creamy pudding of rice and raisins, which became my favorite.

As we finished our food, a few of the men went into the cabins and returned with some strange-looking wood pieces that had strings attached. Jeannie laughed when I grimaced at the sharp squeals. "The men are tuning their fiddles," she explained as they screeched away.

Two other men settled themselves with tin plates between their knees and large spoons in their hands, and then everyone was quiet. I looked around and couldn't imagine what was to come next.

"*Un, deux, trois,*" one of the fiddlers counted as he stomped his foot, and jangled music erupted. Whoops sounded from all around, and when a young man came toward us, Jeannie jumped up to meet him. I guessed him to be René by the way he kissed her when he took her hand.

"Now we dance," Jeannie called back to me. I thought the rhythm of the music too fast, but I was proven wrong when the couple joined the others in what Lucille called a jig. René bounced Jeannie into the air as they danced, and from the way the two laughed and held each other, I could see their love.

I was feeling relaxed and happy, and after I drained the cup of punch someone filled my cup again. Farwell sat down beside me and put his hand on mine before I could raise the cup again. "Better go slow with that," he said, and when I saw he didn't have a mug of his own, I offered him some of mine. He shook his head. "I don't drink alcohol . . . anymore," he said.

"Alcohol?"

"There's rum in that drink. That's booze," he said.

I looked at him in shock. I had grown up with Father's warnings against drink, and I well remembered the effect of it on the braves the day of my marriage. I set the cup down on the ground next to my feet and sat on my hands while I waited for what was to come next. Would I start to yell or look for guns to shoot? I waited, but as I watched Jeannie dance, I only felt happy. Relieved, I smiled at Farwell.

"Are you ready to go?" he asked, reaching for my hand. "They'll be dancing all night."

I felt light-headed when I stood and was glad to be holding Farwell's steadying hand as we waved goodbye and walked toward our camp. Along the way he stopped, and when he took me in his arms, I welcomed his kisses in a way that shook me.

"Have you ever been with a man?" Farwell asked after we began to walk again.

"No," I said, and he seemed surprised.

At our camp, he walked me to my lodge and then abruptly disappeared after announcing that he was going to check on the horses. I hesitated at the door of my tipi, wondering what had happened. I had expected that he would stay with me, and I pondered again the strange ways of white men. Still feeling the effects of the rum, I decided that I might as well go to sleep. Inside my lodge I flung off my clothes—something I had never done before—and climbed into my bed.

Later, when the door flap opened, I saw that it was Farwell. He silently removed his clothes, and when he came over, I held up the blanket to let him slip in beside me.

He had been wise in taking his time with me. When he pulled me to him and kissed me, I felt how much he wanted me, and now I wanted him. "It's been hard to wait for you," he whispered, and an unexpected warmth coursed through my body. My new husband was as patient as he was gentle, and because of it, lovemaking was more pleasurable than I had ever imagined it would be.

CHAPTER TWELVE

1872

THE FOLLOWING MORNING, we went to bathe again, and soon we were entwined on the riverbank. Farwell meant to go to Fort Benton that day, but our attraction to each other convinced him otherwise.

"Why do you call me Farwell?" he asked as we lay spent next to each other.

"That's your name," I said.

"You can call me Abe, you know?" he said.

"I like Farwell." It was the name I had come to know him by and was the name I heard others call him as well.

"Well, then, you call me whatever you like," he said, and kissed me again.

JEANNIE AND LUCILLE found me the next day, after he had left.

"*Bonjour*, Mary," Lucille called out before the two came through the bushes.

"Hi, Mary," Jeannie said. "The men just brought in some buffalo, and the women wanted to know if you would like to come and help us dry the meat and make pemmican? Of course, we'll give you some in return so you'll have a good supply for your trip north."

I glanced around my camp. I had already stacked the wood I would need for a few nights. I had washed our clothes the day before, my bay's leg was cared for, and my horses were watered and fed. My meals were taken care of, as Farwell had arranged for the Métis to keep me supplied with meat. I had brought plenty of dried turnips and wild carrots—both food staples of the Crow, and he had shown me where to find what he called vegetables—carrots, potatoes, and onions—in the back of his wagon.

Jeannie looked at me hopefully. "It would be nice to have someone to work with who is my age. All the others are older or younger, like this little sister of mine." Lucille looked up at her with adoring eyes.

"Yes, I come," I said, eager to spend more time with Jeannie.

My new friend looked at me, smiling. "I think you have come to know your husband? You look happy."

My face turned hot and she giggled. "You'll tell me later," she said.

THE YARD WAS taken over with the women butchering the buffalo. Some were already cutting portions of the meat into thin strips and hanging them over large racks to dry.

"*Bonjour*, Crow Mary," they called in greeting, and Jeannie explained they had decided on that name to set me apart from one of their own, also named Mary. "Good," I said, and nodded my agreement. This was a name I liked. It left no doubt who my people were.

As we walked through the yard an older man was coming out of his log cabin. "*Merde*," Jeannie muttered when she saw him heading toward us. "You can never tell what he's thinking with that big white beard covering his face."

The man walked slowly, dragging his one foot behind, followed by a scruffy-looking dog. "You won't like him," Jeannie warned, "but my mother-in-law will have my hide if I don't stop to say hello."

"Who you got here?" he asked.

"Hello, M'sieu Dubois," Jeannie said. "This is my new friend, Crow Mary."

He scowled. "You Crow?"

I nodded.

He spit at the ground. "Dirty Crow," he said, and limped away.

"You old pecker," Jeannie said under her breath, then leaned close to me. "Don't worry about him. He's just a miserable old Métis fur trader. His Sioux wife and two children were killed years ago during a battle with the Crow. They put an arrow in his leg, too, so he really hates them. Actually, he hates everyone. The only thing he cares about is his damn dog."

I felt a shiver of fear but remembered the rifle I had propped inside my tipi.

FARWELL WAS AWAY for four more days, and each morning I was glad to go to the Métis camp to help make pemmican. Those days were hot and the sky was cloudless—perfect weather for hanging and drying the thinly sliced meat, but my eyes opened wide when I saw how many mounds of dried juneberries were waiting to be crushed. Later, in a final step of making pemmican, buffalo bones would be boiled and the fat skimmed off to be mixed with the pulverized meat and berries. That mixture—a rich and nutritious food—would stay preserved for many months. It was a food we Crow relied on, and now I saw that these people did as well. But I was surprised at the amount they made.

Jeannie and I separated ourselves from the others so that as we ground the dried fruit, we could talk with some privacy.

"You make much pemmican," I said.

"*Merde.* I know. It's a chore. But we don't just make it for ourselves. We sell it to the big trading companies whose men rely on it. They say that one pound of our pemmican will feed a man better than eight pounds of fresh meat, and we have a hard time keeping up with the demand," she said with some pride. "Besides, even if we don't sell it, it keeps for up to three years."

I had Crow friends, but I already felt a bond with Jeannie that I had never before felt with a girl of my own age. I *did* want to talk to her about what went on between me and Farwell at night, but I certainly didn't have the words for that—either in English or in Crow.

I loved to listen to her talk. At first, she was hard to follow, because she spoke quickly and often forgot herself as she slipped from one language to another.

"You talk English and French?" I asked.

"And Cree," she said.

"How you learn?"

"I was taught by the Grey Nuns," she said. "At the orphanage up in Canada. My father abandoned my mother, and when my mother died they took me in. I was just a baby. Some of the nuns were good to me, but there were some, *cruelle* . . . but I don't talk about that." She shuddered and shook her head at the thought. "They wanted me to be a nun like them, and they were training me to be a teacher, but last year, the year I turned sixteen, I met René one morning at the market and he saved me from all that business. Imagine. We fell in love over onions and potatoes. God be praised," she said, smiling.

"What that is, 'God be praised'?"

She laughed. "It means I was raised by Catholic nuns."

"My English . . . ," I said.

"Your English is surprisingly good, but I'll make a deal with you. I'll teach you English," she said, "if you will teach me to speak Crow? I'll bet you will learn faster than I will."

In that way, my education began as a game, with each of us trying to remember more than the other. If either of us had difficulty understanding certain words, we relied on sign language to get us through. Jeannie was not sparing in her corrections and neither was I, and because of that we both learned quickly.

OUR FRIENDSHIP GREW daily, and soon the two of us looked forward to working alone, as increasingly we talked about the more intimate side of marriage. Both of us laughed guiltily as we compared our limited knowledge, though I had less experience than she did.

"Do you like *faire l'amour*?" she asked one day, raising her eyebrows. "To make love?" she translated.

My face flushed and I nodded. "Do you?"

"*Ah, oui*," she said with such enthusiasm that we both laughed aloud. "How much do you like it?" she asked.

I thought for a few moments. "Not so much like rice and raisins," I said, mentioning my new favorite food, of which I could not get enough.

My answer sent her into peals of laughter. "Ah! God be praised," she said after she dried her eyes. Then she closed them again and leaned her head back and moaned. "Mmmm, husband. You are almost as good as rice and raisins."

We laughed until we went weak, and in the days that followed, all it took was for one of us to mention rice and raisins to set the other off.

CHAPTER THIRTEEN

1872

JEANNIE AND I spent the bulk of our days pulverizing endless amounts of dried meat and berries, then adding the fat and pouring the mixture into parfleches. I don't know how many of those rawhide bags we filled, but we produced more pemmican than I had ever seen.

One day, Jeannie went out into the woods to "see to nature," as she taught me to say in English, when Mama Rosa came over to where I sat in the shade of a log house. Though she often glared at us, on the whole, she left us to ourselves, so I was surprised when she leaned down toward my ear.

"You go home! Farwell, he no good," she hissed.

I looked at her in surprise.

"You go back to Crow. Farwell, he sell whiskey. He no good."

"Mama Rosa." Jeannie came from out of the woods. "Is something wrong?"

Her mother-in-law gave her a quick glance before she hurried away.

"What was she complaining about this time?" Jeannie sighed as she sat down again and picked up her stone to grind more berries.

I was shaken. "She say Farwell sell *whiskey*."

"Well, of course he does. He's a fur trader."

"He sell whiskey to Indians?"

"I would guess he *sells* it to whoever wants to buy it."

"But he say he don't drink whiskey."

"*Doesn't.* He said he *doesn't* drink whiskey," she corrected. "One has nothing to do with the other. Selling it is part of his business."

My chest felt tight. "But whiskey? It is bad!"

"Only when you drink too much of it."

"But Father—"

"Didn't you say he was a chief?"

I nodded.

"Then you see why he would be against it. When Indians get ahold of it, they sometimes drink too much. But we drink it here all the time. You liked the rum punch, didn't you, and that's liquor same as whiskey?"

"Yes," I said, but now I was not only scared, I was confused. Had Father known that Farwell sold whiskey? And if Father disapproved of liquor so strongly, why had he encouraged me to marry a man who sold it? Was I the price he paid for getting more rifles?

Jeannie nudged my shoulder. "Mary. Don't worry about it. There's nothing wrong with liquor. René always has some in our house." She ground hard at the berries, shaking her head. "That Mama Rosa. She wants everybody to be as miserable as she is."

THAT NIGHT, I was sitting by my small campfire, still uneasy about Mama Rosa's warning, when I heard the rustle of dry grass and my growing puppy's low growl. I had my rifle raised when I heard Jeannie softly calling for me.

She came through the trees. "I was hoping you wouldn't shoot," she said. She pulled a tall bottle from underneath her shawl. "René's in Fort Benton with Farwell, and I didn't think Mama Rosa would ever go to sleep. Do you have some cups?" she asked.

Wondering at her intention, I went for two of our tin coffee mugs and handed them over. She uncorked the bottle and poured a mugful for each of us. "I knew you were still worried about what Mama Rosa had to say, so I asked Lisette to make us some rum punch. I didn't bring whiskey because the taste is vile, but rum is liquor, too, and I want you to see that there's nothing to be afraid of. Let's just drink all we want. I've never done that before because René's mother is always watching me." She lifted her mug toward me. "*A ta santé*!" she said and then took a gulp.

I liked the taste as much as I had the first time I drank it, and it was fun to share it with Jeannie. We were both giddy by the time we drained our second mug, and when Jeannie poured a third, she spilled some on my moccasin. We both thought this was the funniest thing, and we couldn't stop laughing. Though I was already light-headed, I drained my mug along with Jeannie. Suddenly my friend jumped up and grabbed hold of my hands. "Let's dance."

I remembered my grandfather's cheery song and I began to sing. "Oh, a-hunting we will go, a-hunting we . . ."

Jeannie squealed. "I know that song!" and together we sang and swung each other around as Grandfather had swung me. But I hadn't had a bellyful of rum punch when I danced with him, and now I fell into a dizzy heap, pulling Jeannie down with me. Laughing, we lay back on the grass and looked up at a sky that seemed bigger and more vast than ever.

"Oh, Mary, I love having you for a friend," she said.

"*Diiawáchissik*," I said.

"*Dia wah ti siik*? Does that mean I love you?" she asked.

"*Éeh*," I agreed.

Jeannie's eyes closed. "Come," I said, shaking her and pulling her to her feet. I knew she had to get home, and when she stood it was clear that she would need my help to walk. We set out with the two of us hanging onto each other, but we didn't get far before she doubled over and vomited. "Ohhh," she moaned after her stomach emptied. "Jus' lemme sleep here tonight."

I supposed that was the best idea and dragged her to my lodge. After I settled her, I gathered my guns and covered them with a blanket behind my pallet. I didn't want Jeannie waking in the night and getting hold of a gun.

"WHAT HAPPENED?" THE sun was almost up when Jeannie shook me awake.

It took me a while to remember what she was doing in my lodge.

"*Merde.* This tipi is spinning." She held her head as she sat beside my pallet. "We drank too much. Mama Rosa will be getting up soon. What am I going to do?" She looked at me with alarm.

"Tell her you got a bad stomach and you go out, *see to nature.*"

She smiled as though I had given her a wonderful gift. "God be praised. Good idea. And I won't be lying, either. My stomach is still queasy. How about you?"

"I get sick, too," I said, and told her how during the night I had to rush from the lodge before my stomach emptied.

"Well, that was a first for me, and I won't be too quick to try that again. How about you?"

I gave an exaggerated moan, and we exchanged pinched smiles. She smoothed back her hair that had come loose from her braid and then shook out her dress when she stood. "Say goodbye. You might never see me again. Rosa's going to kill me," she said, ducking out the door.

My stomach wanted nothing to do with food that morning. Instead, I sat and sipped a cup of water as I thought about the night before. I smiled when I remembered the two of us dancing and singing, but the idea of rum punch nauseated me. It reminded me of eating fresh chokecherries when I was a child. When we picked the berries, the adults warned us not to eat too many of them, but most of us had to make that mistake at least once. I remembered my bowels being so stopped up that I cried for two days with stomach pain. I didn't like chokecherries to this day, and I doubted I would ever drink rum punch again, either.

FARWELL CAME HOME that night, after being away for five days. "I'm only here for tonight and tomorrow," he said, slipping from his horse. "I hope you weren't bored."

His embrace was so tight I found it hard to breathe and I wondered if I still smelled of rum. I thought again of his involvement with the whiskey trade, but when he kissed me, I couldn't help kissing him back. Later, when we were lying together, he buried his face in my neck and breathed in deeply. "You smell of the river," he said. "I didn't know that a smell had color, but you smell of blue."

"You smell like soap," I said, running my fingers through his thick brown hair. It was a scent he always carried, and now that I knew what it was, I found it pleasant. What color was he? I wondered, but then he kissed my neck. I lifted toward him as his kisses traveled down my body, and all thoughts of color vanished when once again I became lost in pleasure.

Farwell stayed home Sunday, and later that afternoon he joined the Métis men who were shooting at targets, each one declaring himself to be a better shot than the next. I was with the women, helping them prepare the food, when Jeannie's husband called her over.

"Watch this," René said proudly to the other men as he handed his rifle over to his wife. Jeannie lifted the gun to her shoulder, and René threw a tin can into the air. She pulled the trigger and the bullet blew it apart. Then she handed him back the rifle and calmly returned to us at the fire. She winked at me as all the men whooped.

I knew what was coming next when Farwell called my name. I went, as Jeannie had done, aimed the rifle, and hit the tin can as it flew through the air. The same admiring whoops followed, and when I got back to the fireside, Jeannie gave me a wide grin. I felt a warmth toward her then that I had never before felt for another woman, and I wondered if this is what it felt like to have a sister. I was beginning to dread the idea of leaving her behind.

THE NEXT TIME Farwell returned from Fort Benton, he presented me with a brand-new handgun. "It's a Colt 45. You've got a rifle, but you should have one of these," he said, handing it over. "A rifle shoots three times as far as a revolver like this, but this is easier to handle and you can carry it on your belt."

I was delighted to have it, and when René came to help Farwell replace one of the wheels on the wagon, I took a run over to Jeannie's to show her my new gun.

"Oh, Mary. This is your very own?" she said, turning it over in her hands and brushing her fingers over the polished wooden handle. "It's still heavy, but it's so much lighter than a rifle."

"Do you have one?" I asked.

"Oh no," she said. "We don't have that kind of money. Even René doesn't have one as nice as this." She tried to hand it back, but I had seen her need.

"You keep it," I said.

"I couldn't. What would Farwell . . . ?"

But I insisted.

Later, I explained to a surprised Farwell that I had given Jeannie my gun.

"But it was a gift. I thought you liked it," he said.

"*Éeh.*" I nodded.

"Then why did you give it away?"

"That is Crow way," I said. "When we get gift, if others need it, we give to them."

Farwell's eyebrows lifted. "You don't say? So is that why your mother has your silver bracelet?"

"*Éeh,*" I said.

"I'll be darned. Well, I guess that's one way to handle it. Another way, the white man's way, is when a gift is given to you, you keep it for yourself." He smiled then and shook his head before he kissed me. "Still, I have to say, I like your generosity. I know how much you liked that revolver."

On his next return from Fort Benton, he brought not only another six-shooter for me but also plenty of ammunition for practice. "I want you to learn to shoot this handgun as well as you do a rifle," he said.

I took his advice seriously, and I practiced as often as I could. Out a distance from our lodge, Farwell had set up pieces of logs as targets, and Jeannie joined me whenever she was able. We loved to challenge each other, to see not just who could repeatedly hit the targets, but also who could outdo the other in speed when reloading the six-bullet chambers. These guns couldn't shoot the same distance as a rifle, but the kick to our shoulders was still strong, so we had to limit our practice.

"Why do you bring your horses over here whenever we practice with our guns?" Jeannie asked one day, as I tethered my horses close by.

"So they hear guns."

"Oh. Then if you have to shoot when you're riding, they won't be afraid of the sound?"

"*Éeh.*" I nodded.

MY PUPPY WAS growing tall and gangly and was a wonderful comfort whenever Farwell was away. I couldn't decide what to call him, and I still hadn't named him the day Jeannie reached down to pat his head. "Your dog needs a name," she said.

"Like what?" I asked.

"How about Pierre?" she suggested. "It's a good name, and that way you'll think of me every time you call for him."

"Then I call him Pierre," I said, liking the sound of it, though I should have guessed she was up to some mischief by the way she hid her smile.

Pierre was soon responding to his name. He was usually at my side, but recently he had met M'sieu Dubois's dog, who was friendly enough, though he was a scruffy-looking animal, with hair missing in large patches on his black-and-white coat. He was twice the size of Pierre, but the two got along well and often wandered off together. I didn't mind that my dog had found a friend, especially since Pierre always returned for his evening meal. However, one evening he did not show up, and I spent the night restless and worried.

The morning sky was just starting to turn orange when I took my revolver and slipped onto Snow's back. I knew the path along the river that the two dogs usually took, and I rode out, calling for Pierre over and over. As the sun rose, so too did my fear. Had he run into a bear? But there were mountain lions, too, and one could easily make short work of a human, never mind a dog. I was out farther from our camp than I had ever been and was about to turn back when Snow answered a whinny. I swung around, and at the sight of an approaching horseman, my hand went to my gun.

M'sieu Dubois's scowl was as deep as the riverbank next to us. "Where those dogs?" he asked.

I shrugged. "Pierre . . ."

"Why you call your dog Pierre?" he growled.

"Jeannie said it is good name."

"That damn Jeannie." Before I had a chance to defend her, he pursed his lips and sent out a piercing whistle. I clung to my startled horse when he did it again.

"If the damn wolfers get my dog, I kill them," he said, just as the two dogs came bounding out from the thick underbrush that lined the riverbank. Wet and dirty, Pierre came racing over to me, and I scolded him even as I dismounted and wrapped him in my arms.

M'sieu Dubois gave another shrill whistle, and his dog followed on his horse's heels as he rode off.

CHAPTER FOURTEEN

1872

OUR LODGE, SECLUDED by pines and dense shrubbery, stood far enough away from the Métis settlement that we were not within sight nor easy shouting distance. This gave Farwell and me the privacy we enjoyed as lovers, but one early evening, with my husband away in Fort Benton, it felt isolated and lonely. Jeannie was helping her mother-in-law, and Pierre was off visiting his buddy. I no longer worried about where my dog was, for in the evenings M'sieu Dubois now tied his dog up to keep him from roaming. Pierre was either visiting his friend or with me.

I had straightened everything in my lodge, cleaned the campsite, and gathered plenty of firewood in preparation for Farwell's return the following day. But it was still light, so with nothing else to do, I decided to try some target practice on my own.

I was buckling on my gun belt when the pungent scent of animal pelts became so strong that I stepped out of my lodge to look for the source. A large man startled me when he walked up from the back side of my tipi, and I drew my gun.

"Whoa!" He threw his hands up. "Put that gun away! I'm here to see Abe."

His voice was deep and heavy, suited to his size. His nose was broad and flat, his chin long, and his ears large, even for a head big enough to fit his frame. This was a huge man, taller even than my father, and wide across both the shoulders and hips.

I kept the gun on him. "Who are you?" I asked.

"Name's Sam Stiller."

"What you want?" I asked.

"I'm a friend of Abe's. You Farwell's squaw?"

I nodded, hating the way he said the word "squaw," which I knew was no compliment.

"Well, I'm here looking for him."

"Farwell come tomorrow," I said, regretting my words as soon as they were out.

"Is that right?" He dropped his big hands. "Put that gun away. What's he thinkin', givin' a squaw a gun?"

Unsure of what to do but not wanting to threaten a friend of Farwell's, I reluctantly holstered my gun. He glanced back when his packhorse whinnied, likely complaining about the weight of the wolf pelts on his back. The man looked around again. "Well, guess I'll have to wait. I'll just tie up for the night over there," he said, pointing back behind my tipi. "Think you could fix me up with some grub?"

It was a custom for our people to offer food to visitors, and even though I didn't like the look of this man, I felt it was something I should do. As I built up my outdoor fire and made some fry bread, he set up his camp close enough to mine that I could hear his spurs jangle as he worked.

He returned with a bottle of whiskey.

"You got a cup, I'll give you some," he said, and winked.

"I don't drink liquor," I said.

"Come on, I never did know a squaw not to booze," he said.

I shook my head.

He shrugged, sat, and removed his black hat. It was the first time I saw a head of curly hair. Under other circumstances I might have stared at this unusual feature, but concerned that he might misunderstand my look as one of interest, I quickly turned away as he poured whiskey into his tin cup. He drank it down in a few large gulps and exhaled deeply after each swallow. "This stuff has a bite!" he said as he refilled his cup. "Here, try some," he said, offering to share.

"No," I answered, handing over a plate of pemmican and hot fry bread.

He was careful in his way of eating, much like Farwell, but while he ate, he finished off more of the drink. "Seems like you talk some English?"

I nodded.

He sat looking me over.

"Have to say I never did see Farwell as a squaw man," he said. "Course, you got a mighty fine shape to you."

I busied myself cleaning the frying pan, but his eyes stayed on me.

"So where'd he find you?"

Wanting him to leave, I didn't answer, but then his voice turned hard. "I guess you didn't hear. I asked where he found you?"

"I am Crow," I said, hoping he didn't hear the tremor in my voice.

There was a long silence before he slapped his hat back on his head and stood, his large frame silhouetted against the setting sun. The size of him was startling.

I was crouched down over the fire when he came over with his plate. When I took it from him, he leaned down and roughly pinched my cheek. I pushed his hand away and rubbed the burning spot on my face.

"Come on," he said, "don't go tellin' me that hurt. I was just playin' with ya." He stood for a while looking over the camp before he turned back to me. "Tell you what. You change your mind, why don't you come see me later tonight? And don't worry about Farwell. Don't think he'd mind sharing a squaw with an old friend."

To my relief he began to walk away, but then he looked back. "You know where to find me," he said.

I argued with myself after he left. Was it possible that this was Farwell's friend? Should I go to Jeannie or sit with my guns? And could it be true that Farwell wouldn't mind sharing a woman? I was married to my husband for less than a moon, and it struck me once again how little I knew about him.

I sat all night with my gun in my lap, too afraid to sleep. At sunrise

I heard footsteps outside my lodge. I readied my revolver, but as my heart raced, the footsteps turned back. Shortly after, I heard Sam Stiller leave with his horses, and later I found his note weighted under a stone outside the door to my lodge.

> *Farwell. Can't go into town or stay hereabouts—heard the sheriff is looking for me. I'll be needing more ammo, so if you can pick it up for me, I'll catch you on the trail or I'll find you up at your new post. Your squaw gave me some grub but was none too friendly. You got to train her better. Stiller*

My grandfather had taught me how to read his English alphabet, but I wasn't good at putting words together, so I gave the note to Jeannie. After she read it aloud she stood back to look at me in disbelief. "Sam Stiller was here?" she asked.

"*Éeh*," I said, wondering how much to say.

"Why does the note say you were none too friendly?"

"He want me to drink whiskey. I say no."

"Weren't you scared?" she asked.

I nodded, and she gave me a hug. "Oh, Mary, why didn't you come to me?"

I shrugged. "I had my gun," I said.

"Well, if he ever shows up again, you come stay with me until he goes. He is not a good man. If M'sieu Dubois had known he was around, there would have been a problem. Those two hate each other."

"Why?"

"M'sieu Dubois claims he once poisoned one of his dogs. Stiller is one of the worst of those wolfers."

"Wolfers?" I asked.

"Those are men who use strychnine on a buffalo carcass. Wolves and coyotes and other animals come to eat the poisoned carcass. They all die, and the wolfers take the pelts and sell them to the fur traders. The Métis and Indians hate them so much because often our dogs eat at the carcass and die, too."

I was relieved when Jeannie stayed with me for the rest of the day. We practiced shooting, went swimming, and later, as Jeannie braided my hair, I told her I wanted to learn how to read. I didn't like that I hadn't been able to understand Sam Stiller's note.

"I'll make up some alphabet and study cards for you," she said, "and you can start there."

"WHO IS THIS?" Farwell asked when he returned. I tugged at the red shawl that Jeannie had put over my shoulders, then nervously fingered the ribbons she had attached to my singular braid. It felt odd to have my hair pulled back, but I hoped that by dressing more like Jeannie I would show my new husband that I was adjusting to his world.

"You look mighty pretty," he said, cheerier than usual.

"*Merci, M'sieu,*" I said, and gave the small curtsey that Jeannie had taught.

He laughed. "And now you are learning to speak French?" he asked playfully.

"Jeannie is a good teacher," I said.

"And you are a good student." He kissed me, then stepped back to get a better look at me. "*Damn.* You sure are a pretty woman. And I can't believe how quickly you are picking English up."

"Come, eat some *grub*," I said, taking his hand and leading him to the fireside. He gave a wide smile when he saw the pan of fried potatoes and onions. He had plenty of this unfamiliar food in his supplies, and Jeannie had taught me how to cut the slices thin and then brown them together in fat until they were cooked through with crispy edges. She taught me, too, how to season the dish with salt and pepper.

Farwell ate like a hungry man and shook his head at me when he handed over his empty plate. "We'll make a white woman out of you yet," he said.

I shot him a look. "I am Crow," I said, suddenly wary.

"Come sit," he said, patting the seat beside him. He took my hand to kiss it, but I pulled it away. "I am Crow," I repeated.

"Of course you are Crow. What I meant was that I am glad to see you learning some of our ways."

"Stiller come here," I blurted out.

"Stiller? What did he want?"

I handed over the note and waited. Farwell read it, balled it up, and threw it onto the fire. "Did you feed him?"

I nodded, afraid of what was to come. If a Crow wife was unfriendly to her husband's good friend, there would have been trouble.

"I'd be obliged if you'd treat him well when he shows up. We've known each other a long time—since the war back east. He got me out of a real tight spot then, in fact I guess it's fair to say he saved my life, and for that I owe him." Farwell thought for a while, then shook his head. "Last I saw him, he was hitting the bottle pretty heavy. Was he drinking when he was here?"

"Yes," I said.

"Did he want you to drink with him?"

I hesitated, unsure of how much to tell him.

Farwell's eyes opened wide. "Did you drink with him?"

"No."

"Good," Farwell said. "I don't want you drinking that stuff, and especially not with him."

"What does he mean when Stiller say you *share a squaw*?" I blurted out what had been bothering me.

Farwell's face turned a deep red. "He had no business saying that. There was liquor involved," he mumbled.

This might have been my opening to ask him about his selling whiskey, but he suddenly jumped up. "I have some good news." he said, pulling me to my feet. "It's time to pack up. We're leaving for the north, day after tomorrow."

Though I knew it was coming, this was unexpected. I wished I could share his excitement, but instead I thought of how much I would miss Jeannie.

❀   ❀   ❀

THE MORNING FARWELL and I left the Métis settlement, everyone turned out to say farewell. Even M'sieu Dubois came, and I felt his glare. I watched as my husband shook hands with the other men, and then he came to M'sieu Dubois. "M'sieu Pierre," he said, clapping the older man on his shoulder. "Always good to work with you. I'll see you and your men with the supplies in a few weeks."

M'sieu Dubois's name was *Pierre*? I sent Jeannie a look of surprise. She grinned and hurried over to give me a hug.

"Don't be angry," she whispered. "He deserved it."

How could I be angry with her? Leaving her was almost as hard as leaving my family.

"I will miss you, Crow Mary," she said, squeezing me tight.

"I will miss you," I said, near tears.

She pushed back from me, her face joyful. "But guess what? I'll see you again in a few weeks."

"What? How?" I asked.

She laughed. "I was saving it for a surprise. I'm coming with René and the other men when they bring the supplies up to Farwell's fort."

She leaned in to whisper, "Can you believe M'sieu Dubois agreed that I could come along to do the cooking?"

"You cook for all those men?"

"God be praised. I don't mind. It will give me a break from making pemmican," she said. "And René has family at the Métis settlement up there. He said it is only a few miles away from where Farwell is building his fur-trading post. Of course, we will only stay with you a couple of days, but there will be enough time for us to catch up and for you to show me your new home." She remembered the package she held in her hand. "Here. I made some study cards for you. They'll help you learn to read. I wrote out each letter of the alphabet, and then I drew a picture beside it. There's a list of words, too. Ask Farwell for help if you can't figure them out."

I thanked her and carefully tucked the package into a parfleche that held my personal things. Then I mounted Snow and Jeannie handed over the reins of my packhorses. "Travel safely, Crow Mary. I will miss you," she said, brushing away tears with the back of her hand. "*Kalachíi diiawákaawiik.*"

"*Éeh*, I will see you again," I replied, and turned my horse to follow my husband.

"Enjoy your rice and raisins," I heard her call, but my throat was too tight to reply.

CHAPTER FIFTEEN

1872

FARWELL RODE ON the small wagon, pulled by a team of two horses, and after I saw the way he bounced over the ruts and rocks, I was happy that I had chosen to ride my horse and to trail my packhorses. That first day, my main concern was to keep my horses from stepping into one of the treacherous holes dug by the badgers and scurrying prairie dogs. It was hard to focus because tears blurred my eyes long after we left. It was difficult leaving Jeannie, but I was also aware that as we headed north, I was moving farther away from my mother.

Farwell, though, was in high spirits, and when he realized my unhappiness, he called out, "Come on, Mary. Sing with me! Oh, a-hunting we will go . . ." He sang with such gusto that I joined in, and Grandfather's song soon cheered me as much as it had when I was a little girl.

We traveled far that first day, covering a long stretch of flat land while following a rutted trail made by other wagons, though we didn't see any. More flat land with sagebrush lay ahead, but finally, in the glow of sunset, we came to a creek with swift running water where Farwell reined in his team. There was good thick grass for the horses to graze, and my mouth watered when I saw some plump ripe plums dangling from thick shrubs along the water.

As I prepared to take my lodgepoles from his wagon, Farwell stopped me. "How about we sleep under the stars?" he asked. "Looks like it'll be a pleasant night—no rain, not too cool."

I was happy with that idea, and as he took care of the horses, I gathered wood and started a fire. I dug through the supplies and found some cast-iron frying pans, and by the time Farwell had finished his chores, I was dishing out pemmican and some hot fry bread onto our tin plates. Jeannie had taught me the use of a fork, and though I didn't like how it felt cold in my mouth, Farwell seemed pleased that I was using one.

After we finished eating, Farwell went to the buckboard, and when he came back, he carried two pretty blue and white tin bowls and a glass jar of something orange. "I brought along plenty of these peaches," he said. "It's my favorite food." He twisted off the top, tipped the jar toward the bowls, and out plopped pieces of the orange fruit. He drizzled the sweet-smelling juice over the peaches and handed one of the bowls to me. "Tell me what you think?" he said, handing me a spoon and waiting for me to take a taste. The tart sweetness made my mouth tingle, and Farwell's favorite food became one of mine as well.

That first night I lay under my husband's arm with Pierre snuggled against my feet. Our horses were close by, and each of us had our revolver and a rifle at our side.

The night was dark, with only a sliver of a moon, yet I felt protected and cared for. It occurred to me that I hadn't thought about Big Cloud in many days.

"Mary," Farwell said, "can I ask you a question?"

"*Éeh*," I said.

"You are a quiet person," he said. "You have little to say, and that is fine, but do you have any questions for me?"

Had I not spent the last weeks with outspoken Jeannie, I might not have asked, "Why you want a Indian wife?"

He gave a deep sigh. "Well, mostly because I wanted someone who knows how to live in this country. White women find this land too hard. And when the Indians come to trade, they will like that I have an Indian wife. You'll recognize the good pelts, and you'll be able to talk to them better than I will, at least through hand signals that all of you Indians seem to know so well. And look at how quick you are picking up English. Either Jeannie is one amazing teacher or you are one incredible student."

"Jeannie say I am good student," I said.

He laughed and gave me a squeeze. "Another thing I like about you is how confident you are. And there is that—that determination of yours. Some might call it stubborn, but I call it having a mind of your own." He glanced over toward our wagon. "At least you seem to know when to give in. I was glad you finally agreed to put the bulk of your things on the buckboard."

"It is not so hard for my horses," I said.

He sighed deeply again and hugged me tight, my head against his chest. "Mary, I got lucky when I found you. From the first time I saw you I thought you were beautiful, but I didn't think I'd be falling for you like this."

"PEACHES," I MURMURED, waking to an orange sky.

Farwell laughed. "You're right! It is the color of peaches," he said. "I never thought of that before."

I went down to the water to wash up, and on the way back, wary of snakes, I grabbed a stick and wacked at the bushes before gathering a skirt full of dark ripe plums. On my return I was surprised to see that Farwell had a fire burning and a pot of coffee ready for us to drink. I didn't really like black coffee, and when I told Farwell this, he smiled.

"I'll just bet I have something that will change your mind," he said, springing up. He returned from the wagon with a small tin. "I want you to try this. It's called condensed milk," he said as he shook the can and then punctured it twice with his pocketknife. "Hold on," he said, and poured a good measure of the steaming black coffee into one of the tin cups. He then added a generous amount of the thick white cream before he gave it a final stir. "Here," he said. "Try this."

I took one sip and then another before I gave a satisfied smile. We sat next to each other on a fallen log while we softened leftover fry bread from the night before by dipping it into our coffee. As we ate he studied the brightening sky. "We made good time yesterday—must have come about twenty-five miles. Looks like we'll have another good day today, and if the weather holds, we should make it to Cypress Hills in another six days or so."

I offered him a ripe plum before I took one for myself. I wondered how Farwell had decided where to set up his fur-trading post. In our culture, before we would move location, the chiefs and the elders all gathered to smoke and pray and decide where to lead us. It wasn't our way to question the leadership, but the night before Farwell seemed to welcome my questions, so I took a chance and asked him why we were going all the way up to Canada.

"Mainly, we're going up to trade in the Cypress Hills because it's in Whoop-Up country."

"Why it's called *Whoop-Up*?"

"Well, I reckon the straight answer is that it's a place far enough up north where we can still trade for whiskey."

At that I looked away from him. Suddenly, the last bit of coffee tasted bitter in my mouth.

"Down here, trading liquor to the Indians for fur pelts has been outlawed for years, and the law will come down hard on you if you're caught. Government claimed it was unfair of the fur traders to give the Indians liquor before they did their trade, and I agree. That's why I never give out liquor before I do a trade with any of my customers—Indian or Métis."

I took in a deep breath. "But why trade whiskey to Indians? My father say that is no good."

"And he's right. It often isn't. But up north, across the border in Canada, that is what they want for their pelts, and if I don't trade for it, someone else who doesn't give a damn will cheat them. At least I'm fair."

But I still didn't understand why he didn't just stay in the Fort Benton area and not use whiskey for trade.

"Because up north is where the real money is, and that's what I'm after." He looked down, and after a slight hesitation, he looked at me again. "You know, Mary, there are some things in my past I'm not proud of. Six years ago, a couple years after the war, I came out here from New York to work for a big firm. I was hired to build forts for their trading business. I built some big places. Fort Peck up on the Missouri was one of them, but all along, my goal was to buy a ranch. I worked hard and saved everything I made, but then . . . well . . ."

He looked off and shook his head at the memory. "I'll tell you about it another time. It's hard to talk about, and for now I'll just say that I lost it all. It would have taken years to earn that amount again in construction, and by then I had seen how fast money could be made in fur trading, so I thought I'd give it a try. Turns out I was good at it. Word got around that I was fair, and the Indians and Métis came to me."

He put his coffee mug on the ground, reached for my hand, and kissed it. "I still want that ranch, Mary, and if we work hard by trading up north, we'll be able to buy it in a couple of years." He stood. "We should get moving. We have a lot of miles to cover, and I want to get there before the other traders."

"Other traders?" I asked. Until now I had imagined a small singular camp similar to the one Farwell had set up outside our village.

"Yah. Most, though, have no idea what they're getting themselves into, so I'm not too worried about the competition."

He went for the horses, and as I took care of the fire and packed up our camp, I thought of what he had said. Again, I wondered if Father had known that Farwell used alcohol for trade.

In these last years I had heard Horse Guard speak of ruined camps where whiskey had brought nothing but destruction. Yet, since leaving my family, I had met the Métis and saw that they often drank liquor and their settlement was thriving. I wondered if maybe Father had seen only a few bad camps and his judgment was based on that.

Then, too, I had knowledge of my own about alcohol, but Jeannie and I had promised to keep our rum punch night to ourselves.

CHAPTER SIXTEEN

1872

THAT EARLY SEPTEMBER, in the moon that plums fall, it grew cold at night, but the sun warmed us each day. The leaves of the cottonwoods were already turning yellow, but when the sun was overhead it was still strong enough to make the idea of shade a pleasant one. Farwell was knowledgeable about this vast Montana territory, and he often pointed to the hills and the mountains that surrounded us while giving me their English names. Bear Paw Mountains, Sweet Grass Hills—pretty names, I thought.

We had been following a deeply marked trail but when it branched off into two, we took the one less rutted. "This one will save us time. The other one's for the bull trains," Farwell said.

The new trail led us up and over green hills where we often surprised herds of antelope in the low valleys. The timid animals soon sped away onto higher land to better observe us.

By the next day we were again in the flat prairie of fading grass and chirping prairie dogs, when we came across a large herd of buffalo. There, huge bulls, unfazed by our passage, continued to roll in their wide deep wallow, stirring up billowing dust, while the massive herd contentedly grazed nearby.

And so we continued, over beautiful land that rolled and flattened, then rolled again, until three days in, while still in the Montana territories, we came to the cloudy Milk River. The crossing there was wider than the streams we had forded before, though the silty water looked shallow enough for easy passage. Still, I climbed down from my horse and gave the river some dried meat, while I asked the water spirits for their help in our crossing. Farwell observed me with curiosity but said nothing.

WE SAW THE buzzards circling and smelled the decaying carcasses before we came upon them in a shallow gully. The feeding buzzards weren't bothered by us and stayed picking at the entrails of three buffalo that lay rotting, missing only their tongues and some ribs that had been cut away. Buffalo tongue and ribs were delicacies for all the Plains tribes, but no Indians would have wasted these animals in this way.

I stared in dismay. "Who did this?" I asked.

Farwell didn't meet my eyes. "Had to be some white men. Wolfers most likely. They don't have the respect for the buffalo that you Indians do. They see the huge herds, and because they are so plentiful, they feel they can take just the choicest part and leave the rest."

"But . . . the hide and the . . ." The waste was almost more than I could stomach, and I tasted bile as I rode away as quickly as I could. Who would disrespect these life-giving animals in this way?

We Crow used every part of the buffalo: the tongue, a delicacy that was boiled and eaten as a treat; the tail that we used as a fly swatter or a whip; the hooves that we boiled for glue; the sinews to sew our clothes; the horn cups from which we drank; the shoulder blades we used as scraping tools—everything—everything we needed came from the buffalo.

Who were these men that Farwell knew, and what else were they capable of doing? I wondered.

WE WERE STILL a few days away from the Cypress Hills. All day we had been following the trail through vast grasslands, out in the open prairie, but by early evening we came upon a good place to set up camp for the night. We found shelter amidst some shrubs and willows that grew alongside a stream, and as I set about gathering firewood, the frogs greeted Farwell as he watered the horses. He was tethering them, and I already had a fire going when my husband suddenly looked up and then shielded his eyes from the setting sun. "I think that's a rider coming up," he said as he went for his rifle. I reached down and was reassured to feel my six-shooter still attached to my belt. Though Farwell said he had a good working relationship with most tribes, one never knew how a raiding party of Sioux or Blackfoot might respond to two travelers with especially fine horses.

"It looks like he's alone," Farwell reported, and as the figure drew closer, he set his gun aside. "It's Stiller. I can always tell it's him, not only by his size, but by the size of that damn big horse he rides. He's kicking up some dust, though. Might be someone on his tail."

We couldn't see anyone behind him, though, so as Farwell waved him in, I added more pemmican to the pan to fry it the way Farwell liked. I dreaded seeing Stiller again, and I kept busy as the two men greeted each other, slapping each other on the back.

"You were coming up pretty hard. I thought maybe you were trying to outrun that sheriff from Benton? I heard about that poker game," Farwell said.

Stiller gave a loud laugh. "Nah, it's not the sheriff I'm worried about. I heard there might be some Sioux over this stretch, and I don't always get along too well with those boys. If it's all right, I'll join you for the night."

"Good to see you, old friend." Farwell patted his shoulder again. "I know what you mean about those Sioux. I have to say, so far we've been lucky. Haven't seen hide nor hair of 'em."

I, too, hated the Sioux, but not enough to welcome the sight of this man. Fact was, I'd rather have taken on four Sioux warriors than have to face Sam Stiller again. I would have just shot the Sioux and had Farwell thanking me for it.

"Thought you might be ranchin' by now, Abe. Lost wind of you for a couple of years, but sure good to see you again."

"Got that note you left with Mary. Thought you might've waited for me?" Farwell said.

"I had some hides to get rid of, and I couldn't go into Benton—that sheriff, you know, so headed south. Now, with winter coming, thought I'd go back up north. It's a distance to travel, but those hides up in

Canada are the best—thick and heavy. Those animals know how to get ready for the snow. Say, did you bring my ammo?"

"Yup, got it in the wagon."

I stayed busy while the two watered and tied up Stiller's horses and then did their business before they came over to eat.

"I guess you already met Mary?" Farwell asked.

"Yup, sure did. Hello, Mary," he said, nodding at me. "Good to see you again."

I looked over at the man, finding it hard to believe his easy words. He smiled, and I wondered if Farwell saw how his cool gray eyes did not match his upturned mouth.

"Damn!" he said. "Almost forgot." His spurs clinked when he went for his saddlebags and returned with a bottle of whiskey. He lifted it in the air. "I got a full bottle here, but between the three of us I think we can bring it down some. What do you say?"

He held the bottle out to Farwell. "You got some cups, or we just drink it straight from the bottle?"

My husband put his palm up in the air. "Actually, we're going to pass on that. I don't want Mary to get a taste for it, and I don't drink whiskey anymore," Farwell said.

Stiller snorted. "Come on, Abe. I don't believe it. Go get yourself a cup."

"Afraid I still have to say no," Farwell said. "That stuff's like poison to me."

"Drinking out here? What harm can it do?"

"I just don't want to get started again. Seems once I start, I don't quit."

Stiller shook his head. "Well, suit yourself, but I'm not goin' to let that stop me."

"No," said Farwell, "you go right ahead and drink up."

Though I took no part in it, I listened to their conversation as I heaped pemmican and fry bread onto the tin plates and then handed them over to the men. *Once I start, I don't stop.* Farwell's words made me uneasy.

"So I understand you're setting up a trading post again? I don't know how you have the patience to work with those Injuns," Stiller said. "I don't find them all that bright."

"Oh no, they're intelligent. What complicates it is that every tribe speaks a different language, and each one is hard to learn. Lucky I know hand talk, but most Indians are so fast that it's hard to keep up."

"Never did learn those hand signs. Those heathens don't speak English, they got no business with me. Told 'em so, right to their face. And they had nothing to say about it, either. Just mumbled some crap to each other."

After Farwell stole a glance at me, he quickly got to his feet. "Say, would you have a look at one of my horses?" he said to Stiller. "His one hoof is worrying me, and I don't want him coming up lame."

They went off together, and I wondered if Farwell had seen me fingering my knife. I had never scalped a man, but I knew how to do it.

STILLER DRANK INTO the night, and the more liquor he put into himself, the more he became frustrated that Farwell wouldn't drink with him. "Come on, Abe. Don't you remember the good times we had?"

It was when Stiller began to share remembrances of the past that Farwell grew restless. "Did you tell Mary, here, 'bout you and me in that bloody war out east, fightin' side by side—you gettin' hit at Gettysburg and me there to pick you up. Didn't know I could run that fast, carryin' weight like yours, but hell, a man got bullets chasin' him, he'll pick up speed right quick."

"I'll never forget that you saved my life, and I'll always be grateful to you for it," Farwell said.

"Come on, Abe. Have some of this gut warmer with me for old times' sake. Wasn't for you, I wouldn't even be out here. You were the one wanted me to come. Remember? 'It's a wide-open country out here,' you wrote, 'with all kinds of money to be made.'"

"I do remember, and I stand by it," Farwell agreed.

"Well, I'm sure glad you hadn't quit the sauce when I first got here. We had us some wild times. I'll never forget that one squaw up at Fort . . ."

Farwell leapt up. "Stiller, I think it's time we get some sleep."

Stiller looked over at me. "Hell, Abe, no disrespect. Fact is, I got to say this one you got here is mighty fine. There's talk in town that you got a preacher involved, but nobody can figure why you'd do that. These squaws know which side their bread is buttered on. Oh, well, you get tired of this one, you just let me know."

Farwell waved him to his feet. "Come on. Time to hit the sack. Where are you heading tomorrow?"

"I'm going your way, but since it looks like there's no trouble with the Sioux, and now that I got my ammo, I'll go on ahead," Stiller said. "I can move faster than you with draggin' that wagon."

Hearing his answer, I breathed a sigh of relief. We bedded down, a distance from him, but even with all the fresh night air, a stink lingered when he took off his boots.

AFTER STILLER RODE out, Farwell and I drank our morning coffee in silence as we watched squawking geese fly overhead, already heading south to escape the cold weather we were heading toward. It wasn't just Stiller who had left a cloud of gray hanging over us. Until now there had been only sunny skies, but this morning there were some darker clouds looming. "I've got a good hat for you and some canvas to pull around you if it rains," Farwell said, taking a swallow of coffee. "Long as it doesn't storm too hard," he said, studying the sky. "I hate riding a horse through a storm out in this open country. Saw a horse and rider get hit by lightning—killed them both—and I never want to see that again."

I gave him a startled look.

"But don't worry," he said quickly, "these clouds look high enough. I'm thinking this will just blow over. And if it starts to storm, we'll pull up in some lower ravine and wait it out."

But we got lucky, and by the end of the day, there was an orange sunset. That night, as we prepared to settle under a sky so big that it might have swallowed us, I greeted the sacred stars as I always did, with my palms open. Then I slipped under the snug buffalo rug that I shared with Farwell. He pulled me close and pointed up at the sky. "Look how bright the Big Dipper is tonight."

I tugged his arm down. "Don't point," I said, and reached for a nearby willow twig, then handed it over. "Use this. Don't point with fingers," I said. "First Maker gives us stars, so they are sacred."

"If you say so," he said, using the willow stick to outline the stars he called the Big Dipper.

"The Big Dipper? We call them Seven Brothers. At night they give Crow warriors direction and they help tell time."

"Really?" he said. "You can tell time from them?"

"*Éeh.*"

"I'll be darned," he said.

We lay quietly studying the sky until I broke the silence. "Farwell?"

"Yes, Mary?"

"What you say to Stiller . . ."

He released a long sigh. "What's that?"

"You drink whiskey?"

He stiffened. "I did. But it's almost two years now since I stopped. Remember how I told you I lost all my money?"

"*Éeh.*"

"Well, that's how I did it. I went on a two-week bender up in Fort Peck and it damn near killed me. I was so liquored up over those weeks that I don't remember much of it—all I know is, I lost everything I'd saved."

I was quiet as I thought this through.

"But I don't want you to worry," he continued. "I promise that I'll never touch that stuff again."

It was easy enough to believe him when I thought of his steadfast refusal of Stiller's bottle.

"Do you trust me, Mary?" he said. "I want you to trust me."

I heard the need in his voice, and I rose up on my elbow and leaned over to kiss him. "I trust you," I said, before pushing the covers back and trailing my fingers across his shoulders and down his bare chest. It was a full moon, and I liked to see the pleasure on his face. "Old Woman watches," I teased.

"Old Woman?" he asked. "You mean the moon?"

"Yes," I whispered as my hand continued to journey. "She is giver of life."

Later, I lay awake as Farwell slept. I had never guessed that white men could also have a problem like that with whiskey. But then why did they sell it? Somehow, I had believed that white men knew more than my people. They had so many things that we did not—things we needed like guns, beads, tools, blankets and kettles and frying pans. Yet if they knew more than we did, why didn't they know how much whiskey to drink? Then there was the awful way they had wasted those buffalo. Did they know nothing about the sacredness of life? What else, I wondered, didn't I know about the Yellow Eyes?

I looked over at Farwell in his sleep. In the moonlight he looked much younger than his thirty-four snows. What was he like as a child? What would he be like as a father? I wondered if I would be like my mother and have only one or two children.

I studied the Old Woman's face, and in her shadows, I saw the familiar figure of a woman hanging meat up to dry. Since Old Woman gave life, that night I explained to her that though I wanted children, I was only sixteen snows, and I was not yet ready for them. I needed to first know more about my husband. I asked if she might wait and bless me with one when the time was right. She is known to be a benevolent Old Woman, and I felt sure that she would honor my request.

CHAPTER SEVENTEEN

1872

WE WERE TRAVELING through open prairie when we stopped for a rest.

"Just look at this," Farwell said, removing his hat and gazing upward. "Yesterday we thought there might be a storm, and today there isn't a cloud in the sky." I loved that my husband appreciated Mother Earth as much as I did, and together we looked out on a vast sky as clear a blue as I had ever seen. An autumn breeze came from the west and rippled through the grass that was now the color of our creamed coffee. "Back home in Pennsylvania, I heard and read of this vast prairie land, but I never imagined the beauty of it."

"Why you leave home? Why you come here, Farwell?" I asked.

He answered me as he looked out over the prairie.

"My mother died when my little brother was born," he said. "A few days later, he died, too. I was ten years old and I still think about them almost every day. My father married again, to a woman who had three of her own children, and . . . let's just say, she didn't like me. When I was fifteen I was sent to a school in New York, where my father wanted me to be a lawyer or something to do with business. I gave it a try for a few years, but it wasn't for me, so I quit and took up building houses. I was good at it, and pretty soon I was hired on to build bigger buildings, like hotels. Then came the war, and I signed up. That was bloody hell. I'll tell you anything you want to know about my family, but I won't talk about the war. I was twenty-three when I fought at Gettysburg, and when the war ended and a job offer came through to build Fort Peck, I hightailed it out here to the West."

I understood why he didn't want to talk about a war. I remembered only too well the battle I had seen at Arrow Creek when Grandmother died. I still had bad dreams about it.

ON OUR SIXTH day of travel, Farwell pointed to a dark edge of pines in the far distance. "Look up ahead, Mary. There's good water up there, and that's where we'll camp tonight. By tomorrow we should reach the Cypress Hills."

By early evening we were setting up camp. Farwell tied a picket line between two trees and secured the horses there, closer to us than usual. "Now that we're near the Cypress Hills we have to really be on the lookout. The Blackfoot call this place the Grizzly Bear Hills. Keep your eyes open and your rifle handy when you go down to the water and into any trees."

I heard what he said and would be certain to carry my gun, but I was glad that Pierre always stayed close to my side.

As evening fell, I grew quiet with a growing sense of dread, but not because of grizzlies. The next day I would meet more Yellow Eyes, and I hated the idea of seeing Sam Stiller again. Farwell tried to tease me out of my mood, but I ignored him. After we ate, he went to the wagon and returned with a few brown leathery pieces of food that I hadn't seen before. "Try these," he said. "They're dried apple slices. Maybe they'll help you feel better."

I tasted one. "I like this," I said. The unfamiliar fruit was sweet and chewy, and after I ate the last one, I asked for more.

"I'm saving them for the trade store. I only have one small barrel, and I'll need them in case the supplies are late."

"But I *want* more," I said irritably, surprising both of us.

He looked at me with astonishment. "I'm sorry, Mary, but I can't spare them."

In a huff, I set about cleaning the dishes. I was tired and my back and thighs ached from the long day's ride.

"Call of nature," he said, taking a small shovel as he went off into the dark. "And I'll give you a little time to yourself," he mumbled.

I was setting the dishes back in the wagon when Pierre's low growl warned me that there was something or someone in the nearby pine trees. I quickly reached for my loaded rifle. This was not only the land of grizzlies, this was also Cree and Assiniboine territory, and all were enemies to fear. I followed Pierre's stare into the dense, dark trees until I caught sight of a shadow moving low to the ground. Pierre growled as it crept forward.

I looked behind into the dark to see where Farwell had gone. Where was he? If it was an enemy, had they already got to him? The shadow stopped moving, as though aware that I had seen him. Gradually, I edged closer to the wagon, hoping for more cover. There! It was moving again, and the horses, sensing danger, began to stamp and snort. As the shadow grew closer, I steadied the rifle against my shoulder. I still couldn't tell the size of it, nor whether it was man or animal. If it was a large grizzly, one shot would not bring him down. If it was an enemy, and if they had already killed Farwell, there would be others. I dared not take my eyes off the movement in front of me.

Pierre's growl deepened. A lone dog was little help with a bear, and at the worst he could provoke an attack. "Quiet!" I said. Snarling, he dropped next to me as he had been taught. A twig snapped as the threatening figure inched toward the horses. Snow whinnied as she and the other horses fought the picket line that secured them. I took aim when I saw the flash of yellow eyes, then pulled in a deep breath as I steadied myself and fired. The shadow leapt with the impact of the bullet, but what had I hit? When I saw no other movement, I slowly made my way toward the trees with my rifle at the ready.

"Mary!" I heard Farwell's call, and by the time he reached us, I was checking to see if the mountain lion was dead. It was longer than Farwell was tall, and its paws were bigger than my hands. I had never seen one of this size before, and it made me wonder what the grizzlies looked like up here.

"Damn! You all right?" Farwell stared at the lion. "Whoa! That's one hell of a big cat."

"How much apple slices do you give me for the pelt?" I asked, unsheathing my skinning knife while Farwell threw back his head and laughed.

CHAPTER EIGHTEEN

1872

THE RUTTED TRAIL had led us all the way from Fort Benton to where Farwell and I now paused on a high ridge facing north. After traveling the flat prairie for days, I was unprepared for this view of the Cypress Hills. I hadn't expected such vast beauty of lush green hills that rolled into one another, seemingly without end. A multitude of wild animals would be sheltered in the slopes and valleys, hidden in the dense stands of willows, poplar, and spruce. And how abundant were the lodgepole pines, those straight trees so perfect for tipis or making travois for our travels.

A breeze floating toward us from the hills brought the scent of wild rose and the ripening berries of the purple-leaved chokecherry bushes that grew thick along the hillsides. To the east, in the far distance and on the flat prairie, were buffalo, grazing on the nutritious short grass.

I was relieved to see this dark herd of many hundreds. How could I have been worried that the buffalo would ever disappear?

An elk's bugle rang out over the hills, as though claiming this land. For him, rutting season was just beginning. Snow lowered her head and ate grass as I sat back in my saddle. Farwell, from his seat on the wagon, pointed down to a small silver-blue river that wound around the rolling hills like one of Jeannie's ribbons. "That's the North Fork of the Milk River," he said. "Isn't this one of the most beautiful places you've ever seen?"

I nodded, not wanting to take from my husband's happiness, but even here, the uneasiness I felt the night before would not lift. *Yes, this place is beautiful*, I thought, *but what and who does it shelter?* Grizzlies were one thing to fear, but I had known of them all my life. The human wolfers were new to me.

We traveled northwest, into the Cypress Hills, and by late afternoon we arrived at Farwell's chosen site. There we were met by a group of at least ten men, and to my relief, Stiller was not among them. These Métis men, from a village about three miles to the east, had been hired by Farwell and were logging spruce trees in preparation for building the trading post. They already had stacks of logs so high that I wondered what they would possibly do with all the cut trees.

"Our boss and his wife here. Now we got to get to work," one joked as he pointed our wagon toward their campsite.

Farwell led us a distance away from their camp so we might have our privacy, but a man from the Métis camp site saw us and hurried over.

"I'm Simon, de cook." The man eagerly shook Farwell's hand. Simon was short, not much taller than Jeannie, and like her, everything about him was full of life. He wore the bright red Métis sash around his sizable waist, but he also wore a hat of muskrat fur that looked too small for his head.

"Good to meet you, Simon," my husband said. "I heard you'll do the hunting as well as the cooking?"

He broke into a grin. "I shoot de deer, elk, and buffalo, and I cook 'em." He looked toward me. "You like to cook?"

"This is my wife, Mary Farwell," my husband said.

At this, Simon removed his hat. "Bonjour, Marie," he said, nodding before he quickly slapped his hat firmly back atop his balding head. "You like to cook?" he asked again.

"*Éeh*, I—"

"My wife can help you out, but once we get set up, she'll mostly be helping me with the trading. Madame Lebombarde will be coming in a few days to give you a hand with the cooking."

"Ah, Madame Lebombarde. She cooks good."

Farwell handed Simon the reins to the wagon. "Can you take care of the horses?" he asked, and then turned to me. "I'm going up to see how the men are doing. Can you get us settled?"

"*Éeh, itchik*," I agreed, then caught myself. "Yes, good," I repeated in English, and Farwell left before Simon had time to unhitch the horses.

"*Itchik*, that means good?" Simon asked as we led the horses down to the water. This small river was cold and clear and deep enough to easily provide for us, our animals, and the wildlife.

"Yes," I said, as we both laughed at Pierre, who was wild with delight, barking and leaping around in the shallow water and making a pest of himself to the horses.

"You have *itchik* man in Farwell and he take *itchik* care of his woman," he said. I already liked Simon for his attempt to use my language.

"You are Crow, right?" he asked, pointing to my moccasins. "I figure from your beading."

"Yes," I said, suddenly proud. "I am Crow."

That evening, Farwell had me sit next to him when we ate at the Métis campsite. I was glad that Jeannie had schooled me in how to use a knife and a fork, as I noticed most of the men used these tools. Simon had cooked the elk steaks perfectly, and the sweet meat, seasoned with salt and pepper, was as tender as any I had ever eaten.

In this setting, Farwell was the chief. This was a group that liked to laugh, and as we ate, one of the men teased Farwell about being "caught by a woman."

His response was quick. "Nope. I caught her," he said, looking at me with tenderness. "Not only is Mary beautiful, but she can cook, and you should see her with a gun."

MY DAYS WERE busy helping Simon prepare meals for the men that were building Farwell's fort. I was astounded at the size of the place and how quickly the men were getting the log structures up. I had not expected that there would be so many buildings, nor had I imagined that they would be surrounded by the stockade, easily twice my height. It made me wonder if Farwell was preparing for trade or for battle.

About three weeks after our arrival, I was coming into the fort from our lodge when I heard my husband's call. "Mary. Up here." He greeted me from atop a high lookout, newly built into a corner of the stockade. "Come through the gates," he directed, and from there he waved me toward a ladder. "Come on up here with me."

I was fine climbing up, but standing next to him on the narrow platform I clung to the posts, uneasy at being up this high. "Look," Farwell said, turning my attention to the buildings and the yard below.

"It's big," I said.

"It measures sixty-eight feet by eighty feet," he said, clearly proud of numbers that had little meaning for me. "I wanted you to see from up here how I've laid it out. Look, over by the front gates—that's a big enough space to bring the horses in at night. We'll have up to thirty head, and they'll all need shelter."

"From grizzlies and mountain lions?" I guessed.

"Well, yeah, but it's the Indians, too. Once they do some trading and get a taste of liquor, they often want more of it—even if they don't have any more pelts to trade. Times like that they might feel entitled to take a horse or two."

He pointed toward the largest of the four sod-roofed buildings below. "That one will have windows. That's where we'll eat and gather. The Lebombardes will sleep in there at night. They're older and they'll have the warmth of a stove. And that small building behind it. That's ours. We'll sleep there and I'll do my bookkeeping there, too. See that lean-to attached to the main building? That's where we'll put the kitchen, and that pit they've dug beside it is the root cellar that'll hold our vegetables."

"But my tipi . . . ," I began.

He laughed. "Mary, your tipi covers at least twenty feet. There's no room for it in the yard. Besides, we'll have a snug place of our own. Just wait and see."

Farwell turned his attention to the other buildings. "That long one is the storage shed for the pelts, and that bigger building in the corner—well, that'll be the trading store." He looked at me with pride. "So that, my dear, is Farwell's Fort."

"Why do you call it a fort?"

He shrugged. "Up here these posts are called forts. Back where we're from, they're called trading posts."

From our high perch we also had a better view of another fort going up directly across the river from us. That one was smaller, and though it too had a wall surrounding the buildings, those logs were uneven in height, and you could see that the whole place was built with less care. I asked Farwell if he wasn't concerned about competition this close to him.

"Nah." He shook his head. "Heck, I know of at least thirteen other whiskey traders within three miles of here, and if it's a good season there'll be plenty of pelts to go around." He nodded toward the other fort. "Moses Solomon's putting that place up. He's close, about forty feet from the river, same as us. Handy for the water supply so I can't object to that. Also, he buys a lot of supplies from me, and it's easy for his men to cross the river here with the water only about three feet deep. But am I worried about competition from him? Nah. Solomon's not much liked by the Indians—he's one of those who give out liquor and then cheat them by weighting the scales. It doesn't take long for word to get around, and then they come to me."

Nervous at this height, I was ready to get down, but Farwell took me by the shoulders and turned me toward the surrounding hills. "Hang on," he said, "I really want you to see the view from up here."

Looking out, I almost forgot to be scared of the height. It was the beginning of October, the moon when the redwing blackbirds gather. The grass had faded to a light brown, and the bright yellow leaves of the willows and the aspen trees stood out against the vivid green of the spruce and pine. Though the sun shone, a cool breeze was coming in from the west, and the woody scent of the changing season was as familiar to me as an old friend.

"Look at that!" Farwell pointed into the distance toward a coulee. There, hidden below a ridge, a massive grizzly was slowly making its way toward a young buffalo calf and its unsuspecting mother.

I gripped Farwell's arm, and we both held our breath until the creeping bear finally leapt. He got hold of the calf, and as it bawled in terror a huge bull appeared out of nowhere. Head down, he went for the bear. The calf scrambled free, but the attacked grizzly caught hold of the bull with his deadly paws. The bull bellowed and pulled away, and though blood ran from his torn hide, he charged a second time. Again his horns hit their mark, but after the bear dropped, his angry roar reached us when he rose again to fight. Dust billowed as the two battled, but in the end, the bear stumbled to the edge of the hill and slid down into the coulee before the wounded buffalo bull dropped to his knees. Farwell whooped as he squeezed me tight. "That was something, wasn't it?"

I had seen bears before, but even from this distance I knew I had never seen one this size. How close did they come to camp? I wondered.

"I'll take one of the men and get out there. We can't have an injured grizzly or buffalo bull this close to camp."

"I come," I said, and though I could see a fleeting moment of doubt in his glance, it passed when he saw my determination.

WE WERE STILL a distance from the berry bushes when Farwell raised his hand. Snow picked up on my nerves and her body went tight. As we readied our rifles and slowly moved in, there was a rustling in the bushes, and the wounded grizzly appeared. We both lifted our rifles. "Shoot," Farwell called, "he's going to charge." Snow quivered in fear, but she held steady as I took aim and shot. Farwell's rifle boomed as well, and the bear went down. My heart was hammering as Farwell cautiously approached the giant animal, easily three times the size of my husband. Our braves had come back many times from a successful bear hunt, but I had never seen one this large.

"He's done," Farwell said in relief, and I could see he was as shaken as I. "Now we have to see to the bull."

We left the grizzly as we urged our horses over the top of the ridge. The rest of the herd had left, and though the bull was down, on seeing us, the massive animal stumbled to his feet. Blood seeped from his opened side as he turned toward Snow and shook his mighty head. As he snorted and prepared to charge, I saw then the fury that Big Cloud must have faced, and my whole body went weak. I stared in terror, unable to move or lift my rifle.

I heard the labored breaths of the charging bull when Farwell's gun blasted. As the animal went to its knees, Farwell shot again before he dismounted. "I think he's dead!" he called out as he approached the animal cautiously. He poked the silent bull with his rifle to make certain. "It's okay, Mary, he's dead."

I slipped from Snow's back and steadied myself against her until my own legs held me properly. Had Farwell seen that I had frozen? How could that have happened, especially after all Red Fox had taught me?

I stood alongside Snow, running my hand along her warm neck as I stared out at the valley.

Farwell came over to me. "Are you all right?" he asked, putting his arm across my shoulders. "That was a big bull, and when he turned on you like that . . . well, I don't blame you for being scared."

Still, I said nothing. From this rise I could see our fort, standing large and strong across the river from Solomon's crooked-looking stockade, and a terrible dread washed over me. I wanted to ask Farwell to forget about this place and to leave with me now, before the snow came. Since our arrival, I had been having dreams—violent dreams. Every morning before my prayers, I would spit the dreams out over my left hand, rejecting them, but they'd return the next night.

Overhead, an eagle screeched as she swooped down, then soared and screeched again as she swung by a second time. Was her nest close by, or was she, too, warning us of danger?

I turned to Farwell and tried to find the English words.

He pulled me to him. "Don't worry. You just froze, that's all," he said. "Every man I know has had a time when something like that has happened to him."

"It was a big bull," I said, resting my head on his shoulder, trying to sort out my feelings.

Farwell grunted. "You can say that again. He scared the devil out of me, too." He hugged me tight before releasing me. "But now I need to get back to work. We've got to finish up these buildings before Pierre shows up with the windows and the rest of the supplies."

I looked back at the bull.

"I'll send Simon and another man up for the meat," Farwell said.

I gave him a swift look as I mounted Snow. "No, I will come back with Simon," I said, not about to let go of both a bear and buffalo hide that was mine.

CHAPTER NINETEEN

1872

ALEXIS AND NANCY Lebombarde arrived the next day, and all the Métis workers gathered around to greet them. Farwell had told me about Alexis Lebombarde and how well he was known in this territory. He liked to say that the prairie was his home, and because he knew the land so well, he was often hired by white men to lead expeditions where his hunting, tracking, and knowledge of Indian people proved invaluable.

Alexis Lebombarde was fluent in English and French as well as Sioux, Cree, and Assiniboine. He worked as an interpreter and my husband had paid well to have him and his wife come to work at Farwell's Fort. The two were a handsome couple. Both were stocky, but her generous curves were rounded and soft, covered in a high-necked dress of blue and green, while his frame, outfitted in Métis style, was as powerfully built as that of a younger man.

When Farwell introduced me as his wife, Alexis removed his fur hat and nodded. His gray hair settled around his shoulders as his brown face creased into a smile. "Madame Farwell," he said. That name still felt very odd to me, but when he confidently greeted me in Crow, I understood why he was so well liked.

Madame stood back while her husband addressed me, and as she waited, she took the green shawl covering her head and placed it carefully around her shoulders. Her hair, braided and coiled at the back of her neck, was as pure a white as I had ever seen. She must have been very proud of it, for she smoothed it when she saw my admiring glance. "Madame Farwell." She nodded in greeting, but her pleasantness ended there when she refused my offer to help her set up her camp. Later, after the couple was settled, Madame found Simon and me preparing the evening meal.

She came over to where I was cutting the buffalo meat into steaks. "Madame Farwell, this is what I was hired for," she said, taking the large knife from my hand. "You go ahead and leave this to me."

In my culture we respected what older women had to say, so I left the two of them and went back to work on the bear and buffalo hides. But I was troubled. Back with my people, my role was well defined. But here the cooking was done by others, and I would have no lodge to care for when we moved inside the stockade. What would I do then?

MY ANSWER CAME the very next day when the bull trains lumbered in. The wagons not only brought the rest of the materials to complete the log buildings, but they were piled high with all the supplies needed for trade in the Indian store.

M'sieu Dubois's dog came bounding ahead to greet Pierre, who had grown and was now almost the same size as his friend. The two chased each other around my feet in circles of joy.

"Mary!" Jeannie waved from the front wagon before she leapt down and came running to grab hold of me. She paid no attention to the men who were staring at us, and as tiny as she was, she lifted me up in the air. "I missed you so much," she said, hugging me tight. She set me back on my feet and looked me over. "God be praised. You look so good."

I laughed at her exuberance and hugged her back. "You look good, too," I said. And she did. Her face was full and her cheeks pink.

She leaned toward my ear. "Guess what?" she said. "I've enjoyed rice and raisins so much that I think I'm going to have *un bébé*," she whispered.

"A baby!"

She put her finger to her lips. "Shhh. You're the first person I've told. René doesn't even know yet."

"You don't tell him?"

"No. If he knew, neither he nor M'sieu Dubois would have let me come along."

AFTER WE GOT Jeannie's lodge up, the two of us went over to see the fort. "I can't believe how big it is," Jeannie said. "Look at the size of that stockade."

"I don't like that wall," I said.

She looked at me in surprise. "Why?" she asked. "It'll keep you safe."

"From what?"

Jeannie shrugged. "Things can get rough up here," she said.

"Rough? What do you mean?"

"A lot of these men are wolfers, and Indians and wolfers usually aren't a good mix."

I tried to let go of that thought as I led us through the open gates and past the men who were unpacking the wagons. There I pointed out the building that would hold the pelts and then the large building across from it—the one that was awaiting windows and where everyone would eat. Behind that building, in the far corner of the stockade, was the finished trade store, but I took Jeannie to the small cabin that sat between the two larger buildings.

"This one is for me and Farwell," I said, and pushed the heavy door open, only to step back in surprise. "What is this?" I asked, staring at the wooden frame that took up much of the space in the room.

"It's your bed. We brought it with the supplies," Jeannie said. "I'm surprised the men got it in here already." She picked up a strange-looking tool. "It's a rope bed, and here is the key. You'll need it to tighten the ropes every couple of nights."

I pointed in disbelief at the cords running across the bottom of the wooden frame. "We sleep on rope?"

She grinned and went to a corner of the room. "Here, help me put this pallet on."

"Why we don't sleep on the ground?" I asked as we struggled to pull the straw mattress up and over the ropes.

"You don't sleep on the ground this far up north. You would get too cold on a dirt floor," she said. "Besides, in here you'll be nice and warm with that little cast-iron stove over there."

The door sat open, and I closed it to make a point. "Look. Too dark," I said, then opened it again.

"Yes, *it is* too dark," she said, emphasizing her words as she pointed to a small table. "That is why you always keep a kerosene lamp here." She continued to look around. "Oh, that's good. Look at all those pegs that they put into the wall for you to hang your clothes."

But my thoughts were still on the closed-in room. How could we breathe with the door shut all night? How would the fresh air come in? I was about to ask her about that but I forgot when Farwell found us.

"It looks smaller with the bed in here," he said.

"It's cozy though," Jeannie said, and Farwell smiled and nodded in agreement. "I came to ask if you would help Mary unpack some of the goods and set up the Indian store. This will be her first time, and I know she could use the help."

"I'll do my best," Jeannie said enthusiastically, and we followed him out the door.

Like all the new buildings, the Indian store smelled pleasantly of fresh-cut wood. This building didn't have windows, either, but it did have two doors. We entered through the door that opened from the inside of the fort, and then Farwell unbolted the back door and swung it open. Beyond it was a meadow, with no stockade to hide the countryside. All three of us squinted into the strong sun.

"Leave this door open while you're working," he said. "It will give you the light you need."

"Is this the door where your customers will come through?" Jeannie asked Farwell.

"Yes," he said. "They can come right in to see the goods."

"I've never seen a trading post that doesn't use a wicket," she said.

"A wicket?" I asked.

"It's like a big window where the customer can look in at the goods, but it has bars on it so they can't get into the store," Farwell answered.

"It can eliminate a whole lot of problems, but I like my customers to see what they are getting."

He took a deep breath and looked around at all the unopened boxes and barrels and crates. "I'll leave the two of you to sort through all this and put some of the things up on the shelves. Do you think that you'll need someone else to help?"

"Not yet. Let us get started and then we'll let you know," Jeannie said. "Mary can reach the high shelves and I'll get the low ones."

"Don't make my Mary work too hard." Farwell winked at me.

"I won't if you won't make my René work too hard," she answered, laughing, and it wasn't the first time that I envied her ease with people.

As soon as he left, Jeannie turned to me with a teasing smile. "Mary, he is so in love with you. René has known Farwell for a while now, and he said that he has never seen him this happy. And you've only been married a few months. Imagine how he'll feel when you have a baby with him?"

I smiled and said nothing in return. I didn't want her to think that I didn't want children, nor did I want to take away from Jeannie's happiness with her own baby coming, so I didn't tell her that I had asked the Old Woman Moon to wait with that blessing.

Jeannie looked around and then rubbed her hands together. "Do you want to get started? I've never seen so many trade goods before. Have you?"

"No," I said, bewildered at the tremendous bounty.

"Since the barrels of flour and coffee and sugar are over there, let's make that the food section. I see the chests of tea, but I know there is more food they'll be bringing in, so why don't we start over here with the fabric and . . . oh," she interrupted herself, "look at all these beautiful buttons. Indians *and* the Métis will love these."

There were bone buttons, glass buttons, steel buttons, and finally clay buttons that were meant to be covered with fabric. Excited to see what else there was, I began to unpack stacks of red, blue, and white blankets, most with stripes that I had yet to learn the meaning of. "Look," I said, slipping my arms into the sleeves when I realized that some of the striped white blankets had sleeves.

"That's a capote," Jeannie said. "It's made from those woolen blankets, and it's popular with the Métis as a winter coat."

I wrapped the blanket coat around me and put the hood up. It would be a warm cover for the winter, and I wondered if Farwell would give me one in trade. I left it on as Jeannie showed me how to line up the many bolts of fabric along a shelf. "Try to keep the colors together like this," she said. "That's the way I've seen it done in other shops." She was right. All the fabric lined up together—the reds and blues and browns, and other patterned in many colors—looked pretty, and soon I had a full shelf.

Jeannie began to unpack the readymade clothes, and we giggled when she held up a pair of men's cotton drawers. "These are pretty ugly," she said as she swung them in the air. I took off the coat when I couldn't resist trying on a man's red flannel shirt.

"That red looks good on you," Jeannie said, and because I liked the easy way of buttons instead of ties, I wondered again about trading with Farwell.

There were women's white hose—"for the Métis women," Jeannie said. "That fancy Madame Lebombarde probably has five pair," she said, scrunching up her face.

Madame had been as cool with her as she had been with me, and Jeannie felt the sting. "She knows I'm an orphan, so she thinks she's better than me."

"And me?"

"You mean why doesn't she like you?"

"*Éeh*."

"Two reasons. First, your husband is her employer, and that sort of makes you her boss, and second because you are Indian."

"But *she* is Indian."

"Only part, like me, so she thinks that's better. Don't worry about her, though. Some people always have to feel as though they are better than others. I pity those people because if they say things to try to make others feel bad it's because they don't feel good about themselves."

"You pity Madame?" I asked.

"No, she's a fool," Jeannie said, and with that turned back to her work.

I found some white glazed plates and two large yellow bowls. "Look, Jeannie," I said, holding them up.

"Oh, those are some nice-looking bowls. Let's put all the dishes over by the food stuff," she said. "Those bowls and white plates are for the Métis, but see those tin plates and cups? And those knives and forks and spoons? Some of the Indians will want those. They'll hammer down the spoons for necklaces and earrings and sometimes they use them to decorate their bags or shields."

I was overwhelmed by the wealth of goods, and throughout the day I was grateful that Jeannie was there to guide me. I thought of my family often as I unpacked the boxes. We set the guns next to countless boxes of ammunition, alongside rows of large butcher knives and axes. Father, I imagined, would have walked past the leather bridles and halters and gone straight to the many rifles and revolvers available for trade. Finally, we turned our attention to the boxes of soap.

"Here, smell." I put an oily square bar under Jeannie's nose.

She sniffed it. "That's castile soap. Sometimes it's scented with pine."

"Farwell use it."

"He *uses* it."

I nodded at her correction.

"It's what we used in the orphanage and it's what the Métis use. A lot of them will come from the village, and they'll buy up boxes of this stuff."

"The village a few miles away?" I asked.

"*Oui*. It's where René and I will go for a few days after we leave here. I wanted to stay here with you, but René said that he has relatives there who want to meet me. They are all big hunters in that village, so they'll likely be over here to trade. Oh," she said, opening another box. "Look at these bottles of ink and all that paper. Maybe you could write to me."

I hesitated, unsure.

"You can use those study cards that I made for you," she said.

"*Éeh*." I often laughed at the animals and stick figures that she had drawn, and I studied the words under her drawings almost every day. "I write my name, but writing hard," I said, and as soon as she scrunched her face, I corrected myself. "Writing *is* hard."

She beamed. "See. You figured it out. Study those words and copy them, and then you can write to me."

"You write to me in Crow," I said.

"I thought you said that you don't have a written language?"

"We don't," I said, and we chuckled.

She sighed. "I'm really going to miss you, and now that I'll have a baby, I don't know when I'll see you again. How about if I write to you first? Would you try to write back?"

"Yes," I agreed.

"Maybe Farwell will help you?"

"I can do it." I knew that by the end of winter those study cards would be ragged from use.

"Great," she said, and hugged me. Then she placed her hands on her hips. "Look at all this. We'd better keep going."

Together we emptied crate after crate, stopping often to show each other a new find. I held up strand after strand of red, blue, green, yellow, and white beads for Jeannie to see.

I thought of my mother and how she would have loved them, along with the thread, the thimbles, and the ribbons. There was so much to unpack that we finally had to stop for the day.

On the second day, we discovered that the men had brought in more food. We stacked bottles of sweet syrup, tins of oysters and sardines, jars of brandied peaches and tangy pickles, and tins of my favorite condensed milk. Then, to my delight, I came upon a whole barrel filled with dried apples.

"God be praised!" I called over, holding up a string of the dried fruit.

"What is it?" Jeannie squinted. "Oh, I love dried apples. We use them to make apple pie, but we don't get them very often."

I told her about the evening when Farwell and I had the argument about the dried apples, and then her eyes opened wide when I told her about the mountain lion. My mouth watered as I held up one of the many heavy loops of the chewy dried fruit. "Can we eat?" I asked.

Jeannie looked toward the closed front door. "Well, they belong to your husband, so I guess you can do what you want."

I didn't need more encouragement. "Here," I said, offering some to my friend and then taking some for myself. The first bite was chewy and tangy, and I closed my eyes to savor it. At first, we ate while glancing at the door, but in time, with no one coming, we began to work and eat at the same time. Finally, Jeannie rubbed her stomach and moaned. "I can't eat any more of those apples," she said. "My stomach hurts."

I had already eaten more than enough, but because I loved the fruit so much, I ate a few more. Just as I swallowed a last piece, Farwell strode in.

He came over and put his arm around me before he kissed my cheek. "Hmm. I smell apples," he said, and then he saw the hanging strings of the dried fruit. "Oh, you found them. Mary, your favorite." With great pleasure, he held a strand up to me. "Now that the barrel is here, my dear wife, you can eat as many of these as you like," he said. He looked at Jeannie. "Damn apple slices made for an unhappy evening on our trip up here."

Jeannie grimaced as she watched Farwell hand slices of the fruit over to me.

"Go ahead, Mary. Have some. Eat as many as you want," he said kindly. "Just don't eat too many at one time. They can upset your stomach."

"*Ahoo*," I said, holding a few slices of the leatherlike fruit in my hand.

Jeannie watched me as I nibbled, but when Farwell offered them to her, she rubbed her stomach. "No, *merci*. I'm pregnant," she murmured. "They don't agree with me."

Farwell looked startled at her news. "Oh," he said. "René didn't say."

"He doesn't know," she whispered. "Please don't tell him," she added.

Farwell looked at me, then back at Jeannie, before he handed the rest of the string over to me.

He left quickly, shaking his head.

Jeannie had her hand over her mouth. "Do you think he will say anything to René?"

"Why you tell him?" I asked.

"*Merde.* I just couldn't eat another piece of that dried apple, and that was the only excuse I could think of," she whispered back.

With that we both held our bloated stomachs and laughed.

CHAPTER TWENTY

1872

THE MORNING THAT Jeannie and René were to leave, Farwell had me take my friend to the Indian store. "She was a big help to us," he said. "Why don't you give her a few things to take home." Jeannie held the kerosene lamp as I unlocked the door to the store. I was excited to give her a gift, and I asked her to pick out anything that she might want.

"I don't know what to get," she said, looking about at the large, overfilled room.

"Maybe something for a baby?" I suggested.

"Oh, that's a good idea," she said. "Some of that flannel, maybe."

As we passed by, Jeannie tapped on some round-bellied wooden barrels. "They must have brought in the whiskey last night," she said, and I smelled the sharp tang of it. I also noticed some tiny blue bottles on the shelf above the whiskey. We hadn't put them there, but they were pretty, and I was about to reach for one, when Jeannie grabbed my hand. "Oh, no, Mary. Don't touch those," she said. "That stuff's so dangerous."

"What is it?" I asked.

"See the label? It's strychnine. I guess Farwell sells it to wolfers."

A chill went down the back of my neck.

"Mary, come help me cut some flannel. René is waiting."

"You tell him about the baby?" I asked.

"Not yet," she said. "I'll wait until we get home. Otherwise he won't want me to have fun."

I encouraged her to look around for something more as I cut a good-sized piece of flannel.

"Maybe I'll take a red shirt for René, and some ribbons for Lucille," she said. "Oh, and some of that embroidery thread for my mother-in-law."

"For Mama Rosa?" I asked, surprised.

She shrugged and smiled. "Maybe she'll be nicer to me."

As she looked about, I folded together the shirt, ribbons, and thread, and then, before I wrapped it all in brown paper, I added a pair of white stockings as a surprise and a box of cartridges for her handgun.

Outside, René was waiting for us with Jeannie's saddled horse. The two of them were going over to the Métis settlement for a few days, and from there they would travel back to their home.

René and Farwell were saying goodbye when Jeannie leaned down from atop her horse. "Guess who will be coming back with us but returning here for the winter? M'sieu Dubois."

"What?"

"*Oui.* He's bringing back more supplies, and he'll stay here until the spring."

"*Merde*," I said, emphasizing the word in the same way Jeannie had. She was still grinning when they rode away.

Farwell found me later at the top of the lookout tower. Even though I was afraid of the height, I clung to the posts so I could watch Jeannie ride off into the rolling hills. "Can you still see them?" Farwell asked as he slipped his arms around my waist and kissed my neck. I sniffed, and Farwell leaned around to look into my face. "Were you crying? What's wrong, Mary?"

I shook my head because I couldn't explain myself.

"What's wrong? This isn't like you. Did you want to go back with them? I'd be heartbroken if you did."

"No," I reassured him. "I want you."

"You'll see your friend again in the spring when we go back." He tried to take me in his arms, but I was too afraid of the height to let go of the posts. "Come on, sweetheart," he said as he helped me down the high ladder. "I wish I could spend more time with you, but today we're putting in the windows. Why don't you take Snow out for a ride? Just take your rifle and stay close by."

Even if I had been able to find the words, what could Farwell have done? The dark cloud I had felt since our arrival at the Cypress Hills had lessened while Jeannie was here, but as soon as she rode away, it returned. With Pierre at my heels, I left the fort and went back to my lodge to gather some clean clothes, some blankets, and my revolver. Then I followed the winding river down until I arrived at my private bathing area. I needed to pray.

Just as Mother and Grandmother had taught me, I cut some long willow branches and used them to form a small rounded frame for a sweat lodge. This I covered with my blankets. After I gathered rocks from the riverbank and heated them in a fire, I used forked branches to move the hot rocks inside, where I drizzled water over them. As steam filled the small hut, I removed my clothes and went inside to pray.

"Please," I begged the First Maker, "I feel that something bad is coming. Please send an animal spirit to help me through." I prayed until I was wet from the heat. When I climbed out, I went to the river, and there I took great care to cleanse every part of my body. When I finished, I felt better, though the dark feeling still lingered.

That night I dreamt of a bear—a huge grizzly—it might have been the one I killed. He came at me through a forest of dark pines, and when he rose in front of me, his mighty paws slashed the air. "Why are you afraid?" he roared. "You carry my heart, and my strength is with you." I woke up as he crashed away into the forest.

I lay awake and thought back to when Simon and I had gone to butcher the buffalo and the bear. Simon worked on the buffalo while I started work on the bear. Before I began, I praised the bear for his brave fight and thanked him for his meat. I remembered Red Fox telling me what our braves did when they had this opportunity, and I found the bear's heart. I took a small slice of it, and as I ate, I asked for the grizzly to give me his strength. This night he had returned to remind me.

Farwell slept as I rose from our pallet. It was just before sunrise, dark-face time, the holiest time of night, when I went out to pray. I thanked the First Maker for answering my prayer so swiftly, and though there was still a heaviness, I also felt assured that I would have help if I needed it.

As THE FORT continued to take shape, Simon asked me to assist with the cooking again, and I was happy to do so. The kitchen was conveniently set up in a lean-to outside the main cabin. There Madame, Simon, and I worked on rough-cut tables alongside a large cast-iron stove and an open fire. When we were alone, Madame scarcely spoke to me, and when she learned that I did not understand French, she used that language to communicate with Simon. Madame referred to Farwell as the master of the place, and when he was around, she made a great show of being friendly to me. Simon saw her tricks, but he did his best to stay out of it.

The men now ate inside the completed main cabin. This was the only building to have windows and wooden floors, and we served the men their meals on a long pine table with benches on either side. There were more benches and two small tables along the walls with a wood-burning stove that kept the room warm. This was also the room where Alexis and Madame Lebombarde slept. I had reluctantly agreed to move into the small log cabin with Farwell, where I did my best to adjust to being closed up at night. There was some flickering light from the small stove, but every night as I tightened the ropes on that sinking bed, I envied the Lebombardes their pallets of thick buffalo hides that they kept stacked in a corner of the dining room. How I missed my stored pallet and tipi and the comforting scent of Mother Earth.

We HAD BEEN in the Cypress Hills for five weeks when George Hammond and Rosalie arrived from Fort Benton. Farwell had told me that Hammond was hired to be his right-hand man, but I didn't like him from the start. He was tall, with a narrow face and long nose, a bushy mustache, and small brown eyes. When he took off his wide-brimmed hat, his dark hair was cut close to his head. The man had a stern look about him, though he softened somewhat when he introduced the woman on his arm. Rosalie was Métis and dressed like Jeannie. She was as tall as me, around my age, and I liked her immediately when she smiled.

George Hammond looked surprised when Farwell introduced me as his wife. "You got yourself a preacher involved?"

"We did," Farwell said.

Rosalie took Hammond's hand. "We're only married 'in the way of the country,' but George promised me next year we would find a preacher."

Hammond's face flushed.

Farwell saved him further embarrassment. "Rosalie, George said you are willing to help with the cooking?"

"*Ah, oui*, I am a good cook," she said.

Farwell turned to me. "Mary, George, here, will be in charge of the fort if I need to be away. The rest of the time he'll have his hands full taking care of the store. Hammond, I've got you staying in the Indian store. It's the best I can do."

"Good enough. C'mon, Rosie, let's get us unpacked," Hammond said, and the girl waved back to me as he led her away.

The next morning, I introduced Rosalie to Madame Lebombarde. Right away, Madame began an animated conversation in French that lasted throughout the morning, and from then on neither spoke English in the kitchen. In that way, Madame made sure that I was solidly left out of their twosome.

As time went on, I began to better understand the structure of our community. Farwell was chief of this fort, but I saw that he was alone in making all the decisions. It concerned me that there didn't seem to be a council of men for him to turn to for help.

As a chief, Father relied on a council of other men whenever there was a decision to be made. Father also had peacekeepers from the men's societies—usually chosen from the one that was most successful in horse raids and battles. It was they who decided on appropriate punishment for any upsets within the community. I remembered a time when a group of young men put themselves and our village in danger by going out on a raid without permission. On their return, the peacemakers decreed that they live away from the village for a full moon. It was a hardship for both the young men and their relatives, but in having our society set up in this way, Father was relieved of making a difficult decision, as some of his young relatives were in that group.

But here, all the men came to Farwell with their problems. Twice, already, men had been drunk and Farwell had to break up their fight. Though it appeared that Farwell had everything under control, I wondered at the weight of it. Still, my respect for my husband grew daily, and I was especially grateful that he did not drink whiskey with the other men when they sat to play poker after the evening meal.

BY LATE OCTOBER, in the moon when the blackbirds gather, snow already covered the hills, and the Métis and Indians began to arrive with their pelts. Farwell had me join him, and together with Alexis Lebombarde, we went out to greet them. I knew good pelts when I saw them, and I was pleased that my husband valued my opinion. These were superior, wolf pelts as thick and silky as I had ever seen, and stacks of quality buffalo hides. As Farwell had anticipated, the Cree and Nakoda liked that he had an Indian wife.

Winter advanced, and as the snow piled up I watched the Indian camps come and go. Not all camps drank liquor, and some nights were quiet. Yet in one sad camp, both the women and the men had a taste for liquor, and when their small village finally left, they were hungover and downcast, with little to show for their past year's hard labor. All had been sacrificed for a few days of drunkenness.

ONE NIGHT I was deep asleep when an explosion went off somewhere nearby. I sat up in alarm. Our dark bedroom offered little light, and for a terrible moment I was a little girl back again at the battle at Arrow Creek. I heard battle cries and frenzied whoops and gunfire. When I heard Farwell's voice, I remembered where I was, but the terrible noise continued.

"It's okay, Mary," he said, reaching for me. "It's just some of the Indians shooting up their guns. They're drunk."

He went back to sleep but I lay awake most of that night, worrying about dangerous stray bullets that might strike the innocent inside their tipis. The next day everything seemed peaceful enough, but the next night was a repeat of the night before.

Again I woke Farwell, but this time I was angry. "Why do you give them that whiskey? Why they cannot trade for some of the other goods?"

He yawned. "I told you, Mary. If we don't give them what they want, they'll go across the river to Solomon's place. He gets them liquored up and cheats 'em. We don't do that." He rolled to his side and went back to sleep.

A few weeks later there came a night that so many guns were shooting off that even Farwell lay awake. I asked him again why these people kept drinking the whiskey, even though they could see how it was harming themselves and their people. He didn't answer for a long while, but when he did he spoke in a quiet voice. "I think some of them are like me. Get one drink of whiskey in them and they can't stop."

I leaned up on my elbow, angry with him. "Then why give it to them?"

Farwell reached for me and pulled me down alongside him. He was quiet a long while before he answered. "I've been thinking about that, Mary. Maybe because I'm getting older, or maybe having you here has made me see things different, but I'm starting to wonder if it's time to get out of this business. Even if we do well this year, we'll still have to do this for one more season, but then we'd have enough money to buy a ranch. After that I promise you that we'll move closer to your people and live a more settled life."

Later, after Farwell fell asleep with me tight in his arms I stayed awake, thinking of his plans and listening to the gunshots.

CHAPTER TWENTY-ONE

1872–1873

THE TRADE STORE was not yet open for business the morning I went in to get some flour that Simon needed for pancakes. In the light of a kerosene lamp, I saw George Hammond leaning over an open keg of whiskey.

"Rosalie, shut the door," he barked, his back to me.

I had just left Rosalie with Madame, and though I disliked being alone with him, I closed the door and went to get the flour. As I slipped past him, I saw that he was adding something to the barrel of whiskey. I stopped to watch him for a minute, but I couldn't believe what I was seeing. Farwell had told me that the traders added water and molasses to the liquor that they sold to the Indians, but it looked as though Hammond was using the little blue bottle that Jeanine had warned me about.

"*What are you—?*" I grabbed at his long arm, and, startled, he shoved at me with his elbow. As I fell back, I tried to catch myself by taking hold of a shelf, but it broke free from the wall, and with it all the tin plates and cups came crashing down. I felt a sharp pain in my shoulder when I landed on the floor.

Hammond glared at me where I sat, surrounded by a mess of cups and plates. "What the hell, Mary! You pushed me and I almost added too much."

I rubbed my throbbing shoulder where the shelf had hit me and tried to make sense of what I had seen.

"Are you hurt?" he asked, his voice cold. A tin cup rolled from my lap and jangled to the floor as I got to my feet.

"That's strychnine," I accused, pointing to the poison in his hand. "You use it to kill Indians?"

"Don't be ridiculous. You don't know what you are talking about."

"Wolfers use strychnine to kill," I said.

He put the wooden lid back onto the keg and then looked at the clutter on the floor. "What did you come in here for?" he asked. "Why don't you get it and then leave. Now I'll have to clean this mess up."

But I left without the flour and rushed to find Farwell in our bedroom. He was sitting at the small table, working numbers in his ledgers by the light of the kerosene lamp. He did this work here and kept these books in our room, for privacy, he said. Now he looked up at me. "What's wrong?" he asked.

It was hard to find the English words. "George Hammond, he . . . he put strychnine . . . in whiskey!" I finally said.

"I know," he said. "But just a little."

I couldn't believe his words. "You want to kill the Indians?"

Farwell closed his ledger and set it to the side. "No, Mary, of course not. It's what the Indians want."

"They want to die like wolves?"

"The amount we put in doesn't kill them. It just gives them what they've come to expect. It makes their hands and feet go numb. If they drink whiskey and they don't have some tingling in their feet and hands, they think they're being cheated."

I sat on the edge of the bed, too stunned to reply.

Farwell came over and sat beside me. He reached for my hand, but I pulled it away. "Mary, most of the whiskey traders do this. They've been doing it for years."

I shook my head in disbelief. "Jeannie said strychnine kills you."

"Maybe Jeannie doesn't know that it's also used in some white man's medicine. If it's used right, it doesn't harm anyone. You'll have to trust me on this."

I stared at him. Was it true that white people put strychnine in their medicine? I didn't know him to lie.

He sighed. "Look, I know my world has to be confusing for you at times. Heck, sometimes I don't even know which end is up. But I can assure you that no Indians have died of this."

I needed to believe him. In the Crow culture, you were nothing if you were a liar. I had to trust that this was true for the Yellow Eyes as well. But . . .

A knock on the door interrupted us. Farwell was needed.

I hated to go back into the store, but Simon was waiting for the flour. Hammond glanced at me from where he was hammering back the shelf that had been pulled out of the wall. "I suppose you told your husband that I'm trying to kill Indians?"

I didn't answer him, but went straight for the flour barrel as he whacked at a nail. "I hope he set you straight," he called to me. "Course, I'm not saying that most of those horse thieves don't deserve to die."

I hadn't liked George Hammond before, but now I had a reason.

BECAUSE I DID not understand or speak French, it was assumed I did not understand much English, either. Everyone spoke freely around me, and one day while serving the morning meal to the last of the stragglers, I overheard a conversation between three men who worked for Farwell.

"I'm hearing there's extra cash to be made over at Solomon's place. One a his men put down a buffalo carcass not too far away, laced it with that white stuff, and they say those wolves, they're dropping like flies. Foxes, too, and some good-sized lions. They're bringing 'em in so fast, they're looking for help to get those hides off."

One of the men groaned. "I don't know about you, but I got plenty to do right here."

The man with the fewest teeth answered. "Me too. That damn Farwell works us too hard. Between shoveling snow, chopping all that wood, and taking care of the stock . . ."

"Best watch what you say. That's his woman there."

"Ah, she's just a squaw. She don't get none a this."

"She's a looker, though."

The three agreed. "Hey, Injun Mary," one of them called over to me where I was clearing plates. "Hey, you. Mary. How 'bout you bring that coffee over here?"

"*Crow Mary*," I said to him without turning around.

"Good enough," he said. "I'll call you Crow Mary if you'll give me some a that dang coffee."

Thinking I didn't understand, he mimed pouring coffee, and I brought over the pot. While I poured, the one with the few teeth gave me a leering smile. "You no speak English?"

I shook my head.

"I bet you got some nice diddies under that dress a yours," he said, and the other two chuckled. "You let me know anytime you wanna share your buffalo rug."

I answered in Crow, "I would curl up to a hungry grizzly before I would share my buffalo rug with you."

He liked that I was talking to him, and his grin grew even wider. "See boys, she likes me," he said.

"Your breath stinks like a skunk on a bad day," I said, and left as the three argued about what my Crow words meant.

That evening I asked Farwell if he knew about the nearby wolfers.

"I'm sure there are plenty out there. Almost all these fellas around here do some wolfing. They stand to make a lot of money."

"What do they do with all the wolf skins?"

"They get shipped east," he said. "Last year the boats from Fort Benton shipped out over thirty thousand wolf pelts and over a hundred and fifty thousand buffalo hides."

We Crow counted in groups of ten, and I had learned how to count the white man's way from my grandfather, but these numbers were beyond me. "What do they do with so many buffalo hides?"

"Well, it used to be they wanted them for sleigh blankets and coats, but now they're using the buffalo hides for industry. Back in the cities they use these big machines, make all kinds of things. Clothes, for example. And since they found out how tough the buffalo skins are, they use them to make belts for these machines, and they need an endless supply."

"Belts like this?" I asked, hooking my thumb into my wide buffalo belt from where I hung my skinning knife and my Colt 45, whenever it was needed.

"Well, I suppose they're cut about the same," he said.

It wasn't a surprise to me that other people found the buffalo as useful as our people did, but this news left me with an uneasy feeling. There had been much talk among our Crow men about the thinning buffalo herds. It used to be easy to find the animals, but now it sometimes took days, and when a herd was found, they said there weren't as many.

And I hadn't forgotten the terrible waste I saw the day that Farwell and I had passed by the buffalo carcasses.

TOWARD THE END of November, in the moon when leaves are on the ground, M'sieu Dubois and his men arrived with a second delivery of supplies. The arrival of the bull train was a happy event, and everyone went out to greet the wagons. To Pierre's delight, his old friend, M'sieu Dubois's dog, leapt from the wagon to greet him. Even the men were amused by the two dogs' excitement as they chased and tumbled over each other in their happy reunion.

M'sieu Dubois looked at me as though he had something to say, but I didn't like the way his dark eyes followed me, and I kept my distance. After dinner that night, though, he followed me out to the kitchen area. "Crow Mary," he called, and pulled out a letter from his coat pocket. "I bring this from Jeannie."

I was astonished at the wonderful surprise. "*Ahoo*," I mumbled before I left him. As soon as I reached our cabin, I set the kerosene lamp down, and before I even took off my shawl I opened Jeannie's letter.

"I feel—[she drew a picture of a very pregnant woman].

"I eat—[she drew a picture of a bowl of what was clearly rice and raisins].

"I don't eat—[she drew a ring of apple slices with a large X over it].

"I shoot my gun—[she drew three men weeping while a woman triumphantly held her gun in the air].

"I miss you—[four hearts were drawn and colored in red]."

I studied every line, laughing and tracing her drawings with my fingers over and over again.

I DRESSED QUICKLY the next morning. The men who had come with the wagon train had spent the night, and Simon needed all three of us women to help prepare and serve the morning meal. Dark clouds hung low, warning us of upcoming snow. The biting wind blew hard, and though the cook stove was burning hot, I was glad for my thick woolen shawl. Simon greeted me with a grin and nodded toward the main cabin. "Dey all still sleeping."

I wasn't surprised. When I left, bottles were being passed around, but those men must have been squeezed in tight. "All in there?" I asked.

"All but M'sieu Dubois. He sleep out by his wagon, away from de snoring."

"Won't he freeze out there?" I asked.

"He's got a fire going."

We had finished serving the men their bacon and pancakes and were dishing out what remained of the apple pies from the night before, when someone mentioned M'sieu Dubois's absence. One of the men spoke up. "Took his dogs and slept out by the wagons. Likes to be on his own."

For a moment I wondered where Pierre was, but then reassured myself that he was surely snuggled up with his pal beside a warm campfire. But Farwell had a troubled look when he left the table.

Both Farwell's workers and the hands who had come with M'sieu Dubois were irritable, suffering the effects of the whiskey from the night before. Two of them began a loud argument about which one of them would have a last piece of apple pie, and finally all the men decided that the argument should be settled with an arm-wrestling contest. The room erupted in shouts as the two men shed their vests and jackets. I stood back to watch, but Rosalie and Madame Lebombarde made for the door.

The men tossed coins onto the table and wagered bets, while the two wrestlers rolled up their sleeves and seated themselves across from each other. Just as the two men clasped hands, Farwell came through the door. "Mary," he called, waving me over, but I shook my head. I wanted to watch. It interested me to see that these men were doing just what the Crow men did—gambling and trying to get the better of one another.

"Mary. Come!" he called again, and then finally came over to reach for my arm. A loud roar went up, and I looked back in frustration as he tugged me out the open door. I wanted to see who had won.

Out in the kitchen area, I first saw both Rosalie and Madame standing and gaping toward the open gates of the fort. When I followed their gaze, I choked back a scream before I pulled away from Farwell and ran toward M'sieu Dubois. He was walking slowly toward us through the snow with Pierre lying across his arms.

"What did you *do* to him?" I screamed.

"It the damn wolfers," he said. "The dogs got into the wolfer's buffalo. They got mine too."

I stared at Pierre's arched body. Dried blood outlined his mouth, frozen into a grimace of pain. My dog's death had not been easy.

"I find out who do this, I shoot them," he said.

"*I'll* shoot them!" I shouted.

"No." Farwell stepped forward. "Neither of you will shoot anyone. It was an accident."

I waved Farwell back before I took Pierre from M'sieu Dubois. The old man gently handed him over before he slowly walked away, his head down and his shoulders stooped.

I AVOIDED M'SIEU Dubois until he left for the Métis settlement a few days later. Though I still didn't trust the old man, I felt bad that he had lost his dog, too, but I didn't know what to say to him. I knew he must be feeling the same heartbreak as I when I woke up each morning and realized that Pierre was gone. And each day I grew angrier. My fury at his death festered over the next week, and I railed to Farwell one morning as we dressed for the day.

"Those damn wolfers," I said as I tightened my belt around my waist.

Farwell's eyes widened. "Women don't say that word *damn*."

"Damn, damn, *damn*," I said, pleased with his startled look.

He took in a deep breath. "Look," he said, "there's nothing we can do about this. A lot of men do wolfing up here. It's just how it is."

With nowhere to put my fury, I stomped off to help serve the morning meal.

That night, after I again refused to make love, Farwell rolled toward me and stroked my shoulder. "Let's do something fun tomorrow. You haven't used a gun since you shot that bear. Why don't we go out and set up some targets? You always liked to do that with Jeannie."

I couldn't find a reason to say no—in fact, the idea seemed like a good one, so I followed him the next day as we tramped through the snow, making our way up the river in the opposite direction of the Indian camps and the forts. There Farwell hung pieces of canvas on trees and challenged me to use my revolver to hit them.

When I imagined them to be wolfers, I hit each one. Farwell joined in and we began to place bets against each other. We were enjoying ourselves when Hammond called to Farwell from outside the fort's gate. "Abe, you need to see these pelts. They just came in."

"Damn," Farwell said. "This was fun. It's good to see you laugh. I'll go, but why don't you stay if you want." He looked up at the gray sky. "More snow is on the way, and who knows when we can do this again."

It felt good to be away from the closed-in fort and the loneliness and isolation that I often felt there, so I decided to stay. My arm and shoulder were getting sore, but I kept on shooting, moving farther and farther away from the targets, until I heard some low voices. I looked up to see a few men from Solomon's fort gathered to watch me from across the river. I ignored them and continued to shoot until I heard a loud whistle. This time when I looked up, I saw Sam Stiller in the bunch. The man stood out from the others, and not just because of his size. Even at a distance I could see the smirk on his face.

I hurried back and found Farwell in the storage room with Hammond. "Stiller's back," I said, and on seeing me, Hammond made an excuse to leave. He didn't like me, and I didn't like him. Our encounter over the whiskey had soured me against him, but I also didn't like the rough way he spoke to Rosalie.

Farwell nodded while he continued his tally of the pelts. "Yah, he's staying over at Solomon's. He's been wolfing and brought in some good-looking pelts."

"I *knew* it. He killed Pierre."

Farwell set his papers down on a stack of pelts and looked at me. "Mary, you can't blame him. Other men up here are wolfing, too. I am really sorry Pierre died, but I promise I'll get you another dog the next time I go to Fort Benton."

"I don't want *another* dog. I want Pierre," I said, and for the first time since my dog's death, I fell into my husband's arms and cried.

CHAPTER TWENTY-TWO

1873

SNOW FELL ENDLESSLY throughout the winter, and with the wind came high drifts. What a relief it was when finally in May, the moon when chokecherries are in bloom, a Chinook swept in and began to melt the snow. I opened the door to our cabin to let the warm air in, and as I shook out our blankets, I happily thought of how I would soon see Jeannie. In a few weeks we would be loading the pelts and heading back to Fort Benton, and then possibly visit my parents.

Now I looked up, startled to see Farwell hurrying toward me. "Mary. Come! There's a bunch of Nakoda just arrived, and Lebombarde says they're in pretty rough shape."

"Rough shape?" I asked.

"He says they're starving. They've come from the north, up in the Battle River area—a good three hundred miles from here. They said it was a rough winter up there with no game, and I guess they've been traveling for a few months now. Lebombarde says that they lost at least thirty people along the way."

"*Thirty* people?"

"Let's go see what we can do."

I grabbed my heavy shawl, and the two of us took the shortest route toward the new camp. We crossed the water in the shallowest spot and came up to Solomon's fort. From there we turned right and quickly crossed a shallow coulee to get to the small hill where the unfortunate

Nakoda had arrived. There I saw women setting up lodges—I counted about twenty-five, while men dragging travois were still trailing in.

Farwell and I joined Lebombarde, who was talking to a group of survivors. I had never known starvation, and I was shocked to see their gaunt, lined faces.

Lebombarde turned to us. "They need food. They ate all the dogs and most of the horses. The four horses they got left are too weak to go out to hunt."

We learned from one of the braves that on his early arrival he had gone to Solomon's for food but had been turned away. The warrior spit the words out in disgust, and I understood his anger. Farwell and I hurried back to our fort, where he instructed Simon to deliver some cuts of the elk he had brought in the day before. Then we returned with some pemmican for the survivors.

Lebombarde interpreted the words of an older man. "Little Soldier, here, says he's the chief. Up north, where they were camped, it was a bad winter, with no game to be found. When they ran out of food they started heading here to the Cypress Hills, where they knew to find elk and deer. Along the way, when they got to the old campsites, they looked for old bones to dig up to make soup. They even boiled stuff like this." Lebombarde pointed to our parfleche bag made of buckskin that held the pemmican. "But worse, the chief says, was leaving behind those who died or those too old or sick who didn't want to go on."

The old chief was looking at his feet as he recounted this and I understood his pain. I couldn't imagine having to leave behind a loved one in that frozen land, or having to sacrifice Snow or Pierre for food. I looked about at these brave people, who, without their prized dogs and horses, had come here dragging the heavy travois loaded down with their sick and elderly, as well as their lodges and belongings.

I approached a young woman who sat off from the others, her head shorn and her arms circling her drawn-up knees, but she refused my offer of pemmican. An older woman came over and told me to let her be. Through sign talk I learned that the young woman had lost her baby along the way because she had no milk.

❊   ❊   ❊

I FELT A deep kinship with these suffering people and in the days that followed I returned with food and to help with the sick. Little Soldier's wife, The Woman Who Eats Grizzly Bear, always greeted me with a smile, but whenever I met the chief, he looked tired and sad—as though he still carried the burden of leaving behind the sick and the dead.

In those first days I came to know a group of five women—all who were related and shared a very close bond. The Woman Who Eats Grizzly Bear, her mother, Grey Claw, and her mother's sister, One Wing, were always there to help me with distributing the food.

But it was The Woman Who Eats Grizzly Bear's younger sister, Song Woman, who impressed me the most. She was the young woman with a shorn head and big brown eyes—the one who had lost her newborn on the journey.

Song Woman had recovered enough to ask me for bear grease, and it was her tenderness, in spite of her own loss, that struck me as I watched her apply it to those with frostbitten limbs. The fifth woman, Paw, helped her cousin Song Woman with this task, though she carried an infant boy on her back and had a young daughter, Little Hawk, always closely trailing her.

This child, Little Hawk, no more than six snows and with a baby doll that she clung to, soon charmed me. One day I saw how she watched Song Woman helping others, and when Song Woman sat to rest, the little girl approached her and offered the grieving mother her doll. Though Song Woman refused the offer, I was affected by the generous nature of this child, and the following day I brought fabric and beading so Little Hawk might sew another dress for her doll. The child's mouth opened in surprise when I gave her the beads and the red fabric, and we were soon joined by the other women for whom I had brought some beads as well. As they sat with me to divide them up, we did our best to communicate. I'd learned from Grandmother and her friend Sees Much that laughter was healing, so I grew brave and had them giggling when I attempted to speak their language.

❀   ❀   ❀

THERE WERE ABOUT one hundred and fifty survivors, and about fifty of them were braves. When some of their men were strong enough to hunt, their four remaining horses were not fit to ride, so Farwell loaned them two of his own. That morning Simon and I were talking with my husband as he finished his morning meal, when two of the men from Solomon's fort rushed through the gates of our fort, armed with pistols and rifles and shouting for Farwell.

He met them at the door. "What's the problem, boys?"

"We saw some braves ride out, and those thievin' Injuns got your horses," said the small skinny man with the tall black hat.

Farwell held his hand up to reassure them. "Nobody stole any horses. I loaned them a couple to hunt game."

The two stared at him. "You what?"

"Come on in, boys. Have some coffee," Farwell said.

I continued clearing the tables as the two took their seats across from my husband, while Simon went out to get coffee. The smell wafting from the two was so strong that I wondered how Farwell could keep eating.

The small man spoke again. "You know you's just settin' us all up for trouble. You think them thievin' Stonies will give them horses back?"

I had heard the Nakoda called the Assiniboine, but this was the first time I heard them called Stonies, and I wondered about this name.

"I do," Farwell said.

"Those damn Injuns think nothin' of takin' a horse. You know damn well they do it all the time and then brag about it. They need to learn, you steal a horse from a white man, you get lynched." For a small man he had a big voice.

Farwell was careful in his answer. "I appreciate you looking out for me like this, but nobody stole my horses. These people need to get back on their feet, and I'm only trying to help them out."

"They're horse thieves, the lot of 'em. And you know it, too."

Farwell's voice took on a hard edge. "They're only horse thieves if they've stolen your horses, and I *gave* them mine."

Simon had not yet brought in the coffee, but Farwell stood and waited for the other two to rise. "Well, boys, I thank you for looking out for me. Now I got to get back to work."

AT THE BEGINNING of the second week, Paw, with her baby boy attached to her back, and her daughter, Little Hawk, came to greet me as I approached the village. "Men get buffalo," Paw signed excitedly. "You eat with us."

"*Éeh*," I agreed, and Little Hawk took my hand as they led me over to where the women were doing the cooking. Their lodges were slowly becoming decorated with colorful quillwork, and the breeze caught the tassels covered with porcupine quills that were attached to the smoke flaps.

The whole community felt alive with hope that day, and the women all greeted me as they continued to dig a pit alongside the fire. When it was deep and wide enough, they lined it with a large piece of hide cut from the neck of the buffalo, and after pinning the hide in place with some rib bones, they filled it with water. Two of the women then took red-hot stones from the fire and slipped them in to heat the water, while others cut chunks of meat. As the water began to boil and the meat was put in, other hot stones were added to keep the water at a simmer. This continued until the meal was tender.

So this is why the white men call them Stonies, I thought. As the stew simmered, the women insisted I sit, and the chief's wife, The Woman Who Eats Grizzly Bear, presented me with some of the freshly roasted buffalo tongue, a treat usually given to the head men of the village. The slices of tongue were roasted perfectly, and later, when Song Woman handed me a tortoiseshell bowl filled with the stone-cooked stew, her wavering smile was as sweet and tender as the meat she served me. This way of cooking was new to me, but my eyes filled as I ate it. So much about these people and this meal felt like home.

ALMOST TWO MORE weeks passed, and though I was no longer needed in the same way, I still went every afternoon to spend time with the five

Nakoda women I had come to know. The Woman Who Eats Grizzly Bear and her younger sister, Song Woman, with her shorn head and large, wounded eyes, were almost always cooking. Their soft-spoken mother, Grey Claw, and their mother's quiet sister, One Wing, were usually sewing or beading. Paw, along with caring for her baby and Little Hawk, was there to help out whoever needed her most.

There were only a few days left before we would be leaving for Fort Benton, and I knew we would soon say goodbye. It surprised me how close I felt to these five women, and by the way they always welcomed me, it appeared they felt the same. This day I had another packet of beads for them and as we sat together, Little Hawk approached me with a shy smile. Her little girl hands fluttered around her head, and when she in turn touched my head and began to chatter, I understood that she was asking for permission to fashion my hair into the Nakoda style. Since meeting Jeannie, I had been wearing my hair as she had, with one long braid down my back, and with new clothes from our store, most days I dressed similar to the Métis women.

I nodded consent and closed my eyes as the young girl gently worked the comb through my hair, and I thought of how I missed my mother, whom I hadn't seen for almost ten months. Little Hawk carefully parted and braided my hair—the same way I had worn it since childhood. But now she took each long braid and, using sinew, secured each into a loop before draping them over the front of my shoulders. She stood back to smile at her finished work, and as one all the women murmured, "*Éeh, itchik.*" With their attempt at my language, my eyes welled up.

THE NAKODA SURVIVORS were an enterprising people, and it wasn't long before some were trading pelts at the Indian store. Though our trading season was coming to a close, there was still plenty of good stock left to choose from, so when I learned some men from Little Soldier's camp were trading for liquor, I confronted Farwell that night as we got ready for bed.

"Why you don't stop them?" I asked as I hung my dress on the nearest wall peg.

"They're free to trade for whatever they want."

"But they—"

"I know. I know the condition they were in, Mary, but that isn't our business."

"But—"

"Nothing we can do about it." Farwell got into bed and held up a corner of the blanket to invite me in. "There's already been problems with them over at Solomon's. They claim he cheated them by weighting his scales when they went to trade him some pelts."

But with alcohol in the camp I was worried about my women friends, and I said so as I lay down in bed next to my husband.

"If it will make you feel any better," he said, "I'll talk with Hammond tomorrow and see if he can try to steer them away from the whiskey."

"Thank you," I said, rising up on one elbow and kissing him. We had been married less than a year, but Farwell had made it easy for me to love him. He had been a good chief, and he was caring, not only for me, but for others as well. Yet though I felt safe in his arms, I couldn't sleep that night.

CHAPTER TWENTY-THREE

1873

W E HAD REACHED the last day of May, the moon when chokecherries are in bloom, and I was excited. That evening, just as the sun was setting, the Métis had arrived with their freight wagons, and the packing would begin in the morning. Within a day or so we would be heading to Fort Benton. The weather was co-operating, and if it held, it would be an easy trip back.

Both Farwell and I were in a celebratory mood that night, and we had just climbed into bed and were kissing when someone rapped on the door.

"Abe," Hammond called. "Got a man out here. Just came riding in. He's wanting to see you. He says there's some trouble with our Stonies taking his horses."

Farwell looked at me and sighed. "Stay right here. I'll be back."

After he left, I lay back and thought of our marriage. I liked that Farwell considered us a team. Earlier in the day, we were together in our bedroom, where he sat at the small table studying his balance sheets. I was perched on the bed, repairing a tear in his shirt, when he turned to me with a smile. "I knew this season was good, but it was even better than what I'd hoped for. One more year like this and we will have our ranch. You are my lucky charm," he said, his smile tender.

"Charm?" I asked.

"You bring me good luck. In the past it would have taken at least two years to get this number of pelts. One more season like this and we'll be finished up here. Then no more trading for whiskey," he said.

Remembering that promise, I now awaited Farwell's return under the covers. I smiled to myself when I thought over the past ten months of our marriage. I no longer was surprised at how often my husband wanted me, nor at how often I wanted him. We had come to care for each other in a way that I don't believe either of us had expected. We were in love.

I AWOKE WHEN Farwell returned much later that night, and I was surprised that he made no move toward me when he climbed into bed. The smell of the kerosene lingered, as it always did when the lamp was shut down, and happily I reminded myself that within a night or two we would be sleeping out in the fresh air and under the sacred stars. There I would wake again to the dark-face time—that sacred predawn time that I could not recognize when sleeping in a room shut off from all natural light.

As I lay there, I realized from Farwell's breathing that he, too, was not asleep.

I rolled toward him. "Farwell, you awake?"

"Yes, I am." He lifted his arm and pulled me close to him.

"*Diiawáchissik*," I said.

"I love you, too," he said, and kissed the top of my head.

I stroked his face. "Go to sleep."

"I would, but I can't stop thinking about this guy Hardwick who just came in from Fort Benton."

I rose onto my elbow and tried to make out Farwell's face in the dark room. For me, words told you what someone might want you to know, but their face more often held the deeper truth.

"I know who he is, but I haven't had anything to do with him until now. He's got a bad reputation—thinks he's above the law, and now that I've met him, I can tell he's looking for a fight."

"Is he a trader?"

"No, a wolfer. I know you already hate them—but this fella's different. Some of these men do wolfing for a season or two, to make money to fund a business. Solomon's done it, Hammond's done it—heck, Stiller still does it. But this Hardwick—he has a bad reputation. They say he kills for sport, and he especially hates Indians."

"Why?"

"Not certain, but a few years ago the Arapaho got ahold of him, and when he escaped, they got ahold of him a second time. You can be sure they were none too gentle before he somehow got away again."

"And now he's here. . . ."

Farwell grunted. "He seems hell-bent on confronting the Nakoda. He claims they stole his horses. He's with a group of wolfers, all of them out of Fort Benton, and they're camping not too far from here. He said they were out wolfing when they had twenty-some of their horses stolen. They had to hoof it back on foot to Fort Benton to get new horses to ride, and now they're out looking for the horse thieves. They're here because they think that it was the Nakoda that took them."

"Our Nakoda don't have horses."

"That's what I told him, but just to be on the safe side, I invited him to bring all his men in tomorrow morning for a meal. Hopefully some food in their bellies will put them in a good mood. Once they've eaten, I'll take them over and show them firsthand how few horses our Nakoda have, and how the ones they do have are crowbait."

"Let's go talk to the Nakoda now," I said, throwing the covers back, but Farwell stopped me as I began to climb out of bed.

"No, Mary, nothing will happen tonight. And I want you to stay out of this. These aren't fellas you want to mess with."

I WAS FLIPPING pancakes when Hardwick's gang rode in through the gates. To get a better look, I raised my hand to shield my eyes from the early morning sun. Their mounts were nothing to look at, but then I remembered that somewhere there were some happy Indians who had had a successful raid. Seeing these no-good wolfers, I realized that whichever Indians had taken the horses had made a big mistake. They should have taken their guns, too.

I had seen armed men before, but the firearms that these men had attached to their saddles and hips were nothing but the finest cartridge weapons and repeating rifles. There was not one slow, old-fashioned muzzle loader between them.

"Come on in." Farwell waved them into the cabin once they'd tied their horses to the rail.

As the twelve rough-looking Yellow Eyes filed past our lean-to kitchen, one of them, good-looking for a blond-haired, blue-eyed man, tipped his hat to me and the other two women. "Name's Evans," he said smiling, and I wondered how such a friendly man got mixed up with this bunch.

After they were seated, I went in with a platter of stacked pancakes that I set on the table.

As I went out for the coffee, Madame brought in bowls of fried potatoes and Rosalie followed with a heaping platter of buffalo steaks, but both women hurried out as soon as they set the food down. The men, smelling of sweat and dirt, held out their mugs as I poured the coffee.

As usual, when Farwell took a seat, he removed his hat, and the others followed his lead, though there was one who did not. Without being told, I rightly guessed him to be Hardwick, and when I approached the man to offer him coffee, one look into his icy eyes told me all I needed to know. He was younger than I expected him to be, at least ten years younger than Farwell's thirty-five snows, but I had seen men like this before, and age had little to do with it. Here was a warrior who had lost count of his kill.

A dark blue and white kerchief tied under his hat covered what was likely a legacy from the Arapahos. I knew a partial scalp when I saw one, and when I leaned over to fill his mug, Hardwick saw that I knew and he hated me for it.

"Boys," Farwell called, nodding toward me. "Until now I've been known as a bachelor. Well, I've changed that. I'd like you to meet Crow Mary, here. My wife."

There were a few glances and murmurs of acknowledgment, but no one stopped reaching for food.

"Didn't take you for a squaw man, Abe," one of the men answered.

"I got lucky," Farwell said. "My wife's been a big help to me up here, and it doesn't hurt that she can handle a gun better than any man I've ever seen."

A few of the men looked at me with mild curiosity, but soon their attention was back on their food. Farwell took his opportunity to speak. "I want you boys to know, these Indians camped here didn't take your horses. Just last night, George Hammond—I think some of you know him, he's run the store here all season—had one of his horses wander off, and don't you know, two of our Stonies brought it back this morning."

"And he ain't lying," Hammond said, coming through the door. He was greeted well enough by those who knew him. "Abe asked me to stop in and tell you about this. Have to say it was a big surprise to me, having horse thieves like that delivering my horse, but they were sure happy to get that whiskey in reward."

As Hammond sat and I poured him some coffee, I heard another voice from the doorway.

"Well, I'll be damned! We heard you fellas was here." My breath caught when Sam Stiller came into the room.

"Well, crap. If it ain't the devil hisself. Sam Stiller!"

Stiller held out a dented tin cup, sloshing liquid into the air. "I've been helpin' the boys over at Solomon's get packed up. He's finished his trading with the Injuns—they're getting skunked on his liquor right now—and Solomon sent me over to tell you he got hisself some liquor left. He's sellin' it mighty cheap and was wonderin' if any a you was interested?"

One of the men at the table answered for all the others. "Shoot. Don't suppose anybody here needs to get that invite twice!"

A hand pounded the table. "Son o' bitch. Let's go, men. Let's show these girls up here how to drink."

The departing men were all jovial as they thanked Farwell for the meal. "You coming for a drink, George?" one of the men asked Hammond.

"Don't know why not," he said.

While the others went for their horses, Hardwick stopped to talk to Farwell. It was the first time I had heard him speak, and now I was surprised at his voice that had an odd high pitch. "I'm guessing you're right. Earlier I was over looking round at that camp of them Stonies and I didn't see no horses, 'less they've got them hidden. Trouble is, you never know with those sneaky bastards."

"I can vouch for them," Farwell said. "They've all been here for a while now, and most were so weak and sick they couldn't ride, never mind steal horses."

"Well, guess we'll let it go then," Hardwick said. "Thanks for the grub."

"Good enough," Farwell said, and looked relieved. Then he went to join M'sieu Dubois, who had arrived from the Métis village with his men, oxen, and the freight wagons, and they were ready to begin packing up.

As I collected the dishes I noticed both Rosalie and Madame off to the side talking to Simon, and though I could not hear what they were whispering about, they did not look happy. Soon after, a driver and cart were arranged and the two women left quickly. Both claimed to be tired out from the busy season and wanted to rest at the nearby Métis village for a day or so before their husbands would come for them. But it wasn't hard to guess that their quick departure had something to do with Hardwick's gang being here.

CHAPTER TWENTY-FOUR

1873

FARWELL HAD GIVEN me a trunk for our clothing and personal belongings, and I went to pack up our room, but before I finished, I decided to make a quick visit to the women in the Nakoda camp one last time. If all went well we would be leaving early the following day, and I wanted a chance to say goodbye.

I hurried to the trade store before it was emptied, and there I took some blue ribbons for Little Hawk, some strings of dried apples, and plenty of beads for the others. All this I rolled into a red blanket and tied it tight before I went out into the busy yard.

There was a festive feeling in the air as the Métis men passed round a bottle of whiskey while they prepared the wagons for travel. Already they were cleaning out the trade store and loading leftover barrels of goods. I didn't see Farwell as I wound my way past the wagons and toward the open gates, but I did see M'sieu Dubois supervising his crew as I walked by.

Outside the confinement of the fort, I lifted my face to feel the golden fingers of Old Man Sun. It was the first day of June—the moon when the katydids sing—and how good the warmth felt. A robin flew out from a stand of wolf willow, and I wondered how many tiny blue eggs were in her nest. I could hardly wait to see Jeannie and her new baby, who might have been born by now.

It would have been a shorter route to the Nakoda camp if I had crossed the river to Solomon's fort and then passed through the coulee and up the small hill to their camp, but I didn't want to run into Stiller or any of Hardwick's men. Instead, I took the path that ran on our side of the water and followed it past my secluded bathing spot and then to a dense shelter of trees, where I could cross the river unseen. There I waded across the shallow water, and with my awkward bundle I clumsily scrambled up the steep embankment and through the shrubs and trees.

The riverbank was close by the Nakoda camp, and as I made my way toward it, I saw Little Hawk peeking out from Little Soldier's tipi. I waved to her, but she didn't return my smile. Instead, she made a run for me, grabbed my hand, and pulled me toward their lodge.

As I followed Little Hawk into the tipi, I was met with the smell of whiskey and urine. Little Soldier, the man who had worked so hard to restore health to his suffering village, was lying on the ground, facedown in a drunken stupor. It was then, after I began to hear raised voices coming from the surrounding village, that I remembered Hammond had given whiskey to the men who had returned his horse.

Little Soldier's wife, The Woman Who Eats Grizzly Bear, and her younger sister, Song Woman, were pleading with him, trying to pull him to his feet.

Paw, feeding her infant boy, sat next to the door, beside her two aunts. Embarrassed that I should see their chief in this condition, they dropped their heads when I glanced their way. I would have left immediately, but Little Hawk's trembling hand held me in place. I foolishly thought to comfort the child with the gifts I had brought, but as I opened the red blanket, the arguing outside escalated. I was handing her the ribbons just as a gun blasted nearby. Paw grabbed for her daughter and pulled her to the floor as the other women all threw themselves down to the ground as well. Instinctively, I reached for my revolver, but with a shock I realized that in my rush to get here I had left it behind. Scared for my life, I didn't say goodbye before I dashed out.

I sprinted back the same way I had come, but when I got to the river, I took the steep bank too fast and slipped, sliding down the slippery moss until my foot caught on a tree root. I lay there, my ankle throbbing, while back at the camp, the angry shouts were growing louder.

Through the din, I thought I heard my husband's voice, so I elbowed my way back up the riverbank to look out. Sure enough, there was Farwell, approaching an irate group of Nakoda braves.

He called out to them in English, "Hammond thinks you took his horse again. That's why he was up here trying to take two of yours. He thinks you're trying to get more whiskey."

The braves understood little of what Farwell was saying, but through shouts and wild hand talk they tried to tell him how they had just got rid of Hammond, who had been in their camp attempting to take two of their four horses.

Hammond, none too steady on his feet, was with a group of wolfers and men from Hardwick's gang who stood down alongside the coulee, their backs to Solomon's fort. They were within shouting distance, and from their safe position, the drunken men began to exchange insults with the Nakoda. One group was as drunk as the other, and Farwell stood in the middle, trying to keep the peace. I knew he understood little of the Nakoda language, and I was about to run out and try to help, when a shrill voice stopped me.

"Farwell, get out of the damned way or you'll get shot!" It was Hardwick's high-pitched shout. He was crouched in the coulee along with others who had joined him, and their rifles were pointed toward the Nakoda braves and in Farwell's direction.

My husband swung toward the ravine and raised his hand. "Wait! Don't shoot. You can see for yourself that they don't have Hammond's horse."

"Get out of the ga-damned way!" Hardwick yelled again.

"I said don't shoot!" Farwell shouted again before he turned back to the braves. "Get your families out of here," he warned, before he left at a run. "I'm going for Lebombarde. Just hold your fire!" he called out to Hardwick's gang as he sprinted past them and toward our fort. "He'll talk to the Stonies. He'll get this mess straightened out."

Little Soldier's leadership was desperately needed, but the door cover to his lodge remained closed. The braves began to shed their clothes in preparation for battle, while the women, who saw what was coming, frantically began to pull their children into their lodges or run with them into the woods.

I stared toward the coulee. Hardwick's hat and scarf-covered head was easy to recognize, but it wasn't just the wolfers who had climbed into the ravine with their guns. Hammond was there, too, and others from Solomon's fort. Would they actually start to shoot at this exposed camp? As though in answer, a rifle blasted from the coulee, followed by a volley of bullets.

Screams followed, and I watched in horror as Nakoda women, children, and men fell, but when a bullet whizzed by my own head, I threw myself down against the riverbank and covered my ears in an attempt to keep out the cries of the wounded and dying. What should I do? Dare I make a run for our fort? But there was shooting everywhere. And where was Farwell? Had they shot him? Surely he would be stopping this if he were still alive?

There was a thud not a hundred paces away, and at the sound of a strangulated voice, I cautiously peeked over the edge and saw a young man twitch in agony and then grow still.

Past his torn body, two old women ran hand in hand—they might have been Grandmother and Sees Much. "Run!" I shouted, and they almost made it to the river before they were both struck, still holding hands as they fell. I dropped my head and moaned.

I wanted to get back to our fort, but with bullets zinging by, I pushed tight against the riverbank and forced myself to wait. The warriors were doing their best to defend their village with their old muzzle loaders and bows, but they were no match against the repeating rifles of Hardwick's group. More than once I heard the whisper of moccasined feet as warriors crept by to shoot at the coulee from different vantage points. Whenever the gunfire stopped, I thought I would run, but that was when the Nakoda women and children raced from their lodges and out toward the trees, and then the bullets came faster and thicker than ever.

I waited as the sporadic shooting continued. I was terrified whenever I thought about Farwell and that he might be lying somewhere wounded or even dead. Again and again, I fought the urge to run, but I dared not stand and make myself known. I had worn my buckskin dress that day, and I was wearing my hair in the style of the Nakoda. If Hardwick's men were to catch a glimpse of me, they would see me as a target. Finally, when I could no longer stand to hear the moans and cries of the suffering wounded, I made the decision to move.

Slowly and carefully, I began to inch my way along the river and through the dense shrubs toward our fort, aware that any movement from the bushes could bring a rain of bullets.

I hadn't gone far, but I was getting close to my bathing spot, when some warriors, hidden by shrubs in front of me, began to shoot toward the coulee. When the return fire came, a branch next to my head was shattered. Terror-struck, I dove into a small hollow on the riverbank and curled into it. That is where I stayed, too frightened to move, while erratic firing continued for the rest of that long afternoon.

Finally, as sunset came, so did quiet. Cautiously I pushed back the branches and crawled up to look over the edge of the riverbank. I forced myself to look past the strewn bodies and toward Little Soldier's lodge. I felt a moment of relief when I saw that it was still standing, though it was leaning to the side. The top, though, was shredded with bullet holes. Surely my friends inside the lodge had stayed flat on their stomachs to avoid being shot.

But then my breath caught. From out of nowhere, three of the wolfers appeared and were approaching Little Soldier's lodge. My body went cold as I watched them lift the tipi door cover and, one by one, pull out the five women and the two children. When Little Soldier was tossed out, he stumbled and fell, but as he struggled to his feet the wolfer behind him kicked him back down. Little Soldier rose again, but that same man, the one with long black hair and a big black mustache, pulled a gun from his hip and fired into Little Soldier's chest.

For a terrible moment, I saw my grandmother's death again, and I struggled to keep my wail from joining those of the terrified women. Little Soldier's wife threw herself across her husband's body, and when the man turned his gun on her, One Wing began to scream while Song Woman and Paw tried to hide Little Hawk between them.

Desperate, I buried my face in my hands. My whole body shook as I waited for the gunshots, but when none came, I looked again.

Now the men had the five women corralled and were pushing them toward Solomon's fort. One of the men was so drunk that he stumbled and fell, pulling Song Woman down with him. She pulled free, and when she began to crawl away, the man tried to catch her by grabbing at her shorn head. One of the other wolfers, laughing at his drunken friend, caught Song Woman by her arm and yanked her to her feet before he pushed her forward.

Paw, with her young baby on her back and her little girl's hand gripped tight, was the only one of the women who looked alert enough to be seeking a way of escape. When she had a chance, she leaned down and spoke into Little Hawk's ear. Then she tried to turn her daughter toward the river, and I finally had my chance. I stood and waved my arm, my heart pounding. I dared not call out and I hoped that Paw saw me, but it was dusk and with my tan dress I wasn't easy to see.

"Send her to me," I whispered, willing the mother to read my mind. But either she hadn't seen me or the child was too scared to run, and the mother and her two children were shoved forward. I crept along the riverbank, following the group until the men pushed the other women though the gates of Solomon's fort.

Paw, with Little Hawk, was dragging behind, with only one drunken man to keep them moving. Suddenly the mother turned and jammed her foot against the man's knee. He went down but grabbed hold of her dress while she pushed Little Hawk away.

The baby on her back screamed while Paw shouted at her daughter to run. But the child stood still, too terrified to move, and watched as the drunken man dragged her mother into the fort.

Again, I scrambled up, but this time I called out to the little girl. She caught sight of me and raced across the grass. When she reached me, though, she began to cry and desperately call out for her mother. Afraid that her frantic calls would alert one of the wolfers, I grabbed hold of her small hand and quickly pulled her with me toward the river. Blinded by her tears, she kept stumbling, and after she almost fell down the riverbank, I scooped her up into my arms. She clung to me as I waded through waist-high water, and once safely across, I kept hold of her and set out at a run. The child was small but heavy enough that by the time I got to the gates of our fort, my arms were burning and I found it hard to catch my breath.

The yard was in chaos, with men anxiously calling to one another as they rushed about, loading up the wagons. M'sieu Dubois, overseeing them, caught sight of me.

"Farwell?" I shouted my question to the old man, while sheltering Little Hawk against my pounding chest.

He came toward me. "He out looking for you," he said.

"He's alive?" I gasped, trying not to weep in relief.

"*Oui,*" he reassured me. He reached for the child, but she clung to me.

"Her mother . . ." I pointed toward Solomon's fort, still catching my breath. "They have her."

M'sieu Dubois waved over a large burly man. "We already take some of her people to the Métis village. Louis, here, he take her. He live there. He know the best way over."

"But if he goes past Solomon's fort and they see her . . . ," I said.

"Louis know the way round that Solomon's place."

It was the first time I had met Louis, a big man with a face hidden by a dark beard, but he seemed to know his mission before it was assigned. M'sieu Dubois hurried us into the trade store, where he picked up a blanket before he opened the back door. When Louis reached for her, Little Hawk dug her head into my neck and began to scream again for her mother.

"Shh, shh." I tried to soothe her as he took her from me, but once in his arms she stopped crying, as though too frightened for tears. We quickly wrapped the shivering child in the blanket before Louis, with his silent bundle, sprinted out the back door.

I STOOD IN our cabin holding on to the edge of the bed to keep my legs from buckling. I was shivering and trying to gather my thoughts when I realized that first I needed to get dry. I had just changed out of my wet clothes when Farwell rushed through the door. "Mary! Damn! I've been looking all over for you. I was about to go over to Solomon's, but Pierre said you . . ."

I threw myself into his arms. "I thought they *killed* you."

He held me tight. "Where were you?"

"By the water. I couldn't . . . ," I said.

"By the *river*? Lord! You could've been shot," he said, and held me tighter still.

I clung to him, breathing in his familiar scent. "Why did they start shooting?" I asked.

"They were all drunk. Most of them still are. Hammond convinced them that the Stonies had stolen his horse again, thinking they would get another reward of whiskey. But the horse had wandered off, and Lebombarde found it out back behind our fort. All this killing was . . . God, it was all for nothing."

"They took some women to Solomon's. We have to go get them."

He pulled away from me to look into my face. "What women?"

"Nakoda women—my friends. Five of them."

His jaw clenched. "They took them into the fort? You sure?"

"Yes. They got Song Woman and One Wing and Paw—"

"Damn," he said. He held his head for a minute, then shook it. "There's nothing we can do. I can't go there. Those men are all drunk, and they're not about to give up any women."

"Then I'll go," I said, and moved toward where my gun belt was hanging on a peg.

Farwell grabbed hold of my arm so tight that it hurt. "No, you won't," he said, his tone hard. "You will not leave this cabin without me." He took hold of my shoulders and turned me to face him. "Mary, I'll lock you in this room before I'll let you go over there. The fact that you're my wife makes no difference to these men. They wouldn't think twice about killing you. Hell, they'd kill any one of us if we tried to get those women out."

"Then take some of the Métis with you."

"They'd kill us all, Mary. They're all drunk, and they're just looking for an excuse for more sport."

"But . . ."

"There is nothing more to be done for those women. Right now, I have to think about how to get everyone out of here as quickly as I can. We might have a day or two before the Nakoda come back with friends—there are camps all over the place around here—and when they come, they won't care whose side we're on. To them, right now, we're the enemy, and they'll kill every one of us. We're going to have to work through the night so we can get our wagons packed up and ready to leave early tomorrow. In the morning I'll see if I can get Hardwick's gang to stick around until we pull out. We're going to need them for protection."

"But . . . the women . . ."

"Mary, you have to forget about them. By now, they're probably . . ."

I sank down onto the bed. Farwell stroked the top of my head. "I'm sorry, Mary, but I have to go. There's too much out there that needs seeing to."

I nodded. I wanted him to stop touching my head. I wanted him to leave. All I could think of was Song Woman frantically trying to crawl away. I had to help her.

At the door Farwell turned back. "I'll need you to help Simon get some grub ready in the morning. We're going to have to feed Hardwick's gang again if they agree to stay."

"*Éeh*," I said.

CHAPTER TWENTY-FIVE

1873

DURING THE NIGHT I waited for the men to finish clearing out the trade store. What was happening to the captured women? Were they still alive? I tried not to think of that as I cleaned my revolver and another one of Farwell's, carefully loading a bullet into each of their six chambers. Twelve bullets would have to do, I thought. My belt was heavy with my skinning knife and a gun on each side, so I buckled it tight. Finally, when I was almost certain they had emptied the store, I peeked out of our cabin.

Torches and lamps lit the yard, and though I caught a glimpse of M'sieu Dubois, Farwell wasn't around. I stepped out and ran. The bolt was tight and heavy on the door to the Indian store, and as I fought to open it, I heard the labored breathing and the heavy drag of M'sieu Dubois's foot as he approached.

Quickly I slipped in, but not before the old man caught hold of the door and followed me inside. The lantern he carried lit his face in a way that made him look fierce, but my fear of him was gone. I put my finger to my lips. "Don't tell Farwell that you saw me," I said. "They got five Nakoda women at Solomon's fort, and I am going to get them."

"They kill you," he said.

I patted my two guns.

He shook his head. "Abe find out I let you go, he take my hide."

"Don't tell him."

"I come, too," he said.

"No." I didn't look at his lame leg, but I said the truth. "I'll have to move fast."

As I lifted the heavy bolt on the back door, he stepped in front of me, trying to block me. "Crow Mary. *Merde*! Those drunk men—"

"You bring Louis here," I said as I pushed past him. "He can take them to the Métis village." I got away before he could limp after me.

I WOULD HAVE been seen if I had taken the direct route across the water to Solomon's fort, so I ran farther up the river until I hit a stand of pine where I hoped I would have good cover. A sliver of moon gave me enough light to see where the water was shallow, but I was grateful for the dark shadows of the woods as I edged my way across the stream and up the far bank. From there I peered out.

When I saw how close I was to Solomon's fort, my legs went weak and I sank to my knees. I thought of the way the men inside had shot the two old Nakoda women in the back. I thought, too, of Hardwick, and how he would welcome a chance to take my life.

And then I remembered Stiller. Was he in there? Had he been in the ravine? I didn't think so, but now I couldn't remember. I reminded myself to breathe and took in gulps of the cold air. Everything in me told me to turn back, but I thought of Song Woman and Little Soldier's wife. I remembered, too, the kindness of their soft-spoken mother and her gentle sister. And Paw—would they have already killed her baby?

I was terrified when I rose to go, and I dropped down again when I began to retch. I had never been this afraid. After my stomach emptied, I forced myself back onto my feet to look out at Solomon's fort. The log wall stood against a blue-black sky, and it was then I realized it was dark-face time, the holiest time of night. The morning star would soon appear, and shortly after, the sun would rise. I prayed then, and as I pleaded with the First Maker for help, I remembered that I carried the heart of a mighty bear. Recalling how our warriors prepared for battle, I gave a low fierce growl as I called on the ferocious animal for his strength. I thought of Grandmother, and her friend Sees Much, at the battle of

Arrow Creek, and the courage of my people who had fought there for their lives against all odds.

"*Awe alaxáashih*! Hold firm," I told myself. I had heard this call during that battle over and over again, and as I felt my strength rise, I crept through the grass toward the fort. I stopped at the sound of a voice coming from up ahead, but I saw nothing. Then slowly, step by step, I moved forward until I was close enough to see more clearly. A lantern hung on a post, and in the dim light I could make out a woman, sitting slumped over outside the open gate of Solomon's fort. Her head was down on her knees while a man swayed over her with a bottle in his hand. "Here. Drink up," he said, and I recognized the dark-haired man with the big black mustache—the one who had killed Little Soldier.

She spit her reply onto his bare feet.

He grabbed her by the hair and forced the bottle into her mouth, then tipped it back. "Swallow," he said, "and stay put 'til I come back for you. You leave, I'll kill them other squaws." He straightened as best he could before he staggered back into the fort. The woman watched him leave, then leaned over to vomit. She didn't bother to wipe her mouth before she dropped her head back against the wall, and I recognized the older woman, Grey Claw, the kind mother of Little Soldier's wife.

At seventeen snows, I had already known terror and despair, but I had never known this kind of rage. I drew my revolver and the weight felt good.

When I reached the brutalized woman, she stared at me in disbelief. I quickly pulled her to her feet, and with hand talk I asked her where the other women were. After she pointed to two nearby sheds, I sent her in the direction of the riverbank. Then I slipped into the yard.

Already there was a hint of morning and enough light to see the door of the first small shed that Grey Claw had pointed out. I eased toward it and then carefully lifted the latch. Inside, stacks of pelts were piled high, but ahead, on the dirt floor, a large naked man heaved himself into a whimpering woman. It was Song Woman, and from the size of him I guessed that the man was Stiller. I didn't stop to think but darted forward and slammed the butt of my gun into the back of his head.

"Damn!" he said, twisting around, but another hard crack made him topple. He was out, bleeding from the head but still breathing, so I gagged him with his shirt while Song Woman rolled away. She was still shaking violently after she pulled on her dress, but she was able to help me use the rope from a bundle of pelts to tie his hands and feet and then secure them together. We quickly left the small building, and then I sent Song Woman out the gate while I went on to the next cabin.

That was a larger building. The door was already cracked open, and from inside I heard a man's voice. ". . . ain't got no fight left in 'em. We need ourselves some new . . ."

The words were slurred, but they were enough to rekindle my rage. This time I stepped into the room with both guns drawn. The heat coming off the wood-burning stove was stifling, and the stench of stale whiskey and rutting was thick in the air.

"What the hell . . . ?" Four partially clothed men were scattered about the room. With a quick glance I saw two of them were seated on floor pallets, and their weapons were not within reach. There was only one rifle that could be gotten, leaning against the wall next to Evans—the friendly man I had once thought good-looking. Now he was so drunk that he could scarcely lift his head from a buffalo rug. But the fourth man who staggered to his feet scared me the most. His black oiled mustache glinted in the firelight, and his chest, covered in black hair, made him look like a bear. The man who had shot Little Soldier wouldn't think twice about killing me.

"Vincent! Grab that gun," one of the men called over to him.

"No!" I said, and aimed for Vincent. "I'll shoot." Startled, he threw his arms up in an act of surrender, but he was so drunk that when his arms went up, he stumbled and fell back against the wall.

Little Soldier's wife began to rise as soon as she saw me, but One Wing, her older aunt, stayed on the floor.

"I want the women," I said. I kept my one gun on Vincent, who was struggling to stand, and then turned my other revolver on the man eyeing a rifle. "I'll shoot," I said. I hoped they were too drunk to realize that if I pulled the trigger, others would come running—and that would be the end of me and the women.

"Hell with 'em," Vincent slurred as he fell back again. "Let 'em go. We're done with 'em anyway."

"Quick." I motioned, trying to hurry the two women along, but One Wing was having a hard time getting to her feet. Little Soldier's wife took a blanket from the floor and covered her dazed aunt, then pulled her out the door.

"You come, I'll shoot," I warned the men again as I backed out, but it looked like none were going to give it a try.

Once out of the fort, I did my best to hurry the two along, but One Wing was finding it difficult to walk. It wasn't much easier for Little Soldier's wife, but between the two of us we managed to half drag One Wing to the river. There she gasped when her feet hit the cold water, and, confused, she pulled away. "Come," I said, grabbing her by her elbow, but she struck at me until her niece calmed her. Finally, we crossed the water where we found the others, terrified and huddled together. It was then I realized we were missing one. Through hand talk I asked about Paw and I choked back a sob when I learned she had escaped earlier with her baby. But there was no time to waste.

Our fort was an easy run, but none of these women were in shape to move fast. I moved them deeper into the pines before I handed Little Soldier's wife one of my guns. "I come back," I signed, and then I ran for Farwell's fort.

I wanted to cry in relief when I saw the silhouette of M'sieu Dubois's Louis waiting outside the door of the trading store. He was watching for me, and after I waved at him, I leaned over to catch my breath. By the time I straightened, the bearded man was loping toward me.

I led him to the women, hidden in the pines, where they were all crowded around One Wing. They had used a corner of the blanket as padding between her legs, but it was blood soaked. Louis saw immediately what needed to be done and did his best to be careful when he lifted the injured woman into his arms. Little Soldier's wife handed my gun back to me and then grasped my arm. "*Pilamaya*," she said, and I understood her words of gratitude.

"*Vite!*" Louis called to the women in a loud whisper before he set out at a quick pace. I stared after them as they left, helping one another stay on their feet. They were alive, but what they had endured left me with a sorrow so deep I felt drained. When they were safely away, I stepped out of the cover of the trees and was startled to see a sky of vivid pink and orange. The colors of the sunrise had never been more intense and glowing. It would be a beautiful day.

I suddenly longed for my mother. I needed to be in her arms. "Mama," I wanted to ask her, "how is it possible that such beauty can exist after the horror of what has happened?"

I WAS FURIOUS with Farwell that he had not come with me, and I was glad not to see him as I hurried through the gates and toward our cabin. The yard was filled with somber men frantically loading the wagons.

"Can you come help?" Simon called when he caught sight of me. I remembered then he was alone, cooking for all the men, and he needed me.

"*Éeh*," I answered, but first I went into my room. The warmth in the room felt good, and though I changed my wet leggings and moccasins, I didn't change my dress or remove my guns before I went out again.

Simon had been cooking most of the night, and his stew of elk meat with beans would be satisfying enough to hold the men through a long day. Because I had not been there earlier to help him, I expected him to be brusque with me. Instead, he gave me a look that I could only interpret as kind. "Our men ate already. Now Farwell go to get Hardwick's men."

I tried to brace myself. Farwell had said that he needed Hardwick and his men to protect us until the wagons were loaded, and then to escort us until we were safely on our way to Fort Benton, but I wondered if they would be game to help after what I had done. M'sieu Dubois made his way over to me and removed his hat to give me a nod. "Crow Mary. You are a woman like my wife, brave and strong. I take my hat off to you."

"*Ahoo*," I said to him, just as Farwell came through the gates leading

Hardwick and four of his men, all of them with their repeating rifles in their arms and guns on their hips.

"M'sieu Pierre," Farwell called out. "These men have agreed to stand guard while we get our wagons loaded, but first I've promised them a meal. I'm hoping to get packed up and out of here by noon."

He led the five men over to the kitchen lean-to, where I was waiting to serve the stew. Two of the men had looked into the barrel of my gun. One was Evans, who still looked drunk, and though I didn't have a name for the other one, I felt dizzy with relief to see that neither Vincent nor Stiller was among them.

"Mary, can you serve up some of that grub? These fellas agreed to watch out for us until we roll out." Farwell noted my solemn face and then my two guns. He gave a short laugh. "Watch out, boys. I see my wife is double loaded today."

Farwell's laugh made me furious. Both Evans and his companion looked around as though uninterested. Farwell, oblivious to their discomfort, continued. "You boys know of Jerry Potts?"

"Yah, we know a him," one of the others replied. "Ain't no better shot."

"I've got men over at Solomon's betting that my Mary, here, can beat Potts on a draw. What gets me is how darn accurate she is every time." I couldn't mistake his look of pride, but his timing sure was bad.

"Anything in particular she likes to shoot?" Hardwick asked Farwell.

"Mary?" Farwell turned to me.

"I shoot little things," I said, looking at Evans and his buddy, and from the way the two avoided my eyes I guessed they hadn't told Hardwick of my visit.

"Little things?" In spite of himself, Hardwick looked at me curiously.

"Little peckers," I said, grateful to Jeannie for her schooling.

Farwell shot me a stunned look.

Hardwick's grin was humorless. "Well, Abe, glad she's all yours. This one don't sound too tame to me."

CHAPTER TWENTY-SIX

1873

W E WERE AWAY by late morning, and as we headed out, I thought Hardwick's men, riding alongside our loaded wagons, looked plenty nervous for a gang that was used to killing. No one knew where the Nakoda had gone, and it was possible that they could show up with friends at any moment. Behind us, dark smoke plumed into the blue sky. Before they left, Solomon's men set flame to their fort and to what remained of the massacre site. I was glad to see it all burned to the ground after I caught the grisly sight of Little Soldier's decapitated head stuck on a lodgepole in the middle of what was left of the Nakoda camp.

Farwell and his men set flame to our fort as well, and as we pulled away, I asked Farwell why he was burning his fort up. "Traders do it every year when they leave so somebody can't get up here next year and claim a place to get an early start," he said, and again the Yellow Eyes reasoning made little sense to me.

Under the ground in Solomon's fort, Hardwick's men had buried the body of their friend who was shot and killed during the massacre. As they lamented his death, I thought of those two old women who were shot in the back as they were trying to run away. I had seen what they had done to Little Soldier's body, but what had happened to the others? By Farwell's count, at least fifteen to twenty Nakoda—men, women, and children—had been slaughtered, and he had no idea how many had been injured.

Hardwick's gang stayed with us until our wagons were well on the way, and while we continued to travel south toward Fort Benton, they turned east, still determined to find their stolen horses. Our travel was slow, but the early June weather was mild. Simon was along to do the cooking, and M'sieu Dubois managed the crew, but the mood was subdued and that was unusual for the typically jovial Métis men. I had been relieved to learn that Louis had got all the women to safety at the Métis village, but I wondered if they would ever get past what they had suffered.

At night, I had difficulty sleeping, even under my beloved stars. It was agony for me to think about what the women had endured, and every time I remembered Song Woman I thought of Sam Stiller and wondered when he might come looking for me.

Farwell, too, was moody and withdrawn. After a few days I began to wonder if someone had told him about my freeing the captive women. Was he angry with me about that? *Well*, I thought, *I'm angry, too.* How could he have left the Nakoda women to such a horrible fate? What kind of man was he really? I was no longer sure how I felt about my husband. In fact, I was thinking that maybe I would leave him once I got to Jeannie's village and then make my way back to my family.

We were about a week out of the Cypress Hills the afternoon Farwell asked if I would ride with him ahead of the wagons. I agreed, and because the plodding oxen were so slow, it wasn't long before Farwell and I were a good distance away.

"Why don't we walk for a while? I don't want to get too far ahead," Farwell said before dismounting, and in answer I slid down from Snow. As we led our horses alongside the rutted trail, we were as awkward with each other as we had been almost a year before when we had first met.

"Mary?"

I looked out over the greening sunlit prairie, waiting for him to speak.

"I know you are disappointed in me. And you have every right to be. Everything that happened was . . . look, when I saw what was coming, I went right to the Nakoda. I tried to warn them, Mary, and then I went to get Lebombarde to get his help. But we were too late."

"When those wolfers started shooting at the Nakoda, why didn't you shoot at Hardwick's men?" I asked.

"We would have been killed. There were too many of them. All of Hardwick's men, Solomon's men—even George Hammond was involved."

"So you do nothing when the Yellow Eyes kill Indians?"

He sighed deeply. "No, Mary. No. I've never seen something like this before. I've known a lot of these men and worked with them for years. I'd even considered a few, like Hammond, to be my friend. Sure, some are rough characters, but the ones I thought I knew—even drunk—I wouldn't have expected this of them." He shook his head in bewilderment. "All I can do is promise you that I'm finished with trading for whiskey and that I will do what I have to do to bring justice to the Nakoda."

"Justice?" I asked. "What do you mean?"

"I mean that these white men will be held accountable. They will have to answer for what they did."

I asked him what he planned to do.

"First, I have to get to Fort Benton to sell these pelts so I can pay everyone. Then I'm going to have to report this to the authorities—to the law, up in Fort Peck. I sure don't want to. I'll be turning in men I've worked with for years, but I don't see that I have a choice. And I'll have to be careful. If any of them find out what I'm planning to do, I'm good as dead."

"Me too, maybe," I said.

"They have no reason to harm you."

I wasn't sure if this was the time, but I decided he should know. "No. Me too. Maybe they want to kill me."

He stopped walking. "What are you saying?"

"I went to Solomon's and took the women."

"You *what*?"

"I went over and I got the women out."

Farwell's face drained of color. He opened his mouth to say something, but closed it again. He turned away and looked out across the vast prairie, then took off his worn leather hat and wiped his brow with his forearm. After setting his hat back on his head, he silently handed the reins of his horse over to me and walked away. He went out a long distance and stood there for a while. In the distance the oxcarts squealed as they gained ground.

On Farwell's return, he took me in his arms. "I don't know what I would have done if something had happened to you." His voice was tender. "Mary, you're young, but I never thought of you as foolish. Didn't you know that they could have killed you?"

I pulled away. "I had my guns."

He stared in disbelief. "Those men are dangerous, especially all tanked up like that. But it sure was damn brave of you to go over there," he said.

"Come with me now to go kill them. Let's finish them off! That is what the Crow do."

Farwell shook his head. He took his horse's reins back from me, and we continued walking. "I know what Indians would do. Hell, that's why we had to get out of there before the Nakoda came back. But no, we can't do that. White people don't kill like that."

Now I stopped to stare. "Hardwick and his men, they're not white?" I asked.

"Yah, but up here in Whoop-Up country, most of these men think there are no laws, and they thought that the Stonies had stolen their horses. You know that for the Indians, stealing horses is almost a sport, but the white men see it as a crime and they hang people for it. Look, this mess has to be dealt with through the courts. It'll take time, but I think you'll come to see that the white man's way of doing things is a lot less violent than the way your people live."

"But I'll take my guns and come with you. You won't go alone."

His look was pained. "Is that it? You think I'm afraid?"

I looked away at the blue cloudless sky. "Éeh," I said.

His hand cupped my chin, and he turned my face toward him. "Mary," he said, "I am not a coward. What happened there . . . I tried my best to stop it. I know I'm not without blame—and I have to do something to make it right. But I have to do it my way."

It was true—he had been in the line of fire when he tried to stop the shooting. He had been brave. He had not been drunk like the others. Now he pulled me into his arms again and held me so tight that I could feel his heart beating.

"Please, Mary, I need you to believe me and to trust me. I don't ever want to lose you," he said.

I knew his words to be sincere, and I decided to stay married to him.

WE CRESTED A hill as we grew closer to Jeannie's community. It wasn't a big hill, but it was high enough to give us a long view. Dark clouds overhead gave an occasional rumble, but across the vast grasslands, and through the grayness of the day, there, on the rim of a valley, I saw a lone figure. When I pointed it out to Farwell, he handed me his field glass. Excitedly I gave him a report of blue skirts whipping in the wind and a red shawl that Jeannie was waving.

I don't suppose Farwell was surprised when I suddenly gave Snow her head and left him behind. Choking back tears, I rode at a gallop, not realizing until now how much I needed to see my friend. Jeannie alone would understand the horror of what I had experienced.

Snow, tired of the slow travel, now flew, and as we grew close, I looked for Jeannie to be holding a bundle—sure that her baby had already been born. But then I saw her trim figure and realized that with a possible storm threatening, she must have left her newborn behind. I dismounted as she ran to me, and when we hugged, I held myself back from swinging her, as she had done to me the last time we had met. Jeannie felt too frail to handle.

"She wasn't big enough to live," my friend whispered. "She came too soon."

We sat then, alongside Snow as she nibbled the grass. "When?" I asked.

"About three weeks ago." The shadows under her large brown eyes told me of her suffering. "Oh, Mary, it was all my fault, wasn't it? I should never have gone on the trip."

I took a deep breath in, thinking through my words, not wanting them to fail her. "No, Jeannie." I spoke with certainty. "That's not true. It wasn't your fault. Sometimes babies aren't ready to stay."

"But I keep thinking of her being all alone."

"She isn't alone. There are many grandmothers to care for your little one at the Other Side Camp until you come for her."

"Do you think so? Many grandmothers?" she asked.

"Yes," I said, "the Other Side Camp is full of grandmothers, and they all love babies. When you are ready, we will talk to Old Woman Moon and ask for a baby that is ready to stay."

"We will?" she asked, her eyes trusting.

"Yes," I said. "We will, and you will have one."

"God be praised," she whispered.

Later that evening, the two of us walked out to where her baby was buried. The marker at the grave was a small wooden cross, and leaning against it was a little horse figure made of yellow fabric.

"Mama Rosa made that for her," Jeannie said. "Lucille made a doll for her, but I buried that with her. I couldn't put her in the ground all alone," she said. We sat together then, on the early spring grass, and I held my friend as she wept.

FARWELL RETURNED FROM Fort Benton a day earlier than planned. "Hammond and some of the others have been going around the saloons and bragging about the number of Indians they killed up in the Cypress Hills." He was irate, pacing back and forth in front of our lodge. "I have to get up to Fort Peck, where I can report the massacre before this gets even more muddied up."

"When do we go?" I asked, disappointed to learn that I'd be leaving Jeannie again so soon.

"Mary, Fort Peck is even farther away than the Cypress Hills. It's still in Montana territory, but it's all the way up the Missouri River. It'll be a hard ride, and I need to get there as soon as possible. It could be a month or so before I'm back. Would you be all right to stay here with Jeannie and her people if I went on my own? You'll have both René and M'sieu Pierre to look out for you."

"Who will go with you?" I asked, knowing that our braves almost always traveled with others.

"I'll go alone. Stiller's the only one I know for sure didn't do any of the shooting, and he's about the only friend I have left. But he's nowhere to be found. Any of the others . . . well, short of bragging, they're acting like nothing happened." He shook his head.

"So this is the 'justice' you talked about?"

"No. If they take me seriously up in Fort Peck, there'll be a trial and I'll have to testify in court against these men. But setting a trial up will take time, so when I get back from Fort Peck, first thing I'll have to do is find some work. We still need more money to get that ranch."

That was the first night since we had left the Cypress Hills that Farwell reached for me, but as he caressed me, I started to cry. Farwell pulled me close. "What is it, Mary?" he asked.

"I keep seeing those men with the Nakoda women . . . what they were doing . . . I can't stop seeing them like that."

"Shh, sweetheart," my husband whispered as he held me. "You need to put that out of your head. Those men were drunk, and they were acting like animals. Just try not to think about it anymore. You saved the women."

Farwell was patient, and made secure by his comforting, I again welcomed his tender kisses. I suspect our lovemaking that night was healing for both of us, though after Farwell slept, I lay awake wondering how an act so full of tenderness could also be so brutal.

At sunrise, I waved goodbye to Farwell's lonely figure. A month without him seemed a long time. I felt safe enough now, but what would happen to us after he reported the men? Wouldn't we be in serious danger?

PART THREE

CHAPTER TWENTY-SEVEN

1875

IN THE MOON when the berries begin to turn red, July 1875, more than two years after Farwell returned from Fort Peck, where he had reported the massacre, one day he came home from Fort Benton to our camp in the Métis village. It was late afternoon and he was accompanied by a man dressed in a striking red jacket and riding a large bay gelding.

"Mary!" Farwell called as he leapt from his horse, as excited as I had ever seen him. "I've been waiting over two years, but now it's going to happen. Major Irvine, here, came from Canada. He's arrested Hardwick and Evans and three others, and there's going to be a trial."

The man watched from his saddle as my husband swung me around and set me back on my feet. "Major," Farwell said, "come on down and meet my wife, Mary. She rides and shoots like a man, and she's as brave as they come, but she's all woman."

He glanced toward the fire, where a haunch of deer roasted alongside plenty of onions and potatoes, just as my husband liked it. "And you're about to see that she's the best cook around," he added.

The man dismounted, his polished black boots and the gold buttons of his jacket catching the sunlight. He nodded as he came forward. "I'm pleased to meet you, Mrs. Farwell," he said.

Major Acheson Gosford Irvine of the North West Mounted Police was a tall, thin man with a full, square-shaped dark red beard and a soft low voice. He reminded me of a Crow brave in that his face did not give away his feelings.

While the men were settling in, Jeannie and René showed up. Jeannie was carrying a precious bundle, her baby girl, Marie, who was already a year old, and I asked them to join us for the meal. After Farwell introduced everyone, we all sat to eat at the rough log table my husband had built to fit under an arbor of willow branches. Farwell eagerly filled us in on the news. "Major Irvine, here, came down from Canada with just one other fella to help him. Can you imagine? The two of them thought they were going to arrest the whole bunch of Hardwick's Benton gang all on their own." Farwell gave a quick laugh.

"Well, the truth is, we thought we were just dealing with some hoodlums," said Major Irvine. "At least we knew not to come dressed in these uniforms, and until we arrested the men, we kept our identity and purpose to ourselves. We had good luck early on when we were introduced to a guide, Alexis Lebombarde, who said he knew the Sioux and could guarantee safe travel for me and my orderly. Along the way, one night he told us about the massacre and how he had been there and seen everything. I kept my mouth shut—he had no idea who he was talking to, but now I have him as a witness. And he was well worth his three dollars a day—you can see that I still have my hair." He gave a slight smile and ran his long fingers through his thinning but close-cropped red-brown hair. "It wasn't until I got here and started to ask around that I found out that Hardwick, Evans, and most of the other boys were not of a type to submit meekly. That's when I decided it might be best if I found some help, other than my man Woods, but it didn't take long to find out there was nobody in Fort Benton in a hurry to offer assistance in rounding these men up."

"What did you do?" René asked.

"Well, as luck would have it, I was able to recruit some visiting men from the US cavalry. With their help, we got hold of Hardwick and Evans and three others who were getting liquored up in the saloons. Right now, those military men and their prisoners are on their way to Helena for an extradition hearing."

René, Jeannie, and I exchanged looks.

"It's a court proceeding where they'll prove that these men committed a crime in Canada and should be put on trial up there," Farwell added. "I just hope my testimony will be enough to make that happen."

"Well, I have Alexis Lebombarde to testify, too," Irvine said. "Between the two of you, we should have a good case."

Farwell shook his head. "I'm still surprised that Lebombarde agreed to testify."

"Can't say it was his idea," Irvine said.

"But there were more than five men shooting that day. Do they have Vincent?" I asked.

"No, he scattered along with the rest of the others," Farwell said. "Hardwick and Evans pretty much headed up the whole thing anyway, so at least we've got them."

EVEN THOUGH THE mining town of Helena was one hundred and eighty miles away from Fort Benton and had just been made the capital of the Montana territory, it was a lot like Fort Benton. The town had attracted people who were rough and rowdy. Saloons and brothels lined the streets, and harsh piano music jangled out their doors. I had hoped we would camp outside Helena, but Major Irvine insisted that we stay in rooms he had arranged for us near his own quarters. Soon I would understand why.

In our room that evening, Farwell read aloud to me from the newspapers that he had picked up in the town. "Listen to this, Mary. They actually have an article written by one of the prisoners—they don't say which one—but here's what he's claiming. *'Abe Farwell, under pretense of going for his interpreter, left us to fight for our lives. Now we are charged with the crime of murder and will be handed over to the Canadian government, who will gladly convict us upon the purchased evidence of this cowardly informant.'*" Farwell threw the paper to the floor. "So that's what they're calling me? A cowardly informant." Angry as he was, he shook open another newspaper. "This one says that Hardwick and all the other men are bound to be found innocent because they were likely fighting for their lives against brutal savages." Farwell tossed that paper to the floor as well.

"Savages?" I asked. "They were the ones who shot the women and children in the back. They were the ones who killed Little Soldier and then cut . . . cut his head off and stuck it on a tipi pole."

After spending time with Jeannie's people, I had finally stopped having terrible dreams about the massacre, but that night, they began again.

In the courtroom, the crowd was squeezed in tight. The smell of liquor and sweat was almost more than I could take. "Squaw-man," I heard someone say to Farwell as we made our way down the aisle to the front row. "Traitor!" someone else shouted, spitting on the floor. Farwell leaned toward me. "Why don't I take you back? This could turn sour. Irvine can post one of the guards and you can wait for me in the room. You'll be safe there."

I wanted to reach for his hand, but I knew that if anyone saw us touching, it would go worse for him. "No," I said. "I'm staying." I needed to see for myself how justice would come for Little Soldier's people. That was what Farwell had promised.

After we settled on the wooden bench, I looked up to see the prisoners sitting together at the front and within easy view of us. Hardwick, his hat pulled tight over his scarf-covered head, glared at Farwell, while the tall blond man, Evans, kept his eyes on me. Beside Evans sat a man who later took the stand and called himself Harper, and he, too, stared at me. Both Evans and Harper had been with the women that night, and from the way they were regarding me, I figured they remembered me with my guns. My stomach turned over when I thought again of what they had done to the women and I willed myself to meet their eyes until they both looked away. I didn't recognize the other two prisoners.

The judge, Chief Justice D. S. Wade of Helena, pounded a hammer on his table and the crowd grew quiet. Colonel Wilbur F. Sanders was presenting the Canadian case for extradition, and he spoke with great vigor. He gestured to the prisoners and called them "Belly river wolfers, outlaws, smugglers, cutthroats, horse thieves, and squaw-men."

After his speech, Farwell's name was called. As he walked to the stand, jeers erupted from the crowd. As I looked around, I saw more than one revolver, and I worried that someone might take a shot at him. The judge finally silenced the courtroom and my husband recounted what had happened—how both the wolfers and the Nakoda were drunk, how George Hammond had accused the Nakoda of stealing his horse, and how he, Farwell, had tried to keep the peace. But when he said that the accused prisoners had jumped into the coulee and were the first to start shooting at the defenseless Nakoda, it became impossible to hear him speak above the roar of protests coming from the onlookers.

FARWELL SLEPT LITTLE that night, and in the coming days, as the hearing dragged on, he was called back onto the stand a number of times. The problem was that neither Lebombarde nor Farwell was able to say he had seen any of the accused shoot and kill any specific Nakoda woman or man. Farwell did volunteer that he saw a man named Vincent kill Little Soldier, but Vincent was not one of the accused in the courtroom.

When Hardwick finally swaggered to the stand, the packed room erupted into cheers. Given the name the Green River Renegade, and known as a notorious outlaw, here in this tough town he was seen as a hero. When, in that high-pitched voice of his, he told a story claiming Farwell was a coward who had left them to fight for their lives while the drunken Nakoda attacked them, men waved their fists in the air, shouting "Coward!" and "Traitor!" at Farwell. Evans told a similar story, and Harper, so meek in his replies to the court that he was reminded to speak up three times, repeated the lies.

The last two prisoners did not testify, as they claimed they had not taken part in the shooting.

I wished I had shot them all when I had the chance.

IN THE FINAL days, character witnesses who claimed to know my husband personally or through business dealings were brought to the stand. Farwell trembled in rage as these men, most of whom he said he had never met, declared him a liar and a whiskey trader.

Finally, after seventeen long days, we were called to the court to hear what Justice Wade had ruled. He gave a long speech that I struggled to follow, but when the overcrowded courtroom erupted in jubilant shouts, I realized that all five men were free to go. Farwell's face went white, and a cold chill went through me. What would happen now? There was no question that our lives were in danger.

I watched as Hardwick and Evans were lifted onto the shoulders of their cronies and carried about as though they were heroes. Major Irvine made his way over and accompanied us through the frenzied spectators jeering at Farwell, some of whom were threatening to hang him.

Amidst the turmoil, the three of us made our way to our hotel room. There I perched on the edge of our bed next to Farwell while the major pulled over a chair and sat across from us. He was quiet a long time before he leaned across and patted my husband's slumped shoulder. "Abe, this is not over. We may not be able to get Hardwick and these four men, but I've had some good news from Canada. The police picked up three more of the men who were involved in the massacre up in the Cypress Hills, and they're being held in jail for trial."

Farwell didn't bother to look at him and instead sat with his head in his hands. I had never seen my husband this done in.

"Did you hear me, Abe?" Irvine said again. "Up in Canada they have Hughs, Vogel, and Carr in custody," Irvine said. "Those were some of the men you reported. You said they were there. You saw them shooting, right?"

"Yeah, for what good that does," Farwell muttered.

"There'll be a trial in Winnipeg, and there those fellas will be convicted for sure."

Farwell slowly shook his head. "Look. If the courts didn't find Hardwick guilty enough to extradite, they won't find anyone else guilty."

"Abe, I know this is a lot to ask, but I need you to consider coming to Canada for the trial. The North West Mounted Police just built Fort Macleod up in the North-West Territories—about two hundred miles west of the Cypress Hills. I'll be heading back there first thing in the morning with the four mounted police who came down for the hearing. Come with us and we can guarantee your safety," he said. "From there we'll have to go to Winnipeg for the trial. That's about a month's travel from Fort Macleod, but it's the closest court where they can try a case this serious. I'll need you again as a key witness."

Farwell leapt to his feet. "Damn it all! And what about my wife?" he shouted. "Am I just supposed to leave her here? I won't do that. I can't leave her behind, especially now. It won't be safe for her here, either."

Irvine took a while before he turned to me. "Mrs. Farwell. I've been thinking about this. After today, I'm wondering if I might be able to use you as a witness as well. Were you there? Did you see the massacre?"

"*Éeh*," I said. "Yes."

He thought this through aloud. "It'll be hard to convince . . . You're not only a woman, but you're . . . you're an Indian woman. But, Mrs. Farwell, would you be willing to testify in Canada if I needed you to?"

"No!" Farwell objected. "She's not going to go through what I just did."

"She won't. We'll have a better case, and the courts will have some order there," Irvine said. "And the Canadians will be on your side. They're plenty sick of the lawless scoundrels in Whoop-Up country."

But I was angry, too, and I could speak for myself. I looked at my husband, who had believed so strongly in the Yellow Eyes' court system. If he had just listened to me . . . and now our lives were in danger. We had little choice but to see this through.

"I'll come," I said firmly.

When Irvine looked to my husband for his approval, I clamped my mouth shut, afraid of what I might say to them both.

"Let me think about it," Farwell said.

After Irvine left, Farwell took his chair opposite me. He rubbed at his face, then sighed when he looked at me. "I don't know what went wrong in that courtroom."

I had no patience left. "It was like you were a Crow walking into a camp of the Sioux. They were your enemy from the start."

"But that isn't the way our court system works."

"Looks to me like this one did."

Farwell stood and began to pace between the window and the bed. "I guess that's true, but now what? We're sure not safe down here. Maybe he's right—maybe we should go up with Irvine to Fort Macleod and hope the courts up there will see the truth. What do you think?"

"We'll go with him," I said, and he looked relieved at my answer. We sat quietly for a while, I suppose each of us thinking of what was to come. "Will I see Jeannie again before we go?" I asked.

"I'm afraid not. I think Irvine wants to head out by tomorrow morning, and it's probably smart to leave this town with his protection," he said, glancing out the window. Ever since the trial had ended, the noise outside had only grown louder. Bonfires had been lit and gunfire punctuated the raucous celebrations that were taking place up and down the streets.

"It'll be a while before you see Jeannie again. Do you want me to help you write a letter to her—explain what's going on?" he asked.

"I'll write to her when we get up to the new place," I said. "Then she'll know where to write back to me." I wanted to confide in Jeannie, and I didn't want Farwell looking over my shoulder. Over these past weeks I had come to suspect I might be pregnant, but I wanted to be certain before I told my husband. I was happy with the news, but I wasn't sure how Farwell would feel about it, especially now, given these new circumstances.

CHAPTER TWENTY-EIGHT

1875–1876

AUGUST, THE MOON of the wild plums, is a hot month for travel. Undeterred, we trekked on to Fort Macleod through the unrelenting prairie heat. I was grateful for the cotton dresses that Jeannie and I had sewn, but it was Farwell's rawhide hat that I could not have done without. Whenever we rested, clouds of mosquitoes swarmed, and I wondered how Major Irvine and his four men didn't faint from heat in their bright red jackets.

This trip was nothing like the one that Farwell and I had taken three years before to the Cypress Hills. This time we hurried. The prairie had long stretches of seemingly endless grasslands, but it also held rolling hills and coulees—some, vast ravines with rugged drops—and they could be difficult to maneuver. However, my packhorse carrying my tipi, and my faithful Snow, were as reliable as ever. Major Irvine stopped asking Farwell if his wife had any special requirements as he soon realized that I might have taught his men a thing or two about traveling on horseback across this country.

One afternoon Irvine surprised me when he came to ride alongside me and I stopped singing the Crow lullaby to my secret passenger.

"Mrs. Farwell. I'd like to ask you some questions, if you are agreeable?"

I glanced at my husband, who had joined us, then nodded back at Irvine.

He was blunt in his approach. "Can you tell me what you saw at the massacre?" he asked.

And so I began. The major simply stared when I got to the part about going over to Solomon's fort to rescue the women.

"You mean to tell me that you went over there by yourself?" he asked.

"I had two guns," I said.

It seemed he couldn't take his eyes from me. "You went alone!? And those . . . those men, just like that, they let you take the women from them?"

"I had guns," I said, wondering if he had missed that the first time. He didn't seem to know what to say when he turned to Farwell.

"She went against my orders," my husband said, and when I looked at him, I saw his face was flushed.

Irvine turned back to me, frowning. "You went against your husband's orders?"

I shrugged. "My husband gives orders to white men. I am Crow."

FINALLY, ONE HOT day, after carefully winding our way down a particularly steep ravine, our horses scrambled up the other side, and there in front of us was Fort Macleod.

Farwell gave a sharp whistle of admiration. "When the North West Mounted Police build a fort, they mean business."

"It should hold up. It's a good two hundred feet square, and those palisades around it are twelve feet high," Major Irvine said with satisfaction.

The impressive fort, built on a curve of Old Man River, was surrounded by water on three sides. Beyond it, across the flat sunburned land, stood a range of rugged snowcapped mountains. Outside the fort, a small town fingered out, while up and down the river there were Indian encampments. People and animals were coming and going as we rode through the massive open gates.

Major Irvine waved toward the buildings at the far end. "Down there we have a hospital and some stores, but you'll be staying in one of those log buildings across from the Mounties' quarters."

"No," I said, "I will camp out by the river."

"But you'll be safer in here," Irvine said. "We don't have the whole gang from the massacre rounded up, and we don't know if they're out looking for you."

"I will camp out by the river," I said again.

Irvine and Farwell exchanged a look. Farwell knew to stay quiet, but Irvine tried again. "But that's where the Blackfoot have set up their villages. Aren't the Blackfoot enemy of the Crow?"

"Yes," I said. But I'd had enough of forts.

WE SET UP our lodge in a pretty spot, next to a stand of cottonwoods where I could hear the river sing. Our Blackfoot neighbors were curious and occasionally came to have a look, but they did us no harm.

I waited another moon before I told Farwell of the coming baby. That morning I had wakened to feel a butterfly in my stomach, and it confirmed that I was carrying a life. I couldn't keep the smile from my face, and when Farwell leaned over for a morning kiss, he asked me why I was so happy.

I took his hand and placed it on my stomach. "I'm going to have a baby," I said.

"Are you sure?" His face turned serious.

"*Éeh*," I said.

His eyes grew soft as he cupped my face and gave me a gentle kiss. "Well, that's good," he said. "I hope it will be a girl, just like you." Later he worried. "But how will you travel? We can't have you on horseback for a month all the way out to Winnipeg. And I'm not going to leave you alone here, either."

"We'll know what to do when the time comes," I said, sure that if Old Woman Moon had given us this blessing, she would see to the travel arrangements.

THE MOUNTIES PROVIDED us with food, but when I told Farwell that I craved fresh liver, he went hunting and brought home a deer. It was good eating, and it was that carcass that started my small business, where I fleshed and tanned green hides and then made moccasins and jackets that the Mounties lined up to buy.

Farwell soon found work with them as well, delivering mail to other outposts across the prairie, and he was often away for days at a time.

But I was kept busy. When I wasn't tanning and sewing, I was working on a cradleboard. Had I been with my people, my relatives would have made one as a gift, but I was alone and it was essential that I have one for my baby.

To get started, I needed Farwell's help. "Will this do?" he asked when he proudly presented the sanded piece of flat board exactly as I had requested. "It's forty inches long and twelve inches wide, and see how I rounded it at the top and tapered it down at the bottom just like you asked?"

I smiled as I rubbed the smooth surface. "It is good," I said, and began that day to cover it with the soft buckskin that I had prepared. In the following weeks I worked on the board as often as I could, creating a pocket of buckskin where my baby would rest and be secured by three pairs of wide straps. Those straps were all to be beaded, as was the flat surface above the baby's head.

I worked on the board at every opportunity, but as my waistline filled out, I realized I would need more time to complete it, so I stopped sewing moccasins and shirts for the disappointed Mounties.

Winter came early that far north, and Farwell was often out on the prairie trail, delivering the mail on horseback through ice and snow. Yet he always returned, and though he had grown more pensive, with little to say, he was always happy to see me. Just as I predicted, Farwell need not have worried about our travel, for once again we had a long wait for the Canadian government to set a date for the trial.

As I grew in size and anticipation, I stitched clothing for my baby from fabric I bought at the Mounties' store, and with every spare moment I continued my work on the cradleboard. I had never felt healthier, and most days I was satisfied to be by myself while I stitched on the cradleboard's background of light blue beads. As childbirth grew closer and I began to bead in the last of some dark blue and white designs, my eyes often grew moist with memories of my family.

It had been more than three years since I had last seen my parents, and I wondered how tall my brother must have grown. I longed to see Red Fox as well, but it was my mother I missed the most.

I missed Jeannie, too, and wished she could be with me as I had been with her when little Marie was born. Though I had planned to, I hadn't written to Jeannie on our arrival at Fort Macleod. After I told Farwell about our expected baby, he offered again to write to her, and this time I agreed. Her reply had been happy enough, but it was stilted and formal, as she knew Farwell would be reading it, too. So that is why, one evening, I decided to write to her myself. Between her study cards and her list of words that Farwell had added to, I managed to print out a whole page.

To Jeannie. Soon when the snow melts my baby will come. I don't show this to Farwell. If there is mistakes that is why. I use the study cards. I made some big dresss to cover my big bely that Farwell rubs. He likes it. But he is not the same like before we went to Helina. He is sad. I told Farwell that him and me could stil take those kilers out with our guns. But he got mad. Write to me. I miss you. Crow Mary

DURING MY PREGNANCY, Farwell was tender and attentive to me, but from the beginning he argued that the doctor from the fort should assist me with the birth. I said no. I would not have a white man sitting in my lodge while I was delivering a baby.

"Then who will help you?" he asked.

"The Blackfoot women," I said.

"The Blackfoot women? You think they will come help you?" he asked, surprised.

"Yes," I said, though I had not yet gotten up the courage to ask them.

It was true that at first the Blackfoot women hadn't been friendly when I first met them down along the water where I washed our clothes, but as my belly grew, they began to give me an occasional nod. Then, by February, the moon when the owls lay their eggs, I was running out of time, so I took some blankets to the midwife's lodge.

She scowled at the sight of me, but when she saw my heavy stomach and then my gift of blankets, we worked it out through hand talk that she and her sister would come to help me with the birth. I was relieved, but how I longed for my mother.

On March 15 of 1876, in the moon when ice goes out of the river, our baby was ready to come. As I waited for Farwell to return with the women, I circled the lodge. Each time my stomach grew hard, I wondered if it was time to kneel on the pile of buffalo robes that I had set in front of two stakes.

I had assisted Jeannie with the birth of Marie, and I had also been there to help Mother with her delivery of my little brother, so I had a good idea of what to expect. However, when the pains started to come closer together, I became more anxious. As the tightness came and the searing pain traveled across my belly and down my legs, I fought to breathe. By the time the two Blackfoot women arrived, I was fighting tears. The women sent Farwell away, and while one walked with me, the other prepared a drink that smelled of bear root. I drank it eagerly, and only once, with the final push, did I moan aloud for my mother.

Kindness doesn't require words, and both of the women were that as they received my baby girl into the world. I studied her in awe, smoothing her brown-black hair and smiling into her dark eyes. She gave lusty cries as the women warmed water in their mouth and used it to clean her before they wrapped her in soft buckskin and then packed cattail down around her tiny bottom. Her little arms quivered when they handed her over to me. I had never seen anything more beautiful, and I reached for the hands of the two women who had helped me. Never again would I see the Blackfoot as an enemy.

WHEN THE WOMEN finally allowed Farwell into the lodge, he knelt beside me. He stared at our gift that we had received from Old Woman Moon—the little one that I held in my arms. "Are you both all right?" he whispered. I handed her over so he might see for himself, and one of his tears dropped onto the baby. Farwell quickly wiped it from her soft pink cheek before touching each of her tiny ears, the tip of her perfect nose, and her thick hair. "She's beautiful, Mary." He looked her over and then said decisively, "We'll name her Susan Elizabeth. That was my mother's name and I think she already looks like her. We'll call her Susie."

I thought it nice that he wanted to honor his mother, but to do that so soon was unexpected. "We don't name a baby like that," I said. "We wait a few days, and then a father might name the child. Often, though, we invite a well-known brave to give our child a name."

He smiled down at our tiny bundle. "Well, I am the father, and I've just named my daughter. You'll see that Susie is a perfect name for her."

I stayed silent, but decided to myself that if the name didn't suit her, I would change it when I saw my people again.

I CHERISHED EACH day as I watched my healthy daughter grow. At almost two moons she smiled easily, and I was singing to her about this month of May, the moon when the chokecherries are in bloom, when my husband showed up at our lodge with Major Irvine. Over the winter Farwell had developed a deep respect for the major, whose determination to set things right made my husband optimistic about the upcoming trial. After Major Irvine was offered a seat of honor in one of our willow backrests, he looked uneasily at the baby in my arms. "Mrs. Farwell," he began, "I'm sure your husband has told you that the date's been set, and we'll be leaving for Winnipeg in a few days." He paused, then continued. "I don't know anything about . . . ah, about babies, but I was wondering if I could make a suggestion."

I nodded. He was looking at Susie as though she might take a leap at him.

"You know that we'll be traveling from Fort Macleod all the way to Winnipeg, and it will take us about a month to get there?"

I nodded again. Farwell had already told me this a number of times.

"And we'll be on horseback all the way."

I gave another quick nod. How else would we get there? I wondered. There were only three ways to cross this land: on foot, in a wagon, or on horseback.

"We've decided to take the fastest and easiest route down closer to the border, but that means we'll be in Sioux territory."

Susie's gurgle startled the man. I was tired of nodding and wished he'd get to the point.

"The Sioux are not a friendly people," he said, and I wondered at his understatement. The Sioux were notorious enemies of the Crow, and they were even less fond of the Yellow Eyes. And from what we had heard, they weren't getting any friendlier with the white settlers pushing them from their lands.

"If we must flee the Sioux, there will be times that we may have to ride hard."

I wondered if I should offer to give riding lessons to his men. Some, I had noticed, held themselves too stiff and upright.

He looked down at his hands, then up again, at a loss for words.

I suddenly guessed the reason for his visit. "You want me to leave Susie behind?"

He sighed in relief. "I thought you might object."

I gave him a hard look.

He shifted position in the lean back. "I thought we might arrange for a Blackfoot woman to care for her?"

"No," I answered.

He looked to Farwell for help, but my husband wisely said nothing.

Not knowing women well, the major gave it another try. "But wouldn't it be easier for you to travel without her?"

It was time to put an end to his foolishness. "It would be easier for me not to come," I said.

At least he knew when to quit, and he stood to leave. "I understand," he said, and turned back to Farwell. "Let's hope Lebombarde knows a safe route."

"I'm glad the Mounties found him," Farwell said.

"A man of his reputation isn't that hard to find, but he wasn't so keen to join us. In the end, we didn't give him much choice. We need him as a witness," Irvine said.

"Well, we'll be damn lucky to have him along on the trip. Lebombarde knows that land along the border well, and he's a friend of the Sioux."

"That could be helpful," the major said.

"Helpful"? That wasn't the word I would have used. The major had clearly never been up against a Sioux war party.

Susie started to fuss. It was time for me to nurse her. The major gave her a swift glance and quickly headed for the door. I did not understand these Yellow Eyes. The man looked to be more frightened of this baby than he was of the Sioux.

CHAPTER TWENTY-NINE

1876

I COULD NEVER HAVE imagined a place like Winnipeg. Long before we arrived at what they called the city center, there was building after building connected by boardwalks that lined roads all in a tangle crossing one another, with buggies and coaches and carriages flying by. Amidst it all, oxen lumbered through, pulling loaded carts, and how they found their way I would never know. I kept close to Farwell so Susie and I would not get lost. Every time I thought I had seen the biggest and tallest building, I found out there was another larger one ahead, until we finally reached our hotel. The wooden building looked like three buildings with one piled on top of another, and I wondered how it would hold up if a good wind came. Yet it was a relief to have finally arrived after the monthlong journey on horseback.

Susie, now three moons, had traveled well. She had inconvenienced no one, but my arms and shoulders were often tired as I didn't like to leave her too long in her cradleboard. A good deal of the time I wrapped her in soft buckskin with a strip of stiff buffalo hide to support her head, and then rode with her in a sling or in my arms. Farwell, from the beginning, was a proud father and he carried her, too, though at first the other men were only brave enough to take sidelong peeks at her. The first one to hold her was Major Irvine, and that happened by accident.

Day after day we traveled, unloading and loading the horses every time we made camp. We had been only a week out on the trail, and I could hardly stomach more of the oatmeal flapjacks and canned pork and beans that were staples of these Mounties. No one was happier than I when we came upon a small herd of buffalo and Irvine urged Farwell and Lebombarde to get fresh meat. The two seasoned men rode out together, and within sight of us they soon took down a young cow.

I could almost taste the fresh liver when Farwell waved for my help with the butchering, and in my enthusiasm for fresh meat I forgot Irvine's fear of the baby as I thrust Susie into his arms before I took off at a run.

"Mrs. Farwell," he called after me. "What do I do with it?" I didn't stop to answer, but kept running, afraid that the men might cut into the intestines and contaminate the meat. But Irvine, until now one of the most sensible of men, shouted only louder—and in doing so frightened Susie, who began to wail. "Mrs. Farwell! Just tell me what to do with it. I don't know what to do with it?"

I stopped short, took in a deep breath, and then let it out as I turned back. How foolish he looked, holding a crying baby out as though his arms had been set afire. "Stop yelling and just hold on to her. And don't drop her!" I shouted, then turned again to run.

She was asleep in his arms when I returned, but something changed for the major that day. In the following weeks of hard travel, there were times, usually after an evening meal, when he'd stroll over and ask if I needed him to hold her for a while. Once placed in his arms, she'd coo while he'd shift from foot to foot to rock her, humming and gazing down at her with a tender smile.

NOW, ON OUR arrival in Winnipeg, Irvine and his men left us and rode off to Fort Gary, while we were taken to a hotel that was close enough so we could walk to the courthouse. What a relief it was to get away from the constant company of men and to a place where our little family was finally alone. I was happy to see there was good light in the room from a big window facing south, and after I put Susie in the middle of the large bed, I went to touch the two long panels of dark blue fabric that hung down on either side of the window. "This feels like the box you gave me before we married," I said, stroking it, and Farwell came over to look. "That's velvet," he said. He kissed me on my cheek. "It's good to finally get here, isn't it?"

I glanced back at Susie, who was gazing about at the stillness. Over the last month, while in my arms on horseback or riding in her cradle-board, she was used to rocking, and now she must have been wondering what had happened

"Look, Mary." Farwell pointed out the window. "From here you can see two bakeries, a grocery store, a watchmaker's shop, and a dry goods store."

I was relieved not to see any saloons like those we had passed on the way in, and I told him so.

"Oh, there are plenty of those," he said, "they're just not in this area."

Our room was almost as big as a cabin, but it held only a small table with two chairs and a bed. Off to the side there was a stand with a big blue and white porcelain basin and a large pitcher of water, while under the bed was a chamber pot, the use of which I had become familiar with at Farwell's fort.

"Will the major's men bring us food like they did in Helena?" I asked.

"No, there's a dining room in this building We'll go there to eat."

"I would like to eat here," I said, not wanting to face all those Yellow Eyes for every meal.

"That's fine," he agreed. "I'll go get the meals and bring them to this room if you like. Now, though, I have to go out to the livery and make sure our horses are taken care of." He kissed me, and after he left, I went to the large pitcher and basin. First I bathed Susie, and then I took my own clothes off for a good wash.

WE HAD A day of rest before the trial, and Farwell insisted that Susie and I walk out with him to see some of the city. As we walked down the boardwalks, our moods were light. Susie was growing plump from my breast milk, and at twenty snows, I felt as healthy as I ever had.

Both Farwell and Irvine were sure this trial would have the outcome they were hoping for and daily, my husband talked to me about the relief he would feel when this trial was finally over. I'd been bothered by one thing, though, and now I brought it up: I didn't recognize any of the names of the accused.

"Jim Hughes came up with the Benton gang—he was the one with that long black beard," my husband said. "Remember, you asked me how he could get it to grow that long?" I remembered the man then, eating at the table with black hair growing so far off his face that it fell to his stomach. I had always wanted to give it a good pull. But I didn't remember seeing him the day of the massacre.

"And Philander Vogel and George Bell were living over at Solomon's over the winter. Bell was the one you didn't like because he kept missing the spittoons all the time."

"Oh, him?" I shuddered. "All that . . . ugh. It made me feel sick. Rosalie said she always had to clean up after him when he left the trade store."

"And you must remember Vogel? He's the one who froze his feet—got so drunk that he slept outside in a snowbank?"

I did remember him. I thought of the times I had seen him hobbling around outside the fort when I had felt sorry for him. But I hadn't seen any of these men shooting at the Nakoda, nor had they been with the women.

"Will there be others that I'd know?" I asked. "Will that man Vincent be there? The one who killed Little Soldier?"

"No, he got away with a bunch of others, but at least they've got these three, and they're bound to be found guilty. I saw all three of 'em shooting."

"But what will I say when they ask me what I saw?" I asked.

"*If* you are called up, the main thing is that you just say that you were there and what you saw happen. All you have to do is tell the truth," Farwell assured me.

THE NOISE AND chaos in Winnipeg was disturbing to me.

When the Crow joined up in the summers, we had hundreds of people gathered together, and there was always noise—celebrations or sorrow when the warriors came back from a hunt or a raid, children racing about, adults enjoying games and competitions, and always dances and much singing. But here was the sound of people who had not come together for a celebration. Their faces held little joy, and I heard only occasional laughter.

That first day I stayed close to Farwell as he led me along the crowded wooden walkway to stop in a small store, where we sat to eat something called ice cream. The cold treat was smooth and creamy, and when I ate it quickly Farwell laughed at my enjoyment of this sweet. Though my stomach gurgled for the rest of the day, I would have eaten more if it had been offered. After we finished, we were heading back to our hotel room, when Farwell pulled me into another store. This one was filled with silver pieces.

"I want a ring for my wife," Farwell told the man behind the counter. My husband took Susie from my arms and had me reach over and let the man fit a silver ring on my finger. "And we'll take that bracelet as well," he said, pointing to one that sat under glass and looked similar to the one I had given my mother. The bracelet was heavy, and when I lifted my arm to admire it, Farwell reached for my hand and kissed it.

"I was a lucky man the day I met my Mary," he said to the man behind the table. The man looked me over, and though he smiled as he took Farwell's money, he looked none too comfortable.

FARWELL WAS IN good spirits again the next morning when we met Irvine at the courthouse.

If I had been astounded at the size of our hotel, I was even more so at the size of the courthouse. It was a wooden building, but it looked to be at least four big houses all joined together, and it might have been a fort if it hadn't had so many windows and doors.

"This place houses the jail and government offices, too," Irvine said, but he suddenly looked doubtful when he noticed little Susie. "Do you think she will disrupt the proceedings?" he asked as he led us to the main courtroom.

I looked to Farwell to see if he had heard the question, but my husband was focused on the courtroom, and when I saw the pallor of his face, I, too, looked about and forgot about Irvine.

This courtroom was three times the size of the one in Helena, and it was already packed. I heard loud whispers as Farwell and I were led to some benches toward the front. Once seated, I looked up and saw a group of the strangest-looking white men I had ever seen. I gripped Farwell's arm.

"Who are those men in the black dresses?" I whispered.

"They're lawyers and judges," Farwell whispered back.

"Why is their hair white?" I asked.

"Wigs," he said. "Here in Canada, it's called the Queen's court. They dress the same as they do in England because Canada is under British rule."

That explanation meant little to me, but I didn't bother him with questions after that. He kept glancing over toward where the three prisoners sat, and he had begun again to pick at the cuticles of his thumbnails, a habit that I thought he had quit a while ago.

I jumped when one of the white-haired men suddenly pounded a wooden hammer on a high table to announce that it was June 19, 1876, and that the Canadian Court of the Queen's Bench charged James Hughes, Philander Vogel, and George M. Bell with the murder of Little Soldier and the Assiniboine Natives.

They were charged with "wanton and atrocious slaughter of peaceable and inoffensive people, unsuspicious of attack, and without warning, from concealment (having) shot down forty Indians in cold blood."

Farwell and I exchanged a look. Neither of us had heard before that number of Nakoda had been shot. I had seen for myself the slaughter, so the number didn't surprise me, but how many others had been wounded that day? I thought again of Little Soldier's wife and the women who had been with her. Didn't they matter?

There was a lot of talk after that, with the judge explaining to those present that the sober-looking men in the box were jurors and together they would decide the outcome of the trial. That, I thought, was finally a good idea, as it was similar to the way the Crow called on the wisdom of the elders. Of course, if the Crow had taken charge, none of the guilty men would be alive, so this problem would have been dealt with a long time ago.

I recognized all three prisoners. They sat with downcast eyes, but all wore clean shirts and jackets. Hughes's black beard was now trimmed close to his face. Vogel sat with his feet on a stool, as though he was still suffering from the frozen feet he had fully recovered from. And finally there was Bell, for once not spitting tobacco. He might even have passed for good-looking in that green shirt if it wasn't for his sour look and his brown teeth.

Farwell had also taken extra care washing and shaving himself that morning. He wore a new dark jacket over a vest and a clean white shirt, and though he usually wore moccasins that I made, this day he wore the brown leather boots of the Yellow Eyes. His new black pants fit him well, and he smelled of pine-scented shaving soap.

I had dressed as I usually did, in a similar fashion to Jeannie, with a red calico shirt and a long dark blue skirt over my beaded leggings and moccasins. My blue and red shawl was one Jeannie had embroidered for me, and I had Farwell weave a red ribbon through my long black braid. He had whistled at me that morning when I turned to face him. "You'll be the prettiest one in the courtroom," he said, and my face turned warm.

FARWELL WAS THE first to take the stand. He kept fingering his jacket after he sat, but once he began to answer questions from a Mr. Cornish, the lawyer for the Crown, he grew more settled. "I am thirty-eight years of age," he began. "I carried on business as a trader over the winter of 1873 in the Cypress Hills. . . . "

As he spoke, I began to think about being up on that stand myself. What would I say and what would it be like to have all those white men staring at me the way they were staring at Farwell? My neck grew damp at the thought, but when Susie started to fuss, my attention turned to her. My shirt gave easy access, and after pulling my shawl over to cover her nursing, I settled my baby on my breast.

On the stand, Farwell told again how the massacre had started—how

Hardwick and his men showed up and accused the Nakoda of stealing their horses.

"Were you concerned for the Benton men when they came looking for their stolen horses?" Mr. Cornish asked.

"I didn't have sympathy for them in the loss of their horses, as, with the exception of Hughes," my husband said, nodding toward the prisoner, "their own profession was stealing horses." The tittering and whispering from the crowd quieted when Farwell was asked to identify the prisoners.

He looked again at the men. "Hughes came with the Benton crowd, and I knew both Vogel and Bell, who were wolfers living at Solomon's fort."

Responding to more questions, Farwell told again how both the wolfers and the Nakoda were drunk that day, and how he had tried to keep the peace when Hammond, his own man, got the Benton boys riled up again after he accused the Nakoda of stealing his horse. "I knew trouble was coming, so I went over and tried to straighten it out with the Nakoda—to tell them what was going on. The Indians were worked up, too, but while I was telling them to be careful, the Benton men climbed into the ravine with their weapons and Hardwick called to me, 'Come out or you'll get killed. We're going to open fire on the camp!'

"I left the Nakoda and ran back to the boys in the coulee and told them to wait, that I was going to get Lebombarde to interpret so we could all talk this over with the Nakoda. But when I left to go get him, Hammond fired into the camp. That . . . ," he said, wiping his brow with his hanky, "that started it all."

"Did you see any of the accused doing the shooting?" Mr. Cornish asked.

My husband nodded. "They all joined in. When the firing was going on, Hughes was in the coulee shooting in the direction of the camp. Vogel and Bell were near the coulee but were shooting from farther back."

"All damn lies!" Vogel called out, leaping up, but then remembered his feet were supposed to be injured and sat. The courtroom came alive with talk and everyone jumped when that hammer came down again, but it quieted the room.

Mr. Cornish's question left me feeling worried. I hadn't seen any of these men doing the shooting. In fact, I didn't remember seeing any of them that day at all. If I had to go up there, I hoped I wouldn't be asked that question.

For the rest of that morning Farwell talked about the massacre, until finally the court took a break. I was exhausted from the tension of watching Farwell testify, and I hoped we were finished for the day. We went back to the hotel, where we had something to eat and I attended to Susie.

"Do you want to stay here for the afternoon?" Farwell asked. "It can't be easy trying to keep Susie quiet all day like this."

"She's a good baby," I said, "and I want to come." And I did. I wanted to watch and learn how to act in case it would be my turn to answer the questions.

When we returned, Farwell was called back to the stand, but this time another man, a lawyer for the defense, was questioning him. This man, Mr. Biggs, wore a dress and a white curled wig as well, but he was not friendly, as Mr. Cornish had been. Still, Farwell answered the questions as before.

Neither of us ate much of the stringy steaks and potatoes that night, but after we finished and as I was settling Susie, Farwell left us for a while. "I've got to walk off some of this tension," he said, and I understood what he meant. He was acting nervous as a prairie dog.

"I'll be cross-examined again tomorrow," he explained. "That's when the defense will try to trip me up."

THE FOLLOWING MORNING, again on the stand, my husband was confident in his answers, though at times he grew angry with Mr. Biggs. Farwell's voice rose when he told of how a man named John McFarlane had shot and killed two old women, and how another of the Benton men, Vincent, had killed Little Soldier, but Mr. Biggs was quick to point out that neither of those men was in the courtroom. "Well, the fighting went on all day," Farwell continued. "Toward evening, I went back to Hardwick and asked him again to stop the fighting, but he said, 'No, we've started in and we'll clean them all out if we can.'"

When my husband finally was allowed to step down, Alexis Lebombarde was called to the stand. When asked his address, he said with confidence and pride, "I live anywhere on the prairie." He went on to tell how he had been hired by Farwell as his interpreter over the winter of 1873, and how he had been there when the massacre had happened. His story of what had taken place was vague, though, and he claimed not to have seen much of the action, or who had done the shooting. When asked about the prisoners, he pointed to Hughes. "I do not know him," he said, "and I did not notice Vogel and Bell participating in the fight." Angry shouts of disbelief filled the courtroom, and the hammer came down once again. After there was quiet, Lebombarde was cross-examined but he had little else to say.

Surely he had lied! That left my husband standing alone with his accusations. I trusted Farwell and what he had seen, but I was worried. I hadn't seen these men shooting, either.

Yet hadn't Farwell told me to tell the truth? I would have to ask him about this again before I took the stand.

Lebombarde's testimony had shaken Farwell. He sat rigid, and just as I reached over to touch his hand and remind him to stop picking at his nails, I heard, "The prosecution calls Mary Farwell." With a sharp intake of breath, I straightened in surprise. I wasn't ready, and when I hesitated, Farwell nudged me and then reached for Susie. "Go on," he encouraged.

There were murmurs from the audience when I stood and walked forward. If I had known this was the day I was to testify I would have worn my best elk's-tooth dress, though Farwell had argued against it. "You should wear your Métis clothes," he had said. "I'm afraid that if they see you dressed like an Indian, they'll think that you're siding with the Nakoda."

I didn't agree, but this day I had worn the green calico shirt—one that opened easily for nursing—and a dark blue skirt—a combination he had always liked. After I stepped up onto the stand, I looked out and noticed Susie was fussing. Farwell had put her on his shoulder and was patting her back to soothe her. *Good*, I thought. *He's distracted and he won't see how scared I am.*

The room was filled with Yellow Eyes, most of them whispering and staring at me. My mouth was so dry, I wondered if I would be able to speak. I was afraid, but then I remembered the two old Nakoda women running for their lives, and I thought of Little Soldier's wife and One Wing and Song Woman. I folded my hands in my lap to keep them from trembling while I asked the First Maker to give me the strength to speak.

Mr. Cornish gave me a kind smile when he asked me to tell the court who I was and what I saw the day of the massacre.

"I am the wife of Abel Farwell. I lived at Fort Farwell in the Cypress Hills in 1873 . . . ," I began. It didn't take me long to tell how the Benton men arrived, how Hammond claimed that his horse was stolen by the Nakoda, and how Farwell went to try to help out before the shooting started. But I had no sooner finished than the dreaded question came. Had I seen any of the accused—Vogel, Bell, or Hughes—shooting at the Nakoda? I looked at Farwell, who had his eyes on Susie. Then I looked over at the three accused. All three glowered at me. Nothing would have been easier than for me to lie. I cared little for any of these people or their opinion of me. I wanted to ensure this "justice" that Farwell and Irvine had promised, but I was Crow and I wouldn't lie to do it.

"No, I did not see them that day," I said. When I was asked if any of these men had killed Little Soldier, again I told the truth. "No," I said. The judge hammered his table, and the room went silent again.

When Mr. Biggs came to talk to me, he asked if any Indians had shot at Farwell. "No Indian tried to shoot Farwell," I said. "But I saw some of the wolfers kill Little Soldier and then take his wife and four other women back with them to Solomon's fort. One with her baby got away but the men kept the others and they . . . they used them all night. I saw it when I got the women out."

"Were any of these men involved?" Mr. Biggs asked, nodding over to the accused.

I hesitated. I knew my answer wouldn't be helpful, but again I stayed with the truth. "No," I replied.

Following that, I was asked to step down.

The room was silent when I walked back to my seat. After I sat, I took Susie from Farwell's arms and saw there was blood on her blanket from my husband's thumbs where he'd picked them raw.

BELL TOOK THE stand, and next Vogel limped forward, but neither of them spoke for very long. Both claimed to have been inside the fort during the massacre, though each was certain that the Nakoda had started the battle. In fact, Vogel said, they had been warned the day before that Little Soldier's camp planned to kill all the fur traders before they left so they could steal their pelts.

Hughes did not speak in his defense.

During a break, Major Irvine came over to where Farwell and I sat outside the building. "I just learned that the defense is bringing in James McKay, a member of the provincial government who has assisted in negotiating treaties. He's well thought of in these parts. McKay is a Métis and speaks quite a few of the Indian languages. I'm hoping that might work in our favor, though the word is that Little Soldier once stood up to him and apparently McKay didn't like it."

We didn't have to wait long to find out what James McKay would have to say. As soon as the court resumed, he was called up. All eyes were on the man as he came forward, strutting like someone who thought he was important. I had seen big men, but I never seen anyone this heavyset before. He was dressed as a Métis, with a wide red sash circling his big stomach. Somehow he wedged his way onto the stand.

"I am well acquainted with the Assiniboine Indians," McKay began, using yet another name for the Nakoda. "And I knew Little Soldier well," he continued. "From what I know of the Assiniboine Indians, I have no hesitation in saying that they would rob, pillage, and murder if they had the opportunity. This is the general character of the Assiniboine, most particularly of the camp of Little Soldier."

"Dear God!" Farwell murmured under his breath, and a chill went through me.

McKay sat with a self-satisfied look after his words brought a stunned silence, but even he flinched when Chief Justice Wood, seated at the highest table, furiously slammed his hammer down, demanded that McKay's words be struck from the record, and ordered the jury to disregard them. But the damage had been done.

Soon after, the court was adjourned.

Farwell did not get up as everyone else left the courtroom. Major Irvine's face looked pale against his red beard. "There are twelve men in that jury," he said to Farwell. "They're bound to see the truth here." But my husband, who always had something to say, said nothing.

CHAPTER THIRTY

1876

THE FOLLOWING MORNING, Chief Justice Wood instructed the jury for a long time before he finished with this: "The important question is if any of the prisoners are implicated in the killing of Little Soldier. It is not necessary to prove that any one of them actually killed the chief; it is enough to prove that they acted in a criminal combination with the individuals most directly responsible for the killings. We have the evidence of Farwell against that of Bell and Vogel, with the negative evidence of Lebombarde and Mrs. Farwell."

I felt Farwell stiffen beside me. Last evening and throughout the morning, Farwell spoke little. I knew the strain he was under, so I said nothing in return. Yet I felt secure in what I had said on the stand. I had told the truth.

The jury returned just as we were leaving the courtroom. As everyone hurried back to their seats, Farwell nervously wiped his brow with his hanky.

Tension filled the room as again the judge settled the crowd. Finally, one of the men from the jury stood and read from a note in his hand. "We find it unsafe to convict for want of sufficient evidence of actual participation by the parties under trial. Our verdict is *not guilty.*"

The silence in the courtroom was almost worse than the celebratory shouts and hurrahs from the crowd in Helena. Stunned, I looked at Farwell, but he avoided my eyes. At first, I was frightened. Would any of the accused come looking for us? But then I became angry. I told

Farwell from the beginning that we should take care of this ourselves, but he believed in the Yellow Eyes court system, and he was wrong a second time.

Irvine looked as stricken as Farwell when he accompanied us back to our room. The two men sat across from each other at the small table, while I fed Susie and changed her clout.

"Look, Abe," Irvine said, "I know this is a blow. But in spite of the verdict, this trial had great meaning. It's been shown that the law affords Indians the same protection that we give to any other people—at least here in Canada."

"But what good does it do them if they don't get justice?" Farwell asked.

"I don't have a good answer for that," Irvine said. "I hope, though, that this will bring us closer to providing that in the future." He paused and looked down at his hands before he spoke again. "I won't be going back with you to Fort Macleod, but you'll have the same Mounted Police escort and Lebombarde along to ensure your safety. We've had word that the Sioux and Cheyenne are gathering south of our border, and they're expecting big trouble down there. I think it best that you take another route and stay farther north to avoid any problems."

Farwell sat silent. Over the four years of our marriage, I had seen Farwell discouraged, but he had never looked so beaten down.

Irvine leaned over and took hold of Farwell's shoulder. "Abe, at the least, this mess brought the Mounted Police out to the West. It was largely because of this massacre that we built Fort Macleod, and now we're building Fort Walsh in the Cypress Hills. Both places will have Mounties to police the North-West Territories and rid ourselves of the whiskey traders."

Hearing that, I felt relief. I thought of the Indian camps that had left the Cypress Hills, hungover and downcast, with nothing to show for all their hard work. Now, at least, no more whiskey would be used for trade.

Irvine rose to shake Farwell's hand. "I have to go now. Our men will come around for you tomorrow morning. If I can ever help you out in the future, I will do my best to do so."

Irvine then came over and stood in front of me where I sat on the edge of the bed with Susie in my arms. "You, Mrs. Farwell, are a fine example of a woman. I have never known better." In a surprise gesture, he gently reached down and pulled back the covers from Susie's face. She squirmed and puckered her tiny mouth before she settled back to sleep. Irvine smiled. "One day, please tell little Susie how she won my heart."

IT HAD GROWN dark, but I couldn't sleep. Farwell had gone soon after Irvine had left, and he was still away long into the evening. I had no idea where he was, so I sat on a chair and waited. I was angry—angry about the trial, angry that I had believed Farwell and Irvine in their assurances, and now angry that Farwell had left me alone with Susie in this room. But I was also worried. Was it possible that one of the accused men from the courtroom had murdered him? As the night continued to close in, I began to think that he might not return. What if he had just left me? What would I do? How would I ever find my way home from here?

When I finally heard his footsteps, I ran to the door and flung it open. My relief was short-lived when my husband stumbled into the room, reeking of vomit and whiskey. "Sorry, Mary, I wuz jus . . ." He didn't finish. His pants were streaked with mud, but he couldn't speak well enough to explain what had happened. I got him out of his clothes and washed him up, and he was snoring before I finished the job.

IN THE FOLLOWING days, Farwell refused to tell me what happened that night, and he also refused to talk about the trial. His dark mood only grew worse as we traveled back toward Fort Macleod, and he almost always rode ahead, by himself. He did not encourage conversation with the Mounties, and it didn't help that he and Lebombarde avoided each other. My husband was short with me, something that I was unaccustomed to, and I guessed that he blamed me for the trial ending the way it did.

As we rode, I tucked away my own anger and turned my attention toward my daughter. I did my best to ignore Farwell's sullen mood, and instead I took in the ever-changing countryside. It was July again, the moon when the berries begin to turn red. Most of the days were hot and dry and sunny, but I didn't mind the heat and the flies as I was happy to be traveling back toward what I knew. I was uncertain what Farwell planned for our future, but he was so glum that I was afraid to ask.

Day after day I observed my morose husband until finally, while traveling across a stretch of particularly flat and dry prairie, I pulled up next to Farwell so our horses could walk side by side.

He glanced over. "Want me to hold her for a while?" he asked, nodding toward a sleeping Susie.

"No," I said, and we rode on in silence.

His horse, irritable in the heat, nipped at mine, and Farwell jerked roughly on the reins. I had not often seen my husband act unfairly toward others, and never toward animals.

"Why are you so mad?" I said finally.

I was surprised at how quickly he swung toward me. "Why didn't you tell the court that you saw those three men shooting?"

"Because I didn't see any of them that day. You told me to tell the truth."

"But Lebombarde. He saw it all. I know he did. He was there with me. And he lied."

"But I didn't lie." My voice broke. After the stress of the trial, my own anger, and the hurt of his coldness toward me, I could not hold back my tears. I wiped angrily at my eyes.

His voice softened. "Ah, Mary. Don't cry. I'm sorry." He reached for Snow's reins and pulled me alongside him. "I know you did your best. It's the whole damn thing that makes me so mad. To think that I had you travel so far—and with our baby. I thought it would all be worth it. I thought that finally there would be some justice."

"Why don't you and me go find Hardwick and Vincent?" I asked. "We can shoot them and take what's left of Hardwick's scalp."

He gave me a disgusted look. "Stop talking like an Indian."

"I am an Indian," I shot back.

"Well, you're living in a white man's world, and in our world, we don't act like savages."

I shot him a look. *Savages?* Had he really used that word? I had hated that word ever since Jeannie explained it to me. Snow responded to the pressure of my knees, and she moved ahead quickly.

"Mary, I'm sorry . . . ," Farwell said when he caught up to me.

I kept my face high and forward so he could get a good look at my Indian profile.

"Mary," he tried again. But he had wounded me deeply. I began to sing aloud a Crow song—one we sang to our braves as they rode out to battle. Farwell rode alongside as I sang the song over and over, until he finally interrupted. "Mary, please talk to me. Forgive me. Please."

I stopped singing and spoke, but I refused to look at him. "Savages?" I asked. "After seeing what the wolfers did to Little Soldier and the rest of his camp, you call *my* people savages?"

He sighed deeply. "You're right. I'm sorry. Forgive me. But I'm in a bad way here, and I don't know what to do. It wasn't your testimony that was bad—it was mine. They said that I contradicted myself. I don't know how I did it twice, but I let everybody down—first in Helena, and now in Winnipeg." We rode again in silence, and it was a long while before my husband spoke again. "You know, Mary, maybe there was a kind of justice. I wasn't innocent. I made a lot of money trading for liquor. Now I've got no job and no idea how I'm going to support you and Susie."

"We don't need much," I said, looking down at Susie asleep in my arms. "Just a buffalo now and then. You're a good hunter."

CHAPTER THIRTY-ONE

1877

BECAUSE OF THREATS on Farwell's life, both the Mounties and Farwell were concerned for our safety, so we stayed up in Canada, camped alongside Fort Macleod, for the rest of that year and into the next. Over that time, Farwell carried mail between the outposts that dotted the vast western Canadian prairie, usually traveling for days at a time and through the worst weather. He drove himself until I was afraid he would get sick. My husband refused to talk about the trial, and though he didn't drink again, he was a quiet man now and we were seldom intimate. I tried to be patient.

Susie, though, drew us together with her cheerful ways and her hearty chuckle. Our daughter was a beautiful example of our love, with her father's round face, her brown-black hair, and my dark eyes. Neither of us made a secret of our love for her. She had been an easy infant to care for, and now entering her first year she delighted both of us as she toddled back and forth between us, babbling in delight. "Da-da" was charmed by those, her first words, and with every small achievement he'd scoop her up and carry her into the fort so the Mounties might learn of her latest accomplishment.

A few days after Susie's first birthday, a surprise arrived in a letter that came from Jeannie. It had come to the Mounties at Fort Macleod, and when Farwell brought it to me, I was putting Susie in her cradleboard and asked him to read it aloud, since it was addressed to both of us and I was not yet confident in my reading skills.

Dear Abe and Mary,

Mary, I am writing this letter on behalf of your grandfather, Red Fox, who came to our settlement looking for you. We gave your grandfather a feast to celebrate his welcome, but we were lucky that Sandy was home—he's one of the freighters who works with René. He speaks pretty good Crow, and between the two of us we were able to understand what your grandfather had to say. First, your mother had been sick with measles, but she recovered and everyone else in your family is well. And this was his big news: Mary, Red Fox came to tell you that because of a treaty the Crow now own a huge parcel of land. He wanted you to know in case you might want to come and live there with your family. In your last letter you mentioned that Abe wants to ranch and Red Fox said that you could do that on Crow land because the white government wants the Crow to become farmers. . . .

Farwell stopped reading and looked up at me in disbelief. Then, aloud, he reread the part about the land. "I think she is saying that there is land that we can farm and that it won't cost us anything." He stared at me again. "Mary, if we don't have to pay for the land, I'd have enough money to build a house, outbuildings, even buy some cattle. This might mean that we could get our ranch."

"But where is the land?" I asked.

"We'd have to check in at the government agency, but it's got to be somewhere down in the Crow territory," he said. "That land is perfect for ranching. Damn, Mary! This could be our chance to start again."

For the first time since the trial, I saw what looked like hope on his face. "Is it safe to go down there?" I asked, thinking of the enemies we had made who still lived in the Fort Benton area.

"Hell, we've been up here almost two years. How long am I going to run scared? But are you game?"

"When can we go?" I asked, grinning at him.

He whooped as he lifted me in the air. "That's my girl," he said. Then he set me down and looked deep into my eyes. "It'll be a fresh start," he said, and with his body pressed against mine, he kissed me in a way he hadn't since before the trial.

BY THE END of May, the moon when chokecherries are in bloom, we arrived at the Metis settlement and Jeannie and I were together again. Little Marie was now three snows. This child had the same dark hair and big brown eyes as her mother, but unlike Jeannie, who was joyous and open, her daughter was somber and serious.

"Do you remember me?" I asked the little girl. "You took my name," I said, and her brown eyes opened wide.

"So then what do people call you if I took your name?" she asked.

"They call me Crow Mary."

"Mama said I should call you Madame Farwell."

"How about you call me Crow Mary?"

She agreed and nodded seriously. "What is your baby's name?"

"Her name is Susie," Jeannie said, covering my squirming baby in kisses.

"Will she like me?" Marie asked.

"I think that she will love you like I do your mother. She will love you like a sister."

"A sister? I had a brother, but he died."

I glanced at Jeannie and saw again the toll of another baby's death.

Jeannie looked at me with tears in her eyes. "Oh, Mary, it's so nice to have you home again."

AFTER EVERYONE HAD been fed and our children were both asleep, Jeannie and I sat together outside my lodge door. It was a beautiful night, with the stars sprinkled around a huge white moon.

"It's good to be here," I said.

"Do you feel it was safe enough for the two of you to come down here? René said there's still talk about the Benton men threatening to kill Farwell."

"I'm glad that René is going into town with him tomorrow. I wanted to go along with my guns, but Farwell said he wanted me to stay here with Susie. He has to go for supplies. . . ."

"I guess he'll have to face those men sooner or later. But what about you?" Jeannie asked. "What was the trial like? Everyone here was shocked to hear that they let a woman testify in court, and an Indian at that."

"They didn't talk to me long, and I don't think I helped," I said. "But I only told the truth. I didn't see those three men that day. There were others who did the shooting, and now they're all on the loose."

"Farwell must be worried about that?" Jeannie put her hand on my arm. "He's changed, hasn't he? He's a lot more quiet."

I nodded and looked up at the moon.

"What aren't you telling me?" she asked.

"Farwell got drunk."

"Drunk? When? During the trial?"

"No, after. He got so drunk that he could hardly walk."

"Oh, Mary," she said. "What did you do?"

"I took his clothes off," I said.

She snickered, but quickly covered her mouth with her hand. "I'm sorry, it's just the way you said that."

I tried to smile but I couldn't. "He was sick over himself and he smelled terrible and he still won't talk about it."

"Has he been drinking since then?" she asked.

"No," I admitted. "But I'm worried. He once told me that when he started drinking, he couldn't stop. What if that happens now? It was awful to see him like that."

"Well, when you consider what happened with those two trials, you can't really blame him," Jeannie said. "But I'm sorry for laughing before. This isn't funny."

RENÉ AND FARWELL went into Fort Benton the next day, and Jeannie stayed with me at my camp to await their return. The sun was setting when we heard their singing from a long way off, and it was nice to hear their harmonizing until Jeannie said, "They sound drunk."

The men waved as they came into view, but Farwell was finding it hard to stay in his saddle.

"You fool," Jeannie said when she went to René. "Well, at least you got what you went for," she said, looking at the packhorses that were loaded down. Farwell slid from his horse and caught himself as his knees buckled.

"We just went for one drink, but Stiller was behind the bar and he—" René began.

I interrupted him with more anger than I intended. "Stiller? Sam Stiller?"

Farwell tried to force himself erect. "Stiller says . . . Stiller says tha' massacre wasn' my fault."

René went over and draped Farwell's arm around his shoulder. "Come on. I'll take care of the horses and the supplies after I put you to bed."

While Farwell slept, Jeannie and I helped René unload the horses, but I was furious with Farwell when the three of us sat down to eat.

"Don't be mad, Mary. Farwell, he's taking all of this hard," René said.

"Here, have another cup of coffee," Jeannie said to her husband.

"We got lucky to run into that man Stiller. He came with us to get the supplies, and if it wasn't for him, maybe they don't sell to Farwell." He shook his head. "I don't know. Farwell do plenty of business with these men for all these years, and now they turn their back on him."

"So Stiller runs a bar now?" Jeannie asked the question for me.

René nodded. "After we get the supplies, he took us back to his bar for drinks."

FARWELL HAD A bad headache in the morning, and after he had two cups of coffee he went down to the river to bathe. I didn't know what to say, but I wasn't about to let this go the way I had in Winnipeg. Jeannie, sensing trouble, came early, and she and Marie took Susie to their cabin for the morning. As soon as they left, I went down to the river.

I expected to see Farwell in the water, and I wasn't prepared to see him sitting fully clothed on the riverbank. His eyes were red when he looked up at me, and when I sat next to him, he began to pick at a fingernail. I reached over and took his hand. "Don't," I said, "they'll get sore again like they were up at Fort Macleod."

I felt his deep sadness, but I was angry. Farwell had promised he wouldn't touch liquor. And especially after that night in Winnipeg, when he had been so sick, why would he do this? I had learned my lesson with rum punch and I wasn't about to repeat that.

"Mary, I'm sorry," he began. "I know I've said it before, but this time I promise you I will never drink again. I shouldn't have . . ." He shook his head. "It seems once I get started, I just can't stop."

"Then why start?"

"It was a rough day. Nobody in town wanted to do business with me. If Stiller hadn't shown up when he did, I doubt they'd have even sold me any supplies." He sighed and rubbed at his face. "I knew it would be bad, but I didn't think the whole town would turn on me."

"But why did you drink?" I asked. "Why do you say one thing and do another?"

"It's hard, Mary. Looks to me like I'm the only one who paid a price. Solomon's got himself a bar and Evans has one, too, that he has the nerve to name the Extradition Saloon after that damn trial in Helena. And they're both doing a booming business. Turns out, Stiller's working behind a bar, too, so when he invited us back for a drink, I went. I didn't see anything wrong with one drink, but after a few, I didn't care anymore." He gave a long sigh. "I'm sorry, Mary. What the hell is wrong with me?"

I looked at this man who had been a good chief and a good husband. I knew how the massacre and the trial still weighed on Farwell, and I suspected that he still blamed himself for selling whiskey. And maybe I did, too. But he was my husband and I loved him, and I wanted us to have a good marriage.

"Did you bring your soap?" I asked. He looked at me, disbelieving, as I stood and slipped out of my dress. "Come on," I said, unbuttoning his shirt. "Let's get you cleaned up."

I bathed him then, the way I might have bathed Susie, taking care to wash his hair and to soap his feet. Later, we lay together on the grass. The sun was warm, and Farwell leaned over me to stroke my cheek and then my neck. His eyes filled as he looked at me. "I love you, Mary," he said. "I'll make this up to you." I pulled him toward me and returned his deep kisses.

CHAPTER THIRTY-TWO

1877

IN JUNE, THE moon when the leaves on the trees are fully grown, we followed the handdrawn map that Red Fox had left with Jeannie and René to show us how to get to my family's encampment. It guided us toward the foothills of the Beartooth Mountains, where the government agency had established the Crow reservation. René told us that the reservation had been set up in a treaty with the Crow. But now my people were restricted to this piece of land and could not leave the area without a pass from a government agency.

"Did Red Fox have a pass when he came to see you?" I asked.

René winked. "He said that he did not sign the treaty, so he was not under any obligation."

I smiled. How like Grandfather to think that way. I wondered then about Father and other braves of our tribe who were now bound to live in such a restricted way. Was it possible that they really were willing to live within boundaries when all their lives they had traveled wherever they chose?

Our travel was slow, with our wagon and packhorses loaded down with supplies and our belongings. We followed an old trail south, but when unsure, Grandfather's well-drawn map didn't fail us. As we drew closer to the foothills of the familiar mountains, I breathed in the fresh earthiness of my beloved homeland. "Oh, look," I exclaimed in joy to Farwell as I pointed at the craggy steep terrain. "See that cliff over there. That was one of our buffalo jumps."

"It must have been something to see buffalo herded off a cliff like that."

"There were always braves at the bottom who would kill any that didn't die right away."

"And your people did this every fall?"

"*Éeh.* That was when their fur was thick and the summer grass made for sweet meat. We'd come from the mountains down to the plains where the buffalo were. Our scouts would go first and find them, then the men would decide together how to stampede the herd in the right direction. Some of the buffalo were three times as big as a horse, and they didn't like to be chased off a cliff, and sometimes men got killed."

"It must have been a wild time," Farwell said.

"*Éeh*," I agreed, and as we drew closer to the ragged mountains, my first memory of a buffalo hunt came back so clearly that I could almost hear Grandmother's voice.

I couldn't have been more than four snows, and in my memory Grandmother was showing me how to sharpen a small knife. We women had set up camp away from the bottom of the buffalo jump, alongside running water and with cottonwoods for shelter. First we heard a faint rumbling in the distance, and then came a thundering roar with clouds of dust filling the air. Suddenly the beasts came, tumbling over the cliff, one after another, bellowing out their last cries. I was afraid and reached for Grandmother's hand. "Why are you crying?" I asked her.

"I am thanking the buffalo for giving us their lives so we might live ours," she said.

The men at the base of the hill rushed to kill any animals that still lived, and after they signaled that all was safe, we women and children hurried in with our knives and packhorses. I remember Grandmother sprinkling salty gall over a small strip of fresh kidney and handing it to me. "Here, Goes First, good for the eyes," she said, as she put a piece in her own mouth. Later that night she gave me a piece of fry bread topped with a slice of roasted liver—a delicacy my mouth watered for now.

AFTER A WEEK of travel, we found the Absaroka Indian Agency settled in the shadow of the Beartooth Mountains. A stockade surrounded the offices and stores, while outside the wall there were some log cabins and plenty of Crow tipis. We might have been more closely observed and welcomed if there hadn't been such a ruckus going on over by a cattle pen. By chance I recognized an old friend of Grandmother's, standing alongside her lodge, and I slipped from my horse to see if she could direct me toward my father's camp.

"Goes First!" she repeated when I gave her my name, and she hesitated as she looked over my Métis style dress and my single braid before she reached for my hand. "I hardly recognized you. Your father isn't here," she said, "but let me ask my husband where his camp is."

While I waited for her return, Farwell went into the agency office. Susie, now thirteen moons, was settled in her cradleboard that was attached to my saddle. She peered out with interest at the action, while I looked closer to see what held the crowd's interest. They were gathered around a pen filled with black cattle, the kind I had seen outside Fort Benton—the kind Farwell wanted to raise on his ranch. Atop their impatient buffalo horses, braves, stripped down to breechcloths and moccasins, were dressed to hunt as they eagerly waited for the Yellow Eyes agent to call out a family name and release a cow.

As the animal flew out of the cattle shoot, the braves whooped and gave chase. The cattle were fast, and many gave the men a good run before they were brought down, some by a blast from a rifle and others by a silent but deadly arrow. Then the women cheered, calling out to one another as they went out to butcher the animal, as they had once done with the buffalo. The men returned, excited as their wound-up buffalo horses, ready to give chase again.

As I watched, the old woman returned. "My husband will come soon and tell you how to find your father's camp. It is farther in toward the mountains. Before you go, will you stay and join my family for our feast today?"

"Thank you, but I have not seen my parents in a long while, and I would like to get to their camp before dark. What is it you are celebrating?"

"Oh, we Crow meet up like this every beef day. The agents want us to take the cattle back to our separate villages, but as you know, we like to feast together. It is hard to find game and the buffalo are few, so some days we go hungry, but on the day that the agency gives us our meat supply, there is plenty for all and so we have a day of celebration."

"Do you like the taste of the beef?" I asked, not liking it myself.

"No, the flavor is poor and the meat is stringy, but it fills our stomachs," she said.

While her husband was giving me directions to Father's camp, Farwell returned from the agency building. I had not seen him this excited since we were first married, and after we rode out, he was quick to tell me why. "About fifty miles east of here there's a piece of land that runs along a branch of the Yellowstone River—you call it the Elk River. It's signed up in your name. It sounds like it will be perfect for ranching, and all we have to do is get out there and get set up."

How full of hope we were that day as we rode out to find Father's village.

I FIRST SPOTTED Red Fox's gray horse tied alongside a lodge, and I urged Snow toward it. She whinnied, but before I could call out for him, Grandfather emerged. Unmindful of his reticence in the past to show affection, I leapt from Snow's back and ran toward him. He returned my hug, and when I released him, his kind eyes were filled with tears. "You came," he said.

It had been five years since I had last seen Grandfather, and I couldn't stop smiling.

"Let me see the child." He moved to where Susie watched his approach from her cradleboard. Hearing his voice, I realized how much I had missed the soothing sounds of my native language.

"Where is Father's lodge?" I looked at the one I thought was his because it stood next to Red Fox's, but there was an unfamiliar woman cooking at the fire outside.

"Goes First, you should know that—" Grandfather began, just as a lanky young boy came out of the lodge. Though he was already eleven snows, I recognized my brother. "Strong Bull," I called out, and though his sad face changed to joy when he recognized me, it was clear that something was not right. I had a bad feeling as I undid the cradleboard. "Down, down." Susie struggled to get to the ground, and I quickly handed her over to Farwell.

"Grandfather?" I asked, but Red Fox only shook his head. I ran past the woman at the fire and looked directly into the tipi. There was no one inside. "Who are you?" I asked the unfamiliar woman, and then I noticed her close-cropped hair. What had happened? I was about to shout at Red Fox, when Father came around the side of his lodge. "Goes First," he said, startled to see me. He looked so wan and worn out that it was hard to recognize him. I greeted him with whispered words. "Where is Mother?"

"She is gone," he said, his face lined with grief.

"Gone?" I asked.

"About a year ago, she had what the Yellow Eyes called measles. Many Crow died from it, but she got better. In the first days of the moon of the first thunder she started to cough, and before the end of that moon she left for the Other Side Camp."

I had missed her by only a few weeks.

WHEN FARWELL FOUND me in the woods behind the camp, he carried a howling Susie in his arms. "No, Mary, don't . . . ," he called as he ran toward me. I had hold of my braid and was about to cut it off, when he pulled my skinning knife from me.

"No, Mary! I don't want you cutting your hair, and don't cut your body, either. I've seen squaws outside forts do that. I don't ever want our daughter to see you like that. It will scare her even more."

Susie had wriggled to the ground and grabbed hold of my leg. "Mama! Mama. Up. Up," she wailed.

I scooped her into my arms as I considered my knife that Farwell held in his hand. "But . . . ," I sobbed, "it is how we grieve. My mother is gone!"

Susie, never having seen me cry like this, was so upset that I sat down on the ground and put her to my breast. Farwell sat next to me, his arm across my back. My daughter's face was pink from crying, and I smoothed her damp cheeks as she nursed. But I felt numb. My mother was gone. How would I grieve if I let go of the old way?

"How about you stay here with your family for a while?" Farwell said. "I can go on my own to claim the land and then come back for you in a week or so. That'll give you some time to adjust."

I agreed to my husband's plan, and he left the next morning.

STRIKES THE HAT, my father's new wife, looked wary of me, but though heavily pregnant with her first child, she did everything she could to make Susie and me comfortable in their lodge. Later I noticed how pretty she was, in spite of the fact that she had shorn her hair after the death of my mother.

Strong Bull already carried himself as a young brave. I often saw him studying my one braid and my Métis dress, and if I caught his eye, he might smile but then quickly look away.

I had hoped that Father would be proud of me, married to Farwell, and though he was friendly enough toward my husband, after he left, my father was more distant with me than ever.

On the last night before Farwell was to return, Father joined our family where we sat to eat. Strikes the Hat had done the best she could with what she had, but the bean mixture that we ate smelled sour and the tough beef was a poor substitute for buffalo. While Susie toddled between Red Fox and Strong Bull, passing back and forth the wooden horse Grandfather had carved for her, I did my best to talk to Father.

"It is good to be back here on Crow land," I said.

"We live only on a small piece of Crow land where the agents tell us we must stay. Here, they say, our horses and our game are protected from our enemies. But when the Piegans or the Sioux come and steal our horses, we are told we cannot go off this land to get those horses back. When we do, we are punished and the agents keep food from us."

"Is game scarce here, too?" I asked.

"When we do find buffalo, the herd is small. Even the elk and deer are getting hard to find."

"I saw the people at the agency getting their government cattle," I offered.

"When we agreed with the Yellow Eyes to stay on this land, we were told that we would be supplied food if we could not find enough game. Each time we are given something to eat, they say that should last us until the next moon, but that is not our way. We've always feasted when we have food, and then we hunt again. And now they are telling us that they want us to become farmers and raise *cattle*."

"That is what Farwell wants to do," I said.

"Farwell is a Yellow Eyes. The Crow hunt for their food. Maybe you don't remember?" he asked, eyeing my Métis dress.

"But can't our people learn a different way?" I asked.

"A different way?" He looked toward Strong Bull, who was still playing with Susie. "If our young men become farmers and they are not allowed to go out on horse raids and war parties, how do they earn coups? And if they don't earn coup, how do we choose our chiefs?"

He was frowning, waiting for a response.

"I don't know, Father," I admitted, but I wondered if he now saw me as a Yellow Eyes and disapproved. With Mother gone and a new wife in her place, who would speak to him for me?

When Strikes the Hat brought her husband a cup of marrow broth, he reached for her hand and she sat down next to him. "And hear this," Father said. "They want us to keep just one wife. They tell us we must give away our other wives. Many of our wives are sisters, and they've always lived together. And how does a man choose only one of the families that he has made?"

Strikes the Hat said nothing, but when she lifted her head, I saw the concern on her face.

"Strikes the Hat helped your mother when she was sick. Now they want us to send some of our wives away. If your mother had lived, where would I send Strikes the Hat? Where would she go with our child? And who would care for them?" He shook his head in disbelief, or was it confusion? "There's even talk that the agents will take our children and put them in schools so they learn to live like the white man. What makes these Yellow Eyes think this way?" Again he looked at me as though I might have an answer.

In the distance we heard the pop of guns, and then it came again. I immediately thought it might be a raid until Father spoke. "That shooting is because of whiskey. There's no stopping it. Some of our people have such a taste for it that they are not allowed back into our village. Their relatives are unhappy with me, but I have to do what is right for all of us."

I wondered again if Father knew about Farwell's trading whiskey, and now I plunged in. "Did you know that Farwell sold whiskey?"

Father's eyes met mine. "Did he give it to you?"

"No," I said.

"Does he provide well for you and your child?"

"Yes," I said, "but . . ."

Father stood. "All traders trade whiskey. Farwell gave us guns. He is not like the government agents who lie to us," he said, and then walked off.

How I missed my mother that night, sitting alone in my lodge with Susie. At the age of twenty-one snows, I was no longer the naive girl who had left my family five years before. I had lived in Farwell's world and seen the turmoil there. I had always reassured myself that safety lay back at my father's camp—a haven in my memory. Now I saw the reality. I ran my hand down the smooth ridges of my long braid and thought of Strikes the Hat's shorn head. My mother was gone. Everything had changed.

Where did I belong?

As FARWELL LED us to our new property, I found it hard to believe this was the defeated man who had come back drunk from Fort Benton. Over the two days it took for us to arrive at the land he intended to ranch, the man I had married came back to me.

"There it is, Mary," Farwell said, pointing ahead. "Just look at this land. See how the river runs alongside? We'll always have water." His saddle squeaked as he waved his arm in a wide arc. "And look. There's all this grassland for cattle and horses, and there's plenty of level land to grow crops, too."

"It's beautiful here," I agreed, looking out over the hills of dense grasslands, made prettier still with vivid red and yellow wildflowers. I knew nothing about raising cattle, but I did know that this land could sustain grazing animals. Here grew hearty grass that dried standing up and would not flatten. In the winter, with a wind blowing the snow clear, this grass would supply feed throughout that brutal season. The creek, too, was of a good size. It had some deep streambeds, shadowed by willows and shrubs that would provide shelter and plenty of water, not just for us, but for our horses and Farwell's cattle as well.

Farwell pointed to a low hill, the base of which was surrounded by thickets of wild plum bushes and cottonwoods. "I'd like to put the house over there, on the top of that hill. What do you think?"

"It's good," I said, but when I imagined only one lodge sitting there, it felt lonely. After visiting with Jeannie and then my family, I was reminded how comforting it was to have relatives living close by.

But Farwell's enthusiasm was boundless. "We'll need to get fencing and outbuildings up before the snow, but in a year or two we'll be building ourselves an actual house."

"What do you mean, an actual house?"

"Well, it will still be made of logs, but this place will be a home—closer to those I grew up in, out east. I want Susie to grow up in a civilized home."

I glanced sharply at Farwell. Civilized? When Jeannie had explained the word "savage" to me, she had also explained the word "civilized." It was the first time Farwell had used that word, and I didn't like it. He caught my look. "I mean she needs to learn how to read and write, set a table and eat at one—things like that."

I said nothing, but later, as we were setting up our lodge down the hill and away from where Farwell's cabin would be built, I resolved that now that we were living on Crow land, I would teach Susie the Crow way of life as surely as Farwell might teach her the ways of the Yellow Eyes. I started that very day and spoke to Susie, who held the stakes for our lodge in her lap, as Farwell helped me set up our tipi.

"Soon, when you are old enough, it will be the two of us setting up our tipi. Crow women don't rely on a man to help unless there are no other Crow women around. Crow women are strong, and their home belongs to them," I said to her, glancing at my husband to see if he understood. But he just smiled at Susie, who was gnawing on a wooden peg.

PART FOUR

CHAPTER THIRTY-THREE

1880–1881

I T TOOK FARWELL longer than he had anticipated to build his ranch. My husband hired some men to build a large bunkhouse for the ranch hands, and then they added more barns and corrals and fencing for the horses. A hundred head of black Angus cattle came next, and if things went as planned, the cattle would pasture-graze year-round and only be rounded up for sale. Along with the cattle came four ranch hands, and through it all, I did the cooking for the evening meals. It was hard work, but I kept up with it. Beef was the usual meat that I served, but I was always happiest when one of the men came with an elk or a deer. That I butchered, too, but I kept the hide for myself. It was extra work, but already I was teaching Susie how to scrape and tan a green hide. Meanwhile, the better part of three years passed, and Farwell had still to construct a house. That was fine with me. In fact, I preferred to live in a tipi, and I told him so. But in that golden autumn of 1880, when we found out that I was pregnant again, building a house became a priority for Farwell.

And it might have been built, but a fire, set off by a careless ranch hand with a kerosene lamp, took down the big barn, and that had to be rebuilt instead. During it all, two of the ranch hands left and three more were hired on, but in the end, the house was still not finished in the spring when I was ready to give birth.

❧   ❧   ❧

"THEY'RE HERE, THEY'RE here!" The baby was ready to come any day, and I was relieved to hear Susie's voice when she ran out to greet Red Fox, Strong Bull, and the two Crow women they had brought to help me with the birth.

Though Father had not yet come to visit, Grandfather came often to our ranch. Early on, he won Susie's heart, not just because of his kind ways, but because of the small spotted dog he had given her as a gift. As well, Susie loved the stories he told and the games he played. Strong Bull occasionally came with him, but my brother was quiet and observant, and he didn't have much to do with Susie. However, that spring, when he arrived days before the birth of my second child, Strong Bull had discarded the clothes given out by the government agency, and in leggings, clout, and a beaded buckskin shirt he strutted about as only a proud sixteen-year-old Crow brave can do.

Susie couldn't take her eyes from him. "Papa said that Strong Bull is my uncle," she said one night during the visit.

"That is in the way of the Yellow Eyes. In the Crow way, he is considered your brother," I said.

Her face lit up, pleased with the news. "My brother?" She grinned. "I like that better." The next morning, clothed in her best red dress and with her father's old buckskin hat perched on her head, she found Strong Bull eating a morning meal. She stood back a distance and waited patiently until he finished. When he set his bowl aside, he looked at her and waited for her to speak.

"My mama said that you are my brother," she said in English.

"Can you speak Crow?" he asked.

She repeated herself in the Crow language.

He smiled at her and tipped back her hat. "Yes, I am your brother," he said. "I will always look out for you."

"And I will always look out for *you*," she said, and sat down beside him.

"How old are you now?" he asked.

She held up five fingers, then asked, "How old are you?"

"I'm sixteen snows," he said.

"Oh, I'm five *snows*," she corrected herself.

"That's right," he approved. "Why do you wear your hair like that?" he asked.

"Like how?"

"In one braid. Crow women wear two braids."

"They do?"

"Yes, two braids," he said, giving me a reproachful glance.

Susie jumped up, and when she returned from our lodge, she carried a brush. "Here," she said, sitting at his feet. "Fix my hair so I will look like a Crow girl."

And so began their close bond.

THOUGH IT WAS an easy delivery, I was grateful for the women who came to help, and I hoped they would be pleased with the fine horses that were waiting for them in the corral. Farwell brought Susie with him to see our new baby boy, and my daughter's dark eyes overflowed as she patted his soft face. "Oh, Mama," she cried. "He's so pretty."

Farwell wiped his own tears as he studied his son. "He looks exactly like my little brother did—the one who died. I'm going to name him Marcus Rosebud," he said. "Marcus, for my brother, and Rosebud, after the best creek in the land for trapping beaver."

"Rose-bud, Rose-bud," Susie murmured, delicately touching the baby's puckered mouth. She laughed when he tried to taste her finger. "Let's call him Bud," she said, and so we did.

After the arrival of baby Bud, Farwell put extra effort into completing the house, but there was always a new problem that held it back. He worked nonstop, and I often urged him to ease up.

"I need to work," was his usual reply.

I never asked him what he meant, because I knew how the trial still haunted him. The first time he went for supplies from the nearby town of Park City, he returned in a foul mood. Only days later did he tell me that his reputation for turning in his friends had followed him the two hundred miles from Fort Benton. After that, whenever he went to town for supplies, I always worried that he'd come home drunk.

❀　　❀　　❀

"MARY! LOOK WHO I found," Farwell called out one evening as he came through the cottonwoods and shrubs that sheltered our lodge.

My stomach flipped over when I saw who our visitor was.

"Well, I'll be darned." Sam Stiller winked at me.

"Come sit." Farwell invited his friend over to a small table set up under the shade arbor I had built of willows and brush. "Mary, I told Stiller that he was welcome to a meal. Do you have something to eat?"

"*Éeh*," I said, and as the two continued their talk I went to uncover what was left of the meal I had made earlier for the ranch hands.

"So, like I was tellin' you," Stiller said, "Evan's bar in Benton is doin' good business and so is Solomon's. Hammond married that Rosalie gal, and the rest . . . well, like I said, they're all doing pretty good for themselves."

I reheated a pan of onions and potatoes and sliced in some of the beef roast that Farwell enjoyed so much. It was meat from the cattle he was raising, and he compared the flavor to buffalo, but to me I might have been chewing on a tough skunk.

I willed my hands to keep from shaking when I set the plates of beef and potatoes in front of the two men. "Thanks, Mary," Farwell said.

"This is some mighty fine-lookin' grub. I'm telling you, Abe, there'll come a day I'm gonna have to steal this woman from you."

Farwell laughed. "Afraid she's mine," he said as he picked up his knife and fork.

"Wait," Stiller said as he pulled a leather-covered flask from a vest pocket. "Let's have a swallow of this before we eat."

Farwell put his hand up. "I'll pass."

"Come on." Stiller pushed it toward him. "You weren't on the wagon the last time I saw you."

"I know, but that was four years ago, and it seems once I start, I go off on a toot."

"Well, you won't be able to do that now because this is all the whiskey I have on me." He held up the pocket flask. "Come on, a few swallows to help me celebrate my new job."

"Well . . ." Farwell hesitated. "Maybe just one drink to celebrate." And to my surprise, he took the silver flask and tipped it up.

I felt the anger heating my face as I stared at my husband, but he avoided looking at me.

"So, tell me, how did you get this job?" Farwell asked Stiller as they began to eat.

"You know. Word gets out. And it was posted in the paper," Stiller said. "Government lookin' for Indian agents—men with a strong hand who aren't afraid to live with the Indians on their reserve. Sent them my records from the war and they offered good enough pay, so here I am."

Susie came out of our tipi. "Hi, Papa," she said, and went to stand beside her father. Rex, her dog who never left her side, growled up at Stiller.

"Well, look at this! A little squaw as pretty as her ma," Stiller said.

"I'm not a little squaw!" Susie objected.

"Is that right? What are you then?" Stiller asked.

"I'm five."

"Five? Well, that's different then. Matter of fact, I'm looking for some kids around your age. How'd you like to come with me and go to school?"

"No. I want to stay *here*," Susie said.

"Well, there's a law that says you are going to have to go to school pretty soon, so you might as well come with me now."

At this I dropped the frying pan and rushed over to put my arm around Susie's shoulders. "She stays with me!" I said, glaring at Stiller. "I teach her everything she needs to know." I turned Susie toward the tipi. "Go back into the lodge," I directed.

Susie gave Stiller a last look. "I'm staying here with Mama. Come on, Rex," she said, and with her dog at her heels stomped off to our lodge.

Farwell watched Susie and turned back to Stiller with a smile. "She's like her mother. Knows her mind."

"Well, just so you know, the government is starting to crack down. They're trying to get these kids on the reservation some kind of education. It's the only way these Indians are going to come around—learn how to live a little more civilized."

"Last I heard, they have a school there on the reservation?" Farwell said.

"They do, but the thing is, the Indians won't keep their kids in it. The government finally got smart and opened a big school in some army barracks all the way out in Carlisle, Pennsylvania. Now we just take the kids and send them on a train out there. At least it's far enough away that they stay put. Trouble is, once the kids are at the school, they say it's like pulling hens' teeth, trying to get them to give up their Injun ways. First thing they do is take away their clothes and cut their hair, but they say you'd think those little savages were being scalped by the way they cry and carry on."

I smacked down the pan I was cleaning. I had heard enough. "You don't cut an Indian child's hair. Indians only cut their hair if they are grieving!"

Stiller's eyebrows rose as he passed Farwell the flask.

"And Susie is not going to any school," I added.

My husband took a long swallow of the drink before he turned to me. "Mary, we'll talk about this later."

Stiller watched me closely. "It's not that I have a score to settle here, but it's the law. She'll have to go soon enough." He glanced toward my tipi at the sound of Bud's cry. "Didn't know you had another one," he said to Farwell.

"A son," Farwell said with pride.

"Well, good for you," Stiller said, and passed the flask again. "Two little Indians."

Furious, I went to the lodge to sit with the children until both men left.

FARWELL DID NOT come back to our tipi that night, and for the first time, he stayed up at the bunkhouse. That evening, when the laughter and shouting grew loud, I realized that the men, including Farwell, were all drunk. I was afraid and angry that Farwell was drinking, and thinking of Stiller's threat to take Susie, I slept with both of my guns beside me.

Farwell missed the morning meal, and when he finally showed up in the evening, I was quiet after he joined me at the campfire, where I sat mending a dress of mine.

"What's wrong?" he asked.

I didn't answer him.

"Mary! I asked you what was wrong."

"What's wrong?" I asked. "To start with, I don't trust that Sam Stiller, and I don't know why you do."

"You take him too seriously," he said. "He likes to tease."

"Was he teasing when he talked about taking Susie away to a school?" I asked.

"Well, I hear that they are setting up schools where they are giving the Indian kids a good education. When Susie's older, we'll have to think about sending her to one."

"Why?" I asked.

"Because they'll teach her a lot."

"Like what?" I asked.

"Well, they can teach her how to read and write."

"She can already read and write," I said. "You teach both of us every night when you aren't too tired. And she can speak Crow as good as I can."

"Yes, but it isn't just reading and writing that she needs. It would be good for her to learn how white people live."

Anger loosened my tongue. "Why? So she can see how well their courts work?" My words hit my mark. "And why did you drink?" I added.

"Because I felt like it!" He stood.

"But you said you wouldn't drink again," I called after him when he began to walk away.

He stopped and turned back. "Listen, Mary," he said, his voice hard as a rock. "That was before when I was trading liquor. Now that we're settled here, the ranch hands are right. I can afford to relax a little. They invite me to have some drinks with 'em, that's what I'm gonna do, and I won't let a wife tell me otherwise."

"Where are you going?" I asked.

"To have a drink with the boys!" he said, and left.

CHAPTER THIRTY-FOUR

1881

FARWELL AND I had always worked closely together, but as time went on, he became so engrossed in working with his cattle and finishing the house that there were days when the only time we had a chance to spend time together was at night. I was kept busy as well, caring for the two children and making meals for the hired men. In the evenings, when before my husband and I were often intimate, now Farwell occasionally began to drink with the workers and sleep up at the bunkhouse. During the times we were together, he grew frustrated with me when I didn't share his enthusiasm for the work he was doing. "You said that we have over a hundred head of cattle. Why do you keep getting more?" I often asked.

"I'm trying to get ahead," he explained.

"Get ahead? Ahead of what?"

"It's how I can make more money."

"But we have everything we need. Why do we need more money?"

"So I can keep building onto the ranch."

"But don't you have the ranch you wanted?"

"No. That will take time."

Yet I had my children, and they were my joy. At five snows Susie already was a big help, not only in caring for Bud, but also in helping me when I butchered meat, or cooked the evening meal for all the men. When we had time, with Bud on my back in the cradleboard, Susie and I picked berries and dug wild turnips, just as I had with Mother and Grandmother. But what made me the happiest was that my daughter and I shared a love of horses. Susie had a natural instinct for them beyond her years. From the time she was four snows, she cared for her own pony, leading him from the corral and tethering him beside Snow so they might feed together on the rich grass. Now I taught her to ride whenever I had the time.

Farwell was as loving with Susie as I was, and though he appeared to be fond of Bud, my husband was especially proud of his daughter. Ranch hands came and went, and if one of them was Crow, Farwell often called on Susie to translate. I suppose there was a need, but I also suspected there were times he was just showing off how well his daughter could speak both English and Crow.

I didn't forget Stiller's threat about the Indian school, and I tried to keep Susie close to my side, never knowing when he might show up again. But she was fiercely independent, and I couldn't keep her from spending time up at the house with her father. She was as excited about the building of the log cabin as Farwell was.

"Mama," Susie reported one day. "Wait until you see! There is a kitchen with a big black stove and another big room right next to the kitchen with a table where ten people can sit. Papa said we will all eat there and the ranch hands will, too."

"That sounds . . . nice," I said.

"And guess what? You and Papa will have your own room to sleep in, and Bud and me and Rexy will have our own room, too. But I don't know if I like that."

"Why not?"

"How will I see you when I wake up from a bad dream?"

"Maybe you should ask your papa," I said, and wondered what Farwell would have to say to that.

I HEARD REXY'S barking before I heard Susie's call. "Mama, Mama. Look who's coming!" It was in the early fall, about six months after Bud was born, when Susie came running to announce Red Fox and my brother.

I was elated to see them again, and I couldn't wait to show them how much the baby had grown.

Strong Bull arrived this time leading two horses, one a large beautiful bay, and the other a pretty piebald pony. "Look what I have for you, little sister," he called to Susie.

"For me?" she squealed in delight as she ran toward him.

Farwell came to greet the two men, and Strong Bull proudly presented the horses to my husband, asking that the pony be given to Susie. How proud I was of Strong Bull. My brother would not give a gift to me; instead he gave to me through my husband and my family, just as one day I would let Strong Bull know how I valued him by the way I treated his wife.

Red Fox straightened with pride as he told of Strong Bull's achievement. "Five of our young men, including Strong Bull, went out on a raid, and together they came back with ten Sioux ponies—all beautiful animals. Now Strong Bull gives them as gifts to others, as the Crow have always done."

"Do the Indian agents know about this raid?" Farwell asked.

After I translated, Strong Bull replied with a quick smile. I laughed when I translated his reply. "Not yet."

But Farwell wasn't amused. "Isn't your agreement with the government that they will supply you with food and clothing if you do not go out on raids and travel off your reservation?"

Strong Bull shrugged and answered himself. "I sign no treaty."

Again I laughed, knowing he repeated words of my grandfather, but Farwell shook his head in disapproval. "If they learn about this, they could cut off your camp's food supply."

"The Crow brave raid and hunt. That never stop!" Strong Bull's eyes glinted in anger when he spoke directly to Farwell.

Until now, my brother had shown only respect for my husband, and Strong Bull's heated response surprised us all. The two Crow men Farwell had recently hired were compliant and quiet. They were men who appeared to have accepted the government's restrictions, and I doubted either of them still went out on raids. But those men also appeared defeated, and they seemed to have dealt with the loss of their familiar life by drifting from job to job and getting drunk whenever liquor was available.

"Well, Strong Bull, I'm afraid we can't accept these horses," Farwell said, handing back the reins. "I don't want to start trouble with Stiller and the other agents over this."

I gasped at Farwell's words. It was an insult to refuse a gift given in this way. Susie watched, trying to understand. Her bond with her father was deep, but she worshipped Strong Bull as well.

"Please, Papa," she begged. "He said the spotted one is for me."

But Farwell shook his head. "I'm sorry, Strong Bull," he said. "If I take these horses, I'm going against the agreement that the Crow made with the government. Then we'll both get in trouble."

As I translated his words, I was as angry as my brother. I couldn't believe that my husband would so completely support an unfair rule set up by the Yellow Eyes.

Strong Bull glared at Farwell before he leapt onto his horse. He looked at me but said nothing before he galloped away, taking the gift horses with him. Red Fox shrugged apologetically before he mounted his own horse and followed Strong Bull at a trot.

As they rode away, I swung toward Farwell. "You shouldn't have talked to him like that. You shouldn't have refused his gift."

"Mary, you don't understand. If the military ever gets involved—and they will if they feel that these young braves are getting out of control—they could put him away."

"What do you mean—*put him away*?" Contempt colored my words.

"Lock him up. Put him in jail."

"For what?"

Farwell's voice was cold. "For stealing horses."

"So when the Sioux steal horses from us, the Crow are not supposed to do the same? We are to just let them take what they want? And you heard about our two braves that the Blackfoot killed when our men were out hunting? Our braves aren't supposed to retaliate?" I asked.

"Those Crow men were killed because they were trespassing on Blackfoot territory."

"But you heard why. They had to go that far up north because the game here is getting that scarce and many of our people are hungry!"

"Stop!" Susie grabbed hold of my arm and then Farwell's. She had seldom heard us shout at each other, and we went silent when we saw her tears. She looked back and forth at the two of us, and Farwell, as sorry as I was to see her this upset, squatted down beside her.

"Come on," he said, putting his arm around her shoulders. "Let's go out to the horses and find you a new one to ride."

"But I liked the one Strong Bull had for me," she whimpered.

"I know, but it was an Indian pony and I don't think it was broken yet. I've got one for you that will work out a whole lot better."

"You do?" she asked, wiping her face with her fist.

"Yes," he said. "Let's go have a look at her."

I went to check on Bud, who had been sleeping inside my tipi. Awake now, he smiled at me, and when I picked him up, I kissed him and smelled his sweet baby perfume. His face looked like Farwell's face must have looked at that age, and though I was furious with my husband, my heart was filled with love for this baby boy. I cuddled him and cooed as I took him outside my lodge to nurse while sitting in the warm comfort of Old Man Sun.

It was already September, the moon when the plums fall. Yellow and red colors tinged the rolling hills, but I disliked seeing the barbed-wire fencing that crisscrossed our land. Only weeks before, when a village of Crow traveled by, they bypassed us instead of stopping for a visit. Our fences would have kept their horses from grazing, and our yard offered little room for their lodges to make camp. How disappointed I had been as I watched their caravan wind past our land.

As I sat nursing Bud, Farwell led Susie down to our tipi. She waved to me, atop her new ride. This one, too, was a piebald pony, but he wasn't a gift from my brother.

"Mama, look," Susie called for my approval. I nodded and smiled at her, but I avoided looking at Farwell.

Once again, that night Farwell stayed up at the house to drink with the men and did not come down to sleep in my lodge. And that was fine with me.

❧   ❧   ❧

IN THE WEEKS that followed, Farwell finally completed the house. The day he came for me, he was filled with pride. "Come on, Mary. The house is finished and I want you to see it. We can move in at any time."

I had no desire to live in a white man's cabin and had been dreading this day. I had seen the building go up, but to Farwell's frustration I had stayed away. Now I kept my eyes on the dress I was stitching. "I like my tipi," I said.

"I know you do, and you can always come back to it whenever you like. But winter is on its way, and we have two children to think of. Now come and see the house. I think it's the best work that I've ever done, and I did it all for you, including the furniture that I built."

"Mama, come." Susie grabbed hold of my hand and led the way up the hill. She waved toward the long low bunkhouse. "That place has room for six men," she said, "but Burt doesn't live in the bunkhouse. He lives in a room off the kitchen."

"Burt?" I asked.

Farwell grinned. "He's a surprise. I've hired a man to do the cooking for the hands. I'm trying to make it easier for you," Farwell said. "You can help out whenever you like, but you don't have to cook unless you want to."

I was relieved to know there was help, but I didn't like that Farwell hadn't consulted me about it. Susie opened a door to the house that was so large that three or more tipis could easily have fit inside. To answer Susie and Farwell's eager looks, I said how I liked that all the rooms had floors and windows. "And this is a good table," I said, nodding toward the long yellow pine table that sat in the room next to the kitchen. Farwell smiled. "I made it for you. I thought you might want to do some sewing on it in the wintertime."

He looked pleased when I ran my hand over the smooth finish.

I liked Burt, too. He was an older, heavyset man, who kept his sparse white hair tied back from his round, pleasant face. He greeted us in the kitchen, where he stood next to a big black cooking stove.

"Good to meet you, Mrs. Farwell," he said, reminding me of Major

Irvine when he nodded respectfully. Burt was the first Yellow Eyes I trusted on sight.

WE MOVED INTO the house before the first deep snow, and there we made good use of the pine table my husband had built. Farwell and the hired hands used it for both the morning and evening meal, and after they finished, I sat there to eat with the children. I also appreciated the workspace the table gave me, with plenty of room to cut and sew clothes and moccasins for my family. We had some good evenings around that table, too, when my husband sat with Susie and me and continued to teach us both to read and write.

I often helped Burt prepare food, especially when butchering needed to be done. Then I also dried plenty of thin strips of fresh meat for the ranch hands who liked having the chewy pieces to eat during the day while they were out working with the cattle.

Burt moved slow because of his sore hips, but he got his work done, his meals were good, and he kept the kitchen and house tidy and clean. He was kind to the children, and he further won my favor when I learned that he did not join the others at night to drink whiskey.

"Drink can make a good man bad and a bad man worse," he said one day as I helped him butcher a deer that one of the men had brought in. "Never did like the stuff. I had a son . . . ," he said, but shook his head and said no more.

During that winter, Farwell began to drink almost every evening. As I readied the children for bed, he would make an excuse to go out to the bunkhouse and there join the men who drank. Some nights he slept out there, but some nights, after I was already asleep, he made his way to our bedroom. He would reach for me then, and though the smell and taste of whiskey was sharp on his breath, I returned his kisses because I hoped it might make me feel close to him again. Instead, it left me feeling confused and angry. What happened to his promise to me not to drink? Why had he gone back on his word? I couldn't understand what liquor gave him that I and the children could not.

Through the years, Jeannie and I kept in touch through letters, but I had never told her about the trouble in my marriage. Now, though, my letter writing was more skilled, and after I wrote a more honest account of my life, she sent a reply.

Dear Mary,

You sound unhappy and I don't blame you. God be praised, your two children are in good health, but it seems to me like your husband needs a good paddling. If you lived around here, Marie could do it for you. Remember how she was always so serious? Well, heaven help us, it's starting to look like she has some of the same personality as Mama Rosa. In fact, she even straightens her own grandmère out. At seven years old! And guess what Mama does? She laughs! And you should see Marie with the twins. They're not even three years old yet and they often come to me and say Sisi Marie is making them work too hard. I've actually thought of sending her up to the orphanage so she could help them run it.

Anyway, at least she's a big help and I need it, as I've been eating those damn rice and raisins and you know what that does to me. I still have another three more months to go, but I'm about as wide as I am tall with carrying this one. I'm praying for a boy. René is determined that we produce at least one.

Now, about your problem. I hope you don't mind that I talked this over with René. He thinks that Abe still feels bad about the trial and that drinking helps him forget. René said that wherever he travels, Abe Farwell's name is still mud and he figures that it's the same down there by you. That's got to be hard on Farwell and I doubt the men in this country will ever forget that.

You did say that he is a good father, so I don't suppose there is much you can do about the drinking. I guess you have to take the bad with the good. It sounds like you have a beautiful house and I hope one day I will get to see it. It sounds like heaven to have a room of your own.

Forever your friend,
Jeannie

CHAPTER THIRTY-FIVE

1882–1883

OVER THE WINTER Farwell had promised me a visit to see my family, but by summer I was pregnant again, and for the first time I felt too ill to travel. I couldn't stop thinking of Jeannie and how sick she had felt when she carried her two babies who died.

In late September, the moon when plums fall, Red Fox came again to see us. I was so happy to see him that I greeted him with tears. Soon enough we were setting up his government-issued canvas tipi close to my own where I and the children had been living over the summer.

Weeks later, when an early snow fell, I was overjoyed when he agreed to stay for the winter. As the cold weather descended, Farwell insisted that I move back to the house, but Red Fox would not join us there. I gifted Grandfather with the last two buffalo hides that Farwell and I had stored, and with the children's help, we spread the pelts up the sides of his lodge to better insulate his tipi against the cold. For extra warmth I draped thick gray wolf pelts over each of his backrests.

Even on the stormiest of winter evenings, while Farwell and his ranch hands drank and played cards in the bunkhouse, the children and I tramped down through the snow to visit Red Fox. When we grew close to his lodge and smelled the smoke curling from his tipi into the dark night, Bud would wriggle from my arms and run to take hold of his sister's hand. Coming up on two snows, my son was a healthy child, but he was not as outgoing as Susie, and he always looked for her to take the lead.

"Grandfather. We're here for a story," Susie would call, and both children giggled in delight when Red Fox peeked out from his door. "Did I hear someone call for me?" he asked, pretending not to see them. "Here, Grandfather, we brought you something to eat," they would offer, and then giggle again when he declared his surprise that they were old enough to cook.

He told us stories, those evenings, stories of the Old Woman's Grandchild or Old Man Coyote—the same stories my grandmother had once told me.

Each night he began with, "*Aikeeh*!" "Attention!"

"*Éeh*!" we all answered with great enthusiasm, and then the stories began.

I loved those evenings as much as the children did, and as we snuggled there, I breathed in the pungent scent of the buffalo rugs and listened again to the familiar spit of the night fire. How comforting his lodge was in comparison to the log house that felt so large and empty.

WHEN STILLER VISITED again, I took the children with me to stay in the bedroom until he left, but the next day Farwell came to me to discuss sending Susie to a reservation school.

"No," I said. "Why do you listen to that Sam Stiller? I will not send her away. She is only six snows. She needs to be with me."

"This has nothing to do with Stiller," Farwell argued. "I want my daughter to be educated."

"She knows enough. You teach her all the time and you can keep doing that. She can already read and write and do numbers. If she goes away, how will she learn to cook and take care of a lodge? No, Farwell. She's staying here with me." And maybe because I was pregnant and was sick so much of the time, Farwell dropped the subject. But now I was afraid.

One crisp morning, toward the end of winter, I went down alone to visit Red Fox. After Grandfather put another log on the fire, he waved me over to a lean-back and then waited as I gathered my courage to speak.

"Grandfather," I finally said, "I am troubled."

"Yes?"

"It is about the children," I said, fighting back tears.

He nodded for me to continue.

"I'm worried that Farwell will send Susie to a government school. They would keep her there and try to make her into a Yellow Eyes."

"Yes, I know of the schools," he said. "They've built a wall around the one that they have by the agency so the parents and the relatives of the children can't see in and the children won't cry when they see their families."

"Farwell thinks the school would be good for her. He said she would like it there."

Grandfather shook his head. "It is not a good place. Last year they took my friend Sitting Hawk's only grandson away from her and put him in the school. When she learned he was growing sick from their food, she camped outside and cooked for him and then passed him the food under the fence. But the agents found out, and when she would not leave, they took the boy away to another school. At the new school, the boy got sick and went to the Other Side Camp. Ever since Sitting Hawk came back from the mountains where she went to grieve, she has not been the same." He shook his head again. "Why would Farwell put Susie in a place like that where children die?"

"He said that at the school they will teach her how to become more like a Yellow Eyes. But I don't want that. The Yellow Eyes—their word is no good. They say one thing and then do another. I saw what happened at those trials. They talked about justice for the Nakoda, but it was only words. I don't trust them."

"Your husband is a Yellow Eyes. Do you not trust his words?" he asked.

"I do when he isn't drinking, but now I don't know. He drinks almost every night."

Grandfather nodded. He already knew this. "What did you say to him about taking Susie to the school?"

"I told him that if he would ever mention it again, I would take the children and go to live next to my father's lodge."

Red Fox shook his head. "That won't work. You must convince your husband not to send them away, and you must stay here where you have plenty of food and shelter for your children. Many of the Crow people no longer have that. If their children are taken to the agency school and the parents go to the school to demand their release, they are told that they must go home or they will not get any of the government food or clothing. There is little game to hunt, and many families rely on the food that the agents give them to eat, so they leave brokenhearted and without their children."

"There is a man, a big man, by the name of Sam Stiller," I said.

Grandfather's head swung sharply toward me. "Yes! An agent. He is one who takes children." He paused and his troubled look frightened me. "Granddaughter, how do you know of this man?"

"It is almost ten snows since I stopped him . . . while he was . . . using a woman." I shuddered at the memory.

Grandfather stared at me. "You stopped him?"

"Yes. I hit him over the head with my gun and knocked him out so I could take the woman away."

"Did you get her away?" Grandfather asked.

"I did," I said.

His look was one of pride. "You are brave, Goes First. You carry your grandmother's blood," he said. "But you must be careful. This is a bad man to have as an enemy."

RED FOX LEFT when the snow began to melt, but he promised to return with help before the birth of my child. By the end of June, I began to worry that he might not arrive in time. My baby felt ready to come, and as I prepared my birthing lodge, I began to instruct Susie, who, now seven years old, would already be of help to me if no one else came.

Just in time, Grandfather arrived, and this time he brought my father's wife, Strikes the Hat, and her young daughter, Pretty Coyote. My small sister was already six years old, and Susie was thrilled to have her as a playmate. At first Strikes the Hat was shy with me, but we had no time for that because my baby came right away. It was an easy birth because the infant was so small, but she looked so unlike the other two that I found it hard to believe she was mine.

"Her arms are so small, Mama, and her face is wrinkled like a grandfather," Susie said.

As Farwell knelt beside my pallet, he gave a start when I pulled the blanket back. "She's skinny as a baby squirrel!" he said. Still tired from the birth, I took it as an insult and looked away. He took hold of my chin and turned my face to his.

"Don't worry, Mary, she'll fatten up in time." I couldn't escape the sour smell of whiskey on his breath when he kissed me. "We'll call her Ella," he announced.

"Ella? Why Ella?" I asked.

"Always liked that name," he said.

"But I wanted Grandfather to name her," I objected.

"I name my children," he said as he rose unsteadily to his feet, "and I don't want my kids to have Indian names. Her name's Ella."

By now I knew not to argue with Farwell when he had been drinking, and I was happy to see him go.

The baby was frail and nursed poorly, and I was having difficulty getting my milk to come in. I was frustrated and scared and when I began to cry, Strikes the Hat came and took the baby. My new young mother was kind and reassuring, and a short while later she offered me a drink. "Here, sip this. It's milkweed and it will help," she said. And she was right. A few hours after I drank the green drink, I was producing milk, though it wasn't until days later that I grew more confident that my baby would live.

I had been unwell for much of my pregnancy, and now my recovery from childbirth was slow. I couldn't help wondering if my health and my baby's poor start had anything to do with my growing unhappiness with Farwell.

My relatives stayed with us for five weeks, until Ella and I were both stronger. The night before they left, Farwell joined us where we sat outside our lodge enjoying the warm summer evening. Sipping a cup of whiskey, Farwell began to question my grandfather. I was relieved that I would be translating. This wouldn't be the first time I might have to soften words.

"Red Fox, I don't understand your people." Farwell started in. "Can't they see that their old way isn't working for them? Why won't they settle on a piece of property and make it their own? The government is even willing to give them some cattle so they could start to ranch. Why the hell won't they do it?"

I took a minute and then said to my grandfather in Crow, "My husband says he would like to understand our people better. He wants to know why we refuse to farm and why we won't settle on one piece of earth."

Grandfather listened to my translation, and when I finished, he spoke slowly and carefully, as though explaining something to a child. "You know that the Crow have always set our lodges close to one another in our camp. We have relatives all around to help us celebrate a birth or a successful raid. We have friends to help us when trouble comes. We work together as a family should—like we just did for your wife. We do not care to settle alone on one small piece of land, and then drink whiskey for companionship."

I turned to my husband. "My grandfather says we . . . like to live close by in case we need each other."

"But they need to start raising cattle or they'll all starve!" Farwell's voice rose in anger, and he was already starting to slur his words. "Don' they understand? They'll starve."

I heard the concern veiled in my husband's anger, but Red Fox didn't need a translation. He had heard enough, and he stood up, walked to his tipi, and did not return to the fire that night.

The next morning, as Strikes the Hat and Red Fox prepared to leave, Farwell came with four fine horses laden with blankets and food. It was the Crow way to thank relatives with gifts when they gave their help, but Farwell had brought extra, and I guessed he felt bad for his behavior the night before. It pleased me to see that our gifts were accepted, and I hoped my husband would be forgiven.

Farwell stood beside me when we waved goodbye. I had Ella in my arms, so Susie had to catch hold of Bud when he realized they were leaving. "No, don't go, Fa-Fa," he cried, plaintively reaching his arms out for Red Fox.

"Come here, Bud," Farwell said and, in an effort to soothe him, he took his two-year-old son in his arms. But Bud didn't want his father and began to kick until Farwell set him down.

As Red Fox turned his horse away, Bud ran to his sister, and when he leaned against her legs and bawled, she tried to comfort him. Again, Farwell reached for his son, but Susie, holding back tears of her own, pushed him away. "Leave him be, Papa," she said, "Bud doesn't like you."

Farwell looked stricken by Bud's rejection and Susie's words.

"It's your damn whiskey," I said, and walked away.

FARWELL SLEPT UP at the house that night, and late the next afternoon, Burt came down to get me. "Abe's not feeling well," he said, "and he's asking for you."

I had never known Farwell to be sick enough to be in bed during the day, and when I came through the doorway of the bedroom, he reached out a hand that was damp and trembling. "Mary," he said. "I'm going to stop drinking. I've done it before. But I'll be sick. Just don't leave me alone."

Over the next days he was as sick a man as I had ever seen. It was frightening to see him shake and vomit the way he did, and through it all he begged me to stay with him.

Burt stepped in to help with both Farwell and the children, and between the two of us we worked to keep the sour smell out of the room and my husband clean and dry. At times Farwell's whole body shook, his teeth chattering, and on the second day, when the shaking was especially strong, I was startled to hear Burt ask Farwell if he would like a drink of whiskey. "Just one shot and no more after that," Burt said. "It will make it easier on you."

"No," my husband said. "I've got to quit the damn stuff. Don't give me any now. I can make it through." The vomiting and the tremors left him weak and exhausted, but by the third day he was drinking broth, and by the end of the week he insisted on getting back to work.

"All he did was stop drinking. Why did he get so sick?" I asked Burt when the two of us, butchering a deer, saw Farwell sitting by the corral. He looked pale and exhausted after repairing a wagon wheel.

"He had two years of solid boozing. We're just lucky it wasn't worse."

In the early days of Farwell's recovery, he was more caring toward me than he had been in years, but once he was stronger and back at work, and especially in the evenings when the ranch hands were drinking, he grew restless and argumentative.

I had convinced him to spend the nights with me down in my tipi, where I was determined to keep my family until the snow came. Both Farwell and the children needed the fresh air, and here I felt the baby and I would grow stronger in the open arms of Mother Earth.

The two of us talked more now, and I did my best to listen and to be patient. Over the time when Farwell was getting sober, Burt had told me of conversations that they had had, where my husband spoke of the shame he felt knowing that in all the towns from here to Fort Benton, he was thought of as a traitor and a liar. He hated that the Nakoda had never gotten justice, and he was frustrated, too, to see what was happening to the Crow way of life. He couldn't understand why they refused to take the offer of cattle from the government and to set up a farm like his.

One night he had that conversation with me as well. "Why don't they understand that they will have to learn how to live like white people? It is the only way for them to survive."

I listened as patiently as I could, but after a day of caring for the children and still recovering from Ella's birth, I couldn't hold my tongue. "The only way? Do you still think that the white man's way is the best way? Why, then, are all the men you said would be served justice out there telling lies about you?"

I was sorry as soon as I said it, and after he walked out into the night, I was worried that he'd go for a drink. When he finally returned, I was so relieved to see him sober that I ran to him. "I'm sorry," I said, and when I kissed him, he returned my kiss.

"Oh, Mary," he said, after we pulled apart, "I'm the one who's sorry. I don't know what to think anymore. It's all such a mess."

The air was warm that night, and after I pulled a pallet out from the lodge, we lay together under the stars. When we kissed again, his mouth was free of the taste of whiskey, and though my body had not yet fully returned to itself after the birth of Ella, I set those concerns aside as we began to make love. It felt so reassuring to be in his arms again, but for some reason Farwell couldn't respond. I did my best to encourage him, but he soon lay back with a sigh. "It's no good," he said.

"What's wrong?" I asked, confused.

"Nothing," he said, and stood to take the pallet back into the lodge. I followed, but didn't speak because the children were asleep. Farwell avoided looking at me, so after I checked on the baby, I lay down beside him on our pallet. "Is it because I . . . ?" I whispered.

"Got nothing to do with you," he said, his voice gruff, and I wondered if he was telling the truth.

We tried again in the following nights, but each time Farwell was unable to respond he grew more irritable. Finally, we stopped trying. I wanted to talk to him, to understand what was wrong, but I was afraid that I might learn he was no longer attracted to me. My body was not the same after three children, and maybe this last birth had ruined something for him.

I didn't know what to do. I missed our lovemaking, and I was sure that Farwell did, too. It had always healed past differences and brought us closer together. Now, it seemed, we had little to hold on to.

WITH THE FIRST dusting of snow, I began to prepare for the winter move back up to the cabin, as I had promised Farwell. I was in my tipi packing things up when Susie came running, her little brother in tow. "That man is here again," she said. "He's talking to Papa."

"Which man?" I asked, though I'd already guessed.

"That big one with the big horse. The one who said he was going to take me away to school. I don't want to go with him, Mama."

Bud clung to my skirt as he stared at his sister, whose eyes were large with fear.

"It will be all right," I said to Susie. "Papa won't let him take you."

I felt confident in saying this, since Farwell and I had again recently discussed the idea of school. I had told him about Red Fox's stories, and especially the one about his friend Sitting Hawk and the loss of her grandson.

"Listen, Mary," he said. "I'm sure the stories are exaggerated, but if you feel this strongly, then we'll keep Susie here for now and decide when she's older."

"But what if they just come and take her? That's what Red Fox said they often do."

"Stiller wouldn't touch her without my say-so," he said.

But I didn't trust Stiller, and now I attached a gun to my belt. "You stay down here, Susie, and take care of the little ones. Ella should stay sleeping, and make sure you keep Bud back from the fire." She nodded, and I left the three of them safely inside the tipi while I went up to the house.

When I came in through the kitchen door, the two men seated at the long pine table in the next room didn't notice me. I watched as Farwell lifted the pot of coffee and poured some of the steaming liquid for each of them.

Stiller sat back, taking in the adjoining rooms with the large windows and the honey-colored pine furniture that my husband had built. "You sure got yourself a nice setup here, Abe," Stiller said. "I guess every man dreams of owning a place like this."

"Well, Mary actually owns the land," Farwell said, pouring a cup of the coffee for himself.

"So it's not in your name?"

"No, it came through a land deal with the Crow."

As Farwell set the tin coffee pot down on the table, Stiller pulled a flask from his jacket. Farwell saw the flask and raised a hand. "I'm off the stuff," he said, but Stiller leaned the whiskey toward my husband's cup.

"Oh, come on. You say that every time I see you," Stiller said as he poured.

"No!" I called out as I rushed forward, but my foot caught on the edge of the cowhide that covered the wood floor, and I went sprawling into the room. "Mary," Farwell said as he jumped to his feet.

All I could think of was the whiskey in his coffee as he helped me up. "Don't drink it," I pleaded. I got to my feet, my left knee skinned from the fall.

Stiller smirked. "Well, if don't that beat all. Abe Farwell's squaw telling him what to do."

Farwell's face went red at his friend's words, but I turned on Stiller. "You get out."

The large man gave me a look of surprise before he raised his eyebrows and looked to Farwell.

"Mary, calm down," Farwell said. "Stiller's here on business. He came to buy cattle." He turned to Stiller. "I don't know what got into her," he apologized, and took hold of my arm as he led me to the door. "Go down to the lodge and stay there until I come."

I left, not because I was directed to, but because I was afraid that if I stayed, I might use my gun.

I waited for Farwell to come down to the lodge that night, and when he didn't, I sat outside the lodge and cried. I knew that he was drinking again.

CHAPTER THIRTY-SIX

1886–1887

BUD WAS BESIDE himself when he saw the horses coming over the hill. "Grandfather's coming!" he shouted as he ran to greet him. And sure enough, it was Red Fox. But it was another rider, my brother, who rode over, reached down, grabbed Bud's arm, and lifted my little boy up atop his horse. Bud, at five snows, usually kept his feelings to himself, but this day he waved and laughed aloud as Strong Bull's shining bay trotted toward us, kicking up the yellow autumn leaves that surrounded our ranch. "Look, Mama, look!" Bud called as my heart sang.

It was the fall of 1886, and it had been four long snows since I had last seen my brother. Every year I planned a visit to see my family, but as each season slipped away, Farwell always had an excuse to keep me from going. I had wanted to take the three children on my own, and I tried to reason with Farwell when he wasn't drinking, but drunk or sober, he wouldn't hear of my taking the children for two days of travel on horseback.

Fortunately, Red Fox visited us every few months and always brought news of my family, but Strong Bull had not returned since the time Farwell had refused his gift of the horses. Now, to my delight, my grown brother had arrived, and with him were two of his friends. With Bud in his arms, Strong Bull dismounted, and at twenty snows, he was a commanding presence. Tall and powerfully built, he carried himself with the sureness of one who knew his strength and purpose. Surely, I thought, my brother was destined to be a great chief.

For this visit, the three young braves had shed the government-issued long pants and shirts and instead were shirtless and wore traditional breechcloths with colorfully beaded hip-high leggings and moccasins. None had cut their hair as the government agents wanted, but wore it as my father had always done, with a front section cut short and stiffened with mud, while long braids hung down on either side. The young men were beautiful, and my eyes misted when I remembered Big Cloud.

Strong Bull soon presented gifts to the children. "Look, Mama!" Susie's eyes grew wide when she unsheathed the sharp blade of the deer-bone-handled knife, and I gave my brother a grateful smile. I was around Susie's age of ten snows when Red Fox had given me mine, and now, at thirty snows, it still hung from my belt. Bud looked with awe at his bow and quiver, filled with blunt arrows. "Look! It's my size!" he said, slipping it over his shoulder.

Once again, honoring our Crow tradition, I did not address Strong Bull but turned to Red Fox with my question. "Grandfather, please tell my brother and his friends how welcome they are. I am especially happy to see them clothed as Crow braves."

The young men all straightened in pride, and Strong Bull responded through Red Fox. "Tell my sister that we always shed those clothes whenever we are out of sight of government agents."

"What happens if they find you dressed as a Crow?" I asked, forgetting to speak through Red Fox.

One of the other young men answered. "They'll withhold food from our families or even put us in jail."

"In jail? For dressing in the clothes you have worn all your life?"

"*Éeh*," they agreed.

"They are fools enough to believe that if they can get us to discard our clothing, they can get us to discard our ways," Strong Bull said. He spoke to Grandfather. "Please tell my sister that we have come to speak with her husband."

I nodded. "I will get him, but we will also feast," I said, and sent Susie to tell Burt to slaughter a cow.

Burt, Susie, and I roasted beef ribs to celebrate my brother's arrival. To sweeten the meal, I made some fry bread and a Juneberry pudding, and I was not disappointed when the young men feasted on all these familiar Crow dishes. After they ate, Farwell asked me to come sit next to him by the fire outside my lodge so I might interpret what the young men had to say. "But first," he said, pulling a small bottle of whiskey from his jacket, "let's have some of this."

None of the Crow accepted. Farwell looked surprised at their refusal, but then took a long pull before he set the bottle down. I caught Strong Bull's glance of disapproval and then saw his friends exchange the same look. In response, Farwell took another long drink. "So what are those scars on your chest?" he asked my brother.

I, too, had seen the angry-looking scars, but I knew what they meant, and I wasn't surprised when Strong Bull hesitated in answering this question. My brother glanced at his comrades, and only after nods of agreement from each one did he speak.

"We were invited by the neighboring Cheyenne to a Sun Dance," he said.

"Isn't that one of those things that've been outlawed, that dance?"

"It is a sacred ceremony."

"But those scars?" Farwell asked again.

Strong Bull paused. My brother was wise and kept the explanation simple. "I will tell you only what the white man needs to know. The Sun Dance is a chance to pray to the Creator for blessings. We pierce our muscles in our chest and pull rawhide strings through. After the strings are tied to a pole, we lean back until they break through our flesh and we are set free. We endure this pain to earn blessings."

Farwell took in a deep breath as he looked again at Strong Bull's chest. "I don't know that I could do that," he said.

"Not all men can," I answered quietly. My pride in my brother was great.

"The agents have brought in a priest and others who tell us our beliefs are wrong," my brother continued. "But if it becomes necessary, we will fight for them. There are about a hundred of us who will stand against the agents if we are challenged."

"A *hundred*?" Farwell shook his head. "If you start something, they'll bring in an army of many hundreds to put you down."

Strong Bull straightened his shoulders. "Then we will fight like many warriors."

"They'll kill you all!" Farwell's alarm worried me, but I remembered the battle of Arrow Creek and how badly we were outnumbered. We had won, and so it would be if it became necessary for my brother to fight.

"We are strong, we are brave, and we will live a long time," I said in Crow, and I glanced at my brother just long enough to see the slight smile cross his face when he recognized the words of the lullaby I used to sing to him.

Strong Bull spoke again. "I have come because you are my sister's husband. This year again, they've moved us another one hundred and thirty miles to the east. They say they want us to have a better place for farming, but we know that the Yellow Eyes just wanted to take more of our land. Some of our old men are becoming soft. They are giving up. But we three stand with those who are ready to fight. We have had enough, and we want back our old way of living. Will you help us?"

"What do you want from me?" Farwell asked.

"We will need guns."

Yes! I wanted to shout. *Yes. I will come and take a stand with you! You are right not to believe the Yellow Eyes, for they say one thing and then they do another.* But I did not say those words aloud. They were not for me to say, as Strong Bull had put this question to my husband.

Farwell took a long swallow from his bottle before he asked, "What does Horse Guard say about this?"

"Father will not farm, and he wants to keep the old way just as we do. But he cautions us against fighting."

Farwell drank again and wiped his mouth with the back of his hand. "Your father is right. I can't give you any guns. And I warn you, if you try to fight back, they'll bring in the military and kill all of you."

Strong Bull's face hardened. "They are killing us now. Game is scarce and we are limited in where we can travel, so the men cannot hunt as they once did and the women cannot harvest our familiar food and medicine. What your government gives us to eat makes us sick, and our people are dying of white man's diseases—like my mother."

Suddenly, what was left of Farwell's patience was gone. "Look around you." He waved his arms toward the land. "Is it so terrible to live on a place like this and manage some cattle? You young ones are just going to have to get up off your duffs and start to learn how to farm. It's the only way that the Crow will survive!"

As I translated, I tried to soften Farwell's words, but his stern tone had already said too much. All three of the young men exchanged angry looks until, as one, they stood up and went for their horses.

I WAS HEARTBROKEN, as were the children, to see the men go. I hadn't seen my brother in years, and I knew what it had taken for him to come ask Farwell for help. Grandfather left with them, too, and since it was late fall, I was sure I wouldn't see him again until the spring.

After they were gone, I got the children settled in the tipi and then, still furious, I went up to find Farwell in the cabin. I didn't care that he was likely drunk. When I found him alone in the house sitting at the table, I was shaking with anger. "Why did you do that? Why didn't you offer to help Strong Bull?"

Farwell, drunk, grew maudlin. "Can't help him, Mary. If he tries to fight, they'll kill him." He stumbled to his feet and tried to embrace me.

"Stop," I said, pushing him away. I desperately needed him to act like a chief and help my brother. He came at me again and tried to take me in his arms. Furious, I slapped his face. It took both of us a minute to realize what I had done, and I braced myself for his retaliation. Instead, he turned and walked out into the night.

OUR MARRIAGE WAS crumbling, and I didn't know what to do. When the snow came I wanted to stay in my tipi, but for the children's sake, I moved us back into the house. After my brother's visit, Farwell drank more than ever, and though he often slept in the bunkhouse, one night he came to our bedroom and climbed on top of me. Disgusted at the whiskey smell coming off him, I pushed him away, but when he kept pawing at me, I shoved him hard and he fell off the bed.

For a drunk man, he was swift. Furious, he rose and pulled me from the bed. "Then get out and stay out," he slurred as he pushed me from the room. With little recourse, for the rest of the winter months, I slept on a pallet in the children's bedroom.

WHAT FOLLOWED WAS a long hard winter. Twice Farwell was so weak and sick from drink that he couldn't leave his bed. We had three hired men, none of whom I trusted to do their job, so the first time Farwell was down, I took over the care of the horses and had our herd of twenty-five pastured close to the barns where my children could help me see to them. Susie was almost eleven snows and was as skilled at handling horses as I was. Bud, though not yet six, helped as well, carrying water and hay, so while Burt looked out for Ella, the two older children and I made certain that the horses stayed in good shape.

Surprisingly, Farwell did not object to my taking over the care of the horses, and even after he was well and working again, he wanted me to continue. He did, however, object to what he called my "interference with the cattle" and harshly told me that I was to let the hired men see to them. At that time, we still had about seventy head of cattle out on the range, so I could only hope that the ranch hands would do their job when my husband was unable to do his.

Burt was now central to our family. There were days when he moved slow and I knew his hips were especially sore. He never complained, but those days I gave him a Crow remedy of milkweed with water, and after he drank it down, he said he had some relief. But it was the special attention he gave to Ella that I was most grateful for. My youngest daughter, at three, was still tiny and somewhat frail, and she grew to love Burt as she might have a father. Thanks to him, that winter we had fun as well, when in the long, snow-bound evenings, Burt taught us how to play card games. He read to us, too, and had Susie do the same. Even Farwell sat in some evenings to listen to the two of them bring alive the stories of *Robinson Crusoe* and *David*

Copperfield, two books Burt treasured and kept in his room off the kitchen.

But it was also Burt who cleaned up after Farwell and at times put him to bed at night, so in the morning the children were spared from seeing their father sprawled out in his own vomit.

WITH SPRING'S ARRIVAL, I waited for Red Fox to return. I moved us out to my tipi again, and in spite of his difficulty walking, Burt helped carry some of my supplies down the hill. "Thank you for helping us," I told him. "I don't think too many would stick around for this mess."

"I had a son who died of the drink, and I always wondered if I could've done more. I keep hoping that Abe will stop. Besides, I have nowhere else to go." He gave a crooked smile. "I think it's good if you still bring the little ones up for breakfast. Maybe it will remind your husband that he has a family depending on him," Burt said.

Most mornings we did see Farwell when I brought the children up for their usual favorite meal of pancakes and syrup. Generally, that early in the morning he had not yet been drinking, and though he was more or less dismissive of me, he always paid attention to Susie and occasionally to Bud, though he completely ignored little Ella. It was as though he didn't claim her, and because she never had had his attention, she didn't look for it. Burt, though, continued to favor Ella, and the two of them had a close bond. Susie remained loyal to her father and relished any time with him that he gave her. I generally allowed her to do as she liked, but one morning, after I saw that Farwell was already unsteady on his feet, I stopped her as she prepared to go out to check fences with him.

"I don't want you to go with your papa today," I said.

"Why?" she demanded.

"Because he is drunk. He could fall off his horse, and then you'd be stuck alone with him, and his horse is not easy to handle."

"I'm good with horses," she argued.

"I don't care," I said. "I don't want you going out with him today."

"You just want to see him dead!" she said, turning her back on me in anger.

"Why would you say something like that?" I snapped back.

She swung toward me, her eyes full of tears. "Because he said that's what you want. He said that you want to take us and go live with the Crow and he won't let you. He said he'd shoot you before he'd let you go."

I stared at her. How could Farwell have known? I had only recently begun to think that when Red Fox returned, I would talk to him again about moving back to Father's village.

"Mama?" Susie grew alarmed at my silence. "Do you think he ever would? Would he ever shoot you?"

"No, Susie," I said, trying to quiet my voice and reassure us both. "That's just his talk when he gets drunk."

ALL SUMMER, AS I waited for Red Fox to come, I wrestled with what to do. I was already thirty-one years old, and the only hope I saw for myself and my children was to leave my marriage. Farwell had broken every promise he had made not to drink again. Now I was worried that he wouldn't keep his promise not to send the children away to school.

I told myself that if I returned to my people, we would be safe. The children would have Red Fox, my father, and my brother as protectors. They would learn the old ways and we would be happy as a family. And so, I waited for Grandfather's return. But summer passed, and then fall, and with no word from Red Fox, each day I grew more worried about his well-being.

Finally, in mid-November, in the moon of the first frost, Grandfather arrived in the snow, half frozen, feverish, and with a deep cough. I was weak with relief that he had come, but he was so sick that I insisted he move into the house with us where I could better care for him. I set him up in the children's room, while they, always happy for a change, bunked in the living room. That first afternoon, Grandfather could only manage sips of liquid, but after he began to chew some Bear Root he began to breathe easier. The next morning I tempted him with a wild turnip porridge he liked, and finally his cough loosened enough for him to speak without choking.

"Oh, Grandfather, it is good to see you doing so well," I said later that morning when I returned to find him sitting up in bed. The children and I had just finished breakfast across from Farwell, who was surprisingly sober. Grandfather's face was still pale, but it was no longer flushed with fever. He motioned for me to close the door. "Come, sit with me, Goes First."

Frost covered the window, and outside the high winds churned the snow into a white frenzy. I was so relieved to have Grandfather here, safe with me in the cabin. The children were in high spirits, running through the house playing hide-and-seek. At four snows, Ella, though tiny, had a squeal that rivaled that of a frightened animal, and I didn't blame Red Fox for wanting the silence. After I closed the door, I pulled up a chair next to his bed.

He smoothed the bedclothes as though gathering his thoughts. "I have something to say," he said. Then he paused for so long that I grew alarmed.

"Does it have something to do with our family? Is it Father?" I finally asked. When Strong Bull last visited, he mentioned more than once that my father was aging.

"No, Goes First," he said, "I have news about your brother."

"What? What is it?"

"Your brother is a true warrior."

"Yes," I said. I settled back into my chair, full of pride, and ready to hear what he had done.

"He wasn't alone. He and his friends joined a group of young men under the leadership of a Crow brave by the name of Sword Bearer. After the Blackfoot stole some of our tribe's horses, these young braves, encouraged by a number of the elders, retaliated and were successful, not only in getting their horses back, but in stealing some horses from the Blackfoot."

"Good for them," I said.

"On their return, they acted as their fathers had always done when they came back from a successful raid. They drove their horses through the camp, shouting out their victory, and shooting their guns in the air."

"I remember times like that," I said, recalling the thrill of Big Cloud lifting me onto his horse as we triumphantly rode through the village. How happy I was to know that Strong Bull had experienced this. I only wished I had been there.

"But the government agent at the Crow Agency, Henry Williamson, a man who understands nothing about the Crow, grew alarmed with what he called 'an uprising' and sent for the army."

My heart thumped hard against my chest.

"It happened as Farwell said it would. The army came and brought cannons and guns. What were our young warriors to do but to take a stand and fight for the right to live as their fathers and grandfathers had always done? Only one from the white man's army died, but Sword Bearer and your brother left for the Other Side Camp. The others were rounded up and taken to prison."

I stared at Grandfather, unable to take this in.

"He fought like a warrior, Goes First. He was a true brave. Surely he would have been a great chief for our people."

"Please, Grandfather. Not Strong . . . not my brother." As my body received the words, I doubled over in pain. A wail escaped me, and I was struggling to breathe when the door flew open and the three children rushed in.

Ella threw her arms around my shoulders and Bud and Susie took my hands. "Mama?" Ella cried. "Mama! What's wrong?" But I couldn't answer.

Red Fox called the children to him. "Come. Come, sit with me," he encouraged all three. "Your mother must take some time to grieve," he said as I stumbled from the room. "Her warrior brother left for the Other Side Camp."

THE NEWS SHATTERED me. I was in my lodge on my knees. I knew one way to survive this pain, and blood dripped from the gashes I had made along my left arm. I was about to do the same with the other, when Farwell rushed in. "Stop!" he said, and grabbed the knife away.

"My brother . . . ," was all I was able to say.

"I know. Red Fox told me." Farwell tore a piece of an old shirt of mine and then knelt beside me to wrap my bleeding arm. "Oh, Mary," he said, and tried to take me in his arms. But I pulled away, unable to take comfort from him. He sat back, shivering. "It's too damn cold in here," he said. "I'm going to get a fire started." When the fire was blazing, he sighed and then came to sit beside me.

"They killed him," I said, disbelieving my own words.

Farwell was quiet as he studied me. "Look, Mary. There's going to be more of this if the Indians don't start to understand what they're up against."

My mouth filled with a bitter taste. "Why don't the Yellow Eyes try to understand us? We have a right to our own beliefs."

"You think any white person is going to understand you cutting yourself like this? If it's too much for me to understand, what will others think?" Again, he tried to put his arms around me, but this time I was more forceful when I pushed him away and he fell back.

His voice was cold as he got to his feet. "I want you up in the house by tonight. Just make sure you get your arm cleaned up and pull yourself together before the kids see you. You don't want them to go to school, yet this is what you teach them? I won't have my children learning to behave like this."

CHAPTER THIRTY-SEVEN

1889

AFTER MY BROTHER'S death, I gave up on the idea of leaving Farwell. Tensions were high at the Crow Agency, and I knew that for the safety of the children we must remain here at the ranch. However, that summer, with or without Farwell's permission, I decided I would at least take them to visit my father and Red Fox. The children were old enough for the trip—this month Ella was already six snows—and they all were in good health, so I waited for a time when Farwell was sober enough to tell him of our plans.

I chose an early morning in June, the moon when the katydids sing. Farwell was still at the table, though he had already finished his meal when I arrived with the children. His eyes were puffy and his skin had a yellowish tinge, but I didn't smell whiskey in the coffee he was drinking. Burt brought in the pancakes and as Susie helped the younger two, I began to explain about the trip while Farwell sat back and listened.

"It'll take us a few days of travel to get there, and I'll need to take the wagon to bring my family some—"

"You aren't going anywhere. I need you all here to take care of the horses."

It was true that I and the children were now responsible for the horses.

"The herd is in good condition," I said. "I have to see Father. He's already sixty-five snows. Before Red Fox left, he told me Father's health is bad and that my brother's death was hard on him."

"Go then, but the children stay here with me."

Burt poured Farwell some fresh coffee. "I could help you out while they're away," Burt offered.

"They're staying here," Farwell answered, and with a glance of sympathy toward me, Burt shuffled back to the kitchen.

Farwell then turned on me. "You think I don't know what you are trying to do? Do you think I don't know that you wouldn't come back? Well, you go ahead, but the kids stay here with me. They're mine. In any court of law, I have the legal rights to them. And I'll tell you this. They'll never be living with a bunch of people who refuse to learn how to take care of themselves."

Susie was the only one who dared speak. "Mama, were you going to keep us there?"

"No," I said, and I spoke the truth, though I wasn't sure if my daughter believed me. At thirteen snows, Susie was beginning to question everything I did. Or had she guessed that I had confided in Red Fox about leaving Farwell? But I had heard Grandfather's advice when he had cautioned me. "Keep the children here where they are safe from disease and have plenty to eat. And as long as they have Farwell, they will not be taken to the schools."

We all got up from the table except for Susie. "I'm going to stay with Papa and help him out today," she said. There was little I could do about that, though I knew that Farwell would surely be drunk by noon. I looked at this husband I had once loved so much. I couldn't remember the last time I had seen him smile. His face was drawn, his blue eyes were dull, and he looked tired and mean. We had three healthy children, one as dear as the next, and yet he kept choosing whiskey over his family. Bud and Ella had never known him as a caring father, and though Susie was loyal to him, she was often confused and frightened when he was sick. If he didn't stop drinking, I saw what was coming. And what would happen if Farwell died? He was all that stood between Stiller and my children.

❀ ❀ ❀

THAT SUMMER WAS hot and dry, and one scorching afternoon, Susie and Bud came into the house looking for Ella.

The two of us were at the pine table, where I was teaching my youngest daughter to bead a shirt as my mother had taught me. More so than Susie, Ella loved detailed handwork such as this, but she set it down quickly, excited to learn that Farwell had told the children they could spend the afternoon swimming, down by the river. It was a distance away, and though they had already been once this summer, I was surprised that he was letting them go again, as he generally wanted the children to stay close to home. I guessed he felt guilty that he had disappointed them by not allowing them to take a trip with me.

"Is Papa going with you?" I asked.

"No, but he said we should take the wagon," Susie said, and I looked through the open door to see Farwell up by the corral, hitching up the small wagon.

"Why not take your horses?" I asked.

"Papa said that in this heat we should only take one horse. We're to make sure we put him in the shade, but I already knew that. He wants us to go back to that swimming hole on the Clark's Fork," she said, "so he knows where we are."

Ella, who loved to swim, clapped her hands. "Mama, you come with us so I can show you how good I can swim?"

Bud answered her. "No, Ella. Papa said that Mama's staying here to keep an eye on that mare in the corral. Marco went into town, and Papa has to go out to check on the cattle."

Ella looked at me and I nodded reluctantly. It was true. There was a mare that I was watching who was about to foal, though I guessed she still had a day or two. I might have gone, but I didn't want to start an argument with Farwell to spoil the children's day.

"But I want you to come," Ella said, hugging me around my waist.

"Next time I will," I promised. We all hated to disappoint Ella. She was still tiny for her age, but Ella's ways were so gentle and sweet that we all doted on her.

I walked with the children to where Farwell had the horse and wagon tied up by the corral.

"Papa, aren't you going to say goodbye?" Susie called out to Farwell, who was already atop his own horse and about to ride away. He was still sitting his horse all right, but I could tell from the way he spoke that he wasn't sober.

"Things to do, Susie girl," he said. "Need to get out to that far field to check the cattle."

He looked toward the corral and would not meet my eye, so I knew he felt guilty for having me stay back. "Mary, you keep an eye on that mare. I'll be gone all day, but Marco should be back from town soon if you need help."

I didn't reply. Marco, our last remaining ranch hand, was useless, except for his visits to town when he supplied Farwell with his whiskey. Later, the two would have plenty to drink, and I could be sure that Farwell, too, would be unavailable if I needed him when the mare was ready to foal.

As Farwell rode off, Susie exchanged a knowing look with me, but I held my tongue against her father. "Do you need me to stay?" she asked, knowing that if the mare had problems I would be on my own.

"No, I don't think she'll foal for another day or so," I said. "You go ahead and have a good time. But stay near the riverbank. No going in over your heads!"

"We won't, Mama." Ella took her seat between her brother and sister. "Bye-bye, Mama," she waved, tipping back the brim of one of Susie's treasured hats.

"Make sure you two watch out for Ella," I said to Bud as I handed over a basket of bread and cheese and some small apple pies that Burt had quickly packed for them. "If the water is high enough, that current can be strong."

"Don't worry, Mama," Bud said. "We'll look out for her." Bud tossed his long hair from his face and gave me a rare smile. How proud I was of my son. At eight snows, he was not a warrior like my brother or my father. He was more like Red Fox—wise and steady, and a quiet observer. "Come on, Rex," he encouraged their faithful dog to leap into the wagon box.

"Don't let him get into the food," I said as Rex sniffed the basket.

"See you later, Mama," Susie said, and gave me a smile as she snapped the reins against the horse's flank and the wagon pulled away.

I WAS SITTING at the yellow pine table and beading new moccasins for Bud. From where I sat, I could see some of the horses in the corral, and I enjoyed the occasional breeze that blew in through the open door. When I heard a cry, I dropped a string of blue beads, and as they rolled across the floor, I tried not to slip on them as I rushed to the door. There I saw Ella running through the tall grass, and I ran out to meet her.

"They shot . . ." Her body heaved as she struggled to speak.

"What?"

"They shot Rexy . . ."

"Who did?" I fought to stay calm. "Where's Susie and Bud?"

"They took them! They took them!"

My heart slammed against my chest. "Who?" I asked, holding her back from me to look into her eyes. "Who took them?"

"That man. Those men who came with him."

"Which men?"

"Those men," she cried. "The big one that said he was going to take us to the school and two others. Bud tried to get to the wagon and . . . and Susie kicked at the man, so he tied her hands. Rexy started to bite, and . . . they, they sho . . ." Ella gasped. "They shot him," she sobbed.

"Ella! Where are Susie and Bud?"

She tried to gather herself. "They tied Bud's hands, too, before they put him on the horse. Susie yelled at me to swim across the river. I was scared but she kept yelling, 'Go, Ella! Go. You can do it. Swim across!' So I did, Mama, I did. I swam all the way across, but when I got to the other side, I looked back and they were gone. The men took them away on their horses."

My child was wet and shaking so hard that I carried her down to my lodge and tried to calm both of us as I dried her. Then I loaded my two revolvers.

"I'm going to leave you with Burt so I can go get them back," I said to Ella.

"No!" she shouted, clinging to me. "Don't leave me, Mama! Don't leave me."

Her cries were so desperate that I couldn't abandon her, so with my guns on my belt and the two of us astride our fastest gelding, I galloped for the river. Once there, the hoof prints were easy to see. I counted three horses, so I knew the agents had the children on their mounts. That might have slowed them, but if I were to follow, I couldn't shoot. My heart pounded against my chest when I saw that their trail led north toward Billings and the train station. My instinct was to race after them, but even if I caught up, what would I do? And would they then take Ella?

I needed Farwell. Drunk or not, he could get them back.

Rexy's body lay next to one of the rear wagon wheels, but I didn't take the time to pick him up. How I wished that the children had taken their horses—they would have had a better chance to escape. All three rode like the wind. As these thoughts came, so, too, did a fearful suspicion. Why *had* Farwell told them to take the wagon? They had never done that before.

I tried to reassure a weeping Ella, but my hands shook so badly that it was hard to hold on to both her and the reins as we galloped home.

I SAW FARWELL'S horse in the corral, and with Ella in hand I raced to the house. "Where's Farwell?" I called out to Burt.

"Out in the bunkhouse. Marco just got back with the supplies."

"Can you watch out for Ella while I go to see him?"

"Sure. Come here, Ella girl," he said, and scooped her up to sit her on the kitchen table.

"Why are you crying?" he asked her. "And where are the other two?"

"They took them . . . ," Ella whimpered, and I left, with no time to explain.

❀   ❀   ❀

I STARTLED BOTH of the men when I threw open the bunkhouse door. The place smelled of old boots and unwashed clothes and fresh whiskey.

"Quick. You have to come," I said to Farwell, who was stretched out on one of the bunks. "They took Susie and Bud."

"What about Ella?" Farwell asked as he sat up.

"What about Ella?" I repeated. What did he mean?

"Didn't they take her, too?" he asked.

His question almost knocked me to the floor. I put my hand on the wall of the bunkhouse to steady myself. "Did you know about this?" I asked.

But he didn't answer.

"You did?" I whispered.

He gave a slight nod.

My legs went weak and I sat on the nearest cot. He stood and poured more whiskey into his tin mug, then brought it over. "Here, drink some of this," he said, but I swung my arm at him and the cup flew. Marco wisely left the building.

I was finding it hard to breathe. Surely Farwell wouldn't betray me and the children like this? The thought of it sickened me.

"Come with me. We can still get them back!" I begged.

Farwell took a long drink from the open bottle as he moved away from me to sit. "They had to go, Mary. There's a law that says our kids have to go to school, and I knew you'd never agree to it. Stiller said this was the best way to do it."

"Then I'll go by myself and find Stiller and I'll get them back," I said.

"Forget about trying that. It won't work. I signed permission for the three of them to be taken out to that school in Pennsylvania, and as their father I have the legal say-so." He sighed before he went on. "I looked into that Carlisle school, and it's a good one. The guy Pratt who runs it has the same idea that I do. Indian kids need to learn how to live in the white man's world, and that's what he'll train them for. This is the best thing for both of them, and they'll be back in a few years with an education."

I stood, and as I moved toward him I unsheathed my knife. "How drunk were you when you signed the papers?"

Farwell stood as I stepped toward him, and he raised his hand as a warning. "Mary, you still have Ella. I'll let you keep her here. But something happens to me, you'll go to jail. Then they'll take her, too. Is that what you want?"

My whole body shook with rage, but I heard what he said and stopped myself. He was right. With him gone, what would keep Stiller from coming back for Ella?

"Those kids had to go, Mary. The law said so. You'll see in time that it's a good thing."

I was finding it hard to breathe, so I left then, still clutching my knife as I walked out the door.

CHAPTER THIRTY-EIGHT

1889

As fall approached, I waited again for Red Fox. Ella and I were living down in my lodge, and I never let her out of my sight. Burt kept us supplied with food, but one day when I saw we were running low on flour and salt, I decided to take Ella and go up to the house to get it myself.

I hadn't expected to see Farwell at the pine table sipping a cup of marrow broth. When he saw us come in through the kitchen door, he stood in greeting. "Hello, Ella," he called.

"Hello, Papa," she said, though she shrank against me.

"How you been, Mary?" he tried, but I had nothing to say.

Over the summer I had seen him only in passing when Ella and I cared for the horses, but looking at him now, this close up, I was shocked to see now how his clothes hung off his frame and that his thinning hair was almost white. His skin was a yellowish brown, and at fifty-one years, Farwell looked older than Red Fox, who was easily twenty snows beyond that number. I had been married to this man for seventeen years, and I no longer recognized him.

"Come in here," he asked, his voice meek. "Come and say hello."

"No," I said, and we left without any flour or salt.

Days later, I saw Stiller's horse in the corral, and when Burt came for me in the afternoon, I had both guns on my belt.

"You better come quick," he said. "They've been drinking, and Farwell's real sick this time. It's best you leave her here," he added, looking at Ella.

I handed him one of my guns and pointed to my rifle. "I'll go up, but you stay here with Ella and shoot if anyone tries to take her."

"She'll be safe," Burt promised.

When I reached the bunkhouse, Stiller was kneeling over Farwell, who lay on the floor. "C'mon, buddy," he was saying while trying to lift Farwell to his feet.

"Just leave him until it passes," I said, seeing Farwell's arms and legs jerk uncontrollably.

My enemy looked relieved when he saw me. "He's been like this for a while."

"It'll stop. It's happened before," I said.

After Farwell's body began to relax, I had Stiller lift him onto a cot, and he stood back while I cleaned the white spittle from my husband's mouth. As Farwell regained his senses, he looked about, dazed. When he recognized me, he grabbed hold of my hand. "Don't go, Mary," he begged. "Stay with me."

"I have to watch out for Ella," I said, glancing back at Stiller.

"I'm not here to take your kid. I just came to visit my friend," he said.

I would never trust Sam Stiller, but I trusted Burt to shoot if he had to, so I finished cleaning Farwell up. He was so weak and looked so done that after Stiller left, I sat down next to him and let him hold my hand. I knew he couldn't live long in this state. I hated him now, yet I pitied him, too.

Clinging to me, he'd close his eyes and nod off, only to wake again. Then he'd mumble my name and grip my hand tighter before falling back to sleep.

It was already dusk when I stepped out of the bunkhouse. Neither Ella nor I had eaten since morning, so I stopped at the house to see if Burt had some bread and jam that I could take down for an easy meal. I went in through the back door, and the first thing I saw on the kitchen table was a couple bottles of whiskey. Where had they come from? Either Stiller had left them or it was a new delivery that Marco had brought in.

I was ready to smash the bottles, when I heard a chair shuffle in the next room and then a cough. When I looked in, there was Stiller, seated in the shadows alongside the pine table.

"Mary . . . ," he said when he saw me. "How is he? I hope . . ."

"What do you want?" I asked, too drained from the day to be afraid.

"Come, sit for a minute. I want to talk is all," he said.

I leaned against the frame of kitchen door. "I can hear you from here."

"If I'd a known he was that bad off, I wouldn't have brought that whiskey."

When I didn't reply, he tried a new approach. "Listen, Mary, I've been thinking . . ."

I tensed up.

"You know I've got a score to settle with you, right? A man doesn't forget when a woman cracks him over the head and hog-ties him."

"And a woman doesn't forget seeing another woman being . . ."

"We were all drunk," he said, shifting in his chair.

"Drunk." I spit out the word and turned to leave.

"Look, how about you forget what I was doing, and I'll forget about you whopping me over the head."

"And then what?"

He smiled a crooked smile. "Come on, you know I've always had an eye for you. All I'm asking is that you be nice to me."

"Nice?"

"Have a drink with me? Then maybe we can get more friendly?"

"And then what?"

"Well, seeing Abe like this got me thinking. Fact is, it sobered me right up. It don't look to me as though he'll be around much longer, and I'm gettin' mighty tired of the agent job. I've always had a hankerin' for ranching—in fact I think I'd be pretty good at it. Figured with you ownin' this place and me lookin' for a change . . ."

As he talked, I considered him. The chair he sat on was made to fit ordinary-sized men like Farwell, not a man of Stiller's size, and with his large booted feet stretched forward he appeared even larger than I remembered. His beefy fingers slid back and forth on the table until, made uncomfortable by my stare, he lifted his hand to run it through his hair. I don't know if others smelled it, but to me he would always stink of rotting wolf pelts.

"And if I'm not friendly?" I asked.

"See, if I'm around, I can help keep your Ella here with you, but if I'm not . . ."

Ah! There was the Stiller I knew. A cold chill went up my back. Farwell had told me that he had signed a paper giving the agency the right to send all three kids to the Indian school. "Come on, Mary, I'm giving you a chance here."

A daring thought came to me, and I spoke before I could stop myself. "Maybe you're right. You're a strong man. You could probably do a good job around here."

He straightened up in the chair.

"But I'll need some time to think about this," I said.

"How about I come back a week from today," he said.

"If . . . you and me get . . . friendly, what about the other agents? Won't they come looking for Ella?"

He laughed. "Hell, no, they don't come out this far looking for kids."

I turned toward the window and saw the darkening sky. I forced myself to breathe. When I turned back, I lowered my voice. "When did you say you'd come back?" I asked.

"I'll be here next Thursday. Rain or shine."

"So when you come, why don't you meet me down at my lodge?" I said. "I'll have Burt keep Ella up here for the afternoon."

He gave a wide grin. "Now that's something to look forward to." He watched, but when I couldn't force myself to return his smile, his voice hardened. "You wouldn't be thinking of pulling a fast one on me, would you?"

"Why would I do that? I know what's happening with my husband, and the day is coming when I'll be needing a man around here to run the place. If you're game, why not? Maybe this could work out for me."

"Sure could," he said, and his voice turned soft. "I always remember that night at that campfire. I knew you were looking at me already then.

You touched my fingers when you handed me that bowl of stew and, man, the sparks. And to top it off, turns out you can cook. Sure would like to have you cooking for me all the time."

I had no remembrance of our fingers touching, but I kept that to myself. "How about I make a good stew for you when you come," I added, wondering if I could shoot him as he ate.

"Now that I'd like!" He stood, and as he came forward, I stiffened in preparation for his hands on me. We both jumped when the kitchen door swung open behind us and Marco's voice called out, "Hey, Farwell. I got the booze."

The ranch hand's eyes grew large when he took us in.

That was my moment, and I didn't waste it. I moved quick, away from Stiller, and reached for a bottle of whiskey. I raised it in the air, hoping to further entice him. "I'll keep this safe until next Thursday," I said as I left, and Stiller gave a surprised smile.

IN THE FOLLOWING days, all I could think about was how I could get rid of him. I would stand little chance if I used a knife. A gun would be my last resort. The shots would be heard, and if Farwell and Marco weren't drunk enough, they were bound to investigate. That left poisoning the food or the whiskey, but how would I do that?

I remembered how the wolfers had used strychnine, but I had no way of getting hold of it. I supposed I could send Marco to town, but he reported everything to Farwell, so that ended that. Then, suddenly, on Thursday, after I had Stiller's stew already cooking, and as I was cleaning my guns, I remembered the storage room where Farwell had locked away some goods left over from our trading post. Though years had passed, I wondered if I might find some strychnine there.

Burt was in the kitchen working bread dough. "Burt, do you know where the keys are for that storage room at the back of the big barn?" I asked.

"Sure," he said. He went to his room and returned with a jangling ring of keys. "Here, it's one of these," he said, handing them over. He looked at me and then at Ella, who clung to my hand. "Ella, why don't you help me make some bread?" he asked, and when she nodded, he lifted her up and set her on a high stool next to the table. He cut off a piece of dough and handed it to her as he addressed me.

"That door might be hard to open. It's always been off-limits to anyone but the boss, and I don't think he's been in there for years."

I watched him toss more flour onto the table and then show Ella how to push the heel of her hand into the dough. "Burt, can Ella stay here with you for the afternoon?"

He raised his eyebrows in surprise, but was quick to agree. "Don't see why not," he said. As Ella worked the small piece of dough he had given her, Burt took a knife and cut a large mound into four pieces and began to knead one of them. "Later we'll bake something sweet here in the kitchen, won't we, Ella Bella?" She gave a slight smile at his pet name. I hated to see the dark circles under her eyes. Still shaken at the way her brother and sister were stolen away, Ella clung to me every night when she cried for them.

Burt shaped one of the loaves and settled it into a greased pan. "Will you be all right on your own?" he asked, keeping his eyes on his work, and I wondered how much he guessed.

"I'll be okay as long as I know that Ella is safe with you."

"She'll be safe." He nodded toward his rifle leaning in the corner. "Here, girlie, this is how you shape the dough," he said to Ella.

ASSURED OF MY daughter's safety, I wasn't much concerned about Farwell and Marco, since both, Burt said, had been drinking since morning. As I went toward the barn, for the first time I noticed the yellowing leaves on the trees, and I realized that Grandfather would be coming soon. But would I be alive to greet him?

I hadn't dug a grave. Stiller was cruel, but he wasn't stupid. The hard work of digging a hole that size would have to come later, but I figured I'd be worked up and my nerves would give me the fuel I needed.

It was dark and hot at the back of the big barn, and I had to roll aside a heavy wagon wheel that leaned against the entry to the locked storage room. Finally, the rusty lock clicked and the log door moaned open. I brushed aside cobwebs and worked my way through what was left from our past. And there, on the second-highest shelf, were two tiny blue bottles of strychnine.

My hand shook when I reached for one. How much did I need to kill a man? I wondered. I shrugged and tipped the entire contents into the bottle of whiskey I had saved for Stiller. "Dead is dead," I told myself. "You can't overkill him."

A cold shiver ran through me as I shook the bottle and remembered Farwell's words of warning to Strong Bull on his last visit. "Mary, you tell your brother and his friends that they better not mess with any of the Indian agents. They're considered government, and if an agent gets killed, they'll hang any suspects in front of the whole tribe."

I was locking up again when I saw the horses circling the corral, answering a whinny that came from the direction of my tipi. Was Stiller already waiting? Suddenly weak from fear, I leaned against the wall. I was no match for this man! I was as good as dead. But then I remembered what he had done to Song Woman and what would happen to Ella, and I forced myself to straighten. I took some deep breaths as I gave the whiskey bottle a last shake.

"*Awe alaxáashih*! Hold firm!" I said, and then I went out to greet him.

CHAPTER THIRTY-NINE

1889

I GRIPPED THE BOTTLE as I raced to my lodge, but I stopped suddenly when I saw that it wasn't Stiller waiting there for me. Instead, it was Red Fox standing alongside my tipi. I was too startled and frightened to wonder why he was dressed as though he had been hunting. Wearing only a breechcloth and moccasins, his aged shoulders and chest sagged even as he straightened and lifted his bow in the air to greet me.

"Grandfather," I cried, and ran toward him, waving frantically. I needed him to leave, but he ignored my wild gestures and instead gave me a broad smile.

"I want you to go," I panted when I reached him. "Quick, go away for the day and then come back tomorrow—"

"Goes First," he interrupted. "I have good news."

"Grandfather . . . ," I tried again. "I need you to go. Come back tomorrow." I fought the urge to take him by his shoulders when he didn't move.

"I was hunting with your brother's friends," he began. "And we found a snake."

"Grandfather, please! Listen to me. . . ."

"The snake was a large one, as big as a man. As big as that man Stiller." Grandfather's eyes were filled with life. "A snake's death cannot be blamed on the Crow when it is found in Sioux territory, with a Sioux arrow through his heart. His fine big horse, too, was released on Sioux land, so a Sioux warrior is likely riding it by now." Grandfather chuckled. "But those Sioux are smart. Who knows, they might trade the horse to their enemy, and then a Blackfoot would be chased down by the government." Grandfather laughed aloud.

As the meaning of his words settled in, I sat down, gripping my bottle of poisoned whiskey. "But how did you know?" I asked.

"He was a snake with a big mouth, and one of your brother's friends overheard his talk about you. Those young braves all wanted to earn a coup, but they gave me first chance and I hit my mark. I think they were disappointed." He grunted. "So now I am here to tell you that the snake will not return, nor will he or his horse be found on Crow land."

My whole body began to tremble as I took in his words. Red Fox came over and sat next to me. "You are safe, granddaughter," he said, and waited as I wiped away tears of relief.

"Thank you," I finally managed to whisper.

"There is no need to thank me. Old hearts come alive when they have purpose," he said, "and today mine beats like that of a young warrior."

Red Fox sniffed the air as he nodded toward the simmering stew I had prepared for Stiller. "A feast is called for, and I'd even eat some of that miserable-tasting beef you have over in that pot, if it was offered to me," he said. I set the bottle of whiskey to the side as I rose to get him a bowl of the food. "Don't touch that!" I said sharply when he gave the bottle a hard look. "That was for the snake," I said.

He gave me a mischievous smile as he took the bowl of stew from me. "Ah, Goes First, defending my people makes a man hungry. But I have a question for you."

"Yes, Grandfather?"

"Before I take a mouthful of this food, I would like to know how heavily seasoned it is. Might it be too heavily seasoned for your family?" he asked with a grin.

I grinned back. "Oh, the seasoning in my stew is good, but don't drink my whiskey."

"HE'S SICK AGAIN," Burt said the afternoon he came for me, "and he keeps asking for you."

I left Ella with Red Fox and stomped up to the bunkhouse, furious with Farwell for drinking and doing this to himself once again. Burt followed, but the incline of the land was hard on his sore joints, so I went on ahead. As I came up the hill, I took stock of the place, and for the first time I noticed how uncared for it looked. High grass had grown up to the house, and some of the fencing where the horses were pastured was starting to lean. I was going to have to tackle that fencing myself. The cattle ranged far out, and I wondered when Marco had last checked on them. Coyotes and wolves were always on the prowl, and the herd needed our protection. I supposed it was again time for me to try to tell Farwell to hire on another ranch hand, but I dreaded it, for in the past my suggestions led only to arguments. Yet now, as I took this all in, I knew I had to take a stand.

I was ready to do battle when I swung open the bunkhouse door, but I wasn't prepared to see Farwell vomiting blood, and I hurried toward him. He moaned in pain as he clutched his swollen stomach. Burt came then, and though we tried everything we knew to help, Farwell's vomiting continued. Finally, finished retching, he lay back on a cot. "Mary," he said, reaching toward me. "Don't go," he begged, his breathing ragged. He was as pitiful as I had ever seen him. I sat next to him and wiped fresh blood from the corner of his mouth. His eyes, yellow and pained, searched my face. "I'm sorry," he whispered before his eyes closed.

I suddenly felt a terrible fear. He was so close to death. But then what would I do? Where would I go? And *why*? Why had he done this? Why had he traded me and the children for whiskey? I needed answers before he left. "Farwell?" I shook his arm, but it lay heavily at his side. I tried to wake him, shaking his thin wasted body, but when he began to spasm, I pulled back. This time, when the seizure stopped, Farwell was no longer breathing.

Through the startling silence, I stared at what was left of my husband.

"It's done," Burt murmured. Though I knew Farwell's death was coming, I hadn't expected the wash of grief that took me to my knees. There I sobbed, mourning the loss of what might have been.

❧ ❧ ❧

WEEKS LATER, BURT read aloud an article written in *The Weekly River Press*, a newspaper out of Fort Benton.

> "... *an account of the death of Abe Farwell* ... *He died from congestion of the brain, the result of chronic alcoholism.*
>
> *Abe Farwell leaves no friends in this section of Montana, where he is well, but unfavorably known.*
>
> *It was through his lying representations and turning state's evidence that caused the arrest of a number of reputable citizens of Fort Benton for alleged complicity in the so-called 'Cypress Hills Massacre.'* ... *It was during the trial that Farwell made himself famous by his lying statement to secure the conviction of his former friends.*"

Burt slammed the paper down onto the table. His eyes brimmed with tears, while mine stayed dry. "It isn't right that he should be remembered this way," Burt said. "Part of the reason he drank was because of that trial."

"*Éeh*," I agreed. "But he could have stopped drinking anytime."

"Out east they're starting to say that alcoholism is a sickness—a disease—and I'm wondering if maybe it is. I saw how hard he tried not to drink, but I didn't know how to help him any more than I knew how to help my own son." His voice broke.

"You were a good friend to my husband—I think the best he ever had," I said gently. "There was nothing more you could have done for him."

CHAPTER FORTY

1889–1892

OVER THE NEXT two years, men came with offers to buy the ranch, but I refused to leave. I was waiting for the day that my children would come home, and I wanted them to know where to find me. I decided that it made good business sense to keep twenty of our best horses for breeding, and the rest I sold. Farwell's death seemed to have removed Marco's need to drink, and after he asked to stay on and care for the fifty head of cattle that was left, I agreed, provided he never brought whiskey to the place again. To date, he had kept his word.

It was a hot dry afternoon, that summer of 1892, perfect for Ella and me to go down to the river and do our laundry. We had left Red Fox back at the lodge, where he agreed to join us later after he finished cleaning our rifles. The washed clothing was already spread over the willow shrubs to dry, and I was sitting back to watch my daughter wade around in the shallow blue water. At nine snows, she had already suffered deeply, yet she was the gentlest child I had ever known. As she held up different pebbles for me to see, my heart filled with love for her. I vowed again that she would never be taken from me and I glanced over to make sure that my gun was within easy reach. Reassured, I relaxed and sat back to reread Jeannie's latest letter.

Dear Mary,

Well, we made it. The long wagon trip up here to Winnipeg was quite an adventure. My three older girls are all good travelers, but my youngest twins—they're already eleven—can you believe it? Anyway, they squawked plenty and I had to remind them a few times that you rode all this way on horseback with a month-old baby. Honestly, Mary, I don't know how you did it.

Luckily, my Marie was along, and even though her baby is due in a few months, she kept us all organized. She's bossy with her new husband and the two argue a lot, but they are young and in love and he always makes her laugh.

René is happy that we all agreed to make our home with his people in the Red River Settlement. I think it might be the only way we will find a husband for each of our four remaining unmarried daughters— one more headstrong than the other. And can you believe it? I even encouraged Mama Rosa to come with us, though I doubt René or the girls would have left without her.

I think of you so often and I wonder how you . . .

"Mama," Ella called. "Mama, look!"

I squinted, then realized that she was pointing at something behind my back. My revolver was in my hand when I swung around, but then my breath caught, and I gently set my gun back down on the flat rock.

Red Fox was making his way toward us, lit by the golden glow of a setting sun. He walked with his arm around a boy, until the boy broke free and began to run toward us.

I stared in disbelief as I stood to better see. The boy was thin, but he had grown by a few years. Though he no longer had his long hair, he had Farwell's face, and there was no mistaking my son.

Ella flew by me. "Bud, Bud!" she cried, and as I watched my boy open his arms to his sister, I ran to him, too.

"Grandfather told me about Papa," he said as he wept. Then he looked up at me. "At school, they told us that he was the one who sent us there. I hated him for that, but I didn't want him to die."

"None of us did," I said.

❀   ❀   ❀

NEXT TO THE safety of our lodge, I prepared a pan of fry bread along with some steak, and we all three waited while Bud gratefully filled his stomach. In between bites, he'd smile at us, steady and sure of himself, and I couldn't take my eyes from him. He had left as a child, and he had returned a young man. Bud had always looked like Farwell, but at eleven years, with his brown hair cut short, his square face, his blue eyes, and his strong chin, he looked exactly like his father must have looked at that age. For the first time since his death, I wished that Farwell still lived. How proud he would have been of his son.

Ella could not hold herself back, and before Bud finished eating, her questions began. "How did you get here? Did you come by yourself? How long did it take? Where's your horse?"

Bud smiled at his sister and put down the third piece of fry bread he'd been about to eat. "I came with Lone Wolf, a Cheyenne boy from a reservation just over from us. He and I figured out that if we followed the railroad tracks from Pennsylvania back out west, we could make it home."

"Did you ride the train?"

"A couple of times we jumped on, but once I almost fell under the wheels, so after that most of the time we walked."

"Did you have to walk far?" Ella asked.

"We figured we came about eighteen hundred miles," he said. "It took us a long time to get here. There was still snow on the ground when we left, and now . . ." He looked around. "Well, I guess it's late summer?"

"What did you eat?" Ella stared with admiration.

Bud unsheathed a sharp knife. "Susie got this from the kitchen and gave it to me before I left." He held up the finely stitched leather sheath. "She made this from a moccasin that she found in one of the storage rooms." He shook his head at the memory. "She would have got in real trouble if they had found out about the knife, but we sure needed it." He nodded toward Red Fox. "I remembered everything that you showed me, Grandfather. We used this knife to make bows and arrows and to make snares. One time we killed a deer, but we had to leave most of it behind, so after that we stuck with birds and rabbits and squirrels. . . ."

I could wait no longer. "Bud? Where is Susie? Is she coming home, too?"

Bud's blue eyes met mine. "She wanted to stay there, Mama, but she said that when she finishes, she'll come home."

"Finishes?" I asked.

"She's learning how to help sick people. She wants to be a nurse. Back when they took us to the school on the train, all the little ones, even the Dakota and Sioux, were hanging on to Susie like she was their mama. At the school, some of them got the measles, and the only way they would eat or drink was if Susie would come and feed them. After some of them died, that's when Susie said she wanted to be a nurse."

"She didn't care that you left and came back here?" I asked. I felt tears collecting behind my eyes. How could Susie choose to stay away?

He gave a low grunt. "Oh no, she wanted me to stay. When we first got there, they couldn't believe how well I could read and write, and so they started me out working at the school newspaper. Susie liked that. She said it was a good chance for me to learn a trade. But I hated it when I saw how they took pictures of some of the new kids when they first came and were still dressed in their Indian clothes. After the school cut their hair and put them in the school's uniform, they took pictures again. But they sold those pictures—what they called *before-and-after pictures*—so people could see how they were taming the 'savages' at the school."

"Is that why you left?" Grandfather asked.

"No. Me, I don't know myself," he said, using a Crow expression to describe his loneliness. "I was done with all the marching around in those scratchy wool uniforms, and I was tired of getting walloped for going barefoot or for talking Crow. They said they were going to get the Indian out of me, and that was never going to happen. I heard that Lone Wolf had tried to run away once, so I went to him to ask him how to do it. When he found out that I was going to give it a try, he wanted to come, too."

"He had tried before?" Grandfather asked.

"Yah. After his little sister got the measles and died, he ran away. When they caught him, they beat him and then locked him up for a while. He's a few years older than me and still can't read well, but I got ahold of a map and we looked at it every night. We figured out that if we followed the railroad tracks we could make it back home. Then I asked Susie if she would help."

"I thought you said she wanted you to stay?" I said.

He nodded and looked away, toward the river. "She did. When I first told her that I was going to leave, she got mad at me. She said I'd never make it past the guardhouse, and if I did, how would I ever find my way home? She felt better when I told her that Lone Wolf was going with me and about our plan to follow the railroad tracks. She even thought that was a good idea, and then she helped us."

"How? What did she do?"

"She started a fire on the night that we wanted to leave."

"A fire?" Ella and I asked in unison.

Bud nodded and grinned. "She got such a good blaze going in one of the dorm rooms that they had to get the guards from the guardhouse to help put it out. That's how we got through the gates."

"Susie did that?" Ella asked with no little pride.

"She did," he said, smiling again at his adoring little sister. "And the night before I left, she made me promise to tell you that every night when she looks at the moon, she thinks of you and wonders if you still are jumping toward it so you can grow."

Ella's eyes filled. "I miss her," she whispered, and leaned against her brother's arm.

Bud patted her head and then suddenly reached into the pocket of his worn gray jacket. "Oh, Mama. I almost forgot. She sent this for you."

My hand trembled when I reached for the envelope, but when I opened it, the English words blurred. "You read it," I said, handing it back to Bud.

He nodded and began:

Dear Mama,

If you are reading this, then Bud has arrived safely and my prayers were answered. He's young for this journey, but he is wise and strong and I know that Grandfather has prepared him well. Bud and I felt different about being here—I always knew that Papa wanted me to get an education, and I want to make him proud. Bud doesn't know Papa as I do, and I'm sorry for that.

I am staying here, Mama, because I want to be a nurse. I know I'm already sixteen years old and it'll take me a few more years of study, but I promise to return home before I am an old woman of twenty. Maybe then, as a nurse, I can help our people.

Bud said he was afraid of them taking the Crow out of me here, but that can't happen. I have your Crow blood and no one can take that from me.

I am safe and well, Mama, and I look forward to the day when I can take the train back to my family. I am sending Papa his own letter.

Your loving daughter,
Susie

Bud stumbled over the last line that referenced his father, and when he finished, even Grandfather's eyes were moist.

"It's going to be hard on her to find out about . . . ," Bud said, his voice breaking. He choked on a sob, and after Ella hugged him again, he wiped his face dry. Then he carefully folded up the precious letter before he handed it over to me. "I promised her I would write when I got home, so maybe you and I can write to her together and we can tell her about Papa?" he asked.

"Yes," I said, "we'll do that."

BUD WAS SHAKEN by the news of his father's death, but his relief at being home and Red Fox's company helped him adjust. My son was like his father and enjoyed work, and during the next weeks he insisted on taking over many of the chores with the horses that Ella and I had done on our own. I, meanwhile, stayed vigilant and kept my guns at the ready, should any Indian agents come looking for either of my children.

But I also kept thinking of the news Grandfather had brought back earlier that summer—before Bud's return. "They've moved the boundaries of the reservation again," he had said. "This land we stand on is no longer part of the Crow reservation, and you can sell it if you want. You can claim new land for yourself and each of your children, even if they aren't here."

I would have left then—this land that was filled with memories of Farwell's drinking and his slow death, but without Bud and Susie, I hadn't considered leaving, even when Burt had come to me with someone's offer to buy this place. "I'd say it's the most you'll ever get for this ranch," he said. "It's a lot of money and the man said he'd give you cash."

"Cash? Who is he?" I asked.

"He's one tough hombre, I can tell you that. His name's Red-Eye Smith, and he's a well-known gambler and gunslinger. Marco said that in the towns hereabouts and all the way up to Fort Benton, men cross over to the other side of the street when they see him coming," Burt said.

"Tell him I'm not ready to sell."

"Will do," Burt had said.

But now, with Bud's return, I rethought the offer. I remembered what Burt had told me of this Red-Eye Smith's reputation, and I came up with a plan. "Can you send Marco to find that man Smith?" I asked Burt. "See if he still wants to buy the place?"

"There were other offers, too," Burt reminded me.

"No. I want the gunslinger," I said.

Word went out, and in less than a week, the notorious Red-Eye Smith rode in on a horse that looked almost as pretty as he did, with his black hat, silver belt, and glinting spurs. His black horse pranced and whinnied and tossed his glistening mane, and our four corralled horses ran in circles, wanting to have a go at the bold newcomer.

I invited Smith to sit with me at the long pine table, and it didn't take long for the two of us to work out a deal. The dark-eyed man listened as I set out my terms, and though they might have been considered unusual by some, he not only agreed to them, he seemed to consider them an enticement. Smith further surprised me when he stood to leave. He had the devil in his eyes, and he was too handsome for his own good, but it felt reassuring to be admired again. Until now he had called me Mrs. Farwell, but that changed when he reached out to shake my hand.

"So, Crow Mary, we have an agreement. I have to say, though, that I doubt you'll be needing my services. I learned of your reputation up in Fort Benton, and from what I heard, only a fool of a man would dare stand up to you. I, on the other hand, look forward to getting to know you in the future."

THE FOLLOWING DAY I set out with Grandfather, Bud, and Ella for the Crow Agency. When we arrived at the village, built around a cluster of government houses and a small trade store, I left Red Fox outside with the children and went directly into the agent's office. With both guns in place, I opened the door.

Dressed for the occasion, I wore my hair in two long braids, with my leather belt around the waist of my best buckskin dress. Attached to my belt was my sharp skinning knife and my two guns. I had gained back the weight that I had lost when my children were taken, and I straightened to my full height when I stood in the doorway and faced the startled agent, seated behind his desk.

"I'm here to see Stiller," I said.

"What? He's . . . he left," he said. "Who . . ."

"So it's true? The Sioux got him?" I asked.

"Where'd you hear that?"

"Some gunslinger, Red-Eye Smith, came by. He's buying my ranch. Our agreement is he'll watch out for me and my kids if I sell him the place."

"You're selling that ranch? Farwell's ranch?"

So he knew me. "*Éeh*," I said.

"To Smith? Red-Eye Smith?"

I nodded.

"You don't want to mess with that guy. He'll shoot you as soon as look at you," he said.

"That's right," I said. "He will, and that's why I came to warn the man who steals kids."

"Nobody here steals kids."

"Stiller stole mine."

"Well, just so you know, your husband gave permission for us to take your kids."

"Well, just so you know, Farwell's dead, and I am here to tell you that the next time an agent touches any of my kids, they won't live. If I don't get them, Smith will."

The man tried to find words as he moved papers around on his desk, but I soon lost patience. "My son, Bud, found his way home from that damn school out in Pennsylvania, and he's not going back."

The man lifted his head in surprise. "How on earth . . . how did he get back?"

"Nobody's business but his."

"Well, I . . . I suppose if your son doesn't want to take advantage of the opportunity for an education . . ."

"And my youngest daughter won't go there, either."

"The schools have all the kids they can handle. Maybe when she's older she'll want to go to the school here at the agency, but let's just say, that'll be up to her." He looked anxious for me to leave.

"So where do I go to claim land for my Crow children?" I asked, finished with that part of the conversation.

"There's a map over there," he said, pointing to a table in the corner.

I called my family in, and together we studied the large sheet of paper. Bud understood how to read the map, and Grandfather knew the different areas well. After some objections from the agent and then a few strong words from me, the government man agreed to our choice of good grazing land along East Pryor Creek, in the shelter of our sacred mountains. There, with the money from the sale of the ranch, we would have plenty of whatever we needed to raise horses and to help out Father and his family.

IT WAS THE end of August, the moon of the wild plums. I had chosen the mare I was riding for the way she carried herself—eager and proud.

Today she was dressed as beautifully as I, and as she pranced, the light caught the colorful beaded finery of my ancestors. Among my people, horses were highly valued, and I planned to continue breeding and training them. Days earlier we had traveled to the new land, taking old Snow, along with our best horses and a few head of cattle, and the animals were already grazing in their new pastures next to clear running water, shaded by the mountains. There the government had provided us a log cabin, rustic and small in comparison to the one Farwell had built, but with our pine table squeezed in and a cast-iron stove for cooking, it was set up well enough to satisfy Burt.

I didn't look back that day we left Smith's property. Twenty snows had come and gone since I had married Farwell. In that ranch house and the land surrounding it, I left behind the loss of my husband and his battle with alcohol, and I took instead my hard-won freedom. There was land up ahead, Crow land that had my children's names on it, and though ownership meant little to me, I realized that one day it might mean something to my family.

Ella followed behind me, riding her own well-dressed pony, and she, too, was proudly clothed in her best elk's-tooth dress. She lifted an old hat of Susie's that set low over her two black braids, and she waved it back toward her brother. "Get a move on, boys," she called.

Bud lifted his own hat in response, and Burt waved to her from where he sat on the wagon seat alongside my son. Burt was decked out in a new blue plaid shirt and new denim trousers, and though Bud also wore the pants and shirt of a Yellow Eyes, both wore the moccasins of the Crow.

"Haw! Haw!" Bud called, snapping the reins and urging forward the team of horses that pulled our loaded wagon and the packhorses that followed behind, carrying our lodges.

Our old warrior, Red Fox, armed with his bow, traveled last, guarding our backs as he had these many years. Our small procession reminded me of the happy days of my childhood, when the Crow traveled to greet each new season. It was true that we were now restricted to this reservation, but just as Susie suggested, we carried our history and our ancestors within us.

As we wound our way across the rough trail, over one hill and then another, I looked about this beautiful rugged country, wanting to remember every detail of this journey so I might send both Jeannie and Susie a letter telling of nothing less.

Along the edges of our low mountains, sharp ledges jutted out, giving life to the hardy green pines that grew there, defiant and strong. Among those ridges were buffalo jumps—revered places where our people had hunted the great beasts. I wondered if they would come again, those thundering creatures that gave us their lives to supply us with everything we needed. On this day of hope, it seemed possible. Up ahead, yellow meadowlarks sang across the open grassy plains, where coulees sheltered thickets of berry bushes. Blue rivers and creeks ran between banks lined with willows and stands of cottonwood trees, providing drink and shelter for wild animals.

Here was Crow land, where our mountains and our words were sacred. Here was the place Mother Earth had provided for us, and I was finally coming home.

❀ AUTHOR'S NOTE ❀

AROUND THE year 2000, while I was still writing *The Kitchen House*, I went to visit my parents in Saskatchewan. For an outing, we went to visit Fort Walsh in the Cypress Hills, four hours away from home by car. I knew little about the area and even less about why Fort Walsh, the first North West Mounted Police fort built in Saskatchewan, had come into being.

There were docents at the historical site, and I was immediately drawn to a young Indigenous woman, dressed in the garb of her people. She stood on the rise of a hill that overlooked the green, rolling Cypress Hills, and what she had to say went something like this:

"Here, in the Cypress Hills, I was known as Crow Mary. In 1873, I was sixteen years old and newly married to my white fur-trader husband, Abe Farwell, when a massacre of the Nakoda took place. The men responsible were a group of ruthless wolfers and whiskey traders, and after the massacre they took five Nakoda women back to their camp for their amusement. I couldn't save the women from being brutalized, but alone, and armed only with my two guns, I did save them from being murdered."

As she spoke, a deep chill went through me, and I knew that I was meant to write this woman's story. But who was I, a white woman, who knew little about Indigenous culture, to take this on?

Throughout the process of writing *The Kitchen House*, and later, *Glory Over Everything*, I was always encouraged by the warm support of the Black community. Now I reached out to the Crow people. Here, too, I received nothing but strong encouragement and help, first from Crow Mary's great-granddaughter, Nedra Farwell Brown, and then from a Crow historian, a Crow elder, also known as George "Sonny Joe" Reed (One Whose Horse They Wanna Own.) Through George I was introduced to Elias Goes Ahead, another Crow historian, and then Janine Pease (Loves to Pray), the founder of Little Bighorn College and the sensitivity reader for this book. Throughout the many drafts of this story, I was blessed to have Janice Wilson (Bird of Excellence), a Crow elder, patiently guiding me through the many subtleties and nuances of the Crow culture. Not only has Janice been my educator, I believe she would agree that we have become good friends.

There are so many more who gave their help, and I include those in my acknowledgments.

In the writing of this book, there were many times I felt overwhelmed. Crow Mary's story included important history, and I am not an historian. Yet, with so many resources available, I felt driven to continue. However, I remind the reader that this story is fiction based on fact.

Some facts: Abe Farwell, Crow Mary, and their children did live, and Farwell's end came as written. The Cypress Hills Massacre did happen, though I used license to write my version and to fictionalize Mary's experiences there. It is true that Crow Mary did single-handedly save the women and that she was a witness at the trial in Winnipeg, though none of the accused were ever found guilty. However, as a result of the massacre, the North West Mounted Police built Fort Walsh, and whiskey trading was eventually brought to an end.

Crow Mary's two eldest children were stolen, and they were indeed taken to the Carlisle Indian School in Pennsylvania. Bud escaped from Carlisle and never returned, while Susie stayed. After she received a nursing education, she returned home and used this education to benefit her people.

Fiction: Stiller is fiction, as are Jeannie and M'sieu Dubois, though they are very real to me. The way my writing process works is that the characters come only after I have thoroughly done the research. It is as though they wait until I have enough knowledge about their culture, place, and time, and then they appear to play their part.

A note: The Crow people are deeply spiritual, and because their spiritual practices are sacred to them, I kept Crow Mary's spiritual life largely private.

As well, racial slurs are used in the telling of this story. Words such as "squaw" and "Indian" are not meant to offend, but rather, the Crow elders I consulted advised that I could not tell the story effectively without using them.

In the end, my hope in sharing Crow Mary's life is that others are given insight into this courageous woman's life, and that it inspires them as it did me.

✿ ACKNOWLEDGMENTS ✿

How grateful I am to have Rebecca Gradinger as my literary agent. Thank you, Rebecca, for always being at my side.

This book required two editors, and each gave me exactly what I needed. Thank you, Trish Todd and Alexandra Shelly, for seeing me through the many drafts that it took to get us to the finish line. Thank you as well to Sean Delone, assistant editor, and to Daniel Seidel, copy editor, for your much needed help.

Where would I be without my loyal first readers: Judy Chisholm, Ann Kwan, Carlene Baime, Bob Baime, Barbara Walker, Erin Plewes, and Charles Grissom. I've relied on all of you for so many years, and your help has meant so much to me.

Twenty years ago, when I began research for this book, I had no idea how many people I would meet who would so generously add to Crow Mary's story. Those from the United States are listed in approximate order of when I met them: CB Brown and Nedra Farwell Brown, Jackie Bristow, Barbara Landis at the Carlisle Indian Industrial School, Jean Lande, Dianna Lande Means, Monica and Dick Weldon, Minnie Fritzler, George Reed (One Whose Horse They Wanna Own), Elias Goes Ahead, Bernadette Smith and all those at Chief Plenty Coup's Museum, Janine Pease (Loves to Pray), Janice Wilson (Bird of Excellence), Tim McCleary, Tim Bernardis, Chrislyn Nomee Red Star, Ken Robinson, and all at the Fort Benton/Overholser Historical Research Center.

In the last years, some of these precious souls went to the Other Side

Camp, but I like to think that their wisdom and insight live on through this story.

Canada has its own list. Thank you, Robert Clipperton, for your help and the invaluable information you compiled and edited in *The Cypress Hills Massacre*. Your book was a mainstay and one I referred to continuously.

Thank you to Dominique Liboiron, Royce Pettyjohn, Clay Yarshenko, Brian Hubner, Kaylee Beck, and all those affiliated with the Fort Walsh National Historic Site. My gratitude to Margaret Kennedy, Bill and Sherry Caton, Stewart Tasche, and Ashley Hardwick at the Fort Museum/Fort Macleod. Thank you as well to Byree at the Aaniiih Nakoda College Library, and to those who answered my never-ending questions at the Wanuskewin National Heritage Site. And then there were the wonderful librarians at the University of Saskatchewan, who, through the years, located information I might never have found on my own.

Crow Mary's story came together with help from all these people, and I am deeply indebted to each one for their input, their time, and their encouragement. *Ahoo!*